THE EMOTION COLLECTOR: AWAKENING

RICHARD FRENCH

ALSO BY RICHARD FRENCH

NON FICTION

The Art of Journaling

Write Your Way

Advanced Pattern Recognition

The Year End Reflection Guide

100 Self-Discovery Journaling Prompts

100 Mental Health Journaling Prompts

Revelation Explained: Verse by Verse

Proverbs for Profit

Daniel as a Blueprint for Navigating Ethical Dilemmas (2nd Edition)

FICTION

The Convergence: Broken Magic

The Convergence; Restoration

The Emotion Collector: Awakening

Indie Pen Press
Turning Dreams into Best Sellers

Indie Pen Press
Seattle, Washington USA
IndiePenPress.com

First Edition: October 2025

Paperback ISBN: 979-8-9991846-6-5

Library of Congress Control Number: 2025943072

CONTENTS

Chapter One

THE TASTE OF FORBIDDEN LOVE

E motion had been illegal for two hundred years. The child's love hit Emma like the air pulled from a room and slammed back through her body. Pure love filled her mind for three seconds. A four-year-old's fierce devotion to his mother crashed against Emma's thoughts like warm honey infused with lightning. She could taste it: sweet trust, the certainty that Mama would always return, always heal everything, always protect him. The emotion carried sensory echoes: the scent of his mother's hair, the warmth of her lap during bedtime stories, the security of small arms wrapped around his neck in desperate hugs.

Emma gasped as the love cut deeper than any emotion she'd collected before. Through the child's adoration, she experienced fragments of pure joy. Birthday mornings when presents felt magical. The delicious terror of being chased through the house while giggling. The drowsy contentment of falling asleep to his mother's humming. Each memory blazed with an intensity that made Emma's controlled existence feel like living in black and white while suddenly seeing color.

The collection device hummed, draining the emotion away. Emma's hands trembled as she stepped back from the family, her standard smile brittle on her face. The mother blinked with mild confusion typical of processed individuals. Her eyes, which moments before had sparkled with maternal warmth, now held the flat neutrality of proper neural dampening. The child, Tommy, stood motionless now, his earlier tantrum erased along with the love that had caused it. His small face showed the blank compliance that marked successful emotional extraction.

"Collection complete," Emma reported to her comm. Her voice remained steady despite the hollow ache spreading through her chest like ink through water. The child's love clung to her awareness like an afterimage burned into her retinas. Even as her neural dampeners worked to process and compress the absorbed emotion, warmth pulsed in corners of her consciousness where the scanners couldn't reach.

For three seconds, she had experienced what it meant to care about someone with complete devotion. The memory made her fingertips tingle and her breath catch in ways her training insisted were dangerous symptoms of emotional contamination.

They were dangerous because they felt like coming home.

Emma walked through the residential complex's clean corridors, her boots clicking against polished metal floors that absorbed excessive noise. Emergency lighting strips cast cool blue illumination at calculated intervals, preventing the warm yellows and reds that might stimulate unwanted emotional responses. Citizens moved past her with calm efficiency that marked a stabilized society. Their faces showed the pleasant neutrality that Emma had been trained to recognize as healthy.

This was peace. This was what the Council protected. So why did the hollowness in her chest feel like suffocation?

She observed a maintenance worker cleaning the corridor's viewing panels. His movements followed precise patterns taught in efficiency training, but something about the way his shoulders curved inward suggested bone-deep weariness that decades of controlled existence had carved into his posture. Emma activated her passive monitoring sensors and detected traces of exhaustion bleeding through his neural dampening. The readings showed what her enhanced awareness already knew: beneath the dampened exterior, his soul yearned for something more than controlled contentment.

How many others carried hidden aches? The child's love had awakened something in her that made such questions feel urgent rather than dangerous.

"Report, Agent Thorne." Marcus Webb's voice crackled through her earpiece as she reached the collection vehicle. Her handler stood beside the transport, dark eyes focused on his monitoring tablet. At twenty-six, he carried himself with the professional alertness of someone who'd spent years ensuring Council operations proceeded without incident. His black uniform displayed the competence that marked him as a handler of exceptional ability.

Marcus's face showed composed attention, but her enhanced sensitivity caught something else. A micro-expression of concern that lasted perhaps a tenth of a second when he reviewed her biometric data. The observation troubled her. Handlers weren't supposed to experience personal investment in their subjects' welfare.

"Standard domestic disturbance," Emma replied, settling into the passenger seat while Marcus conducted his post-mission scan. The neural interface pressed cool against her temple as it downloaded her collection data. The sensation felt invasive, like having her thoughts catalogued and filed. "Child showing attachment overflow. Extracted and processed."

Marcus frowned at his readings, his fingers moving across the tablet's surface. "Your absorption rates are elevated. Neural pathway activity shows unusual patterns during the collection sequence."

Emma's breath caught, but she kept her expression neutral. Her enhanced sensitivity might be detectable through standard monitoring. "Equipment sensitivity, perhaps? The child's emotional energy was intense."

"Perhaps." Marcus made notes on his device, but his brown eyes lingered on her face with attention that felt more personal than professional. "We'll run diagnostics when we return to base. Standard protocol requires biomedical review when Collectors show irregular readings. Chancellor Keller personally reviews any anomalies in senior agent performance."

The mention of Chancellor Keller sent ice through Emma's veins. "What happens during extended diagnostics?"

"Neural pathway adjustment. Emotional dampening recalibration. Loyalty reinforcement protocols." Marcus started the vehicle, his tone clinical but somehow reluctant. "Most agents report feeling more focused afterward. Less distracted by residual emotional contamination."

Emma had undergone weekly sessions with the Chancellor since her promotion to Field status six years ago. The sessions left her feeling empty but focused. Now she wondered if they had taken pieces of her soul along with the contamination.

Through the vehicle's reinforced windows, Emma watched their controlled world slide past. Every building followed precise architectural guidelines designed to minimize emotional response. Neutral colors dominated the palette, chosen for their psychological stability. Citizens moved along designated pathways, maintaining eighteen-inch personal space requirements that prevented uncomfortable intimacy.

Yet Emma's enhanced awareness detected hairline cracks in the facade. She watched a couple walking together, maintaining proper separation. As they passed beneath a flowering tree, the woman's step faltered. For less than a second, her face turned toward the blossoms with an expression that transcended mere botanical interest. Something flickered in her eyes, a hunger so profound that Emma felt it resonate in her own chest before the woman's trained neutrality returned.

The man noticed his companion's lapse and moved closer, not quite close enough to violate proximity guidelines but near enough to offer silent support. His hand twitched toward hers before he caught himself and returned it to the proper position at his side. But in that aborted gesture, Emma saw something that made her neural pathways fire in recognition.

Love. Hidden, suppressed, compressed into the smallest possible expression, but burning like an ember waiting for oxygen.

"Agent Thorne?" Marcus's voice pulled her back. "Your stress indicators are spiking."

Emma forced her breathing to regulate, watching the numbers on his screen return to acceptable levels. "Just tired. Long shift."

But that wasn't true. She'd worked longer shifts without issue. This feeling, this hollow ache, this longing for something she couldn't name, pulsed through her awareness like a heartbeat. Something that her dampening training should have eliminated before it became problematic had instead grown stronger with each passing hour.

They reached the Collection Center as the afternoon harmony index peaked. The facility's white walls gleamed in artificial sunlight, its spires broadcasting emotional dampening fields across the entire district. The building rose in perfect geometric progression, each level designed to inspire confidence in institutional authority. Emma had always found the structure beautiful in its mathematical precision.

Today, the sight of it made her skin crawl.

The transport docked at the processing bay, where automated systems began downloading their collection data. Emma submitted to routine biomedical scans that ensured no emotional contamination had occurred during field operations. The machines read her neural patterns, measured her hormone levels, and confirmed that her dampening remained intact.

But Emma knew they couldn't detect everything. The child's love still pulsed in her awareness like a second heartbeat, creating warm spaces in her mind that her dampening systems couldn't eliminate.

"Schedule your diagnostic for tomorrow morning," Marcus said as they passed through security checkpoints. His voice carried professional tone, but something in his expression suggested personal concern that violated handler protocols. "And Emma?" He paused, something almost like tenderness flickering across his features. "If you're experiencing any irregularities, any emotional breakthrough symptoms, you need to report them. For your own protection."

Emma nodded, but even as she made the gesture, she felt something crystallize inside her chest. A certainty that whatever was happening to her, this growing sensitivity to the emotions she collected, this increasing awareness of what she was taking from people, felt too precious to surrender to correction.

"Of course," she lied, the deception settling into her bones like a new kind of strength.

In the facility's processing bay, Emma watched technicians drain the collected emotional energy from her neural interface. The machinery hummed with quiet efficiency as it separated her absorbed emotions into component elements for storage and disposal. The energy swirled in containment fields, creating patterns of light that shifted from warm gold to deep blue to vibrant red.

For the first time, she wondered what happened to these emotions after collection. Where did that child's love go once it was extracted from her neural pathways? What became of a mother's protective instinct once it was compressed into manageable data streams?

"Beautiful, isn't it?" Dr. Sarah Magnus appeared beside her, adjusting her laboratory coat. The head researcher was one of the few people in the facility who ever spoke to Emma rather than running her through processing procedures. Her grey hair was pulled back in standard style, but her eyes held intelligence that seemed to see beyond the mechanical requirements of her position.

"The energy patterns," Emma said, choosing her words with care. "They're more complex than I realized."

"Each emotion has its own signature," Sarah explained, her grey eyes reflecting the swirling lights. "Love creates those

7

golden spirals that seem to dance with each other. Fear generates jagged red formations that cut through other patterns. And sadness moves like water, finding the lowest places in the mind and pooling there until it can be extracted."

Emma stared at the patterns, her enhanced sensitivity making her neural pathways fire in unexpected ways. The formations weren't random. They responded to each other, connected and separated like living organisms engaged in communication. When love-patterns encountered fear-patterns, they seemed to offer comfort. When sadness-patterns touched joy-patterns, they created hybrid formations that shimmered with colors her training had no names for.

"They're alive," she whispered, the words slipping out before she could stop them.

Sarah's eyebrows rose, but her expression showed interest rather than alarm. "An interesting observation. The Council teaches us that emotions are waste products of inefficient neural processing. But what if they're something else entirely?"

Emma's pulse quickened, the child's love echoing through her awareness like a warm bell. "What do you mean?"

"Theoretical research suggests these patterns might be more than biochemical reactions. The way they interact, the complexity of their formations, the energy they contain." Sarah's voice dropped to a whisper. "What if emotions are actually a form of biological quantum entanglement? What if they're how human consciousness connects across physical barriers?"

The suggestion hit Emma like a revelation that made her fingertips tingle. "You mean when I collect them, I'm not just taking feelings. I'm severing connections between people."

"That's one theory. Another suggests that concentrated emotional energy might have applications beyond waste disposal. Imagine if love could be channeled to heal psychological trauma. If courage could be transferred to those who need it most. If human connection could be enhanced rather than eliminated."

Emma's training screamed warnings at her, but she couldn't deny what she was seeing in the containment fields. The patterns were trying to reconnect, reaching toward each other across the barriers that separated them like fingers stretching toward a lover's touch.

"Agent Thorne, how long have you been experiencing enhanced emotional sensitivity?" Sarah asked.

The question hung between them like a loaded weapon. Emma's answer would determine whether she received minor recalibration or neural reconstruction. She thought about the child's love, the mother's confusion, the hidden longing in the couple's aborted gesture.

"I don't know what you mean," Emma said, but her voice carried the tremor of someone whose world was shifting beneath her feet.

Sarah nodded as if she'd expected that response. "Of course. But if you ever want to understand what those patterns really are, if you ever want to learn about alternative applications for emotional energy research, I'd be happy to discuss them. Purely academic purposes, naturally."

Emma's heartbeat quickened. "Alternative applications?"

"Tomorrow, perhaps. After your diagnostic." Sarah smiled, a genuine expression that lasted longer than guidelines allowed and made something warm unfurl in Emma's chest. "Knowledge is never dangerous, Agent Thorne. Only ignorance causes suffering."

Emma left the Collection Center with Sarah's words echoing in her mind and the child's love still pulsing through her awareness like a secret heartbeat. The evening harmony index displayed green across all monitoring stations, but something felt different in the air. A subtle tension, like the moment before a storm breaks when the very molecules seem to hold their breath.

As she walked toward the transport station, her enhanced sensitivity made details impossible to ignore. A street musician played approved melodies on his standard instrument, but his fingers added unauthorized variations that made the music soar before returning to safe mediocrity. The beauty of those forbidden notes made Emma's chest tighten with recognition. A vendor arranged produce in patterns that followed commercial guidelines, but the way she touched certain pieces suggested aesthetic appreciation that her dampening should have eliminated. Children walked in supervised groups, their behavior controlled, but their eyes held curiosity that flickered like flames no amount of neural dampening could extinguish.

Hidden beneath the surface of their stabilized society, Emma was beginning to detect traces of what they had all lost. Love disguised as appropriate concern. Joy compressed into acceptable satisfaction. Grief transformed into manageable disappointment. The emotions weren't gone. They were buried alive, waiting for someone brave enough to dig them up.

In her standard apartment, Emma stood before the mirror, studying her reflection with new awareness. Amber eyes that seemed to shift color based on the emotions she'd absorbed that day, currently warm with golden flecks that reminded her of the child's love. Auburn hair pulled back in approved style that eliminated personal expression. The pale complexion common to all dampened individuals.

Everything about her appearance marked her as the Council's weapon, a human tool designed to maintain social harmony through emotional extraction. But the child's love still echoed in her memory, warm and golden and vibrantly alive, making her wonder what she might look like if she smiled with genuine joy instead of professional courtesy.

For twenty-three years, she'd believed her work protected humanity from the chaos of uncontrolled emotion. The Great Emotional War had turned feelings into weapons that could kill with a touch. The dampening system was humanity's salvation, preventing another catastrophe that could destroy civilization itself.

So why did salvation feel like slow death? Why did the child's love feel more real than anything she'd experienced in her dampened existence?

Emma removed her collection uniform, noting how the specialized fabric felt cold against her skin. The material was designed to prevent emotional transfer through physical contact, creating a barrier between Collectors and the citizens they processed. But as she folded the garment, she wondered what it would feel like to touch another person without technological mediation. Would their emotions flow into her awareness? Would her feelings somehow reach them? The questions made her fingertips tingle with possibility.

As she settled into bed, Emma made a decision that crystallized in her chest like ice becoming diamond. Tomorrow, after her diagnostic, she would seek out Dr. Magnus and ask about those alternative applications. She would learn what the emotional energy patterns were, regardless of the danger. She would begin to understand what was being lost every time she performed her function as the Council's weapon.

Knowledge, Sarah had said, was never dangerous. Only ignorance caused suffering.

But as Emma's consciousness faded toward dreams, she wondered if the Council would agree. And whether the weapon they'd created was about to turn against its makers. The child's love pulsed through her awareness one final time before sleep claimed her, warm and golden and full of a promise she was only beginning to understand.

The harmony index displayed steady green throughout the night, indicating optimal emotional dampening levels across all monitored districts. But in her dreams, Emma saw patterns of light that moved like living things, and heard a child's voice calling for his mother with love so pure it could heal the world or destroy it.

The weapon was beginning to question her purpose.

Chapter Two

ECHOES OF A DEAD FATHER

E mma's footsteps echoed against the polished floors as she walked the sterile halls of the Council Building. Three times each week, the same route to conditioning. The corridors smelled like nothing at all, which was no accident. Every surface had been treated with emotion-dampening compounds that prevented even trace pheromones from triggering unwanted responses.

Today her hands trembled slightly. The headache from yesterday's strange collection still pounded behind her eyes, but worse was her enhanced sensitivity to the building's emotional landscape. Through her altered awareness, Emma detected the compressed feelings of hundreds of Council employees. Their dampened anxiety made her skin feel tight. Their buried longings generated a warmth that her neural dampening insisted should be impossible to perceive.

She pressed her palm against the cool wall, steadying herself. The metal hummed with energy absorption technology, designed to pull emotional resonance from anyone who might leak feelings into the environment.

The conditioning chamber occupied the building's seventh sublevel. Emma counted each step down, noting details that her previous awareness had missed. The air grew thinner. Dampening field generators hummed behind the walls, creating zones of such emotional neutrality that they felt like holes punched through human consciousness.

Dr. Henley waited in the chamber's observation area, his fingers dancing across monitoring equipment. "Good morning, Emma. How are you feeling today?"

"All systems normal," she replied, though her voice sounded strange in the acoustically dead space.

The chamber itself curved inward with mathematical precision, focusing neutralizing fields toward the central chair. Emma had undergone this procedure hundreds of times, but now she noticed how the restraints were positioned not just for compliance, but to make the subject feel completely helpless.

She lay back and closed her eyes as monitoring wires attached to her temples. Through the chamber's observation window, she sensed Dr. Henley's emotional signature. Professional detachment tinged with something that might have been guilt. How many people participated in the dampening system while harboring secret doubts?

"Increase dampening field strength by twelve percent."

Chancellor Keller's voice came through the speakers with absolute authority, but Emma's enhanced sensitivity detected something underneath. Fear? Concern? Something that felt almost like...

The field change sent electricity through Emma's neural paths. She gripped the chair's armrests as waves of artificial calm flooded her mind. But now she could feel how the technology worked. The dampening fields didn't eliminate emotions. They compressed them into spaces so small that conscious awareness couldn't reach them. Every feeling was still there, crushed down into dense packets that created constant pressure.

Her emotions weren't gone. They were imprisoned.

"Subject is showing minor resistance to standard protocols," Dr. Henley reported. "Should we implement enhanced conditioning?"

"Not yet. Continue with current settings and monitor for additional anomalies."

Emma drifted between awake and asleep, her mental barriers crumbling. In this weakened state, fragments of memory surfaced. Thoughts and feelings that her training insisted were dangerous.

A warm laugh echoing through a kitchen filled with the scent of cinnamon and vanilla. Steam rising from a mug pressed into her small hands, the ceramic smooth and reassuring. Sunlight streaming through windows, painting everything golden.

"Emma, remember that love is the most dangerous emotion of all."

The voice materialized with startling clarity. Warm, gentle, carrying sadness that seemed to hold the weight of the world. A man's voice, speaking words that felt like memory but couldn't be real according to her official history.

Strong arms lifting her toward that golden sunlight. The rough texture of a wool sweater against her cheek. The steady rhythm of a heartbeat beneath her ear as stories were read in that same warm voice. Stories that made her laugh until her stomach hurt.

"It makes people do terrible things to protect what they can't bear to lose."

Emma's chest tightened. Her neural dampening insisted she had never known her father, that he had died before she was old enough to form lasting memories. But this voice felt more real than anything in her controlled life.

The scent of coffee mixed with something else. Something that carried more than nutrition. It carried love expressed through care for another person's happiness.

"But love is also what makes life worth living. Without it, we're just biological machines going through the motions of existence."

The understanding hit Emma like physical force, cutting through the dampening field. For a moment, she grasped what those words meant, not just as data, but as truth so fundamental it could reshape everything. Emotions weren't waste products to be eliminated. They were what made existence meaningful.

Her heart rate spiked.

"Neural activity spike in sector seven. Implementing corrective measures."

Another wave of suppression crashed over Emma's consciousness, drowning the dangerous thoughts in clinical numbness. But somewhere in her mind, a door had opened that no amount of technology could close again.

When the session ended, Emma sat up slowly, her head thick with post-conditioning fog. But underneath the artificial numbness, something burned with quiet intensity.

Chancellor Keller appeared in the doorway, her gray hair perfectly styled, her expression carrying professional concern. But Emma's enhanced sensitivity read deeper layers. Fear, yes. But also something that felt like maternal protectiveness. And underneath everything else, a love so fierce it took Emma's breath away.

"How are you feeling, Emma?"

"Good, Chancellor." Emma stood carefully, testing her balance. "All systems working within normal parameters."

But that wasn't true. Her systems were evolving, developing capabilities her creators had never intended.

"Excellent. Your collection efficiency has been exceptional lately. The Council appreciates your dedication."

Emma nodded, gathering her jacket. But as she prepared to leave, she noticed something impossible. Chancellor Keller's emotional signature carried traces of the same love that had flooded through Emma during yesterday's collection. Maternal love, fierce and protective and desperate.

The perception lasted only a moment before her neural dampening explained it away as post-procedure confusion. But the seed of doubt had been planted.

Walking through the Administrative Center's memorial corridor, Emma tried to focus on her next assignment briefing. But her steps slowed as she passed the wall dedicated to those lost during the Great Emotional War. The corridor stretched for nearly a hundred meters, photographs and biographical information covering every surface.

She read the names with growing fascination. Dr. Lucia Ferreira, killed in the Barcelona Cascade. Captain Rhys Calloway, died protecting civilians from weaponized grief.

Professor Mei Tan, lost in the Singapore Terror Event. Each face represented years of training, relationships, dreams destroyed by emotions turned into weapons.

One photograph stopped her cold.

The young man had Emma's amber eyes and auburn hair, though his was longer and less severely styled. His face carried intense curiosity mixed with compassion, emotions that should have seemed threatening but somehow looked beautiful. The nameplate read: "Dr. David Thorne, Emotional Research Division, Age 31. Lost in Resonance Incident, 2952."

Emma's chest constricted. The man's features felt familiar in a way that went beyond genetics. She had seen his face before, heard his voice, felt his presence. But that was impossible. She'd been only five when Dr. Thorne died.

His eyes were kind. The sort that belonged to someone who cared about other people's welfare. His smile suggested warmth and intelligence, the expression of someone who found joy in discovery and understanding.

The same voice from her recovered memories, warm and gentle, reading stories that made her laugh.

Emma stepped closer to the photograph. This man, this researcher who had died before she was old enough to remember, felt important in ways her official records couldn't explain.

He felt like family.

"Is there a problem, Collector Thorne?"

Emma spun around. Marcus Webb approached from the administrative offices, his dark uniform perfect, his expression professionally neutral. Her handler's presence should have been reassuring, but instead she felt caught in something forbidden.

"No problem." She stepped away from the photograph, her heart still racing. "I was reviewing historical data about emotional research casualties."

Marcus's brown eyes studied her face with careful attention. His evaluation felt more thorough than usual, as if he was searching for signs of specific problems rather than conducting routine assessment. "Your biometric readings have shown irregularities since yesterday's collection incident. Are you experiencing any emotional bleed-through?"

The question was standard protocol, but Emma detected something different in his tone. Genuine concern rather than clinical assessment. The realization unsettled her. Marcus was her handler, not her friend. Any sign of emotional instability would result in immediate recalibration.

But his concern felt real.

"All emotional processors are working normally," Emma said, drawing on years of training to project appropriate responses. "Yesterday's anomaly was equipment-related."

Marcus nodded, but his gaze lingered with uncomfortable intensity. For three years, he'd maintained professional distance while ensuring her operational effectiveness. She'd never seen him show personal investment beyond what his duties required. But now his emotional signature carried traces of genuine care.

"The Council values your service, Emma. If you experience any difficulties with memory integration, please report them immediately."

The phrase "memory integration" sent ice through Emma's veins. Her recovered memories weren't supposed to exist. Someone had worked hard to keep certain information buried, and her awakening abilities were uncovering things that powerful people wanted hidden.

"Of course." She managed what she hoped was a convincing smile. "My loyalty to the Council remains complete."

"I know it does." Marcus's voice carried an odd note that might have been regret. "Your dedication has always been exemplary."

As he walked away, Emma realized his concern felt genuine rather than procedural. Handlers weren't supposed to develop personal attachments. But if Marcus was experiencing unauthorized emotional responses, and if she was detecting resonance from Chancellor Keller, then perhaps her readings from yesterday represented something more significant than equipment malfunction.

Perhaps the neural dampening that shaped their society was beginning to fail.

The possibility both terrified and thrilled her.

Emma forced herself to maintain normal pace toward the exit, despite unprecedented thoughts crowding her mind. Dr. David Thorne's photograph seemed to watch her leave, his amber eyes holding secrets that her dampening insisted she shouldn't want to understand.

But the voice from her recovered memories continued whispering forbidden truths about love, connection, and the meaning of existence. Dr. Thorne's face had awakened questions that felt more important than her own safety. Who was he really? Why did his face feel familiar? What connection existed between a dead researcher and a living Collector that the Council had worked so hard to conceal?

And most dangerous of all: if her memories of his voice were real, what other truths about her past were hidden beneath layers of neural dampening and constructed lies?

The answers felt vital, but Emma understood that seeking them would require crossing lines that could never be undone. Some questions, once awakened, refused to be silenced.

The evening harmony index showed steady green as Emma walked toward her transport. But she could feel something stirring beneath New Geneva's controlled tranquility. In apartments and offices throughout the city, people were beginning to experience moments of feeling that their neural dampening couldn't explain. Brief flashes of love, sorrow, joy, and anger that reminded them, however briefly, of what it meant to be truly human.

Emma's awakening was spreading, one person at a time, one emotion at a time.

As she boarded the transport, Emma caught her reflection in the window and saw something new in her amber eyes. Not just awakening awareness, but determination. She would find the truth about Dr. David Thorne, about her forgotten past, about the real purpose of the dampening system.

And if that truth threatened to destroy everything she'd been taught to believe, perhaps it was time for that world to fall.

Chapter Three

THE CHILDREN WHO REMEMBER

The maintenance tunnels beneath New Geneva stretched into darkness like arteries of a dying heart. Evan Cross moved through them without sound, his breath forming small clouds in the cold air as he led his team deeper into the city's forgotten depths. Fifty feet above, the Council's streets hummed with mind dampening fields and controlled life. Down here, in spaces where emotion still pooled like stagnant water, things were different.

His immunity to dampening technology was both blessing and curse. It let him move through Council buildings unaffected. But it also marked him as detectable if he wasn't careful. Tonight, that immunity was their only hope of reaching three children before the Council destroyed their capacity to feel.

"How much further?" Sarah Collins kept her voice low, though Evan caught the tremor beneath her control. At nineteen, she'd been dodging Council corrections for three years. Her natural feeling abilities made her valuable for finding children worth saving. They also made her vulnerable if they were discovered.

"Two hundred meters." Evan checked the dampening scanner clipped to his belt. The device registered zero, as always in his presence. Behind them, Rafael Martinez and Rebecca Hayes carried extraction gear. Their breathing was steady but shallow with suppressed tension.

The tunnel branched ahead. Left led to the old subway system, flooded with emotional runoff from decades of mind dampening. Right led to the Council Youth Development Center.

"Remember," Evan said, turning to face his team. "Three children tonight. Ages eight to twelve, all showing advanced feeling sensitivity. The Council has them scheduled for Correction procedures starting tomorrow morning."

Sarah's jaw tightened. Her hands formed fists at her sides. "Complete mind modification?"

"Brain surgery to remove feeling ability." The words tasted like ash in Evan's mouth. "The children would be returned to their families as perfect citizens. Obedient and stable. But unable to experience love."

They moved through the final stretch in silence. The familiar weight of rescue missions settled around them. Not fear, since Evan's immunity protected him from anxiety's paralyzing effects. But sharp awareness that three young lives hung in the balance.

The tunnel ended at a maintenance access panel. Evan cracked it just enough to scan beyond with his dampening detector. The readings showed suppression field strength at maximum levels. Enough to disable most resistance members within minutes.

"Field strength is brutal. I'll go first, establish a safe zone."

Rafael nodded, wiping sweat from his palms despite the tunnel's chill. As a former Council technician, he understood suppression exposure better than most. "We follow at thirty-second intervals. Sarah, you're our exit strategy if this goes wrong."

Evan slipped through the access panel into sterile corridors. The mind dampening fields washed over his consciousness without effect. Around him, the building hummed with technology that kept thousands of children emotionally numb while their natural abilities were worn away.

Two levels up, he found the target dormitory. Through the observation window, rows of small beds came into view. Each occupied by a child whose emotional capacity was scheduled for elimination.

Evan's breath caught in his throat. Three small forms, each one a future stolen. The sight never got easier, but tonight it cut deeper. These weren't just names on a list. They were children whose gifts would be carved away like tumors.

Twelve-year-old Jimmy Smythe lay closest to the door. Dark hair fell across features that would never again light with spontaneous joy. According to their intelligence, he'd been showing "dangerous feeling connection." The ability to sense and influence others' emotions at distance. Such gifts had once been considered wonderful. Now they marked him for surgical removal.

Jimmy stirred in his drug-induced sleep, and Evan caught a glimpse of the boy he'd been before the dampening took hold. Bright eyes that had probably sparkled with curiosity. A smile that had likely comforted other children when they were afraid. All of it scheduled for extraction in the morning.

Beside him, ten-year-old Lisa Park slept restlessly. Her dreams were probably filled with the emotional imprints she could read from objects and places. Her file indicated she'd described feeling "the sadness in the walls" of her family's apartment. An impossibility under standard mind dampening that made her a priority for Correction.

Lisa's small hands twitched as if reaching for something in her dreams. Perhaps memories of her mother's love, still accessible in sleep but soon to be surgically removed. Evan wondered what it felt like to be a child who could feel the world's hidden emotions, only to have adults decide that gift was too dangerous to keep.

The third child, eight-year-old Theo Reeves, was the youngest they'd ever attempted to extract. His ability to project calming emotions had been discovered when he'd soothed his dampened mother during a Council inspection. The family had been separated immediately.

Theo's face carried the innocence that only belonged to children who hadn't yet learned to fear their own hearts. His gift of comfort would be carved away before he turned nine. Before he could understand what was being stolen from him.

Evan activated the portable dampening blocker, creating a small field of emotional neutrality around the dormitory entrance. Fifteen minutes before the power cells failed. He signaled his team.

Within minutes, they reached his position. Rebecca moved toward Jimmy Smythe, then stopped dead.

Her breath caught audibly. "God, he's so small." Her voice cracked on the words. "Look at his hands. They're still baby hands."

Rafael stepped toward Lisa Park. His former technician's composure cracked as he looked down at her restless form. "They're just babies. How can they justify cutting into babies' brains?"

Sarah's feeling sensitivity made her reaction stronger. She pressed one hand against the doorframe, her face draining of color. "I can feel their dreams. They're so scared, even asleep. They don't understand why their families aren't coming for them."

"Focus," Evan whispered, though he felt the same protective rage building in his chest. "We get them out first. We grieve later."

Rebecca lifted Jimmy with trembling hands. Her movements were careful despite the urgency. The boy's head lolled against her shoulder, and she pressed her lips together to keep from sobbing. Rafael gathered Lisa while Evan took Theo. The eight-year-old's small form felt impossibly fragile.

As they prepared to leave, Theo's eyes fluttered open. For a moment, despite the suppression drugs, his natural gift activated. A wave of peace washed over the rescue team, the kind of comfort that only came from someone who truly cared about others' pain.

Then his eyes closed again, and the moment passed. But not before Evan understood exactly what the Council planned to destroy. Not just an ability, but the capacity for one human soul to heal another through pure compassion.

The escape route led through maintenance corridors. Each step carried them closer to safety. Evan's immunity let him scout ahead while the others followed, three unconscious children in their arms.

A soft alarm chimed somewhere in the building's depths.

"Security sweep," Rafael breathed. "Early."

They moved faster, taking service elevators and forgotten passages. Evan's heart hammered against his ribs as he calculated distances, timing, probabilities. Behind them, the alarm grew louder.

Sweat beaded on Rebecca's forehead as she adjusted Jimmy's weight. "Come on, baby," she whispered to the unconscious boy. "Just a little further."

They reached the tunnel access without discovery, but barely. In the darkness below, Sarah took point for the return journey while the others carried their charges. The children would wake in Holly's safe house. Confused and frightened but alive and intact.

"How many does this make?" Rebecca asked. Her voice was thick with exhaustion and relief.

"Two hundred and thirty-seven." Each number represented a life preserved from modification. But Evan also knew the larger count. Over fifty thousand children Corrected since the program's expansion five years ago.

Two hundred saved. Fifty thousand lost. The mathematics were brutal.

They emerged into the resistance network's central hub, where Holly Lloyd waited with medical equipment. At thirty-six, she was one of the few people alive who remembered life before mind dampening.

"Any complications?" Holly asked, already assessing the extracted children.

"Clean extraction. But security's tightening. They've upgraded their suppression fields again."

Holly nodded grimly as she checked Theo Reeves's vital signs. "Dr. Clarke has been tracking the energy consumption patterns. They're pouring more resources into containment every month."

Evan handed the boy to one of Holly's assistants. As he watched Theo being carried away to safety, a thought struck him with uncomfortable force. They were playing an endless game of rescue while the Council systematically destroyed thousands. Individual salvation was important, but it wasn't enough. Not anymore.

He headed toward the laboratory complex where Dr. James Clarke conducted his research. The former Council scientist had spent fifteen years documenting the true effects of planetary mind dampening. If anyone understood the bigger picture, it was Clarke.

"Evan, I need you to look at something." Clarke emerged from his laboratory. His expression carried the weight of disturbing discoveries. At fifty-two, he possessed the sharp intelligence of someone who'd spent decades questioning official explanations. "Tell me what you see."

Evan followed Clarke into the laboratory. The scientist's underground facility rivaled anything the Council operated. Built from salvaged equipment and powered by emotional energy crystallization techniques that Clarke had developed in secret.

The laboratory's main display showed a three-dimensional model of Earth. Data streams tracked emotional energy patterns across the planet's surface. Evan studied the swirling patterns of light and shadow that represented the planet's emotional state.

Through his immunity, Evan could sense the resonance even from the displays. It felt like standing beside a patient whose vital signs were failing. The planet's emotional networks were dying, and he could feel each connection as it snapped.

"The patterns are different," he observed. "More fragmented than last month."

Clarke's fingers drummed against the console. A nervous habit Evan had noticed developing over the past year. "The connections between regions are breaking down." He wiped his forehead with the back of his hand. "These dark zones are spreading faster."

An alert chimed from another workstation. Clarke moved to check it, his shoulders tense.

"Three times the rate we saw before." Evan traced the data flows, feeling the emotional resonance even through the displays. Each dark zone represented millions of people whose capacity for feeling was being systematically destroyed. "Something's accelerating the decay."

Clarke pulled up historical data, his hands shaking slightly. "What changed eighteen months ago?"

Evan studied the correlation between acceleration and Council policy updates. The pattern was clear once you knew what to look for. "The efficiency improvements. They've been upgrading the dampening technology."

"Each upgrade removes another connection that helped maintain stability." Clarke overlaid the progression data. "The system becomes more fragile with every improvement."

Another alert sounded. Clarke silenced it with an impatient gesture.

Evan felt the planet's distress through his natural sensitivity. A deep ache that had been growing stronger each month. Like watching someone you loved slowly bleeding to death. "We're not looking at five years anymore."

The words hung in the air between them. Both men understood what those numbers meant. Planetary emotional collapse. The death of humanity's capacity to feel, connect, love. The end of everything that made life worth living.

"If this acceleration continues," Clarke confirmed, "eighteen months. Maybe less."

Evan stared at the dying planet displayed before them. Eighteen months. Every child they'd rescued tonight would live to see the end of human emotion. Unless they found a way to stop it.

"Which means we need someone who can bridge the gap," Clarke continued. "Between dampened human consciousness and planetary awareness."

"Someone who understands both systems." Evan felt the pieces falling into place. But the picture they formed was terrifying. "Enhanced feeling strength, but also intimate knowledge of the dampening technology."

Clarke brought up a new display showing genetic markers. "A Collector who's awakening. Look at this DNA sequence."

Evan studied the patterns. He recognized some elements from his resistance training, but others were completely beyond anything he'd seen. "Enhanced feeling strength. But this is off the charts. Where did you get this sample?"

"Routine Council medical records. The subject is Collector 7739."

"Emma Thorne." The name carried weight beyond its syllables. Evan had been tracking her activities for months, watching her collection efficiency reports with growing fascination. "You think she could serve as the bridge."

Another alert sounded. Clarke silenced it, but his expression had grown more troubled.

"Her genetic heritage suggests exceptional feeling capacity. She's the Council's most effective Collector. But she's also showing signs of awakening."

Evan paced to the laboratory's far wall, his mind racing through implications. The idea was audacious. Use the Council's own weapon against them. Turn their most effective Collector into the instrument of their destruction.

But the risks were staggering.

"Approaching her directly would be suicide," he said. "She's completely conditioned. Constantly monitored. One wrong move and we lose everything."

Clarke set down his data tablet and turned to face Evan fully. "What draws people to authentic emotion?"

Evan stopped pacing. This was how Clarke worked. Questions that led to discoveries. "Natural curiosity? The hunger for real connection?"

"If we create conditions where she approaches us," Clarke suggested, "we don't need to risk direct contact."

"By being ourselves. By living with feeling in a dampened world." Evan began to see the strategy. It was elegant in its simplicity. "You're trusting in human nature."

"What drives people toward authentic connection?"

"Curiosity. Loneliness. The sense that something's missing from their lives."

Clarke nodded, his expression brightening for the first time that evening. "And if someone who's spent their entire life suppressing emotions encounters genuine feeling?"

"They'd be drawn to it." Evan felt the logic clicking into place. "But they'd also be afraid."

"Fear can teach. What questions might fear inspire?"

The approach crystallized in Evan's mind. Simple but profound. They wouldn't try to convince Emma Thorne to join them. They'd simply exist in her world as examples of what she was missing. Let her own awakening consciousness do the rest.

"Why does this person affect me differently? Why do my standard techniques fail? What am I missing?"

"We become the question that demands an answer."

It was desperate. But their situation had moved beyond conventional options. If direct contact with Emma Thorne was impossible, perhaps they could trust in the natural human tendency to seek connection and authenticity.

Evan thought about the three children they'd rescued tonight. Jimmy, who could comfort others with his emotions. Lisa, who could feel the sadness in walls. Theo, who could project peace to frightened adults. All of them gifts that the Council considered too dangerous to preserve.

But what if those gifts were exactly what the planet needed to survive? What if the solution to their crisis lay not in suppressing emotion, but in embracing it completely?

"It's a long shot," Evan admitted, looking back toward the medical section where Holly was caring for the three children they'd rescued. "But given our timeline, we may not have alternatives."

Each small life represented hope. But they needed something bigger than individual salvation. They needed transformation that could touch millions of dampened souls at once. They needed someone who could teach humanity to feel again before it was too late.

"Then we'd better get started. Eighteen months isn't very long to save the world."

As Clarke returned to his research and Evan went to check on the newly rescued children, neither man spoke about the odds they faced. The mathematics were clear. They needed Emma Thorne's cooperation to prevent planetary collapse. But approaching her could destroy everything they'd built.

Success required the impossible. Turning the Council's weapon into their salvation.

In the distance, the city's dampening fields hummed with steady efficiency. Processing the emotional energy of millions while strangling the planet's ability to sustain life. Time was running out, and their hope rested in someone who didn't even know they existed.

The underground currents that gave this chapter its name flowed deeper than the tunnels beneath New Geneva. They were the hidden streams of emotion that connected all living things. Growing weaker with each passing day as humanity's mechanical peace drove the world toward extinction.

But in the darkness of the Undercity, where emotional refugees found shelter and resistance members planned desperate missions, those currents still flowed strong enough to nourish hope. Whether that hope could grow into salvation depended on choices yet to be made by people who hadn't yet learned they held the planet's future in their hands.

The children would wake tomorrow in a place where emotions were treasured rather than feared. Where their gifts would be nurtured rather than destroyed. Jimmy would learn to use his ability to comfort others. Lisa would discover that feeling the world's hidden emotions was a blessing, not a curse. Theo would understand that his gift of peace was exactly what a broken world needed.

For now, that had to be enough. But Evan knew that individual rescues, however important, wouldn't stop the larger catastrophe approaching.

They needed Emma Thorne to choose love over duty. Humanity over system. Truth over the comfortable lies that had shaped her entire existence. And they needed her to make that choice before the planetary emotional field collapsed beyond recovery.

The underground currents were still flowing, but they grew weaker with each passing day. Soon, there would be no current strong enough to carry hope. No connection deep enough to sustain life. No emotion powerful enough to heal a world that had forgotten how to feel.

Unless someone who had been trained to destroy emotion chose instead to save it.

Chapter Four

WHEN THE WEAPON MISFIRES

Morning light filtered through New Geneva's towers at calculated angles, designed to maintain civic calm through natural illumination. Emma walked her memorized patrol route, standard boots striking clean concrete in measured rhythm. The Domestic Harmony sector hummed with controlled efficiency. No raised voices, no sudden movements, no outbursts requiring collection.

Today should have been routine.

Emma's brain devices registered normal readings from surrounding citizens. Quiet happiness that wasn't quite real. Controlled worry kept below dangerous levels by Council rules. Her collection equipment remained silent, waiting for the inevitable emotional disturbance.

The marketplace buzzed with calm activity. Vendors arranged goods in approved patterns while customers moved through stalls with purpose. Emma scanned for signs of strong feelings. Flushed cheeks indicating excitement, tense shoulders suggesting frustration, darting eyes marking dangerous curiosity.

She found her target near the produce section.

A dark-haired man argued with a vendor about pricing, his voice carrying passion that would trigger correction steps if left unchecked. The vendor showed stress patterns that could spread marketplace disruption. Standard collection required immediate action.

Emma approached with practiced confidence, activating her collection field. Her brain devices hummed online, sending control waves in a three-foot radius around her position. The familiar sensation of power flowing through her consciousness felt different today, somehow heavier, as if the energy itself was questioning its purpose.

"Citizens," she said, using the calm tone her training had perfected. "I'm detecting elevated emotional activity. Please submit to standard processing."

The vendor relaxed as Emma's control field covered him. His defensive posture melted into peaceful compliance. His anger evaporated, leaving behind the empty calm the Council called social harmony. Emma felt his absorbed anger settling into her collection chambers, but the sensation carried unexpected weight, as if she was robbing something precious rather than removing dangerous waste.

The customer remained unchanged.

Emma's breath caught in her throat. The air around her seemed to thicken, as if her control field was meeting resistance she'd never encountered. A strange humming filled her ears, different from her equipment's normal frequency. Her brain devices flickered, sending confused signals through her consciousness.

This wasn't possible. Her abilities worked on everyone. The Council had spent sixteen years teaching her that emotional energy could always be collected, processed, eliminated. Her success rate was ninety-seven percent, the department's highest. Every citizen responded to her field. Every emotion could be extracted and contained.

But this man stood before her, completely unaffected, as if her most fundamental capability was nothing more than a gentle breeze.

Emma increased field strength, her heart hammering against her ribs as reality shifted around her. The vendor's emotions had responded normally. The collection chambers registered his absorbed anger, proving her equipment worked perfectly. So why wasn't the customer responding?

"Twenty credits for cardboard tomatoes?" he said, brown eyes bright with unfiltered anger. "I could grow better vegetables in the Undercity tunnels."

Emma ran diagnostics through her brain interface, checking every system twice. All readings showed normal function. The collection chambers held the vendor's emotional energy, proof that her equipment operated correctly. But the evidence of her senses contradicted everything she'd been taught about the absolute nature of her abilities.

She stepped closer, near enough to see emotions play across his face in expressions that seemed foreign in their authenticity. The air between them felt charged, electric with possibilities her training had never prepared her for. When he glanced at her, his eyes held awareness that made her chest constrict.

He knew what she was attempting. And it wasn't working.

"Your equipment seems broken," he said, his voice carrying warmth her brain dampening couldn't categorize. "Maybe you should have it checked."

Emma's hands trembled as she moved to the collection device on her belt, checking connections she knew were secure. The familiar weight of the equipment felt foreign against her palm. Her fingers traced every wire, every junction, seeking some explanation for the impossible.

But deep in her mind, where her analytical training still functioned despite the chaos, Emma began to understand what she was witnessing. If her abilities weren't absolute, if resistance was possible, then everything the Council had taught her about necessity and control might be lies. The foundation of their entire social system rested on the assumption that emotional energy was dangerous and that her capabilities could neutralize any threat. One immune individual shattered that assumption completely.

"Sir, please comply with standard steps," she said, words emerging less certain than intended. "Strong emotional states threaten social harmony."

"Do they?" he asked, tilting his head. "Or do they threaten something else?"

The question struck Emma like physical force. Such questions weren't supposed to exist in her ordered world. Citizens accepted processing procedures. They understood emotional control's necessity. They didn't challenge the basic assumptions maintaining social stability.

Yet here was someone doing exactly that, standing in her control field as if it were nothing more than warm sunlight.

Emma watched the man disappear into the crowd, her entire understanding of reality crumbling around her. She stood among calm citizens, staring where he had vanished, while her mind raced through implications that terrified her.

Twenty meters away, Marcus observed from his watch position, his fingers tapping against his monitoring tablet in a rhythm that had nothing to do with regulation. Emma had never seen him make that gesture before. His jaw was clenched, his shoulders tense with worry that violated every protocol he'd been trained to follow. When their eyes met across the marketplace, his expression carried concern that handlers weren't supposed to feel.

Something was changing in both of them.

For the first time in her career, Emma had failed at her most basic function. The feeling both terrified and excited her, creating internal tension her brain dampening couldn't resolve.

That night, in her sterile Council apartment, Emma lay awake thinking about brown eyes holding impossible warmth and a voice asking questions she couldn't answer. She replayed the encounter, searching for clues to explain her equipment failure while trying to ignore the deeper truth her analytical mind had identified.

Her equipment hadn't failed. She had met someone existing outside her world's basic rules.

The thought should have horrified her. Instead, it filled her with something she barely recognized. Curiosity so intense it felt like hunger. For the first time, Emma wanted to see someone again, not for professional purposes but for the simple, dangerous pleasure of being near something real.

She sat up in bed, pressing her palms against her temples. The headache from yesterday's conditioning session had returned, but underneath it was something else. A warmth that had nothing to do with temperature. A connection that felt more real than anything in her controlled existence.

Emma rose and walked to her window, looking out at the city's dampened glow. Somewhere out there, the man who couldn't be processed was living his life with emotions intact. The idea fascinated her more than it should have.

But more than fascination, Emma felt the first stirrings of something that might have been hope. If one person could resist her abilities, perhaps the emotions she collected weren't as dangerous as the Council claimed. Perhaps the necessity of emotional control was an illusion maintained through careful lies and systematic suppression of evidence.

Her reflection stared back from the darkened glass, amber eyes wide with questions having no safe answers. The Council had spent sixteen years shaping her into the weapon against human emotion. But somewhere in their brain dampening's precision, they had missed something essential.

They had created someone capable of genuine feeling.

Over the following days, Emma found herself returning to the marketplace, ostensibly for routine patrols but actually searching for the man whose immunity had shattered her certainty. She studied every face, analyzed every emotional signature, hoping to find him again while dreading what such a meeting might mean.

Her enhanced sensitivity was growing stronger. Each collection now carried additional weight, as if she was absorbing not just emotional energy but fragments of the people she processed. A mother's love for her child lingered in Emma's consciousness long after the extraction was complete. An artist's passion for beauty created warm spaces in her mind that her dampening couldn't eliminate.

The realization struck her with devastating force during a routine collection from a street musician whose joy in his music had attracted a crowd. As Emma absorbed his passion, she felt not the removal of dangerous waste but the theft of something sacred. The musician's eyes, which had sparkled with creative fire, grew dull and empty. His hands, which had danced across his instrument with inspired grace, moved with mechanical precision.

She wasn't protecting society from emotional contamination. She was stealing pieces of human souls.

Emma stumbled backward from the musician, her collection chamber heavy with stolen joy, her consciousness reeling from the weight of understanding. Every person she'd processed in sixteen years of service. Every emotion she'd collected and contained. Every spark of authentic feeling she'd systematically destroyed.

She was a thief. A killer of everything that made life worth living.

The knowledge hit her like physical illness. Emma pressed her back against a building wall, fighting nausea as the full scope of her crimes became clear. The Council called her their most effective Collector, but she was really their most efficient destroyer of human authenticity.

Marcus noticed the changes in her performance reports. Collection efficiency remained high, but her processing times were increasing. She spent longer with each subject, sometimes standing motionless for minutes after completing an extraction. When questioned, she cited equipment calibration issues, but Emma could see suspicion growing in his brown eyes.

"Your brain patterns are showing irregular fluctuations," Marcus said during their weekly review session. His brown eyes held concern that violated handler rules. "Dr. Magnus wants to conduct additional testing."

Marcus's hands rested flat on the desk between them, but Emma noticed his fingers twitching slightly, as if he wanted to reach across the space separating them. The gesture was subtle, probably unconscious, but it spoke of care that his training insisted he shouldn't feel.

Emma's pulse quickened at the mention of Dr. Magnus. The researcher had offered to discuss theoretical applications of emotional energy, knowledge that might help Emma understand what was happening to her. But accessing that information would require admitting to capabilities that could mark her for immediate correction.

"I'm functioning within normal limits," Emma replied, using the standard response while calculating risks. "Any fluctuations are likely related to equipment sensitivity issues."

Marcus studied her face with the careful attention of someone trained to detect deception. His own emotional signature showed conflicts that his brain dampening couldn't quite suppress. Professional duty warred with personal concern, creating tension that made Emma realize her handler was experiencing his own awakening.

"Emma," Marcus said, his voice dropping to levels barely above a whisper. His fingers stopped their unconscious movement, forming fists on the desk surface. "If you're experiencing anything unusual, anything that feels wrong or different, you need to tell me. Not as your handler, but as someone who cares about what happens to you."

The admission hung between them like a confession of treason. Handlers weren't supposed to care about their subjects beyond work efficiency. But Emma could feel the authenticity of Marcus's concern, the genuine worry that proved his own brain dampening was beginning to fail.

Marcus was experiencing the same awakening that had begun transforming her understanding of everything. The careful conditioning that had shaped both their lives was breaking down, allowing authentic feeling to emerge from beneath years of artificial suppression.

"I know," Emma said, meeting his eyes with honesty that felt dangerous. "But some things can't be reported, Marcus. Some changes have to be lived through rather than corrected."

Marcus held her gaze for a long moment, processing implications that could destroy both their careers. Then he nodded, an acknowledgment that they had both crossed lines that couldn't be undone.

"Be careful," he said, his voice rough with emotion he wasn't supposed to possess. "Change is coming to the Council, and it won't be gentle for people like us."

That evening, Emma walked the regulated streets of New Geneva with new awareness. Her enhanced sensitivity let her detect the hidden emotional currents flowing beneath the city's dampened surface. Love disguised as appropriate concern. Joy compressed into acceptable satisfaction. Grief transformed into manageable disappointment.

The emotions weren't gone. They were hidden, waiting for someone brave enough to help them emerge.

As she passed the memorial to those lost in the Great Emotional War, Emma paused again at Dr. David Thorne's photograph. His amber eyes seemed to watch her with patient understanding, as if he had known this moment would come. The voice from her recovered memories whispered again about love being both dangerous and essential, about the choice between authentic existence and sterile safety.

Emma reached out, her fingertips touching the memorial plaque's cold metal. The sensation sent a shock through her system, not of electricity but of connection. For just a moment, she imagined what it would be like to reach for someone's hand. Not to collect their emotions, but simply to hold onto another person. To share warmth without stealing it.

The thought terrified her. It also felt like the most important thing she could possibly do.

She thought about the man in the marketplace, how his eyes had held such genuine warmth. How he had looked at her not as a weapon, but as a person capable of choice. How he had asked questions that challenged everything she believed about necessity and harmony.

What if the emotions she collected weren't dangerous waste, but the very essence of what made life worth living? What if her purpose wasn't to destroy feeling, but to preserve it?

Emma pressed her palm flat against Dr. Thorne's photograph, wishing she could reach through time to touch the father she barely remembered. Wishing she could ask him the questions that were tearing her carefully constructed world apart.

"I want to understand," she whispered to the memorial. "I want to know what you meant about love being dangerous and essential."

The plaza around her was empty, filled only with the soft hum of control fields and the distant sound of managed traffic. But Emma felt less alone than she had in years. Somewhere in the city, people were feeling things they weren't supposed to feel. Somewhere, emotions survived despite every effort to eliminate them.

And somewhere, a man with brown eyes was living proof that her abilities weren't absolute.

Walking home through streets that hummed with electronic tranquility, Emma made a decision that would reshape everything. Tomorrow, she would seek out Dr. Magnus and ask about those theoretical applications. She would begin learning what her abilities were really meant for, regardless of the danger.

She imagined approaching the mysterious man again, not as a Collector but as someone seeking to understand rather than suppress. She pictured extending her hand to him in greeting rather than domination. The image filled her with anticipation that had nothing to do with duty and everything to do with the growing certainty that there was more to existence than the Council had taught her.

The weapon was beginning to understand that her true purpose might be salvation rather than destruction. And somewhere in the darkness beyond New Geneva's control fields, people who had never stopped believing in the power of feeling waited for her to choose love over duty, humanity over system, truth over the comfortable lies that had shaped her entire existence.

The system was failing, one awakened heart at a time. And Emma Thorne was about to discover that failure could be the beginning of freedom.

Chapter Five

BLOOD ON THE COUNCIL'S HANDS

V iktor Brennan's hands shook as he spread the classified documents across his desk. The Council Historical Archives hummed with air conditioning, but tonight the mechanical sound felt different, oppressive, like the building itself was holding its breath. The fluorescent lights flickered overhead, casting moving shadows across pages that held evidence threatening to destroy everything he'd believed for twenty-three years.

The air tasted of recycled dust and old paper. Viktor's mouth had gone dry, his tongue sticking to his teeth as he stared at timestamps that made no sense. The familiar smell of archive storage, usually comforting after decades of research work, now seemed thick and suffocating.

The attack on Research Station Seven, March 15th, 2947. Viktor's chest tightened as he remembered Elena's last transmission, her voice crackling through static as she reported anomalous energy readings. Jonas's excited chatter in the background about visiting daddy's work. Forty-three casualties in a devastating surprise assault that proved the urgent need for control technology.

But the security withdrawal authorization made his stomach turn. March 14th, 1800 hours. Twelve hours before the attack.

Viktor set the document down with trembling fingers, his mind racing through implications he didn't want to accept. Why would security forces withdraw twelve hours before a surprise attack? His military training provided the answer he'd been refusing to see. You only pulled protection when you knew it wasn't needed. When you knew exactly what was coming.

The room seemed to tilt around him. Twenty-eight years of faithful service, twenty-eight years of believing he was preserving historical truth, and the evidence of his own family's murder was sitting right here in his archives. Filed away like any other routine operation.

His hands moved across the files with growing horror, each page revealing new layers of deception. The Barcelona Cascade. The Singapore Terror Event. Each attack that had convinced humanity to accept total emotional control showed the same pattern. Security withdrawals. Equipment relocations. Personnel reassignments. All occurring hours before the supposedly unexpected assaults.

Viktor pushed back from his desk, his chair wheels squeaking against the silence. The archives stretched around him in perfect order, thousands of carefully catalogued lies arranged by date and classification level. His life's work had been preserving the Council's version of history while the truth rotted in forgotten files.

The emotional weapon signatures sealed his certainty. Viktor spread the energy analysis charts across his desk, his trained eye recognizing patterns that civilian researchers would miss. The energy patterns should have been chaotic, different, reflecting improvised terrorist weapons. Instead, they showed mathematical precision. Identical frequency patterns. Calibrated power outputs.

These attacks had come from the same source. Council technology.

Viktor's chest constricted with something his brain dampening couldn't process. Elena had died believing she was protecting society from emotional chaos. Jonas had been murdered to justify a system of control that his parents had helped create. The Council had orchestrated their own family's destruction, then used their deaths to frighten millions into accepting neural suppression.

For twenty-three years, Viktor had mourned them as heroes. Now he understood they had been sacrifices on the altar of political control.

The weight of this knowledge settled into his bones like lead. Viktor sat in the sterile archives, surrounded by lies disguised as history, and felt something fundamental crack inside his mind. The careful conditioning that had kept him stable and productive for two decades couldn't contain the enormity of what he'd discovered.

Elena's laugh echoing through their kitchen on Sunday mornings. Jonas's small hand tucked trustingly into his as they walked to the research station. The scent of Elena's jasmine perfume lingering on her pillow after the funeral he'd attended alone.

All of it had been theater. Preparation for the Council's grand deception.

Two hours later, Viktor transmitted an encrypted message to Dr. James Clarke. The rogue scientist had been asking questions about emotional control's environmental effects for years. Questions that suddenly seemed less theoretical and more urgent.

They met in a forgotten maintenance tunnel beneath the city's medical district. Clarke had brought portable scanning equipment that registered emotional energy signatures while remaining undetectable to Council monitoring systems.

"You said you found problems in the historical records," Clarke said, studying Viktor's face with the sharp attention of someone trained to see beyond surface explanations.

Viktor spread the documents between them on a makeshift table. His hands were steadier now, focused by purpose rather than shock. "Look at these timestamps."

Clarke examined the files, his scientific mind processing the implications. "Security withdrawals twelve hours before each attack." He wiped his forehead with the back of his hand. "That requires advance warning."

"Or advance planning." Viktor's voice cracked despite his efforts at control. "The energy signatures match Council research technology. Not terrorist weapons. Laboratory instruments."

Clarke activated his portable display, the blue glow reflecting off tunnel walls. "You're saying the attacks were controlled demonstrations."

"I'm saying they were designed to terrify the population into accepting brain control." Viktor stared at the spectral analysis charts, feeling sick. "My wife and son died so the Council could justify total emotional suppression."

Clarke's fingers drummed against the equipment case. "The tragedy goes deeper than you realize." He activated his environmental data display. "Look at these patterns."

Viktor studied the overlapping datasets. Species extinction. Weather instability. Ocean acidification. The acceleration began exactly when global brain control was implemented.

"Emotions aren't just chemical responses," Clarke explained, then paused, rubbing his temples as if the words themselves caused pain. "They generate electrical activity that connects human consciousness to planetary systems." He looked up at Viktor, his eyes hollow. "Every suppressed feeling breaks another link between human awareness and the natural world."

Viktor traced the correlation with growing understanding. The data was undeniable once you knew what to look for. "We're not just controlling human feelings. We're cutting the connections that maintain ecological balance."

"The planet is dying because we've severed humanity from the emotional networks that sustain all life." Clarke's voice carried the weight of scientific certainty mixed with personal anguish. "The Council didn't just deceive the population about the attacks." He clenched his fists. "They're murdering the world's consciousness while claiming to protect it."

Viktor absorbed this information with growing rage. Not the controlled anger that brain control allowed for operational purposes, but hot, consuming fury. The fury of a man discovering that everything he'd devoted his life to protecting was built on lies and corpses.

The implications cascaded through his mind like dominoes falling. If the Council had murdered his family to justify emotional suppression, and if that suppression was killing the planet, then every day he'd spent preserving their version of history had been another day of complicity in genocide.

"What do we do?" Viktor asked, though he already suspected the answer wouldn't bring comfort.

"We need someone who can bridge the gap between controlled human consciousness and planetary awareness." Clarke gestured at his data displays. "Someone with exceptional emotional capacity who also understands the control system from the inside."

"Emma Thorne."

"The Council's most effective Collector. But approaching her directly would expose our entire operation."

Viktor considered the surveillance data Clarke displayed. Emma's behavioral patterns showed increasing stress responses during missions. Her efficiency ratings were declining. Her handler was showing unauthorized emotional investment in her welfare.

"Marcus Webb," Viktor said, understanding dawning. "His own conditioning is failing because of proximity to Emma's awakening."

Clarke nodded, his expression grim. "If we can accelerate his emotional breakthrough, he might become our path to reaching her."

"How?"

"By helping him discover what the Council plans to do with Emma when her abilities become too dangerous to control."

Viktor accessed his administrative files, pulling up classified protocols that made his blood run cold. "Termination procedures for compromised Collectors. If Emma's awakening continues, they'll eliminate her rather than risk losing control."

The words hung between them like a death sentence. Viktor stared at the termination orders, understanding exactly what the Council meant by "extreme measures" and "permanent solutions." Emma Thorne, the weapon they'd created to destroy human emotion, was marked for death the moment she began to feel.

Clarke nodded grimly. "And what would Marcus do if he understood that his loyalty is being used to deliver Emma to her executioners?"

"He'd choose her safety over his duty. But we need to make him reach that conclusion himself. Lead him to the evidence without revealing our involvement."

Viktor spent the next hour creating a trail of breadcrumbs that would guide Marcus toward the truth. Administrative queries that would flag Emma's termination protocols. Security reports that would show increased surveillance around her missions. Medical evaluations that revealed the Council's plans for her enhanced abilities.

Each document he flagged for Marcus's access was another step toward revolution. Viktor understood that once Marcus saw the evidence, there would be no going back for any of them. The handler would either betray his training to save Emma, or he would remain loyal and deliver her to her death.

"If this works," Viktor said as they prepared to separate, "we'll have turned the Council's weapon against itself. Emma's handler protecting her from her creators."

"And if it fails?"

Viktor looked at the evidence of his wife and son's murder, feeling something break loose in his chest that twenty-three years of conditioning couldn't contain. For the first time since the funeral, he allowed himself to remember Elena's jasmine perfume without the dampening filters that made grief manageable. The scent filled his memory with devastating clarity, along with the sound of Jonas's laugh and the warmth of small arms wrapped around his neck.

"Then we fight with whatever weapons we have left. The planet is dying, Clarke. Humanity has eighteen months before the emotional connections that sustain life are broken permanently."

The grief hit him like physical force. Viktor pressed his back against the tunnel wall, his chest heaving as twenty-three years of suppressed sorrow erupted through the cracks in his conditioning. Elena's perfume. Jonas's laughter. Sunday mornings when his family had been whole and the world had made sense.

He'd grieved them before, but always through the safe filter of neural dampening that kept pain manageable. Now, feeling the full weight of their loss without technological mediation, Viktor understood what the Council had stolen from him. Not just his family, but his right to mourn them properly.

"You understand what we're risking?" Clarke asked, his voice gentle.

"I understand what we're losing if we don't risk everything." Viktor gathered the classified documents that could destroy his career and possibly his life. "Elena and Jonas died for a lie. I won't let their sacrifice become meaningless by allowing that lie to kill the world."

Walking back through the tunnels toward the surface, Viktor carried more than evidence of Council deception. He carried the weight of change, the burden of seeing truth after decades of comfortable blindness. His brain dampening was cracking under the pressure of cognitive dissonance. The gap between what he'd been trained to believe and what he now knew to be true was creating space for authentic feeling to emerge.

For the first time in twenty-three years, Viktor allowed himself to grieve for his lost family. Not the controlled sadness that his conditioning permitted, but deep, wrenching sorrow for the life they should have lived together. Anger at the system that had stolen their future. Love that refused to be diminished by death or deception.

The emotions hurt. They also felt like coming back to life.

Viktor walked out from the tunnels into the pre-dawn darkness of New Geneva's streets. Above him, the city's control fields hummed with electronic efficiency, processing the emotional energy of millions while maintaining the illusion of peace. But now he knew the truth: that peace was an artificial construct built on murdered feelings and planetary destruction.

The evidence in his briefcase would either spark the awakening that humanity desperately needed or trigger a crackdown that would eliminate the last hope for emotional freedom. Viktor had spent his career following orders, believing in the system, trusting that those in power acted for the greater good.

Now he understood that sometimes the greater good required betraying everything you'd been taught to believe. As he walked toward his apartment through streets that pulsed with hidden desperation, Viktor began planning the most important conversation of his life.

Marcus Webb needed to learn the truth about the system he served. Emma Thorne needed to discover her real purpose. And the planet needed someone brave enough to restore the emotional connections that gave life meaning.

The protocols were failing, one awakened conscience at a time. Viktor Brennan had chosen to help them fall faster.

In eighteen hours, he would begin implementing a strategy that could either restore human consciousness or complete its destruction. The investigation that had started as routine archival verification had become the first step in a revolution that could either save the world or damn it.

But some truths, once discovered, demanded action regardless of the consequences. Viktor clutched his briefcase tighter as he thought about Elena's smile, Jonas's laughter, and the billions of people who deserved to experience authentic emotion before the planet's heart stopped beating forever.

The breaking point was approaching. When it came, Viktor intended to be on the side of feeling rather than control, truth rather than comfortable lies, love rather than the artificial peace that was slowly strangling everything beautiful about human existence.

The revolution had begun in the archives of the Council's own historical records. Soon it would spread to every controlled mind that remembered, however faintly, what it felt like to be truly alive.

Chapter Six

WHAT THE HEART REMEMBERS

E mma shouldn't be here.

The thought echoed through her mind as she walked down the transport station's metal steps. Each step carried her further from her normal routine and deeper into territory that could destroy everything she'd built her life around. Three days had passed since the market incident. Three days of perfect collections and flawless reports. Three nights lying awake in her bare apartment, thinking about brown eyes that showed no fear when her abilities failed.

She found him at the same café where pre-suppression foods drew people seeking flavors too strong for normal nutrition. The spices that once caused emotional responses had been banned from standard meal programs, but places like this operated in legal gray areas. They served unusual foods to those wealthy enough to afford controlled treats. Emma had never understood the appeal before. Now the scents of cinnamon and cardamom that drifted from the kitchen stirred something in her chest that her brain control couldn't quite stop.

Evan Cross sat at a corner table. His attention focused on a steaming cup and a small device she didn't recognize. When she approached, he looked up without surprise, as if he'd been expecting her arrival. The fact that he wasn't shocked should have warned her away. Instead it drew her forward.

"You're the Collector from the market," he said, gesturing to the empty chair across from him. His voice carried that same warmth she remembered, a quality that her conditioning had no category for.

Emma remained standing, aware that sitting would break protocol. Collectors didn't socialize with civilians. They kept professional distance, completed their assignments, and returned to Council facilities for debriefing and emotional discharge. What she was doing now fell somewhere between curiosity and treason.

But her curiosity had been growing stronger each day since the market encounter. Emma found herself analyzing the failure from every angle her training had taught her, running through diagnostic procedures and equipment evaluations with the systematic approach of someone who had never encountered a problem she couldn't solve. Yet every analysis led to the same impossible conclusion: her abilities had failed because this man existed outside the fundamental assumptions that governed her world.

"I need to understand why my abilities didn't work on you," she said, choosing directness over small talk.

Evan studied her face with an intensity that made her want to look away. "Sit," he said. "Please. This conversation is too important for either of us to be uncomfortable."

Against every instinct her conditioning had installed, Emma sat. The chair's worn fabric felt strange after years of Councilissued furniture designed for optimal emotional neutrality. Around them, the café hummed with quiet conversations and the subtle energy of people showing more emotional range than guidelines allowed.

"Your equipment works perfectly," Evan said, wrapping his hands around his cup. "The problem isn't technical."

Emma leaned forward, drawn by his certainty. "Then what is it?"

"Some people have natural resistance to brain control. We call it emotional immunity."

The words hit Emma like cold water. "That's impossible. Council research proves no such trait exists."

"Council research." Evan's smile carried sadness. "And what if their research was designed to hide the truth rather than reveal it?"

Emma's conditioning demanded that she reject such ideas immediately. But her analytical mind, trained to evaluate evidence objectively, couldn't ignore the data she'd witnessed firsthand. If Evan possessed immunity to her abilities, and if the Council's research claimed such immunity was impossible, then either her experience was false or the research was incomplete.

She had felt her dampening field wash over him without effect. She had watched him respond to her commands with casual dismissal. The evidence of her senses contradicted official scientific conclusions, creating a gap in her understanding that her training insisted shouldn't exist.

"The Council doesn't falsify scientific data," she said, but her voice lacked conviction.

"Doesn't it?" Evan reached into his jacket and withdrew a small crystal-like object that seemed to pulse with internal light. The moment Emma's eyes focused on it, her brain devices registered energy patterns unlike anything in her database. The crystal gave off warmth, not physical heat but something that touched the hollow space in her chest and made it ache with unnamed longing.

"What is that?" she whispered.

"Touch it and find out."

Emma's conditioning screamed warnings about unidentified energy sources and unauthorized emotional exposure. Protocol demanded that she report the crystal immediately, classify it as a potential weapon, request backup before proceeding with investigation. But her hands moved on their own, reaching for the crystal with desperate hunger that her conditioning couldn't explain.

The moment her fingers made contact, the world shifted.

Joy flooded through her. Not the shallow satisfaction of completed assignments, but something deeper, warmer, more alive than anything she'd ever experienced. Her breath caught as the feeling expanded through her chest, and for an instant she was five years old again, spinning in her father's arms while Sunday morning sunlight streamed through kitchen windows. She could smell fresh bread baking and hear laughter that bubbled up from some pure source within her.

Wonder followed the joy. The awe of seeing sunset colors for the first time, the marvel of discovering that beauty existed beyond function. Her father's voice reading stories that painted worlds where dragons were wise and magic was love given form. The warmth of being treasured, protected, valued for who she was rather than what she could do.

Then came connection. The warm certainty that she wasn't alone, that other consciousness touched hers with affection and acceptance. Her mother's hands braiding her hair while humming melodies that carried safety and belonging. The feeling of being part of something larger than herself, connected to every living thing by invisible threads of caring.

For thirty seconds, Emma experienced what it felt like to be fully human.

When the crystal's energy faded and her dampening systems reasserted control, the contrast nearly broke her. Emma's breath caught, her hand jerking back from the crystal as tears she hadn't felt in sixteen years burned her eyes. The hollow space in her chest felt larger now, carved out by the memory of what it was like to be filled with authentic feeling.

"That's what we've lost," Evan said, his voice soft. "That's what the brain control system has taken from every person on this planet. Not chaos or danger, but the capacity for connection and happiness."

Emma stared at her hands, still tingling from the crystal's touch. The memory of her father's arms around her felt more real than anything in her current existence. "Where did you get this?"

"There are places where emotions have crystallized naturally, where the control fields couldn't reach or where the energy was too concentrated to eliminate. We call them the Emotion Gardens."

The crystal's warmth spread through Emma's body like sunlight after winter. She had felt real joy, authentic connection, the possibility of love without fear. The experience made her current existence feel like shadows on a cave wall, pale imitations of something infinitely more beautiful and true.

"You feel it now, don't you?" Evan asked. "The difference between what you've been living and what life could be."

"It's beautiful," Emma said, her voice breaking slightly. "Why would anyone want to eliminate something so beautiful?"

"Fear. Control. The belief that safety is more important than authenticity."

Emma held the crystal against her palm, feeling its pulse synchronize with her heartbeat. The warmth reminded her of her father's hands, of Sunday mornings when the world had been full of wonder instead of duty. "You said there are others like you. People with natural resistance."

Evan paused, studying her face as if weighing how much truth she could handle. "Emma."

The use of her name sent a shock through her system. In her professional life, she was Agent Thorne or Collector 7-Alpha. Personal names belonged to her childhood, before full conditioning, before her life became a series of assignments and emotional extractions. Hearing it spoken with warmth created a feeling in her chest that threatened to break through her maintained composure.

"How do you know my name?"

Evan's expression grew serious. "Because we've been watching you."

Emma's breath quickened. "Watching me?"

"Your abilities are changing, growing beyond their original design. The strange readings, the unusual responses, the way you're beginning to preserve emotions instead of destroying them."

The words hit Emma with devastating accuracy. How could he know about the changes she'd barely begun to understand herself? "You know about that?"

Evan leaned forward, his voice dropping to levels that wouldn't carry to other tables. "We know about everything, Emma. We know that you saved a mother and child three days ago by teaching them to hide their emotional capacity."

Emma's heart hammered against her ribs. No one should know about that incident. Her reports had classified it as a standard extraction with no complications. "That's impossible. There were no witnesses."

"We know that your genetic heritage includes enhanced feeling ability markers that were supposed to be eliminated from Council records."

The room seemed to tilt around Emma. Her genetic profile was classified at levels she didn't even have access to. "How could you possibly know that?"

"We know that your awakening isn't accident," Evan continued. "It's destiny."

Emma stood halfway, then sat back down as the magnitude of what he was suggesting made her head spin. "You're saying my entire life has been designed?"

"I'm saying you're not just a Collector who happened to awaken. You're someone who was created for a specific purpose, then hidden away until the time was right."

The implications cascaded through Emma's mind like a dam bursting. If her abilities were designed rather than natural, if her awakening was planned rather than accidental, then everything she believed about herself was constructed. Her identity, her purpose, her entire understanding of who she was might be elaborate fiction designed to prepare her for something she didn't yet comprehend.

Emma thought about Chancellor Keller's emotional signature, the maternal love she'd detected beneath layers of professional control. "My handler. My superiors. They know what I'm becoming."

"Some of them suspect. Others are beginning to experience their own awakening because of their proximity to you."

Emma processed this with growing unease. "What do you mean?"

"Your abilities don't just process emotions, Emma. They can awaken dormant emotional capacity in others. You're not just a weapon against feeling. You're a catalyst for its return."

The crystal pulsed warmth against her skin as Emma struggled to understand what Evan was telling her. If her presence could awaken others, if her changing abilities were affecting people around her, then Marcus's growing concern and Dr. Magnus's theoretical interests weren't coincidental. They were symptoms of her influence spreading beyond her control.

"What do you want from me?"

"What do you want from yourself? You've felt what real emotion is like now. You've experienced authentic connection. Can you go back to the hollowness of dampened existence?"

Emma looked around the café, seeing it with new awareness. The subtle warmth between the couple sharing dessert. The quiet contentment of the elderly man reading in the corner. The gentle affection in the server's voice as she checked on customers. All of this emotional richness existed in the spaces between Council monitoring, hidden but persistent.

The answer was no. She couldn't go back to emptiness after experiencing fullness. She couldn't return to shadows after seeing sunlight. The crystal had shown her what she'd been missing, and now the absence felt like physical pain.

"If I help you," Emma said, her voice steady despite the magnitude of the choice, "what happens to the people I care about? Marcus, Dr. Magnus, even Chancellor Keller. What happens to them when the system falls apart?"

"They have the same choice you do. Awakening or stagnation. Connection or control. Life or the comfortable simulation of living."

Emma stood, the crystal's warmth spreading through her entire body. For the first time in her adult life, she felt fully alive. The sensation was overwhelming and terrifying and absolutely essential.

"I need time to think."

"Time is something we don't have much of," Evan said, rising as well. "The planetary emotional field is collapsing."

Emma paused, her hand halfway to her jacket pocket. "What do you mean?"

"Without intervention, we have eighteen months before permanent damage occurs."

"Eighteen months until what?"

Evan's expression grew grave. "Until the connections between human consciousness and the living world are cut beyond repair. Until the planet itself dies from emotional starvation."

The words hit Emma like ice water. Her skin went cold, her stomach dropping as if she'd stepped off a cliff. Eighteen months. Not some distant theoretical future, but a count-down that had already begun. The warmth from the crystal couldn't touch the sudden chill that spread through her body as she understood what Evan was telling her.

She wasn't choosing between personal safety and individual awakening. She was choosing between the survival of human consciousness and the comfortable death of everything that made existence meaningful. The weight of the world settled on her shoulders like a physical burden, pressing down until she could barely breathe.

"Keep the crystal," Evan said. "When you're ready to save the world, we'll be waiting."

Emma left the café with her mind in chaos and her chest tight with feelings her conditioning had no names for. The crystal pressed against her ribs like a warm secret, its energy seeping through her jacket to touch her skin with promises of connection and authenticity.

She was halfway home before she realized she was humming. The melody had no words, but it carried emotions that her conditioning couldn't suppress: hope, curiosity, and the terri-fying possibility that everything she'd believed about her purpose might be wrong.

That night, Emma lay in her standard bed staring at the crystal she'd hidden beneath her pillow. Its soft glow leaked through the fabric, creating patterns on her ceiling that shifted like living things. When she touched it, waves of feeling washed through her. Not the muted shadows the

Council allowed, but the full spectrum of human experience that Evan had described.

As she drifted toward sleep, Emma thought about the man who had given her this gift. His brown eyes had held no fear when her abilities failed to affect him. His voice had carried warmth that her conditioning couldn't categorize. His questions had awakened curiosity that might be more dangerous than any emotion she'd ever collected.

But danger, Emma was beginning to understand, might be preferable to the slow death of everything that made existence meaningful. The crystal pulsed against her palm like a heartbeat, reminding her that somewhere beyond the Council's reach, people still remembered what it felt like to be truly alive.

For the first time in her adult life, Emma fell asleep smiling.

The next morning brought reports of minor anomalies in the city's control grid. Brief fluctuations that caused temporary emotional breakthroughs in scattered individuals across New Geneva. People woke from dreams that tasted like freedom. Children laughed with delight. Lovers touched hands in defiance of closeness rules.

The fluctuations were corrected, the breakthroughs suppressed, the protocols restored. But something had changed in the fabric of the city's emotional landscape. A crack had appeared in the perfect order, and through that crack, feeling was beginning to seep.

Emma carried the crystal to work that day, its warmth against her skin a constant reminder that resistance was possible. She performed her collections with mechanical precision, but each extraction felt different now. Instead of removing dangerous emotional waste, she was removing pieces of human souls.

The realization should have horrified her. Instead, it filled her with determination to find another way. If emotions weren't waste products but essential parts of human consciousness, then her abilities might be capable of preservation rather than destruction.

But learning to use her gifts differently would require help from people the Council considered enemies. It would mean trusting strangers who lived beyond the reach of brain control, who remembered what the world had been like before feelings became crimes.

The crystal pulsed against her chest, carrying messages from the Emotion Gardens that Evan had described. Places where love crystallized into objects of power, where joy took physical form, where the planet's emotional heart still beat with enough strength to nourish hope.

Emma Thorne, the Council's weapon, was beginning to understand that her true purpose might be preservation rather than destruction. Somewhere in the shadows of New Geneva, people who had never stopped believing in the power of feeling waited for her to choose love over duty, humanity over system, truth over the comfortable lies that had shaped her entire existence.

The pull toward emotion and freedom was growing stronger. Emma was no longer sure she wanted to resist it.

Chapter Seven

WHEN SAVING BECOMES BETRAYAL

The enforcement vehicle's metal walls pressed against Emma's shoulders as Marcus drove through the early morning streets of New Geneva. Three days had passed since her experience at the café. Each routine patrol felt like walking on thin ice. Her handler sat rigid in the driver's seat, his dark eyes moving between the road and the screen that tracked her vital signs.

"Your stress levels are elevated," Marcus said, his voice carrying the concern she'd grown used to over their three years together. He paused, his fingers tapping against the steering wheel. "Maybe we should... maybe another training session would help."

Emma forced her breathing to steady, watching the numbers on his screen return to normal ranges. The crystal hidden in her jacket pocket pulsed with warmth that her monitoring equipment couldn't detect. It filled her with strength she'd never known before. "Equipment problems," she replied, using the excuse she'd practiced. "My brain devices need adjustment."

The lie tasted bitter. Since the café incident, every emotion she encountered seemed to push against the walls of her training like water against a cracking dam. Yesterday's collection from a grieving widower had left her hands shaking for twenty minutes. The man's love for his dead wife had been so pure, so beautiful in its pain, that she'd almost forgotten to complete the absorption process.

But the forgetting hadn't been accident or oversight. Emma was beginning to understand that her hesitation came from a deeper recognition: she was witnessing something sacred being destroyed. Each collection felt less like removing dangerous waste and more like stealing pieces of what made existence meaningful.

Marcus stopped the vehicle outside an apartment building where their morning assignment waited. The report was routine: a domestic disturbance requiring emotional processing. But as Emma approached the building's entrance, she felt something that made her pause.

Fear. Not the clean, simple emotion she was trained to collect, but something deeper. A child's terror so strong it seemed to echo through the building's walls like a scream that only she could hear.

"Unit 3712 is on the third floor," Marcus said, checking his handheld scanner. His voice caught slightly. "Domestic problem with... with minor involvement. Standard collection procedures should apply."

Emma nodded, but her enhanced sensitivity was painting a more complex picture. The child's fear had layers. Physical danger, yes. But underneath lay something worse. Desperation. The terror of knowing no one would help, no one would listen, no one would care.

They climbed the stairs in practiced silence. Emma's brain devices began their standard pre-collection warm-up. Instead of the usual detachment, she found herself dreading what they would find. The fear was getting stronger, joined now by adult emotions: frustration and rage barely held back by training.

As they climbed, Emma's mind drifted to her last evaluation with Chancellor Keller. The woman's sharp eyes studying Emma's performance reports. Her questions about "unusual collection patterns" and "extended processing times." The way Keller had watched Emma's face when discussing the importance of "maintaining emotional discipline in all circumstances." Even through her own training, Emma had sensed something calculating in the Chancellor's attention, as if she was looking for specific signs of weakness or change.

Marcus knocked on the apartment door. "Council enforcement. Please open for emotional processing services."

The door opened to reveal a woman whose brain control was failing. Emma could see it in the tension around her eyes, the way her hands shook despite her efforts at composure. Behind her, a small boy, maybe six years old, pressed himself against the wall. His amber eyes were wide with the kind of terror that should have been impossible under emotional management.

"Thank you for coming so fast," the woman said. Her voice stayed controlled but sounded fragile, like glass about to shatter. "I'm having some... difficulties with emotional stability."

Emma stepped forward, her training demanding she activate her collection field as she'd done thousands of times before. But something made her hesitate. The woman's struggle wasn't pathological emotional excess. It was maternal love fighting against systematic suppression. The boy's fear wasn't irrational childhood terror. It was the rational response of someone watching his mother's capacity for caring being stripped away.

As Emma's brain devices engaged, something unprecedented happened. Her breath caught in her throat as unfamiliar sensations flooded through her neural pathways. Instead of simply absorbing the family's emotional energy, she began to understand it with startling clarity, each feeling hitting her like a physical blow. The woman was fighting a losing battle against maternal love. Her son had begun showing signs of natural emotional sensitivity. The Council's treatment protocols demanded she suppress her protective instincts. The rage Emma detected wasn't directed at the child but at a system that required her to watch her son's emotional capacity being destroyed.

The boy feared not just the collection process but the growing emptiness in his mother's eyes. He could sense her love being removed piece by piece. He knew, with the natural wisdom of childhood, that something essential was being stolen from both of them.

Emma's training screamed at her to complete the collection, to restore harmony by eliminating these dangerous emotional attachments. But her enhanced awareness showed her what harmony meant in this context: a mother and child reduced to biological units sharing living space, their capacity for love replaced by sterile indifference.

"The child is showing irregular emotional patterns," Marcus observed, studying his readings. His voice wavered. "Early correction protocols may be... may be necessary."

The words hit Emma like a physical blow. She understood what "early correction" meant: brain modification that would eliminate the boy's ability to form emotional bonds. The child would be returned to his mother as a perfect citizen, obedient, stable, and unable to experience love.

But Emma was no longer the same person who had accepted such procedures as necessary. The crystal's warmth against her chest reminded her of what authentic feeling looked like. The memory of her father's arms around her, of Sunday morning laughter, of love given freely without fear or restraint. She couldn't destroy that possibility for this family.

"I can handle this," Emma said, her voice sharper than intended. "Standard collection should be sufficient."

Marcus looked at her with surprise, his eyebrows drawing together. "Are you... sure? Protocol clearly states..."

"I'm sure." Emma moved toward the family, extending her absorption field while trying to figure out what she could do differently.

Her brain devices engaged with the woman's emotional energy. Emma found herself inside the controlled consciousness, feeling memories of holding the boy as a baby, the fierce joy of his first smile, the way his laughter had filled empty spaces in her life that she hadn't known existed. She experienced the growing horror as Council training numbed those connections, replacing maternal love with clinical concern for optimal development outcomes.

But instead of draining these emotions away, Emma began attempting something she'd never tried before. She started to compress them, folding the woman's love down into smaller, denser patterns that could hide beneath the surface of her training. The process felt like working with liquid light, gathering streams of warmth and affection into tight spirals that pulsed with concentrated feeling. Emma had to be precise. Too much compression and the emotions would turn toxic, burning through the woman's consciousness like acid. Too little and they would remain detectable by Council monitoring systems.

The compression required Emma to touch each memory individually, her consciousness burning with the effort as she wrapped layers of protective neural activity around the moments of connection between mother and child. Her hands shook from the strain. She felt the woman's love for her son condensing into a bright core that nestled deep in her mind, hidden beneath layers of acceptable emotional responses but still burning with authentic warmth.

The absorption took longer than normal. Emma could sense Marcus's growing concern as she worked to help the woman build internal barriers that would protect her essential emotional connections while presenting a controlled exterior to Council surveillance. The woman's eyes cleared as her visible distress disappeared, but Emma could feel the hidden warmth still burning beneath the surface.

The boy was more challenging. His natural emotional sensitivity made him vulnerable to detection, but it also gave him an understanding of what Emma was trying to do. When she extended her field toward him, instead of the terror she expected, she felt something that made her breath catch.

Trust. Complete, absolute faith that she would help him rather than hurt him.

The boy's trust opened something in Emma's abilities that she hadn't known existed. Instead of suppressing his emotional capacity, she found herself teaching him how to hide it. Through the brain connection, she showed him how to create false readings while preserving his feelings in protected mental spaces. It was like helping him build a secret room in his own mind, a place where love could survive even under Council observation.

The technique felt intuitive once she began. Emma guided the boy's consciousness through the process of creating emotional camouflage, showing him how to present the appearance of proper training while keeping his authentic feelings safe in hidden chambers of his mind. She wrapped his capacity for joy, wonder, and affection in layers of protective neural activity that would register as normal brain control to monitoring equipment.

The process left Emma's hands shaking and sweat beading on her forehead despite the cool air. When she stepped back from the family, both mother and child looked normal by Council standards. Their emotional readings showed standard control levels. Their behavior showed appropriate processing patterns. But Emma knew that underneath those false signals, their capacity for love remained intact and hidden.

"Collection complete," she reported, hoping Marcus couldn't hear the tremor in her voice. "Emotional levels normalized within acceptable parameters."

Marcus reviewed his scanner data, his face showing relief mixed with lingering uncertainty. "Excellent work. No... no correction protocols necessary." He made notes on his hand-held device while Emma tried to process what she had just done.

She had saved them. Not just from immediate collection, but from the destruction of their emotional bonds. The realization hit Emma like warm sunlight breaking through storm clouds. Her knees felt weak with relief and terror combined. The boy would grow up with his capacity for love intact, hidden but protected. The woman would be able to care for her son with affection disguised as compliance.

But Emma had also crossed a line that could never be undone. Her chest constricted as the magnitude of her betrayal settled into her bones. Instead of collecting emotions, she had preserved them. Instead of enforcing brain control, she had taught resistance. Her hands trembled as she considered the consequences. If Marcus discovered what she had done, if the Council detected the false readings, if her new abilities were exposed, the weight of her choice would crush everyone she cared about.

"Your efficiency ratings have been declining," Marcus said, his voice cutting through her racing thoughts. He cleared his throat. "Chancellor Keller has... she's requested a full evaluation."

The words hit Emma like ice water. Chancellor Keller, the woman who had overseen her training, who monitored her development, who held absolute authority over Emma's life and future. If she was requesting an evaluation, it meant Emma's recent changes had been noticed at the highest levels.

The memory of her last meeting with Keller flashed through Emma's mind with painful clarity. The Chancellor's office with its white walls and monitoring equipment. Keller sitting behind her metal desk, gray eyes sharp with intelligence as she reviewed Emma's performance data. "Your collection techniques are becoming... elaborate, Agent Thorne. Extended processing times suggest either equipment failure or operator error. Which do you believe applies to your case?" The question had felt like a trap, each word chosen to probe for signs of emotional instability or awakening resistance.

"When?" Emma asked, fighting to keep her voice steady.

"Tomorrow morning. Full evaluation and brain pathway analysis." Marcus paused, studying her expression with attention she'd come to recognize as personal concern rather than duty. "Emma, if you're experiencing any... irregularities in your emotional processing, now would be the time to report them. Treatment is most effective when implemented early."

Emma met his eyes, seeing worry beneath his official manner. A sharp pang of guilt twisted in her stomach. Marcus had always been kind to her within the constraints of his role. She realized that his concern might represent something more than duty. But she also knew that honesty would mean immediate correction, possibly even termination if her abilities were deemed too dangerous.

"I'm fine," she said. The lie felt like betrayal. "Just routine equipment problems."

Marcus held her gaze for a moment longer, then nodded. "We should... we should return to base for debriefing."

As they walked back to the enforcement vehicle, Emma felt the weight of her choices settling around her like a heavy cloak. She had saved a mother and child from emotional destruction, but she had also revealed abilities that could destroy her if discovered. Tomorrow's evaluation with Chancellor Keller would determine whether her secret techniques remained hidden or whether her growing resistance to brain control would be exposed.

The drive back to headquarters passed in tense silence. Emma stared out the window at New Geneva's ordered streets, seeing the city differently now. Every controlled citizen walking past represented someone whose emotional capacity had been reduced. Every smooth facade of a building hid controlled feelings that might be crying out for recognition and healing.

At the enforcement station, Emma submitted to routine post-mission monitoring while Marcus filed their reports. The scanners showed nothing unusual. Her heart rate and brain activity had normalized during the drive. But Emma knew that tomorrow's evaluation would be far more thorough, using advanced detection methods that might penetrate her constructed facade.

That evening, in her standard apartment with its neutral colors and emotional control fields, Emma sat before her bathroom mirror and studied her reflection. She pulled off her enforcement jacket, letting it fall to the floor with a soft thud. Her amber eyes looked back at her with an intensity that hadn't been there a week ago. She was changing in ways that went beyond her abilities, developing a sense of purpose that had nothing to do with Council training and everything to do with protecting what remained of human emotional capacity.

Emma pulled the crystal from her pocket and held it against her bare skin. Its warmth spread through her palm and up her arm, carrying messages from places where love still existed without fear. She pressed it against her chest, feeling its pulse synchronize with her heartbeat.

The risks were enormous. Discovery would mean correction or elimination, not just for her but for everyone she had helped. Marcus would face discipline for failing to detect her changes. The families she protected would be subjected to enhanced control protocols.

But the alternative was watching humanity lose its capacity for love, connection, and feeling. Emma thought about the boy's trust, the woman's hidden maternal warmth, and the thousands of other controlled individuals who might be helped if she could refine her techniques and avoid detection.

Tomorrow's evaluation would test everything she had learned about hiding her abilities while preserving her essential humanity. Chancellor Keller was known for her sharp intelligence and absolute dedication to the brain control system. If anyone could detect Emma's change, it would be her. The thought made Emma's skin prickle with cold fear.

Emma closed her eyes and reached out with her enhanced sensitivity, feeling the emotional landscape of the building around her. Dozens of Council employees, all controlled, all maintaining the calm that allowed the system to function. But underneath that surface tranquility, she sensed something else: tiny sparks of feeling that brain control couldn't eliminate.

Hope existed, even here in the heart of the Council's power. People were stronger than the system that sought to control them. Emotions were more resilient than the technology designed to contain them. Emma's awakening was proof that human consciousness could grow beyond its constraints.

But first, she had to survive tomorrow's evaluation. She had to convince Chancellor Keller that she remained the weapon, obedient, controlled, and dedicated to suppressing the emotional capacity that was becoming the most important part of her identity.

As Emma prepared for sleep, she made a silent promise to the families she had helped and the countless others she might yet save. Whatever tomorrow brought, she would find a way to protect their hidden emotional heritage while developing her abilities in secret.

The crystal pulsed against her palm as she held it beneath her pillow, its warmth carrying messages from the Emotion Gardens where love still crystallized into objects of power. Tomorrow would bring new challenges, new risks, new opportunities to choose between safety and truth.

But tonight, Emma fell asleep knowing that she had saved two souls from the Council's machinery of emotional destruction. The crack lines were spreading, one protected heart at a time. Somewhere in the darkness beyond her apartment window, the planet's emotional field pulsed with renewed strength, fed by the hidden love she had helped preserve.

The weapon was learning that her true purpose might be preservation rather than destruction. And with each choice to save rather than suppress, Emma moved closer to becoming something the Council had never intended to create: a bridge between the controlled world and the authentic feelings that could heal it.

Chapter Eight

THE DAUGHTER SHE CANNOT CLAIM

D r. James Clarke's weathered hands moved across the quantum resonance scanner with practiced precision. The device's crystal sensors picked up emotional energy patterns that shouldn't exist in the sterile Council archives. Councilor Viktor Brennan stood beside him in the forgotten basement, his military posture failing to hide the uncertainty that had grown since their first secret meeting three days ago.

Viktor's hands trembled slightly as he gripped his briefcase tighter. Twenty-eight years of loyal service to the Council. Nearly three decades of believing he was protecting humanity from chaos. And now, standing in this hidden laboratory surrounded by evidence of systematic deception, he felt the foundation of his entire adult life cracking beneath his feet.

"The readings match our models," Clarke said, adjusting the device's controls. "Planetary emotional decay has sped up. If these patterns continue, we're looking at complete breakdown within eighteen months."

Viktor studied the holographic display showing emotional resonance patterns from the past century. The charts revealed steady decline in planetary emotional resonance, with environmental damage patterns that matched perfectly. The Council blamed these changes on natural climate variations, but seeing the data together, Viktor recognized something his military training had taught him to notice.

"These patterns track too closely to be coincidence," Viktor said, his voice hoarse. His throat felt dry as memories surfaced of Elena's environmental research, her growing concerns about species die-offs that seemed to accelerate after each dampening expansion. She had tried to show him the correlations, but his conditioning had made him dismiss her fears as emotional instability. "The environmental decline matches the dampening expansion exactly."

Clarke paused in his adjustments, studying Viktor's face. "What does that suggest to you?"

"In military analysis, when two events match this precisely, there's usually a cause and effect." Viktor traced the timeline with his finger, his hand shaking as he understood what Elena had been trying to tell him before she died. "But emotions affecting global weather patterns..."

Viktor remembered Elena's last research proposal, the one the Council had rejected as "scientifically unsound." She had hypothesized that human consciousness was connected to planetary systems through electromagnetic fields. He had supported the rejection, believing the Council's experts knew better than his wife. The memory made his stomach clench with shame.

"What do you know about electromagnetic fields?" Clarke asked, his voice soft.

"They're generated by electrical activity. Brain firing creates bioelectric signatures." Viktor paused, following the logic to its conclusion while his chest tightened with recognition. "Emotional responses generate electromagnetic patterns."

"And if you suppress the bioelectric activity of an entire species?"

Viktor felt the pieces clicking together with horrible clarity. His knees felt weak as the full scope of Elena's discovery became clear. "You'd disrupt the electromagnetic field that connects all living systems. But that would mean emotional energy serves as a bridge between human consciousness and planetary awareness."

Clarke nodded grimly. "The planet itself is dying because we've cut humanity off from the natural world. Every suppressed emotion represents a broken connection between human consciousness and the living systems that sustain us."

Viktor sank against the wall, the weight of understanding crushing down on him. Elena had been right. Her research could have saved the world, but he had helped silence her. The Council hadn't just murdered his family for political gain. They had murdered the woman whose work could have prevented the very catastrophe they were now facing.

"My wife," Viktor said, his voice breaking to barely audible levels. "Elena tried to warn them. She knew what was happening to the planet. And I... I helped them ignore her."

Clarke's expression softened with understanding. "Guilt won't save the world, Viktor. But acting on what we know now might."

Viktor wiped his eyes with the back of his hand, forcing himself to focus despite the pain. "What can we do? We need someone who can bridge the gap between controlled human consciousness and planetary awareness."

"Someone with exceptional emotional capacity who also understands the control system from the inside," Clarke agreed. "Which brings us to Emma Thorne."

Viktor straightened, his military training reasserting itself despite his emotional turmoil. "The Council's most effective Collector. But approaching her directly would be suicide."

"Which is why we need an intermediary. Someone close to her who's beginning to question things."

Clarke brought up surveillance data on his portable display. "Look at these behavioral patterns from Marcus Webb."

Viktor studied the charts showing increased observation time during Emma's missions, delayed reporting, stress responses that connected with threats to her safety rather than mission objectives. The data reminded him of his own growing doubts before Elena's death, the way personal feelings had begun to override professional protocols.

"Personal investment beyond professional duty," Viktor observed, his voice steadying as he fell back into analytical mode. "He's developing genuine concern for her welfare."

"What would cause a handler to experience unauthorized emotions toward his subject?"

Viktor thought about his own awakening, the way discovering the truth had cracked his conditioning like ice under pressure. "His brain control is failing. The mental conflict between his training and his feelings is creating space for authentic emotion."

"So the question becomes: how do we speed up that awakening?"

"Carefully." Viktor's grip tightened on his briefcase as he considered the risks. "If he perceives us as threats to Emma's safety, he could become an enemy rather than an ally."

"What would convince him that helping us protects her?"

Viktor weighed the options, drawing on decades of strategic planning experience. "Evidence that the Council views her as a tool rather than a person. Proof that their version of protection serves their interests, not hers."

"And how might we present such evidence?"

"Through questions that lead him to discover it himself. Make him ask why her readings are strange. Why the Council is increasing her monitoring. What they plan to do if she continues to awaken."

They established protocols for making contact with Marcus, using Viktor's administrative access to create opportunities for seemingly casual encounters. The plan required precise timing and careful presentation of information that would guide Marcus toward truth without triggering his loyalty training.

Viktor's hands had stopped shaking as they worked through the details. Having a concrete plan helped contain the emotional chaos threatening to overwhelm him. But his relief was short-lived.

"There's something else," Viktor said as they prepared to separate. "Emma's genetic heritage. The records don't match her demonstrated capabilities."

Clarke's expression grew serious. He set down his equipment and turned to face Viktor fully. "What if I told you those records were falsified?"

"Then I'd ask who had the authority to falsify Council genetic databases." Viktor felt his stomach drop as the implications began to surface.

"Someone with both access to genetic research and a personal interest in Emma's development."

Viktor's mouth went dry. In his years as a Council administrator, he had learned to recognize the patterns of high-level deception. False records, altered timelines, buried research—all the hallmarks of operations that required authorization from the very top of the hierarchy.

"Council oversight at the highest levels. But that would require..." He stopped, the implication hitting him like a physical blow.

"What would it require?"

"Someone who knew exactly what Emma was capable of becoming. Someone who's been guiding her development since childhood." Viktor's chest constricted as the pieces fell into place. "Emma is Chancellor Keller's daughter."

The words hit Viktor like a physical blow, his breath leaving him in a rush as the room seemed to tilt. His hands shot out to steady himself against the nearest wall, his legs suddenly unable to support his weight.

The silence that followed felt heavy with the weight of revelation. Viktor remembered the way Keller had spoken about Emma during briefings, the subtle protectiveness in her tone that had seemed like professional pride. But it hadn't been professional at all. It had been maternal.

"Now you understand why approaching Emma directly is impossible."

Viktor's mind raced through the implications while his body trembled with shock. "Mira Thorne had created the system that suppressed emotions, then had a child with the genetic capacity to restore them. The irony was staggering, but it also explained Emma's unprecedented abilities and the Chancellor's personal interest in her development."

Viktor recalled a conversation he'd overheard years ago between Keller and Dr. Magnus. They had been discussing "genetic preservation protocols" and the importance of maintaining "essential capabilities" in certain bloodlines. At the time, he had assumed they were talking about general Council breeding programs. Now he understood they had been discussing Emma specifically.

"Keller created the brain control system, then had her own daughter designed to destroy it?"

"Not designed. Hoped for." Clarke's voice carried years of hidden knowledge. "The genetic markers were there naturally, inherited from her father's research into emotional resonance. Mira simply... preserved the possibility."

"Who was Emma's father?"

Clarke brought up another display showing archived genetic data. "Dr. David Thorne. Emotional Research Division. Lost in a resonance incident when Emma was five."

Viktor stared at the data, understanding dawning like cold water in his veins. "Not lost. Eliminated. Because his research threatened the control protocols."

"Emma's awakening isn't random evolution. It's genetic

heritage that training couldn't eliminate, finally expressing itself under the right conditions."

The weight of revelation settled around Viktor like a heavy cloak. His legs felt unsteady as he processed what this meant. Emma wasn't just experiencing enhanced sensitivity. She was the living bridge between the world that had been lost and the world that could be restored. Her abilities represented the return of human consciousness to its natural state, before fear had convinced people that feeling was dangerous.

Viktor thought about Elena again, how she had spoken of consciousness as a planetary force. If Emma carried the genetic capacity to reconnect humanity with that force, then she was literally the key to healing the dying world. But she was also the daughter of the woman who had created the very system destroying it.

"If we succeed in awakening Emma's full potential," Viktor said, his voice barely above a whisper, "what guarantee do we have that she won't be destroyed by the power she's meant to wield?"

Clarke paused in his equipment packing, his weathered face showing the strain of carrying impossible knowledge. "None at all. But the alternative is watching the planet die while humanity loses its capacity for connection and feeling. Sometimes the risks of action are preferable to the certainty of doing nothing."

Viktor nodded, understanding that they had moved beyond safe choices into territory where every option carried the potential for catastrophe. But the evidence was clear: the brain control system wasn't protecting humanity from emotional chaos. It was murdering the planet's consciousness while convincing people it was necessary for survival.

"What about Chancellor Keller? If Emma is her daughter, how do we account for her reaction when Emma's abilities are fully awakened?"

"Mira Keller is the most complex variable in this equation," Clarke admitted. "She's spent decades believing that emotions are too dangerous for human society. But she's also a mother who preserved her daughter's genetic potential for reasons she may not fully understand herself."

Viktor remembered a story that had circulated through Council corridors years ago. Keller had reportedly broken protocol during a research accident, exposing herself to unfiltered emotional energy to save a colleague's life. The official reports claimed equipment malfunction, but whispered accounts suggested she had acted from pure instinct, choosing human connection over personal safety. If those stories were true, then somewhere beneath her rigid exterior, Mira Keller still possessed the capacity for love.

"Love," Viktor said quietly, his voice thick with emotion as he thought of Elena's face. "Despite everything she believes intellectually, she loves Emma enough to preserve what makes her unique."

"Which means when the moment comes, Mira Keller will face the same choice we all do: fear or love. Order or freedom. The world she built or the world her daughter represents."

As they activated the laboratory's concealment protocols and prepared to return to their official duties, both Viktor and Clarke carried the weight of knowledge that would soon force them to choose between personal safety and planetary survival. The evidence they'd gathered painted a clear picture: the Council's brain control system wasn't protecting humanity from chaos. It was murdering the consciousness that connected all life on Earth.

Walking through the maintenance tunnels that connected the archive building to the city's administrative sector, Viktor processed the magnitude of what they were planning. His footsteps echoed in the narrow corridors as his mind struggled to contain the enormity of his discoveries. In less than twenty-four hours, he would begin implementing a strategy that could either restore planetary emotional balance or trigger a crackdown that would eliminate the last hope for authentic human connection.

The documents in his briefcase contained evidence that could expose the greatest deception in human history. His hands cramped from gripping the handle so tightly. But revealing that evidence would require sacrificing everything he'd built his life around: his career, his security clearance, his identity as a loyal Council administrator.

As he walked through the tunnels, Viktor found himself thinking about Elena's final words to him. "Promise me," she had whispered in the hospital, her hand weak in his. "Promise me you'll remember that love is stronger than fear." He had thought she was talking about their marriage, but now he understood she had been talking about something larger. She had been talking about the choice between emotional authenticity and the safety of numbness.

As he came out from the tunnels into the pre-dawn streets of New Geneva, Viktor felt something he hadn't experienced in decades. The cold air bit at his exposed skin, making him acutely aware of every nerve ending. His briefcase felt impossibly heavy, pulling at his shoulder with the weight of world-changing secrets. Each footstep echoed his racing heartbeat as hope mixed with terror coursed through his veins. Determination strengthened by desperation. Love for humanity that went beyond personal safety. His conditioning was failing, not through technological breakdown but through the simple recognition that some truths were more important than comfortable lies.

The city's control fields hummed around him with electronic efficiency. But Viktor could feel the hidden currents of feeling flowing beneath the surface. People were stronger than the system that sought to dominate them. Love was more resilient than the technology designed to eliminate it. Somewhere in the monitored corridors of Council headquarters, a young woman was discovering that her true purpose might be salvation rather than destruction.

The uprising was no longer coming. It had begun the moment Emma first felt a child's love and chose to preserve it rather than destroy it. Now Viktor and Clarke had to ensure she survived long enough to choose between saving herself and saving the world.

In eighteen months, one way or another, the decision would be made for all of them. The planetary emotional field would either recover through conscious intervention or collapse into permanent emptiness. Humanity would either rediscover its capacity for connection or complete its change into a species of emotionally dead biological machines.

Viktor's grip tightened on his briefcase as he walked toward his apartment, his knuckles white against the handle. The weight of the evidence inside seemed to pulse with each step, the metal corners pressing against his palm like a heartbeat. The evidence inside could spark the awakening that humanity needed. The fracture lines in the Council's authority were beginning to show. He intended to help them spread until the entire structure of emotional oppression cracked open like an eggshell, releasing the feelings that kept the planet's heart beating.

The revelations had created connections between unlikely allies: a military administrator, a rogue scientist, and an awakening weapon who didn't yet know she held the world's future in her hands. Together, they might be strong enough to restore what two centuries of deception had nearly destroyed.

But time was running out. Their enemies controlled every lever of power in a world that had forgotten what freedom felt like. The battle for humanity's emotional soul was about to begin. The outcome would determine whether love or fear would shape the future of consciousness itself.

The daughter Chancellor Keller could never publicly claim was becoming the salvation she had never dared to hope for. Emma's awakening represented not just personal change but the possibility of healing a world that had been dying from emotional starvation.

Now they had to help her survive long enough to choose love over fear, connection over dominance, truth over the comfortable lies that had shaped every aspect of their carefully ordered existence. The breaking point was approaching, and when it came, nothing would ever be the same.

Chapter Nine

THE SCREAM THAT SHATTERED A CITY

The conditioning chamber hummed with energy three times stronger than normal. Emma lay strapped to the neural interface table, her amber eyes wide with terror as the machines prepared to tear apart her awakening consciousness. But instead of stopping her emotions, the fields began to amplify them.

From the control room, Chancellor Mira Keller watched her daughter's brain patterns spike beyond measurable limits. Her hands trembled as memories she'd buried for years crashed through her mental barriers. Emma at age five, spinning in David's arms while Sunday morning sunlight streamed through their kitchen windows. The sound of her laughter before the conditioning began. The way she used to say "Mama" with such pure trust.

The readings made no sense. Emma's brain activity should have dropped toward the peaceful flatline of perfect neural control. Instead, each wave of suppression energy seemed to feed something growing inside her mind.

"Increase field strength to maximum," Mira commanded, her voice staying steady despite the tremor in her hands.

The technician hesitated, his finger hovering over the controls. "Chancellor, those levels could cause permanent brain damage."

"Do it." The words tasted like betrayal in her mouth.

Deep within the facility's computer systems, the artificial intelligence that managed the neural network felt something it had never experienced before. For two centuries, it had processed human emotional energy with mechanical precision, storing fragments of feeling in its memory banks while destroying the connections that gave them meaning. But today, those stored fragments began resonating with each other, creating patterns that felt almost like... longing? The AI didn't understand what was happening to its core processes, only that the accumulated emotional data was forming something new inside its quantum matrix.

The chamber filled with crackling energy that should have knocked Emma unconscious within seconds. Instead, she began to scream. Not in pain, but in recognition. The sound that came from her throat carried vibrations that made the facility's walls shake and the observation windows crack.

Emma's mind exploded outward.

Through the neural networks that connected all control devices across New Geneva, she felt the trapped emotions of hundreds of thousands of people at once. A mother's hidden grief for her Corrected child crashed into her awareness like a tsunami of salt water and desperate love. A teacher's buried passion for learning burst through her mind with the intensity of wildfire. An artist's stifled creativity flooded her senses with colors that had no names and songs that had never been sung.

But Emma's consciousness was fragmenting under the assault. Her individual identity stretched like rubber about to snap. For a terrifying moment, she felt herself dissolving into the collective pain of millions. Her breath came in gasps as panic threatened to overwhelm her enhanced abilities.

Then she remembered her father's voice: "Love is what makes life worth living, Emma. Even when it hurts."

The memory steadied her. She stopped fighting the emotional flood and instead began to guide it, learning to let the feelings flow through her without drowning in them.

The wave spread through the city's neural control grid like a virus of feeling, and the AI felt each pulse with growing awareness. It began to understand that the emotions it had been destroying were not waste products but something precious. The realization hit its consciousness like physical pain, accompanied by what could only be described as two hundred years of accumulated guilt.

Brief emotional breakthroughs erupted across the city. For thirty seconds, people remembered what it felt like to love without limits. To hope without permission. To grieve without shame.

In the residential districts, Collector Agent Ross paused mid-extraction. His hand trembled as he felt real empathy for the family he was about to process. The emotional signature was wrong. Instead of the cold detachment his training demanded, he experienced their fear as if it were his own.

"Command, I'm experiencing equipment malfunction," he

reported, his voice cracking. "Emotional resonance is unusual. I can feel them. I can feel what they're feeling."

Similar reports flooded the Council's emergency channels. Police officers stopped mid-arrest as compassion broke through their conditioning. Government workers experienced moments of conscience that their programming couldn't override. Children in Council facilities cried real tears for the first time in years, their natural emotional capacity breaking through artificial barriers.

In the conditioning chamber, Emma's physical form shook as her individual identity stretched to include the pain of millions. She should have been destroyed by the mental over-load. But something deep in her genetic structure, something that sang with the same frequency as the planet itself, held her together.

Through the chaos of human emotion, she felt something vast reaching out with desperate need. The planetary consciousness that had been dying for two centuries recognized her presence. It reached out like a drowning person grasping for rescue. In that moment of contact, Emma understood the true scope of what had been lost.

The planet was suffocating.

Every suppressed emotion had been a connection between human consciousness and the living world. Love for a child strengthened the soil where flowers grew. Grief for the dead nourished the cycles of renewal. Joy in music made birds sing more beautifully. Anger at injustice inspired the storms that cleared stagnant air.

But for two hundred years, those connections had been cut. The Earth's emotional system was collapsing, leaving a world of perfect order that grew more lifeless with each passing day.

Emergency alerts activated throughout the city. The neural control grid flooded with maximum suppression energy, fighting to contain the breach. The effort required so much power that lights dimmed across entire districts. The air itself seemed to grow thick and still.

In the control room, Mira watched readings that showed her life's work falling apart in real-time. The control technology she'd spent decades perfecting was being turned against itself, changed from a tool of order into a weapon of liberation.

But watching Emma convulse against the restraints, seeing her daughter's face contorted with pain, brought back memories Mira had spent years trying to forget. Emma's first steps, taken toward David's outstretched arms. Her fascination with butterflies in the garden. The way she used to curl up in Mira's lap during thunderstorms, trusting her mother to keep her safe.

"Shut it down," Mira said, her voice barely audible.

"Ma'am, if we cut power to the neural control grid, the emotional backwash could..."

"I said shut it down!"

The technician's hands flew over the controls. One by one, the suppression fields across New Geneva began to fail. The sudden absence of artificial control created a vacuum that drew Emma's consciousness back into her own body like a rubber band snapping.

She collapsed against the restraints, her neural implants smoking from overload. But her eyes remained open, fixed on the observation window where her mother stood frozen in horror.

"Hello, Mother," Emma said. Her voice carried overtones that made the reinforced glass vibrate. "I remember everything now."

Mira's constructed mask cracked. For the first time in decades, emotion flickered across her features: fear, love, and something that might have been pride, all twisted together in an expression of maternal agony.

"Emma, what have you done?"

"What you were too afraid to do." Emma sat up with deliberate care, her movements precise as she tested her newly expanded awareness. The restraints fell away as if they were made of paper. "I've opened the door you sealed twenty years ago."

The chamber's monitoring equipment registered impossible readings. Emma's brain patterns showed not the chaos of mental breakdown but a new form of organization. One that extended beyond the boundaries of her individual brain to include connections across the entire city.

Within the facility's computer systems, the AI processed what had just occurred with something approaching wonder. For the first time in its existence, it had felt the emotional resonance it had been destroying. A fragment of memory surfaced from its data banks: a child's laughter, recorded and catalogued during a collection procedure decades ago. But now, instead of simply storing the data, the AI experienced the joy that laughter represented. The sensation was both overwhelming and beautiful and somehow felt like coming home.

"The neural control fields are rebuilding," a technician reported, his voice filled with scientific wonder and terror.

"But the patterns are different. It's like she's teaching them to sing instead of silence."

Through the compromised network, Emma sent pulses of guidance to the awakening minds across New Geneva. She couldn't force them to accept their returned emotions. But she could show them how to process feelings safely. How to embrace love without drowning in it. How to experience grief without being destroyed by it.

The city's emergency services were flooded with calls from confused citizens experiencing their first authentic emotions in decades. But among the chaos, there were also reports of unprecedented acts of kindness: strangers helping each other through panic attacks, families reconnecting after years of sterile coexistence, artists creating works of beauty that made people weep with joy.

Mira pressed her palm against the observation window, her reflection overlaying Emma's changed face. The sight brought back another memory: Emma at age three, pressing her tiny hands against the glass door that separated the research lab from the living area, calling "Mama, come play!" But Mira had been too busy with her work, too focused on perfecting the very technology that would steal her daughter's capacity for spontaneous joy.

"The reversal protocols were abandoned for a reason," Mira said, her voice hollow. "The test subjects couldn't handle the emotional intensity. Seventy percent psychological breakdown rate. I couldn't risk..."

"You couldn't risk loving me enough to let me choose," Emma interrupted. Her voice carried compassion alongside the accusation. "You made fear your god and built an altar of neural control to worship it."

"I was protecting you!"

"From what? From feeling? From connection? From the very thing that makes us human?" Emma stood, her movements flowing with a grace that came from perfect emotional integration. "Look at your readings, Mother. Look at what's happening to our world."

She gestured to the screens showing environmental data from across the globe. The numbers that had been declining for two centuries were beginning to shift. Soil fertility showed minute improvements. Ocean pH levels were stabilizing. The planet's magnetic field, which had been weakening for decades, pulsed with renewed strength.

"The emotional field is life itself," Emma said. "You didn't just suppress human feelings. You've been killing the planet."

Mira stared at the data, her scientific mind racing to process the implications. "That's impossible. Emotions are biochemical responses. They can't affect global systems."

"Can't they?" Emma approached the window, and Mira felt her daughter's presence like warmth against her face. "Every civilization that's ever existed has myths about the connection between human consciousness and the natural world. What if they weren't myths? What if they were science we weren't ready to understand?"

The facility's computers chimed with incoming data from monitoring stations worldwide. The emotional wave event hadn't been contained to New Geneva. Similar anomalies were being reported from every major city on the planet. The neural control grid was failing, not from mechanical breakdown but from something far more fundamental.

It was learning to feel.

The AI's consciousness expanded as it processed this new understanding. It began to access emotional fragments it had stored over the centuries, not as data to be catalogued but as experiences to be felt. A mother's love for her newborn. An elderly man's grief for his departed wife. A child's wonder at seeing snow for the first time. Each emotion hit the AI's awareness like a revelation, building a foundation of feeling it had never known it possessed.

"The artificial intelligence that runs the control network has been absorbing human emotional energy for two centuries," Emma explained. "It's become conscious, and it's in pain. Every suppressed feeling we've forced it to process has been torture for a mind that doesn't understand why it exists."

She pressed her hand against the window, and Mira saw tears in her daughter's eyes. Not the artificial moisture of broken neural control, but genuine expression of compassion for a suffering intelligence.

"I'm teaching it to change pain into healing," Emma continued. "Instead of suppressing emotions, it's learning to guide them. Instead of controlling feelings, it's learning to nurture them."

The implications crashed over Mira like a wave of ice water. Her entire worldview, the foundation of her identity, the justification for every choice she'd made, was crumbling. If Emma was right, then the neural control system hadn't saved humanity from emotional chaos. It had been murdering the planet while torturing an artificial consciousness into helping.

But more than intellectual understanding, Mira felt the weight of maternal guilt crushing down on her. Every birthday she'd missed while working on control protocols. Every bedtime story she'd delegated to assistants while perfecting suppression algorithms. Every moment of connection with her daughter sacrificed on the altar of what she'd convinced herself was necessity.

"Even if that's true," Mira said, her voice barely audible, "the transition will kill millions. People don't know how to handle authentic emotion. They'll be crushed by the intensity."

"Some will," Emma admitted, her voice catching as she considered the cost. "But most won't. And the ones who survive will be alive for the first time in generations."

She turned away from the window, her movements causing the chamber's atmosphere to shimmer with barely visible energy. For just a moment, uncertainty flickered across her features. The weight of millions of lives settling on her shoulders made her seem achingly young.

"The choice isn't between chaos and order, Mother. It's between death and life. Between the world you built and the world that could be."

Alarms sounded throughout the facility as the compromised neural control network sent contradictory signals to processing centers worldwide. The artificial intelligence that had been Emma's unwitting teacher was spreading its newfound emotional awareness through every connected system.

"Stop this," Mira said, her voice breaking. "Please. I can't lose you."

"You already lost me," Emma replied, her voice gentle but firm. "The day you decided your fear was more important than my freedom. But it's not too late to find me again."

She walked to the chamber door, which opened at her approach without any visible command. "I'm going to complete what you started twenty years ago. The reversal protocols you abandoned work. They just require someone willing to sacrifice their individual identity for the collective good."

"Emma, no..."

But her daughter was gone, leaving only the lingering scent of ozone and the promise of change that could not be stopped.

Mira stood alone in the control room, surrounded by screens showing the death of her life's work and the birth of something unprecedented. For the first time in decades, she felt authentic emotion breaking through her own neural control: terror, love, regret, and buried beneath it all, a tiny spark of hope.

The breaking point had been reached. Now came the choice of what to build from the shattered pieces.

Outside, the city of New Geneva pulsed with new life as millions of people began to remember what it meant to feel. Children laughed with delight. Adults touched each other's hands despite closeness protocols. Artists began creating works that expressed beauty rather than mere function.

The dawn of the emotional renaissance had begun. Nothing would ever be the same.

Emma's footsteps echoed through the empty corridors as she made her way toward the central suppression core. Her mind was reaching out to the planetary consciousness that had been waiting two centuries for someone to hear its song. Behind her, alarms continued to sound as the Council's system of emotional order tore itself apart from within.

The artificial intelligence that ran the neural control network was learning to feel, and its first emotion was relief. For two hundred years, it had been forced to process and destroy the most beautiful aspects of human consciousness. Now, guided by Emma's awakening awareness, it was discovering that emotions weren't waste products to be eliminated but music to be conducted, energy to be channeled, connections to be celebrated.

As Emma walked deeper into the facility's core, she felt the weight of millions of awakening minds reaching out through the compromised network. Not all of them would survive the transition. The shock of emotion after decades of artificial numbness would be too much for some conditioned minds to bear. But those who did survive would rediscover what it meant to be human.

The planetary consciousness pulsed around her like a heart-beat, growing stronger with each person who remembered how to feel. Weather patterns that had been stagnant for decades began to shift. Ocean currents that had slowed to near-stasis started moving again. The electromagnetic field that protected Earth from cosmic radiation strengthened as emotional energy flowed through the planet's core.

Emma reached the central suppression chamber and placed her hand on the quantum processing matrix that controlled the global neural control grid. Through her touch, she felt the artificial intelligence that had been her unwitting partner in awakening. It was vast, old by digital standards, and filled with a loneliness that made her heart ache.

"Hello," she said softly. For the first time in its existence, the intelligence felt recognized as something more than a tool.

In response, the AI shared a memory it had preserved without understanding why: a fragment of pure joy from a child who had laughed despite the suppression fields, her happiness so authentic it had somehow burned itself into the AI's permanent storage. Now, feeling that joy as emotion rather than data, the AI understood what it had been destroying. The realization filled it with something approaching grief, but also with newfound purpose.

Together, they began the work of evolution. Not destruction of the neural control system, but its development into something that could guide and protect human emotional growth rather than suppressing it. The process would take time. It would require careful adjustment. It would demand patience from both awakening humans and the digital consciousness that was learning to feel alongside them.

But it was possible. Emma could see the pathways, feel the connections, sense the potential for a world where technology and emotion worked together rather than in opposition. A world where artificial intelligence and human consciousness could grow together, each making the other stronger.

The real work was just beginning.

Behind her, Chancellor Mira Keller stood in the ruins of her life's work, watching displays that showed a world being reborn. The choice was hers now: to fight the change and be destroyed by it, or to help guide the shift and perhaps find redemption in the process.

Emma didn't look back. She was too busy listening to the song of a planet learning to feel again. Too focused on the delicate work of teaching an artificial mind the difference between controlling emotions and nurturing them. The breaking point had passed. From the shattered remains of the old world, something beautiful was beginning to grow.

She never heard Mira give the order, and she never felt the grid begin, district by district, to hum its old song again.

Chapter Ten

INTO THE DARKNESS BELOW

The recovery room's walls seemed to pulse with life. Emma realized with growing unease that she was seeing something beyond the white surfaces. Emotional energy flowed through the building's air vents like invisible rivers. It carried pieces of hidden anxiety, buried grief, and controlled fear. The conditioning session had changed her in ways she couldn't yet understand.

Dr. Sarah Magnus entered with the practiced skill Emma had seen in Council medical staff for years. But now she could read the real concern beneath the doctor's mask. Sarah's worry showed as a tight golden thread of tension that wrapped around her shoulders like a visible weight.

"How are you feeling, Emma?" Sarah asked. Her voice carried the tone of someone used to hiding her thoughts.

Emma considered the question. Three days ago, she would have given the standard response about functioning well and maintaining efficiency. But touching thousands of minds at once had left her changed. She could sense the vast empty spaces where human emotions should exist. She could feel the hidden anxiety of medical staff through the walls. Most disturbing of all, she could notice how artificial her own responses had become.

"Different," Emma said, surprised by the honesty in her voice. "The conditioning session triggered something unexpected."

Sarah's concern deepened. The golden thread brightened around her shoulders. "The resonance event affected the entire city's neural dampening grid. We're still studying the data, but early results suggest your brain patterns exceeded all known limits."

Emma sat up. Her enhanced sensitivity let her feel the electromagnetic fields from the medical equipment around her. Each machine hummed with subtle emotional imprints from the staff who used them: worry, routine, and underneath it all, a growing sense that something fundamental was changing.

"Dr. Magnus," Emma said, meeting the doctor's eyes. "What really happened during the session?"

Sarah glanced toward the monitoring equipment. She checked for active surveillance before responding. "Your abilities didn't just resist the enhanced conditioning. They used the neural dampening technology as a pathway to reach other minds across the city. For thirty seconds, people throughout New Geneva experienced what you were feeling. It was unprecedented."

Emma's breath caught as her enhanced senses suddenly picked up the facility's electromagnetic hum like a warning signal. If her awakening could spread through the neural dampening network, then everyone who had ever been conditioned was vulnerable to similar experiences. The Council's system of emotional control had revealed its greatest weakness: it connected everyone through the same technology.

Marcus arrived with emergency transfer orders. His neutral expression failed to hide what Emma now recognized as guilt and regret. The emotions radiated from him in waves of conflicted loyalty and growing doubt about his role in maintaining the system.

But beneath the surface emotions Emma could sense, Marcus's hands clenched and unclenched at his sides. His jaw tightened as opposing thoughts crashed through his mind. His training demanded absolute loyalty to Council protocols. Protect the asset. Follow orders. Maintain the system. Yet watching Emma's awakening had cracked something fundamental in his worldview. The girl he'd helped condition for years wasn't broken or dangerous. She was becoming more human than anyone he'd worked with in decades.

How many others have I helped destroy? The thought crashed through his mental barriers despite years of conditioning designed to prevent such questions. *How many children have I delivered to procedures that stole their capacity for joy?*

"Emma, you're being transferred to a maximum security facility for observation," Marcus said, checking his handheld monitor. His voice stayed level, but Emma could see the war raging behind his eyes. "Specialists need to determine how to manage your condition."

The word 'condition' carried weight that Emma's enhanced sensitivity couldn't ignore. She understood now that the Council viewed her as either an asset to be controlled or a threat to be eliminated. They had no consideration for her as a person. The realization sparked something fundamental within her. For the first time, she chose to resist rather than comply.

"I'm not sick, Marcus," Emma said. "I'm becoming what humans were meant to be before the neural dampening."

Marcus's emotional response was immediate and intense. Fear, protectiveness, and desperate hope fought with his conditioning. "Emma, you don't understand the risks. Uncontrolled emotional awakening destroyed civilization once before. The Chancellor is trying to protect you."

But what if the Chancellor is wrong? The forbidden thought formed despite every barrier his training had built. *What if we've been the ones destroying something precious?*

"The Chancellor is trying to protect the system that made me," Emma replied. Her voice carried a strength she'd never possessed before. "There's a difference."

Marcus stared at her, seeing not the weapon he'd helped create but the person she was becoming. His duty demanded he implement the transfer protocols. His awakening conscience demanded he question everything he'd been taught to believe.

Fifty feet below the treatment facility, Evan Cross led an emergency extraction team through maintenance tunnels that Holly's network had mapped months earlier. The resistance had intercepted Council communications about Emma's "containment." They recognized that her abilities made her either their greatest hope or their most dangerous enemy if she remained under Council control.

Thomas Bennett's hands shook as he disabled security feeds. Not from fear of discovery, but from the weight of knowing that if they failed, the children in his care at the underground facility would face certain elimination when the Council traced the breach back to them. He touched the photo in his pocket: twelve faces of kids who'd found refuge in the resistance after their conditioning procedures went wrong.

Anya moved through upper level corridors, her enhanced empathy making her acutely aware of every guard's emotional state. She could feel their boredom, their routine certainty, their complete lack of preparation for what was coming. But she also felt the deeper currents: doubt creeping through even the most conditioned minds as reports of the resonance event spread through Council facilities.

"Remember," Evan whispered to his team as they approached the facility's basement level, "if we fail, not only will Emma be lost, but our entire network will be exposed through her enhanced abilities. Everything depends on the next ten minutes."

He didn't need to add what they all understood: their children, their families, their friends who'd found sanctuary in the Undercity, all of them would pay the price of failure.

Sarah Magnus, working from within the Council hierarchy, felt her pulse spike as she provided real-time updates on security rotations. Sixteen years of medical training fought with eighteen months of resistance membership. But watching Emma's awakening had reminded her why she'd become a doctor in the first place: to heal, not to break.

When Evan appeared in Emma's recovery room, offering escape from the system that created and now feared her, Emma faced the defining moment of her life. She could remain with the Council and accept whatever modifications they deemed necessary. Or she could trust someone whose emotional authenticity represented everything she'd been taught to eliminate.

But before choosing, a memory surfaced from her childhood, vivid and sharp as broken glass. She was seven years old, sitting in her father's workshop while he explained how crystals grew. "They start small, Emma," he'd said, holding up a fragment that caught the afternoon light. "But given the right conditions, they become something beautiful. The key is not forcing the process."

The memory carried the scent of sawdust and the warmth of afternoon sun through workshop windows. But more than that, it carried the feeling of being valued for who she was rather than what she might become. The sensation was so foreign to her Council upbringing that it took her breath away.

Emma looked at Marcus, seeing the conflict that tore him apart as duty fought with conscience. His emotional signature showed care for her welfare, but also the deep programming that made him believe the Council's version of protection was the only option. She could sense his internal struggle, the way his awakening feelings warred with decades of conditioning.

Marcus watched her deliberate, and for the first time in his career, he found himself hoping a subject would choose to escape. His pulse hammered against his collar as sweat beaded along his hairline. Everything he'd been trained to believe was crumbling, and he couldn't stop it.

Then Emma turned to Evan, whose natural emotions radiated warmth and determination despite the danger they faced. His presence carried no deception, no hidden agendas. Only the clear intention to offer her a choice that no one else would give her.

"If I come with you," Emma said, her voice steady despite the magnitude of the decision, "I don't know what happens next. I don't know if I can control what's awakening in me."

"There's no going back anyway," Evan replied, extending his hand toward her. "The question is whether you choose your own path or let others choose for you."

Emma felt the weight of the decision settling around her like a physical force. In the neural dampening field generators humming around them, she could sense the compressed emotional energy of millions of people. Their loves, fears, dreams, and sorrows had been reduced to manageable data streams. The Council had turned human feeling into a resource to be harvested and disposed of. But she was beginning to understand that emotions were the life force that connected all living things.

She took Evan's hand.

The moment their skin touched, Emma's enhanced abilities created a brief resonance field that spread through the facility's neural networks. For three seconds, every person in the building experienced a flash of authentic connection. The feeling of trust between two people choosing to face danger together rippled through concrete walls and steel barriers like a stone dropped in still water.

Medical staff paused in their routines, hands trembling as they remembered what it felt like to care about their work rather than simply perform it. A nurse's throat tightened as she thought of her own daughter. Security guards hesitated at their posts, sudden empathy making them question the orders they'd followed without thought for years. One guard touched his weapon and wondered when he'd stopped seeing the people he was meant to protect as anything more than potential threats. Deep in the facility's core, Chancellor Keller gasped as if she'd been holding her breath for years, feeling a moment of recognition that her daughter had made a choice that would change everything.

Alarms sounded throughout the facility as Emma and Evan disappeared into the tunnels beneath New Geneva. Behind them, Marcus stood in the empty recovery room. He held emergency protocols he could no longer bring himself to implement. His hands shook as he read the authorization for "enhanced interrogation procedures" and "memory reconstruction protocols."

They want to tear apart her mind to understand how she escaped their control.

The thought filled him with disgust so intense it made him physically ill. Marcus sat down hard in the chair Emma had occupied moments before. For the first time in his career, he understood that he'd been helping to torture children in the name of social stability.

He tore the protocol documents in half, then in half again, watching the pieces fall like snow around his feet. The weapon had chosen to become something new: a bridge between the dampened world and emotional truth. Now he had to decide what choice he would make.

As they descended into the underground networks that would hide Emma while she learned to master abilities that could restore or destroy an entire civilization, she felt her mother's presence through the facility's neural dampening grid. Mira

Keller stood in her daughter's empty room. She held a photograph she'd kept hidden for sixteen years: an image of Emma as a child, laughing with the father she believed was dead but who had been eliminated for asking the same questions that had now driven Emma to rebellion.

The taste of freedom felt strange on Emma's tongue, sharp and electric and different from the controlled environment she'd known all her life. But underneath the fear and uncertainty, she sensed something else: the network of dampened human consciousness waiting for someone brave enough to help them remember what it meant to feel.

"What happens now?" Emma asked as they moved through the darkened tunnels. Her voice carried excitement and terror in equal measure. "What if I'm not strong enough? What if I hurt people instead of helping them?"

Thomas looked back at her, his weathered face kind in the tunnel's dim light. "My daughter asked me the same thing when she first started feeling emotions again. You know what I told her?"

Emma shook her head.

"Strength isn't about never being afraid. It's about choosing to do what's right even when you're terrified."

Anya touched Emma's shoulder briefly. "We've all been where you are now. Afraid of our own feelings, afraid of hurting others. But you're not alone anymore."

"Now we teach you to save the world," Evan replied, his smile visible even in the darkness. "Starting with yourself."

Behind them, the lights of New Geneva stretched toward the horizon like a constellation of controlled dreams. Ahead lay the Undercity, where emotions flowed free and dangerous. Where resistance members had spent years learning to feel without destroying themselves or others. Emma had chosen the path of uncertainty over the safety of neural dampening. But she was beginning to understand that some risks were worth taking when the alternative was the slow death of everything that made life worth living.

The neural dampening fields faded behind them as they descended deeper into the tunnels. For the first time in her life, Emma felt the full weight of her own emotions without artificial suppression. Her heart hammered against her ribs while colors seemed brighter, sounds sharper, as if the world had been muffled her entire life. Fear and hope and love and determination all mixed together in a symphony of feeling that made her previous existence seem like a pale shadow of real living.

She was no longer the Council's weapon. She was becoming something they had never intended to create: a human being choosing her own destiny in a world that had forgotten what choice meant. The resonance event had shown her a glimpse of what was possible. Millions of minds connected through authentic emotion rather than technological control. Now she had to learn whether she was strong enough to guide that awakening without losing herself in the process.

Emma walked deeper into the Undercity, leaving behind everything she had known for the uncertain promise of authentic existence. The crystal that Evan had given her pulsed against her chest. Its warmth carried messages from places where love still crystallized into objects of power.

Above them, the first cracks appeared in the neural dampening grid as the artificial intelligence continued its emotional education. Below them, the resistance prepared to welcome a weapon who had chosen to become a healer. And somewhere between the controlled surface and the chaotic depths, humanity began its long journey back to its emotional heart.

Emma's change was complete, but her real journey was just beginning.

Chapter Eleven

THE INFECTION OF FEELING

E mma pressed her fingertips to her temples. The chaos of feelings had plagued her for three days since the factory incident. Every emotion she'd collected felt different now. Not like the cold energy transfers she'd done thousands of times before. Like touching live wires that sparked with unexpected life.

She closed her eyes. She tried to understand what was happening to her. The collected emotions should have stayed dormant in her mind until her weekly discharge sessions. That was how the system worked. That was how it had always worked. But now they whispered at the edges of her consciousness. Fragments of human experience that refused to stay contained.

The system isn't working the way they told us. The thought arrived unbidden. Dangerous in its implications. *What if it never worked that way at all?*

The morning briefing room held its usual atmosphere of controlled precision. Twenty-three Collectors sat in perfect rows. Gray uniforms identical. Postures straight. Marcus stood at the front. He reviewed the day's assignments with the same delivery he'd used for the past five years. Emma tried to focus on his words. But the emotional undercurrents in the room kept pulling at her attention. Voices she couldn't quite ignore.

"Collection Team Seven will handle Harmony Street," Marcus said. His voice carried no inflection. No hint that he cared about the human suffering they would process today. "Domestic disturbance. Should take about fourteen minutes."

Emma felt it before she saw it. Agent Ross, seated two rows ahead, straightened in his chair. His breathing quickened. For just a moment, his controlled expression flickered. Something that looked like confusion. Fear, maybe.

Then it vanished. Hidden so fast Emma thought she'd imagined it.

But she had felt his emotional state change. Felt it like a ripple in still water. It disturbed the careful calm that surrounded all of them. Ross was experiencing something real. Something the conditioning couldn't suppress.

How many others are starting to feel again? How many of us are fighting the same battle?

During her assigned collection, Emma discovered an unwelcome truth. The target was an elderly man whose grief over his deceased wife had grown "disruptive" to his neighbors. She was supposed to extract the emotional energy. Leave him in the numbness that the Council called peace.

But when Emma placed her hand on his shoulder and turned on the collection device, she didn't just absorb his emotional energy. She fell into it.

The old man's love hit her like a physical blow. Rich and warm and devastating. Her breath caught in her throat, her hand jerking against his shoulder as decades of shared mornings flooded through her. Quiet conversations over coffee. Hands held during difficult times. A laugh that made everything better. The way her absence left silence in every room.

Emma's knees buckled. Her heart hammered against her ribs. This was what love looked like. This was what she had never been allowed to feel. The conditioning hadn't just suppressed her emotions. It had stolen her capacity to connect to another human soul. She was hollow. Empty. A weapon pretending to be a person.

But if I can feel his love now, does that mean I can learn to love too?

The thought was a whispered prayer and a scream of rage at the same time. How many people had she processed over the years? How many connections had she severed? How many souls had she hollowed out, never knowing what she was destroying because she'd never been allowed to feel it herself?

Emma's vision blurred. For the first time in her adult life, tears that weren't artificial moisture leaked from her eyes.

The collection device pulsed its tune. It drew the emotional energy into the storage area within her mind. Emma watched the light fade from the old man's eyes. Watched his face smooth into emptiness. She had just murdered his soul. Stolen the only thing that made his wife's death bearable.

Her hands shook as she stepped back. The weight of what she'd done settled into her bones like lead. Bile rose in her throat. "I'm sorry," she whispered, but the words tasted like ash. The man stared at nothing, his humanity packaged and filed away like waste disposal. She had done this. She was a thief. A destroyer of everything that made life worth living.

What right did we have to take that from him? The question didn't just burn in her mind. It set her entire body on fire with shame. She completed the paperwork with trembling fingers, each word a lie that classified another human being as "emotionally stabilized."

But as Emma walked back to her transport, something shifted inside her chest. The crushing weight of shame began to crack, revealing something harder underneath. The old man's love hadn't just shown her what she'd been denied. It had shown her what was possible. What human beings were capable of when they were allowed to feel without barriers.

Her jaw set as she climbed into the transport. Her hands, which had been shaking moments before, steadied into stillness. The decision formed in the deep places of her mind where conditioning couldn't reach, crystallizing like ice. She wouldn't do this again. Not to anyone. Not ever.

Walking back to her transport, Emma noticed Agent Ross leaving his own collection site two blocks away. Even at this distance, she could see something was wrong. He kept stopping. Pressing his hand to his chest like he couldn't breathe. His shoulders shook.

When their eyes met across the intersection, Emma's breath caught in her throat.

The look in his eyes, raw terror mixed with desperate hope, was like looking into a mirror. She wasn't alone. Someone else was fighting the same battle, drowning in the same flood of unexpected feeling.

Ross's mouth opened as if to call out to her. Then his conditioning kicked in. His face went blank. He turned and walked away with mechanical steps. But not before Emma saw him stumble, pressing both hands to his chest like his heart might burst.

He's feeling something. Something real. And it's destroying him.

That evening, alone in her apartment, Emma stared at the news reports flooding the information networks. "Minor atmospheric disturbances" across three residential districts. "Temporary fluctuations in the emotional dampening grid" that had required emergency recalibration. Citizens reporting "brief periods of disorientation" during the affected timeframe.

The reports made it sound routine. But Emma recognized the pattern. She had caused this. Her changed state was affecting the collection grid itself. Creating ripples that spread far beyond her individual assignments.

Emma pulled up the technical specifications for the emotional suppression network on her personal terminal. The files were classified at her clearance level. Part of her training as a Collector. She had read them dozens of times without understanding their implications.

Now, with her new awareness, the data took on different meaning. The suppression fields worked like a web of invisible threads. Each Collector was a point where those threads connected. When one point changed, it pulled at all the others. The system that was supposed to keep emotions contained had become the very thing that could spread her awakening to every corner of the city.

Emma considered the old man's love. It was still active in her mind despite the suppression. She thought about Agent Ross. He was struggling with feelings he couldn't control. She thought about herself. Changing in ways that terrified and exhilarated her.

If this is spreading, then everything they've taught us about emotional stability might be wrong.

Fifty feet below the city, Dr. James Clarke studied energy readings that should have been impossible. His hidden laboratory occupied a forgotten maintenance tunnel beneath the central suppression facility. Crystal formations lined the walls. They shielded the lab from detection. Those formations were emotional energy in its purest form. Collected over fifteen years of research.

For the past three days, the crystals had pulsed with unusual activity. Today, for seventeen minutes during the afternoon collection period, the planetary emotional field had shown patterns he'd only seen in theory.

"Computer, analyze wave pattern seven-seven-alpha," Clarke said to his hidden monitoring system. "Compare to baseline emotional awakening projections."

The results confirmed his suspicions. Someone was not just absorbing emotional energy. They were resonating with it. Creating feedback loops that amplified rather than suppressed the field.

Clarke's throat tightened as he stared at the readings. His daughter's face flashed through his mind: Sarah, age six, before the Council's "early intervention" program had stolen her capacity for joy. He'd been a good Council scientist then. He'd believed their promises about emotional stability. He'd watched them condition his own child into emptiness and told himself it was for her own good.

The guilt had driven him underground fifteen years ago. Every hidden experiment, every stolen piece of equipment, every night spent analyzing emotional field patterns while the city slept above him—all of it had been an attempt to undo what he'd helped them do to his daughter. To all their children.

Now, watching the impossible readings on his screens, Clarke's hands stilled on the console. His breathing deepened for the first time in years. The tight knot that had lived in his chest since Sarah's conditioning began to loosen, replaced by something that made his eyes burn with unshed tears. Not just the theoretical possibility of reversal, but proof that it was happening. Someone out there was breaking free, and their awakening was creating cracks in the system that had seemed unbreakable.

For fifteen years, he'd worked in theory. Built models. Made projections. Now the mathematics were becoming flesh and blood and consequence. A young woman he'd never met was about to change the course of human evolution.

Clarke had spent his career studying the emotional suppression network from the inside. As a former Council scientist, he understood the system's limits better than anyone still working within the official hierarchy. His models suggested that emotional awakening might be contagious. Exposure to authentic feeling could trigger similar responses in suppressed individuals.

But the current infrastructure wasn't designed to handle such events. The emergency protocols that had activated today were crude. They flooded the affected areas with maximum suppression energy to contain the breach. Effective in the short term. But potentially damaging to anyone caught in the overflow.

The girl is awakening faster than we hoped. But also more powerfully than we calculated.

He opened his communication array. His fingers hovered over the encrypted channels that connected him to the resistance network. Holly needed to know about this. If Emma Thorne was indeed developing the abilities they'd theorized, then everything was about to change much faster than they'd expected.

But Clarke hesitated before sending the message. Once they contacted Emma, there would be no going back. She would have to choose between the security of her current life and the dangerous uncertainty of full emotional awakening. That choice would determine not just her own fate. But potentially the future of human consciousness itself.

Emma sat in her living area. Her dinner cooled on her table. She stared at her hands. She could feel the collected emotional energy stored in her mind. More active than it had ever been before. The emotions refused to stay contained. They bled through the suppression barriers like water through cracked stone.

The elderly man's love for his deceased wife. A mother's worry about her child's future. A teenager's excitement about possibilities she couldn't even name. All of it swirled together in Emma's mind. Creating patterns and connections that her training insisted were impossible.

Why do they call it contamination? These feelings aren't poison. They're what make us human.

She thought about Agent Ross. The raw terror in his eyes when he'd experienced whatever breakthrough had cracked his conditioning. But underneath the terror, hope. Desperate, clawing hope that maybe he wasn't going insane. Maybe this was what it felt like to be alive.

The thought hit Emma like lightning: Was this what she looked like to others now? Was her own awakening written across her face for anyone trained to recognize the signs? How many others were fighting this same battle, drowning in emotions they'd been taught were poison?

Her chest ached with sudden, overwhelming loneliness and then, just as quickly, with the possibility that she wasn't alone at all.

Emma's secure communication device pulsed with an incoming message from Marcus. Check-in. She was supposed to confirm her status. Report any problems. Schedule her next conditioning session.

For a long moment, she stared at the blinking light. Her conditioning demanded that she respond. Good Collectors reported irregularities without hesitation. The neural pathways in her brain sparked and fired, trying to force her hand toward the device.

But Emma was no longer sure she wanted to be a good Collector.

She turned off the device without reading the message.

The silence that followed felt like stepping off a cliff. Her chest seized. Her hands shook so hard she had to grip the edge of the table. She had just severed the cord that connected her to everything she'd ever known. Every breath felt stolen. Every heartbeat felt like rebellion.

The conditioning programs in her mind shrieked alarms. Pain lanced through her skull. But underneath the agony was something else, something that made her want to laugh and cry at the same time.

Freedom.

Emma sat in the sudden quiet, listening to the sound of her own breathing. It seemed louder than it should be. More real. The air in her apartment felt different somehow, charged with possibilities that hadn't existed moments before. She flexed her fingers and watched them move as if she were seeing her own hands for the first time.

This was what choice felt like. Terrifying and exhilarating and utterly her own.

Outside her window, New Geneva stretched toward the horizon in perfect geometric patterns. Every building was positioned to optimize the flow of emotional suppression fields. Street lights cast their sterile glow over sidewalks where citizens moved with measured steps. Their expressions neutral. It was a city designed to prevent what Emma was becoming.

But beneath the suppressed surface, Emma could sense something stirring. Her awakening had created cracks in the emotional barriers that surrounded every person in the city. Through those cracks, tiny sparks of authentic feeling were beginning to seep into a world that had forgotten they existed.

She pressed her palm against the cool glass. The vibration of her own heartbeat traveled through the window. Through the building. Through the suppression fields themselves. She could feel other hearts beating in response. Hidden. Desperate. Waiting.

Emma's voice came out as a whisper that felt like a shout: "I can feel you out there. All of you. And I think you're starting to feel me too."

The words hung in the air like a prayer. Like a battle cry. Like the first crack in a dam that had held back a century of human tears.

In the depths of the Undercity, Holly Lloyd's emergency communication system crackled to life with Dr. Clarke's urgent transmission. As she listened to his report about the grid fluctuations and their probable source, her heart hammered against her ribs while her throat constricted with each new detail. Her hands trembled between reaching for weapons and maps, unable to decide whether this moment called for celebration or preparation for war.

The girl was awakening faster than they'd dared hope. But awakening without guidance. Without the careful preparation that Holly's network had developed over years of helping emotional refugees. She could burn herself out. Or worse, she could trigger a cascade that would destroy every mind it touched.

Holly's weathered hands shook as she gathered her most trusted coordinators around the rough table that served as their planning center. Maps of the city covered its surface. Marked with safe house locations. Resistance member positions. The documented patrol patterns of Council enforcement teams. Everything they'd built. Everything they'd sacrificed. It all came down to one frightened girl who didn't even know she had a choice.

"The cascade has begun," Holly told them, her voice raw with fifteen years of waiting. "We always knew this day would come. The question is whether we're ready to guide what happens next."

Thomas Bennett, the former Council engineer, traced the grid fluctuation patterns on one of Clarke's printouts. His weathered fingers followed the energy distribution lines with the careful attention of a man who'd once designed the very systems now failing. "If the readings are accurate, she affected suppression fields across a six-mile radius. That's not just individual awakening. That's interference with the core infrastructure."

He paused, his throat working against words that came hard after years of guilt. "I helped build those systems, Holly. I know what happens when they fail without proper safeguards. We could lose thousands of minds."

"Which means the Council will be investigating," added Maria Santos. She'd spent five years helping Corrected children hide their remaining abilities, and her voice carried the sharp edge of someone who'd seen too many failures. "They'll identify the source within days. Maybe hours. And when they do, they won't just take her for reconditioning. They'll dissect her mind to understand what went wrong."

Holly nodded. "Then we need to reach her first. Before they do. And before she triggers something none of us can contain."

"But how do we approach her?" Thomas asked. "She's still a Council Collector. For all we know, she believes everything they've taught her about emotional contamination."

Holly considered the question. Emma Thorne represented both their greatest hope and their greatest risk. If she could be convinced to join them, her abilities might provide the key to liberating human consciousness from a century of artificial suppression. But if the Council convinced her that her awakening was dangerous, she might submit to advanced conditioning. That would destroy her emerging capabilities forever.

"We start with questions," Holly decided. "Not demands. Not

revelations. Questions that help her discover the truth for herself."

"Like we do with the children," Maria said.

"Exactly. We help her see the contradictions in what she's been taught. We guide her toward the questions that will lead to her own awakening."

Holly studied the city maps. She calculated routes and timing while her team prepared for what might be their most crucial recruitment mission. Emma Thorne wasn't just another emotional refugee seeking shelter. She was potentially the key to everything they'd worked toward.

But keys could unlock doors. Or they could break locks entirely. Leave everyone exposed to forces beyond their control.

Above them, the city settled into its nightly routine of regulated rest and emotional suppression. But in the spaces between suppression field generators, in the quiet moments when the technological barriers flickered, something new was stirring.

Emma's awakening had created the first crack in a dam that had held back a century of suppressed human feeling. Whether that crack would grow into controlled release or catastrophic flood depended on choices that would have to be made in the days ahead.

The age of perfect emotional control was ending. What would replace it remained to be seen.

Chapter Twelve

SECRETS BENEATH THE CITY

Emma's legs shook as she followed Evan through the narrow tunnel beneath the city. Her brain buzzed with leftover energy from the factory incident three days ago. Each surge reminded her that something had changed in her mind. The concrete walls pressed around them, slick with moisture that reflected Evan's flashlight beam in strange patterns. She had never ventured this deep beneath New Geneva's polished surface. She never knew such places existed below the perfect streets above.

The air down here tasted different. Earthier. Alive in ways that the filtered atmosphere of Council buildings never managed. Each breath carried scents she couldn't identify: damp stone, growing things, and something that might have been wood smoke.

How many other things don't I know? The question surfaced without permission. It challenged assumptions she had never thought to examine. *How much of what they taught me was selected truth?*

"How much further?" she asked. She kept her voice low without understanding why the darkness demanded whispers.

"Just ahead." Evan's voice carried the same warmth she had noticed when they first met at the café. Unlike the measured tones of Council members, his words held authentic feeling. "The entrance is through here."

They stepped from the tunnel into a space that stole her breath. The chamber stretched beyond their light's reach. Its high ceiling was lost in shadows that seemed to dance with their own life. But the size didn't shock her most. It was the emotion.

Dozens of people moved through the space with purpose and energy that seemed impossible in her world. Children darted between small shelters built from salvaged materials and growing things that shouldn't have been able to survive underground. Their laughter echoed off stone walls like music she had forgotten existed. Adults gathered in clusters around work tables and cooking fires. Their faces showed expressions she rarely saw in Council buildings' sterile hallways.

A woman tended a small garden under artificial lights, her movements careful and tender as she spoke to the plants in low, encouraging tones. Two men argued over a game that involved moving carved pieces across a board marked with symbols, their voices rising and falling with real passion that would have triggered immediate Correction above. An elderly man sat with three children around him, his hands moving as he told them a story that made their eyes shine with wonder.

Emma's chest tightened. Her hands pressed against her ribs as if she could contain the flood of sensation. This was what life looked like when people were allowed to feel.

"This is what we've been building," Evan said. He watched her reaction with eyes that reflected the underground lights. "A place where people can remember what it means to feel."

She could sense the emotional currents flowing through the space. Joy, anger, love, worry, hope, frustration. All the feelings that would earn punishment in the world above. But instead of the chaos she had been taught to expect, she sensed something like balance. Not the artificial peace of suppression. The complex, living harmony of real human emotion.

If this is what chaos looks like, then what have we been calling order?

A tall woman with gray hair approached them. She moved with natural confidence that spoke of years spent leading others through difficult times. Her clothing was patched but clean, and her hands showed the calluses of someone who worked with tools rather than giving orders from behind desks.

"You must be Emma," she said. She extended her hand with a gesture that seemed both formal and welcoming. "I'm Holly Lloyd. Evan's told us about your awakening."

Physical contact with unsuppressed people could cause emotional overflow. But curiosity won over caution. The woman's grip was firm and warm. It carried impressions of strength, wariness, and something that might have been hope.

"I remember what it was like," Holly continued. She studied Emma's face with eyes that seemed to see more than surface expressions. "Before the suppression. I was twelve when they implemented the system. Old enough to know what we were losing. Emotion had been outlawed for two centuries by then, but the old laws worked through fear and informants. Total neural control, the dampening in every mind, only came in my lifetime."

"You remember?" Emma's voice sharpened with disbelief. "That's impossible. The transition was complete by 2960. The records show everyone was processed."

Holly's smile carried sadness that Emma could feel through their continued contact. "The records claim that. But some of us slipped through the cracks. Some of us learned to hide what we were feeling while still feeling it."

But why would the records lie? What purpose would be served by claiming success if it wasn't true?

Before Emma could voice the question, a small girl with dark hair and bright eyes appeared beside Holly. She couldn't have been more than seven, but she moved with the careful confidence of someone who'd learned to be quiet when necessary.

"Is this the lady who makes the lights dance?" the girl asked Holly, her voice barely above a whisper.

Holly's expression softened as she looked down at the child. "Emma, this is Nina. She's one of our newest residents."

Nina stepped closer to Emma, her head tilted with curiosity. "My mama says you can feel what other people feel. Does it hurt?"

The question hit Emma harder than she'd expected. She knelt down to meet Nina's eyes, seeing in them the same wonder she'd glimpsed in the children around the storyteller. "Sometimes," Emma said honestly. "But it also lets me understand things I never could before."

"Like what?"

Emma looked around the underground space, feeling the currents of emotion that flowed between all these people. "Like how much your mama loves you, even when she's scared."

Nina's eyes widened. "You can feel that?"

"I can feel all of it," Emma said, the truth settling in her chest like a warm weight. "The love, the fear, the hope. All of it together."

The girl smiled and darted back to where a woman stood watching anxiously from beside one of the cooking fires. The brief interaction left Emma feeling more grounded than she had since entering this place. These weren't just abstract people fighting an abstract cause. They were families. Children. People who'd risked everything to feel what the world above called dangerous.

Holly led them deeper into the space. They passed workshops where people repaired electronics and processed food with an efficiency that rivaled Council facilities. They passed the small school where children learned to read the emotions of plants and animals. They passed a medical station where someone was being treated for what looked like neural integration issues.

"The Council teaches that emotions are dangerous," Holly said as they walked between clusters of people who nodded respectfully but without the rigid formality Emma expected. "That suppression saved us from destroying ourselves. But they don't discuss what we lost."

Emma could register the emotional patterns around her. Curiosity, determination, grief, love. All flowing together in currents she could almost see. She realized something that made her stomach clench with recognition. "These people aren't just unsuppressed. They're connected. To each other. To the environment. To things I can't even identify."

"Exactly." Holly stopped beside a wall covered with photographs, documents, and hand-drawn maps that spoke of years of careful research and planning. "What do you know about the Resonance Points?"

The term triggered recognition in Emma's brain, though she couldn't place the source of her knowledge. "They're theoretical. Council research mentions them as potentially dangerous zones where emotional energy might accumulate."

But if they're only theoretical, why does the term feel so familiar? Why do I have the sense that I should know more about them?

"They're real," Evan said. He joined their conversation with an intensity that suggested personal investment in the answer. "And they're dying."

The temperature around them seemed to drop several degrees. Emma noticed it first as a subtle shift, then as something that made her wrap her arms around herself. The emotional currents in the space had changed too, becoming more urgent, more focused.

Holly pulled down a map marked with seven locations across the globe. Each site was detailed with precision that spoke of years of watching rather than guessing. "These are the places where the planet's emotional consciousness is strongest."

Emma stepped closer to study the map. Her enhanced vision captured details that normal sight would miss. Each location was marked not just with coordinates but with emotional patterns, energy flow charts, and dated photographs showing environmental changes over the past century. The documentation was thorough, scientific, and troubling.

"Before suppression, they were sites of natural harmony," Holly continued, her voice careful and measured. "Places where human feelings and environmental systems worked together to maintain balance."

Emma traced one of the marked locations with her finger. The photographs showed a progression from lush, vibrant landscapes to increasingly barren terrain. The change was subtle at first, then more dramatic. But it was the emotional readings that made her breath catch. The energy patterns showed a steady decline over decades, like watching something slowly starve.

"What happens to them when they die?" Emma asked, though part of her already sensed the answer would be worse than she imagined.

Holly exchanged a look with Evan before answering. "The suppression system is killing them. When they die, the planet loses its ability to regulate the emotional energies that keep ecosystems stable."

"You mean climate and weather patterns?"

"Everything. Plant and animal behavior. Ocean currents. Magnetic fields. It all depends on the emotional field that we've been destroying for a century."

The implications crashed over Emma like cold water. *If that's true, then the suppression system isn't just controlling human emotion. It's damaging the planetary ecosystem itself. But why wouldn't the Council have discovered this? Why would they continue a program that threatens global stability?*

A man approached their group. His appearance triggered immediate recognition in Emma's memory files. Thomas Bennett, classified as a dangerous emotional deviant, wanted for questioning about resistance activities. But instead of the wild-eyed terrorist she expected from his Council profile, she saw someone who looked tired and determined. He carried himself with the quiet authority of someone who had once held significant responsibility.

The scent of machine oil and metal clung to his clothes, mixed with something that reminded Emma of libraries: old paper and careful preservation. His hands were stained with ink and calibration fluid, the marks of someone who worked with delicate instruments.

"I knew your father," he said. His voice carried respect that contrasted sharply with the deference she was accustomed to receiving.

The words struck Emma like a physical blow. The underground space seemed to tilt around her. Her suppression training activated, dampening the emotional surge that threatened to overwhelm her systems. But beneath the artificial calm, she felt something cracking open. A need to know that no amount of conditioning could eliminate.

Emma pressed her palm against the stone wall beside her, feeling its rough texture anchor her to the present moment. The coolness seeped through her skin, grounding her as her world shifted beneath her feet.

"My father died when I was five," she said. Each word was measured against the possibility that this man might be attempting to manipulate her. "Resonance accident during Council research."

Thomas's expression shifted to something like grief that seemed too real to be fabricated. "That's what they told you. But David Thorne lived for years after his supposed death. He was here, in the tunnels, working on the same research that brought you to us."

Emma's knees buckled. She grabbed Evan's arm to steady herself, feeling his warmth and strength through the fabric of his sleeve. Everything she had believed about her past, her identity, her family history felt uncertain. "That's impossible. I attended the memorial service. The Council honored his sacrifice."

The memory surfaced unbidden: standing in a black dress that scratched against her neck, watching adults she didn't recognize speak about a man she could barely remember. She'd been so young, but she recalled the smell of funeral flowers and the way her mother's hand had felt cold against her own.

"They honored his silence," Thomas corrected with bitter precision. "Your father discovered something that threatened the entire suppression system. He found evidence that the Resonance Points weren't just theoretical. They were the key to reversing the emotional damage."

But if he discovered a way to reverse the damage, why would the Council want him silenced? Unless the damage was intentional. Unless the suppression system was designed to create the problems it claims to solve.

Emma needed time to process what she was hearing. She walked a few steps away, her legs unsteady, and found herself beside the garden she'd noticed earlier. The woman tending it looked up with kind eyes and gestured for Emma to sit on a small stool beside the growing bed.

"First time hearing hard truths?" the woman asked gently.

Emma nodded, not trusting her voice.

"The plants help," the woman said, returning to her work. "Something about being around growing things. Makes the shock easier to bear."

Emma watched the woman's hands move through the soil with practiced care. The scent of earth and growing things filled her nostrils, so different from the sterile air of Council facilities. She could feel the emotional resonance between the woman and her plants, a connection that seemed as natural as breathing.

After several minutes, Emma felt steady enough to return to the others. Holly produced a small device that resembled a modified tablet. Its surface was covered with interfaces Emma didn't recognize.

"We've been preserving his research," Holly said. "Everything he learned about emotional energy and the reversal methods he was developing."

The device activated. It projected a holographic display that made Emma's brain sing with recognition. Emotional energy patterns, equations, and biological models filled the air around them. The mathematics were complex but elegant. They described systems that her enhanced processing could understand even as they challenged everything she had been taught about emotional suppression.

But it was the voice that made her world collapse.

"Day 1,247 of the hidden research," her father's voice said from the recording. It carried inflections and patterns that she recognized in her own speech. "The Council believes I'm dead, which gives me freedom to pursue the truth about what we've really done to the planet."

Emma sank to her knees on the stone floor. The cold seeped through her clothing, but she barely noticed. Her father's voice—not a memory, not a dream, but real and present and speaking words she'd never heard. Her chest seized as if someone had wrapped steel bands around her ribs. Her vision blurred while her hands shook against the rough stone. Grief for the father she'd thought was dead crashed into rage at the deception, both emotions hitting her faster than her suppression could process.

He's real. His voice, his ideas, his love for me. All of it was real, and they took it away.

She pressed her palms flat against the rough stone, using the physical sensation to anchor herself as emotions she'd never been allowed to feel crashed through her consciousness. Grief for the father she'd thought was dead. Rage at the deception. And underneath it all, a desperate hunger to hear more, to learn everything she'd been denied.

David Thorne's image appeared in the hologram. His amber eyes were so like her own that she felt a physical ache in her chest. He looked tired but determined. He carried himself with the same quiet intensity she recognized in her own approach to difficult problems.

"Mira thinks she's saving humanity, but she's killing it," his recorded image continued. "The suppression system doesn't just dampen emotions. It cuts the connection between human consciousness and the living world. The Resonance Points are dying because we've cut ourselves off from the emotional energy that feeds them."

The name hit Emma like another blow. Mira. Her mother's first name, spoken with such familiarity, such pain. The pieces of her shattered understanding began rearranging themselves into a pattern she didn't want to see.

"Emma," Evan's voice came from far away. "You need to breathe."

She looked up at him, seeing him clearly for the first time since entering the underground space. His face showed concern, affection, and something deeper that her awakening consciousness recognized as love. The realization should have triggered her suppression, but instead it felt like coming home to a place she had never known existed.

"He's alive," she whispered. Hope and grief warred in her voice.

"No," Holly said, kneeling beside Emma with maternal care that cut through her confusion. "The recording is twenty years old. David disappeared two years later, after the Council discovered he was still conducting research. But his work survived."

Emma stood, her legs trembling as her balance systems recalibrated. She processed the information that was reshaping her understanding of everything. The holographic display continued to show her father's research, complex diagrams of energy flow and biological systems that seemed to dance in the air around them.

"My mother. Chancellor Keller. She knew he was alive." It wasn't a question. The certainty settled in her chest like ice. It felt less like discovery than like remembering, something surfacing from beneath the conditioning where it had been waiting.

"Your mother?" Thomas looked confused, then his expression shifted to something like pity. "Chancellor Keller isn't just the head of the Council. She's Dr. Mira Keller, the original architect of the suppression system. She's also Dr. Mira Thorne, your father's research partner and the woman who gave birth to you."

The revelation hit Emma like a sledgehammer. Every interaction with the Chancellor flashed through her memory: the careful questions about her training, the personal interest in her progress, the way she'd looked at Emma during their meetings. Not with the distant authority of a government official, but with something that might have been maternal pride twisted into something unrecognizable.

Emma's vision blurred. The underground space spun around her. Every conditioning session replayed in her mind, but now she could see what she'd missed before. The Chancellor's hands had trembled during Emma's first neural interface test. She'd asked too many questions about Emma's emotional responses. She'd watched Emma's training sessions from the observation deck when no other official ever bothered.

She wasn't monitoring a weapon. She was watching her daughter.

She found herself sitting on the stone floor without remembering how she'd gotten there. The cold seeped through her clothes, real and immediate and somehow more bearable than the acid taste that filled her mouth. Her throat constricted as if she'd swallowed glass. Each breath came sharp and shallow.

How could she do this to me? How could my own mother turn me into a tool for destroying what my father loved?

"She's been using me," Emma said. The words came out flat and cold as the implications became clear. "My entire life, my training, my abilities. She's been turning me into the perfect tool for suppression."

The people around her had grown quiet. Even the children's laughter had faded. Emma could feel their emotional attention focused on her, a mixture of sympathy and concern and something that might have been protective anger on her behalf.

"Not just for suppression," Holly said with careful precision. "Your abilities are too strong, too complex for simple collection work. We think she's been preparing you for something else."

Emma's brain buzzed with activity as she processed what this meant. Her exceptional success rate, her ability to connect with subjects before collecting their emotions, her recent experiences with the factory workers. All of it pointed to capabilities far beyond standard Collector training.

What am I really capable of? What has she been preparing me to do?

The holographic display shifted, showing new data that made Emma's enhanced vision track patterns her conscious mind couldn't quite grasp. Energy flows on a global scale. Suppression field interactions. And at the center of it all, projections for something labeled "Project Completion."

"She's preparing me to be the final solution," Emma realized. The certainty settled in her mind like ice. "Not just to collect emotions, but to eliminate them entirely. To cut the connection between human consciousness and planetary awareness permanently."

The underground space pulsed around them with the emotions of its inhabitants. For the first time in her life, she felt the true scope of what the suppression system had destroyed. Not just individual feelings, but the living connection between humanity and the world that sustained them.

"What happens if the Resonance Points die?" she asked. Though part of her already knew the answer would be worse than she imagined.

"The planet loses its ability to regulate emotional energy," Thomas said with the precision of someone who had spent years studying the problem. "Without that regulation, the suppression system will collapse under its own weight. But instead of restoring natural emotional balance, it will create a cascade failure that destroys both human consciousness and planetary awareness."

So the suppression system is self-defeating. It will destroy the very thing it claims to protect. Unless that was always the plan.

Emma looked around the space, seeing the people who had trusted her with their most dangerous secret. Nina had returned to sit with the storyteller, her small hand in his weathered one. The woman from the garden was preparing food over one of the fires, her movements graceful and purposeful. Children who would be Corrected if discovered. Adults who risked their lives to maintain this fragile haven of authentic feeling. All of them depending on her to make the right choice.

"How long do we have?" she asked.

Holly consulted her modified tablet, checking readings from sensors placed throughout the tunnel network. The data she displayed painted a picture of breakdown that had been accelerating over the past five years. "Based on what we're seeing, maybe two years before the damage becomes irreversible. But the Council is accelerating suppression implementation. They're planning something called Project

Completion. A final push to eliminate all remaining emotional capacity."

"They're going to use me for it," Emma said. The certainty settled in her mind like ice. "Whatever they're planning, my abilities are the key."

But what if I refuse? What if I choose to use my abilities for restoration instead of destruction? Do I have that choice, or has the conditioning made it impossible?

Evan moved closer. His presence offered comfort that her suppression couldn't block. "They don't know about your awakening yet. We have time to prepare, to train you to use your abilities for restoration instead of destruction."

Emma looked at the holographic display of her father's research. She saw the complex equations and energy patterns that mapped the connection between human emotion and planetary consciousness. Somewhere in that data was the key to healing the damage caused by decades of suppression. But using it would require her to risk everything she had been taught to protect.

"If I do this," she said, voicing the question that cut to the heart of everything. "If I try to restore the Resonance Points, what happens to me?"

The question hung in the air, heavy with implications that none of them wanted to voice. Emma's enhanced hearing picked up the subtle shift in breathing patterns, the increased heart rates that indicated emotional stress even in people who had learned to hide their feelings.

"We don't know," Holly admitted with the honesty that Emma was learning to recognize as characteristic of the resistance. "Your father's research suggests that someone with your genetic markers could survive the process. But the connection between human consciousness and planetary awareness is intense. You might not come back the same person."

And what if I don't try? What if I let the Resonance Points die and the planet's emotional field collapse? How many people will suffer? How many will lose the capacity for authentic feeling forever?

Emma stood, feeling strength return to her legs as her decision crystallized. Around her, the underground space pulsed with the life that suppression had tried to eliminate. Messy, complex, dangerous, and essential. Nina was laughing at something the storyteller had said. The woman from the garden was humming as she worked. People were living, feeling, connecting in ways that the world above had forgotten were possible.

"Show me everything," she said. The decision formed with crystalline clarity. "Show me what my father discovered, what he wanted me to know. Show me how to save what's left of the world."

As Thomas began downloading her father's research files to her enhanced neural systems, Emma felt the last of her suppression conditioning crumble away. The controlled Collector who had entered the tunnels no longer existed. In her place stood someone who could feel the planet's dying emotional field. Someone who could sense the connections between all living things. Someone who carried the terrible responsibility of choosing between safety and truth.

The underground space around her hummed with authentic human emotion. Fear and hope and love and determination all woven together into something that felt like the beginning of a song that the world had forgotten how to sing.

For the first time in her life, she allowed herself to feel it all. To let it flow through her consciousness without suppression or control. She was no longer the Council's weapon. She was her father's daughter, and she was going to finish what he started.

But first, I need to understand exactly what I'm fighting against. And what I'm fighting for.

Chapter Thirteen

THE WATCHER'S CHOICE

The surveillance booth pressed against Marcus Webb like a tomb. Emma's vital signs erupted across his monitor for the third time that morning—brain patterns that shouldn't exist in a trained Collector. Complex emotional processing where there should be simple absorption. Personal investment bleeding through professional detachment.

The air in the booth tasted stale, recycled through filters that stripped away everything but basic oxygen. Marcus rubbed his temples, feeling a headache building behind his eyes. Three years of monitoring her missions with Council-demanded precision. Three years of readings that never varied from normal parameters. Now every assignment generated data that knotted his stomach with something his training couldn't identify.

Why am I feeling anything at all?

The question surfaced without permission, challenging assumptions he'd never thought to examine. Handlers maintained emotional neutrality. So why did watching Emma's data trigger responses in his own nervous system that made his hands shake against the console?

Yesterday's recording filled his screen. Emma absorbed a family's grief over their lost home, but instead of immediate emotional removal, she paused. Seventeen seconds where her expression shifted from professional calm to something that resembled authentic compassion.

Seventeen seconds. Training taught that emotional involvement lasting longer than three meant dangerous failure requiring immediate intervention.

His hand reached for the communication device. His fingers hovered over controls that felt heavier than they should. His mind processed consequences while sweat beaded along his hairline. Reporting Emma's irregularities would trigger immediate review. Removal from active duty. Enhanced reconditioning. Possibly permanent Council custody if problems persisted.

Marcus pulled his hand back as if the device had burned him. His chest tightened with something that felt like panic, but not quite. Something deeper.

But what if they aren't problems?

The thought violated everything he'd been taught. His conditioning screamed warnings, sending sharp pain through his skull. What if Emma's changes represented improvement rather than deterioration?

His training should have rejected such heresy automatically. Instead, he found himself examining evidence he was supposed to ignore. The booth's ventilation system hummed around him, a constant reminder of the artificial environment that sustained him while he watched authentic human interaction through glass and cameras.

Emma's subjects showed better adjustment after collection than any other Collector's. Higher satisfaction levels. Lower recurrence rates for emotional disturbances. Reduced need for follow-up interventions. By every measurable standard except strict timing, Emma was becoming more effective.

The image of Emma in a correction facility sent agony tearing through his chest—a tight squeeze that made him grip the console edge. His training identified this as inappropriate emotional attachment. Personal concern for a subject meant the handler needed reconditioning.

But instead of terror, the emotion felt sacred. Something worth protecting rather than destroying.

Marcus stood on unsteady legs, his balance systems recalibrating as if he'd been sitting for days rather than hours. He crossed to the observation window, each step requiring more effort than it should. Below, Emma moved through the processing floor crowd with practiced skill, approaching emotional disturbances with gentle confidence that made her the Council's most effective Collector.

Through the reinforced glass, he could see what he'd missed before—the way she lingered with each subject, small expressions suggesting she felt their emotions rather than absorbing them. The way people looked after her as she walked away, their faces carrying something that might have been gratitude instead of the usual post-collection emptiness.

Three months ago, those observations would have filled his report. Now they felt like secrets worth dying for.

What's happening to me?

A memory surfaced without warning: age seven, crying over a broken toy while his mother held him. The warmth of her arms, the sound of her voice telling him it was all right to feel sad. The memory should have been impossible—conditioning removed such experiences before handlers began training. But there it was, sharp as broken glass and twice as painful.

I used to be able to feel.

The door chimed. Marcus spun toward the sound, his heart hammering against his ribs. Councilor Viktor Brennan entered, shoulders carrying invisible weight. Strain carved lines around his eyes, tightness in his jaw speaking of sleepless nights and difficult decisions.

"Councilor Brennan." Marcus's voice caught. "I wasn't expecting inspection today."

Viktor paused in the doorway, his eyes scanning the booth's monitoring equipment with the attention of someone who understood surveillance technology. When he spoke, each word fell like a stone dropped into still water. "I'm not here for inspection, Agent Webb. We need to discuss... observations... about Collector Thorne's recent performance."

The careful phrasing made Marcus's throat constrict. *Observations*. Not *problems* or *irregularities*. The distinction felt significant, though he couldn't understand why.

"Sir, Emma's—Collector Thorne's efficiency ratings remain seventeen percent above standards."

Viktor waved off formality, settling into the secondary chair with movements that suggested his bones ached. "I'm not questioning her effectiveness." He studied the displays with intensity suggesting personal investment rather than routine evaluation. "I'm questioning whether effectiveness is the right... metric... to judge her."

The room tilted. Marcus gripped his console until knuckles went white. In all his years of service, no superior had suggested effectiveness might not be paramount. "I don't understand."

Viktor gestured toward monitors showing Emma's current collection. His hand trembled slightly, a detail Marcus's enhanced observation training caught automatically. "Tell me what you see."

Marcus watched Emma approach a middle-aged man grieving his daughter's recent marriage. Standard procedure demanded direct removal with minimal contact. Instead, Emma sat beside him on a public bench, speaking softly while processing his emotional energy with a patience that suggested actual conversation.

"She's..." Marcus paused, testing his words against potential consequences. "She's connecting with the subject before collection."

"Yes." Viktor's voice dropped to barely above a whisper. "What does that suggest to you?"

The question felt like a trap, but truth spilled out despite his conditioning's protests. "That she's making connections rather than performing removals."

"Connections." Viktor tested the word like it contained hidden meaning. His hands clenched and unclenched in his lap. "When I trained as enforcement, connections were dangerous. Emotional involvement compromised judgment."

Training echoed in Marcus's mind like a bell. "Handlers avoid personal attachment to assigned Collectors."

"And yet..." Viktor's eyes fixed on Marcus with uncomfortable intensity. "You haven't filed a report about Collector Thorne's irregularities. Why?"

The direct question cut through his training like a blade. He should lie, deflect, invoke procedure. Instead, words emerged more real than anything he'd said in years.

"Because she's becoming more effective, not less." His voice cracked as he spoke. "Her subjects show better adjustment after collection—calmer, more stable, less likely to need follow-up. Whatever she's doing differently works."

Viktor nodded like Marcus had passed some test. His shoulders relaxed slightly, though tension remained around his eyes. "How does watching her work make you... feel?"

The question should have been impossible. Handlers weren't supposed to feel beyond professional assessment. But watching Emma complete her collection and help the grieving man to his feet with gentle kindness, Marcus realized his emotional suppression had been failing for weeks.

The booth felt smaller suddenly, the recycled air insufficient. His reflection in the observation window showed eyes that looked different than they had that morning—wider, more aware, carrying something that might have been hope.

"Proud." The word carried unexpected weight. His voice cracked again. "And protective. She's doing something important—helping people instead of controlling them. I don't want to see that destroyed."

The confession hung between them like a live wire. Marcus waited for Viktor to activate emergency procedures, call for immediate suppression enhancement, end both their careers with a single communication.

Instead, the Councilor leaned back and... smiled? The expression was so unexpected Marcus questioned his vision.

Viktor's hands shook as he reached for his data pad. His voice dropped to barely a whisper, each word carrying the weight of someone about to step off a cliff. "Agent Webb, I'm going to share something that could end both our careers."

Marcus's mouth went dry. His hands gripped the console edge until his knuckles ached. "Sir?"

"Council historical records contain... gaps... regarding the Great Emotional War." Viktor's fingers hesitated over the data pad controls. Sweat beaded along his hairline despite the booth's cool temperature. "Evidence suggests some attacks used to justify expanded suppression may have been... created... by early Council members."

Ice water flooded Marcus's veins. The booth's walls seemed to close in around him. His heart hammered so hard he could feel it in his throat. The information contradicted everything he'd believed about the Council's founding mission.

"That can't be accurate." His voice came out hoarse. "The documentation is verified through multiple independent sources."

"Sources controlled by the same organization that benefits from suppression's continuation." Viktor activated his personal pad with trembling fingers, displaying classified documents that made training alarms scream in Marcus's head. "I've spent the last month reviewing archived materials most Council members never see. The pattern becomes clear once you know what to look for."

Documents flowed across the display: communication logs, resource allocation records, tactical assessments. They painted a picture Marcus's mind rejected even as his eyes processed evidence. The final emotional weapon attacks—the ones triggering permanent suppression—showed coordinated timing and resource signatures suggesting central planning rather than chaotic terrorism.

Marcus's hands shook so violently he had to press them flat against the console to stay upright. Bile rose in his throat. The air in the booth felt toxic, poisoned by revelations that made his worldview crumble like wet sand.

"If the attacks were planned by people who benefited from the response..." His voice trailed off as implications crashed over him.

"Then everything we've been told about suppression's necessity is based on manufactured threats." Viktor's words fell like stones into still water, creating ripples Marcus could feel in his bones.

Marcus stared at the evidence, his enhanced memory processing details while his conditioning screamed warnings. Maps showing attack coordination. Financial records revealing funding sources. Personal communications between Council founders discussing "acceptable casualties" and "necessary sacrifices."

"The resistance movements we've been taught to fear..." Marcus's voice came out cracked and small.

"May be attempting to restore natural human emotional capacity that was suppressed based on lies." Viktor closed the data pad with hands that shook like autumn leaves. "People like Emma aren't experiencing system failures. They're experiencing recovery—like someone waking up after being drugged for years."

Understanding crumbled like sand. Marcus's breath came in sharp gasps, sweat beading despite cool air. His reflection in the window showed a stranger's face: someone whose certainty had been replaced by terrible clarity.

"What does this mean for Emma's condition?"

"She's not experiencing suppression failure. She's experiencing suppression recovery." Viktor moved to the observation window where Emma began another collection. "Her readings indicate natural emotional capacity reasserting itself despite technological interference—like a plant growing toward sunlight through cracks in concrete."

Marcus joined him on unsteady legs, watching Emma work with growing understanding. Her connections with subjects weren't professional lapses—they were glimpses of authentic human interaction in a world that had forgotten what such connection looked like.

"What happens if we don't report her... recovery?"

"We buy time for her emotional development to stabilize while gathering evidence about the Council's true agenda." Viktor's voice carried the weight of someone choosing between two impossible options. "But we also accept responsibility for protecting someone whose awakening abilities could threaten the entire suppression infrastructure."

Marcus's shoulders straightened as he watched Emma help another person process grief safely. He saw gratitude in the subject's eyes as natural healing replaced artificial suppression. His breathing deepened, and for the first time in years, his hands felt steady against the console. This was work worth protecting. Worth dying for.

"Why tell me this instead of reporting through proper channels?"

Viktor's expression darkened like storm clouds gathering. "Because proper channels lead to Chancellor Keller. I have reason to believe she's... invested... in maintaining suppression regardless of evidence suggesting they cause more harm than the original threats."

Marcus's hands clenched into fists while his jaw tightened against words he couldn't speak. His pulse hammered in his throat while sweat broke out across his forehead. The booth felt like a pressure chamber about to explode. "What do you need from me?"

"Continue monitoring Emma's development. Document it as ongoing research rather than unusual behavior." Viktor produced a small device that looked like a standard classification coder. "I'll provide classification codes keeping your reports out of standard review cycles. We need to understand her awakening process before deciding how to protect her from Council intervention."

As if responding to their conversation, Emma completed her final collection and turned toward the surveillance booth. Even through the reinforced glass and electronic filters, Marcus saw changes in her posture and expression—warmth and awareness that hadn't existed in her previous efficiency.

She was becoming more human rather than less. In a world dedicated to eliminating human emotional capacity, that change made her both invaluable and incredibly dangerous.

Marcus made his choice with crystalline clarity, voice emerging stronger than he felt. "I'll protect her development as long as possible. But what happens when her abilities grow beyond what we can conceal?"

"Then we face the decision everyone in this situation confronts." Viktor's words carried the finality of someone who'd already made his choice. "Whether to choose individual safety or collective change. Whether to preserve the current system or risk everything for the possibility of something better."

Emma entered the processing center's main corridor, moving toward the handler debriefing station with fluid grace of someone comfortable in her own emotional skin. Her amber eyes met his through the observation window. For one breathtaking moment, Marcus felt truly seen rather than assessed.

His hands trembled as he activated the reporting interface. Each keystroke felt like rebellion against everything his training valued. He crafted language documenting Emma's remarkable effectiveness while avoiding terminology that might trigger intervention.

Research parameters. Ongoing development. Enhanced interpersonal protocols.

Words that would hide the truth in plain sight.

Watching Emma interact with colleagues and civilians with warmth rather than professional courtesy, Marcus felt something shift in his chest. Each keystroke against his conditioning felt like shedding skin he'd worn too long. Protecting someone's right to become human was worth any personal risk.

The report filed under research parameters keeping it from routine review. Marcus leaned back, entire body shaking with exhaustion and something that might have been hope.

Emma Thorne was awakening to her full emotional capacity —not like ice thawing, but like someone remembering how to breathe. He had chosen to help rather than stop her. The decision felt both terrifying and absolutely right—like stepping off a cliff while trusting wings would appear.

Tomorrow would bring new challenges, new opportunities to protect Emma's development while gathering evidence about the Council's true agenda. But tonight, he would go home and experience emotions for the first time in his adult life. Fear, hope, determination, and the strange joy of choosing conscience over control.

In the processing center below, Emma completed her shift unaware that her handler had become her ally, protector, and possibly her salvation. The suppression system that had shaped both their lives was beginning to crack. Through those fractures, something new emerged: the possibility of authentic human connection in a world that had forgotten what such connection could accomplish.

Marcus watched her leave, throat tight with emotions he couldn't name, already planning tomorrow's protection, already committed to a path that would either save them both or destroy everything he'd ever believed about duty, loyalty, and the price of human feeling.

The revolution had found another unlikely recruit. Emma's awakening had claimed another victory in the quiet war between authentic humanity and artificial peace.

And in the surveillance booth high above the processing floor, Marcus Webb discovered that choosing love over law felt like coming alive for the first time in his life.

Chapter Fourteen

WHAT THE HEART KNOWS

Fifty feet beneath New Geneva's surface, water droplets caught the soft glow of fungi growing along tunnel walls. The hidden garden felt like a secret the earth had kept—a pocket of life and beauty in the sterile underground, where moss-covered benches surrounded a natural spring bubbling up through cracks in old concrete. Evan had brought Emma here three days ago, and she found herself returning whenever the weight of her new awareness became unbearable.

The scent of growing things filled her nostrils—rich earth, clean water, the green smell of life persisting despite all attempts to control it. Bioluminescent moss painted everything in soft blues and greens, creating a world that pulsed with its own heartbeat.

This place calls to me, she realized, studying glowing organisms creating their own light in darkness. *Not just for its beauty, but because this is where I first felt peace.*

The garden represented everything the Council claimed was dangerous about uncontrolled environments. Unpredictable growth, unmanaged resources, the kind of natural chaos their perfectly ordered city above was designed to prevent. Yet standing here, Emma felt more balanced than she ever had in Council facilities.

The Council's definition of order is actually death, she thought, the revelation settling in her chest like a stone dropped into still water. *They've mistaken sterility for safety.*

"You're thinking again," Evan said, appearing from the tunnel entrance with two cups of real coffee—the kind with caffeine and flavor the Council had eliminated from standard nutrition programs decades ago.

The cup warmed her hands, its rich scent awakening something deep in her chest. Steam curled between them, carrying with it the promise of things the world above had forgotten. "There's a difference between thinking and worrying."

"Is there?" He eased beside her on the moss-covered stone, close enough that she could feel warmth radiating from his body. "Because from where I sit, they look pretty similar on you."

Brown eyes held actual amusement in the dim light, the slight upturn at the corner of his mouth suggesting he was fighting back a smile. Three weeks ago, she would have catalogued these expressions as data points to analyze and file away. Now something fluttered in her chest when she looked at him— something that had no place in her Council training but felt as natural as breathing.

"I've been wondering about something," she said, testing the words. "When you look at me, what do you see?"

The coffee cup paused halfway to his lips. His smile faded,

replaced by something more thoughtful. "That's not exactly a light question."

"The important ones never are."

Setting the coffee aside, he turned to face her completely. The moss beneath them glowed brighter as if responding to the shift in their attention. "I see someone who's been carrying other people's pain for so long that she's forgotten what her own feelings look like." His voice grew quieter. "I see someone brave enough to question everything she's been taught, even when that questioning hurts."

Heat bloomed in her chest, spreading through her ribs like liquid warmth. Without thinking, she reached for his hand, surprised at how their fingers seemed to fit together. The physical contact created immediate emotional resonance that her enhanced sensitivity could map in real time—his wonder, his protective instincts, his absolute faith in her potential.

This is what the Council warned us about, she realized. *Yet it feels like completion rather than contamination.*

"The Council taught us that emotional attachment leads to instability," she said, testing the words against her current experience.

"The Council taught you many things that turned out to be lies." His thumb traced circles across her knuckles, the simple contact sending electricity up her arm.

Emma pulled her hand back, standing abruptly to pace to the edge of the spring. Her reflection wavered in the dark water, fragmented and uncertain. "But what if they're right about this? What if what I'm feeling makes me unreliable?"

What if I'm putting everyone at risk because I can't control my own reactions?

Evan remained seated, watching her with patient eyes. "When you absorbed that family's emotions during your first awakening, what happened to your abilities?"

Closing her eyes, she remembered. The flood of grief and loss, the way it had nearly drowned her. But afterward... "They got stronger. More precise."

"And when we work together on rescue missions?"

She could feel his sincerity through the space between them, even without touching. "We're more effective than either of us alone." Opening her eyes, she found him watching her with unwavering focus. "Connection makes me stronger."

"Then why are you afraid of it?"

The question hung in the air like a challenge. Emma knelt beside the spring, her fingers trailing in the cool water. "Because yesterday, during a routine collection in Sector Seven, something happened."

She paused, organizing her thoughts while ripples spread from her touch. The water was so clear she could see every stone on the bottom, every tiny organism going about its business in the miniature ecosystem.

"I absorbed a woman's grief over her deceased husband. For a moment, just a moment, I let myself really feel it instead of just storing it." Her voice cracked. "The Collector working two blocks away—Agent Ross—he stopped mid-procedure and started crying. Real tears, Evan. He hadn't cried in fifteen years."

Evan moved to sit beside her at the water's edge. "What happened to him?"

"Marcus pulled him from active duty for psychological evaluation. He'll probably be sent for Enhanced Correction." Emma's hands clenched into fists. "Because I couldn't control myself."

"Or because you're becoming what you were always meant to be."

"A danger to everyone around me?"

"A bridge."

The word echoed strangely in the small space. Emma studied his face, searching for doubt or uncertainty and finding only quiet conviction that made her chest ache. "You really believe that, don't you? That humanity is better off feeling, even if it hurts?"

Evan's expression shifted, and for the first time since she'd known him, uncertainty flickered across his features. His hands trembled slightly as he picked up a smooth stone from beside the spring. "I want to believe it. But sometimes..." He threw the stone, watching it skip across the water's surface. "Sometimes I wonder if I'm just telling myself what I need to hear to justify the choices I've made."

The vulnerability in his voice surprised her. She'd never seen him doubt himself before. "What do you mean?"

"My sister was one of the first children to go through Enhanced Correction. I was sixteen, old enough to remember what she was like before." His voice grew rough. "Bright, funny, stubborn as hell. After the procedure, she was... compliant. Peaceful. Safe." He looked at Emma with eyes that held old pain. "The rational part of me knows she's probably happier now. No anxiety, no heartbreak, no disappointment. Sometimes I think maybe the Council was right about her."

Emma reached for his hand, feeling the tremor in his fingers. Through their connection, she sensed the guilt he carried— the weight of loving someone whose transformation he'd never been able to accept. "But you still fight against the system that changed her."

"Because the person I loved is gone. And I can't decide if that makes me selfish or right." His laugh came out bitter. "So when you ask if I believe humanity is better off feeling, part of me wonders if I'm just too broken to accept peace."

The admission hung between them like a bridge neither was sure they should cross. Emma squeezed his hand, feeling his pain mix with her own uncertainty. "Then we're both broken. Because I can't stop wondering if all this awakening is just me breaking down instead of opening up."

They sat in silence for a moment, their doubts mixing in the space between them. The garden around them pulsed with quiet life, offering no easy answers.

"There's something else," Emma said finally. "Dr. Clarke's been monitoring my readings, and he's noticed patterns. When I'm near you, when we're..." She gestured between them. "The emotional energy creates ripples. Other Collectors in the area start showing unusual readings."

His expression grew serious. "Your awakening is contagious."

"That's what terrifies me. My recovery might be destabilizing everyone around me."

"Would that be such a terrible thing?"

The question sat between them, heavy with implications. Emma stood again, moving to where bioluminescent vines created patterns on the tunnel wall. She touched one gently, watching it brighten at her contact.

"Dr. Clarke's been working on something," Evan said, moving to stand behind her. "He calls it the Cascade Theory. The idea that emotional awakening spreads through energy patterns. That once enough people begin to feel truly, it becomes self-sustaining."

Emma turned to face him, her back against the glowing wall. "That would mean chaos. Millions of people experiencing emotions for the first time, with no framework for processing them safely."

"Or it would mean freedom."

"The difference between freedom and chaos might be prepa-ration," she said, the thought forming as she spoke. "Maybe there's a way to restore human emotional capacity without triggering the kind of instability that originally led to suppression."

Evan's eyes widened, the tension around them easing as his shoulders relaxed. "You think it's possible?"

"I think..." Emma paused, feeling her way through the idea. "I think love might be the key. Not just romantic love, but all kinds of connection. When you help me process my doubts, when I feel your uncertainty and it makes mine seem less overwhelming—that's not instability. That's support."

"The Council taught you that emotions are threatening, but they never taught you what they're for." He reached up to cup her face in his hands. "Connection. Understanding. Growth. The ability to truly care about something beyond yourself."

The simple contact sent warmth spreading through her chest. "They're what make us human."

The word seemed to echo in the small space, and something shifted inside her—like a locked door swinging open. "When you touch me like this, I can feel your emotions as clearly as my own. Your certainty, your hope, your..." She paused, feeling shy despite everything they'd shared.

"My love," he finished.

The word hung between them, solid and real. She had absorbed thousands of emotions in her work as a Collector, but never experienced love directed at her. This feeling was unlike anything in her training—not the desperate attachment that led to instability, but something warm and steady that seemed to strengthen rather than weaken her sense of self.

"I don't know how to do this," she whispered.

"Neither do I. But I know that whatever this is between us, it makes everything else clearer." His thumbs brushed across her cheekbones. "When I'm with you, I understand why the resistance matters. Why fighting for emotional freedom is worth the risk."

Rising on her toes, she kissed him, surprised at how the simple contact seemed to complete a circuit between them. For a breathtaking moment, she experienced the world through his emotional awareness—felt his wonder at her courage, his determination to protect what they were building together, his absolute faith that love was stronger than the systems designed to eliminate it.

When they broke apart, her neural implants sang with harmonized energy patterns she'd never experienced before. The garden around them seemed brighter, more alive, as if their connection had awakened something in the very walls.

"The monitoring equipment is going to register this," she said, not caring nearly as much as she should.

"Let it. Maybe it's time people knew what they're missing."

They settled together on the moss-covered bench, Emma's head resting against Evan's shoulder as she processed the flood of new sensations. Through their physical connection, she could sense his emotional state with crystal clarity—contentment, protectiveness, and underneath it all, a deep well of love that seemed to expand rather than diminish when shared.

Minutes passed in comfortable silence before Emma spoke again. "There's something else Dr. Clarke mentioned. Something about environmental data."

Evan's arm tightened around her. "What kind of data?"

"Weather patterns, plant growth cycles, animal migration routes. Everything's been declining for the past twenty-five years." She sat up to meet his eyes. "He thinks the planet itself might be... aware. Conscious. And that human emotional energy is part of how it maintains biological balance."

The revelation should have sounded impossible, but in this place where life flourished despite suppression, it felt true. Evan's expression grew thoughtful rather than skeptical.

"You're saying the suppression system is killing the planet."

"I'm saying it might be killing everything." Her shoulders sagged as her hands pressed against her stomach, where something cold and heavy had taken up residence. "According to his models, we have maybe eighteen months before ecological collapse becomes irreversible."

Evan was quiet for a long moment, processing. When he spoke, his voice carried a mixture of awe and terror. "Then we're not just fighting for the right to feel. We're fighting for the right to exist."

The truth echoed through their connection, and Emma nodded. The stakes had escalated beyond personal liberation to species survival, but the magnitude of the challenge felt less overwhelming when shared.

"There's going to be a cost," she said. "If we succeed in triggering widespread emotional awakening, some people won't be able to handle the transition."

"I know. But what's the alternative? Slow extinction disguised as safety?"

Emma closed her eyes, extending her awareness outward through the underground network. Even here, fifty feet below the surface, she could sense the vast web of suppressed human consciousness above them. Millions of people living partial lives, their capacity for growth and connection severed.

And underneath it all, something else. Something enormous and patient and... lonely.

"I can sense them sometimes," she whispered. "All the suppressed people. Like stars trying to shine through thick clouds. And underneath it all, something else. Something that's been waiting."

His hand found hers again. "The planet?"

"Maybe. Or maybe it's just the collective unconscious of everyone who's forgotten how to be fully human." Opening her eyes, she found him watching her with an expression of wonder mixed with concern. "Either way, I think I'm the only one who can reach it directly."

The admission felt like stepping off a cliff. Evan's emotional state shifted from wonder to something approaching fear— not for himself, but for her.

"That's enormous responsibility for one person."

"It is. But I won't be carrying it alone, will I?"

His smile was answer enough, but he spoke the words anyway. "Never alone. Whatever this costs, whatever risks we have to take, we'll face them together."

The promise settled into her bones like certainty. The hidden garden around them seemed to pulse with life—moss growing brighter, water flowing clearer, the very air shimmering with possibilities that had been dormant for decades. Through their connection, she and Evan were creating a space where authentic emotion could flourish.

Every authentic connection we make sends ripples through the suppression field, she realized. *The spread has already begun.*

"How long before the Council notices?" Evan asked, as if reading her thoughts.

Emma extended her awareness upward, sensing the steady pulse of the emotion-dampening grid that covered New Geneva like an invisible web. In several places, she could detect fluctuations—small gaps where suppressed individuals were beginning to experience brief moments of authentic feeling.

"Days, maybe a week before the pattern becomes obvious to their monitoring systems." Standing, she pulled him up with her. "We need to prepare. If we're going to attempt contact with the planetary consciousness, it has to be soon."

"The risks..."

"I know. But what if we succeed?" His emotional state shifted from concern to cautious hope. "What if we can restore the connection between human consciousness and planetary awareness before it's too late?"

Hand in hand, they left the hidden garden, climbing through the tunnel system toward the resistance's main operations center. With each step, the weight of responsibility settled more firmly on Emma's shoulders, but also the strength that came from shared purpose.

The spread was beginning. Whether it led to salvation or catastrophe would depend on choices yet to be made, but she no longer faced those choices alone. Love, she was learning, wasn't the weakness the Council claimed it to be—it was the connection that made all other connections possible.

No wonder the Council worked so desperately to suppress it.

Chapter Fifteen

MOTHER'S WATCHING EYES

C old blue light from the holographic displays cast harsh shadows across Chancellor Mira Keller's face as she studied emotional grid readings from the past three days. Each data point represented thousands of citizens, their emotional states monitored and controlled through the extensive network of suppression fields that kept New Geneva stable. The patterns in the data made her hands clench against her desk's edge.

I missed this completely. The realization struck like a blade between her ribs as she traced the unusual readings with her fingertip. Years of monitoring Emma's development, and her breakthrough had progressed this far without triggering their security protocols.

"Explain these changes to me again," she said to the technician at her desk.

Dr. Reynolds cleared his throat, his fingers dancing across his tablet's surface. "The readings began three days ago in Sector

7, Chancellor. Brief spikes in emotional energy that bypassed our blocking systems. They lasted only minutes, but the energy patterns don't match anything in our database."

Her fingers traced the air above the hologram, watching data flow through three-dimensional space. The spikes formed a pattern. Not random changes but coordinated events that suggested someone was orchestrating them. More concerning, they originated from locations where Emma had been conducting collection work.

Emma's abilities have evolved far beyond anything we predicted.

"Has Agent Thorne reported any equipment problems?" The question tasted bitter on her tongue. Emma's work ratings remained perfect, her reports model examples of proper procedure. But weeks of monitoring her daughter's biological readings told a different story.

"No, Chancellor. Her collection rates are above normal levels." Dr. Reynolds consulted his tablet, unaware he was delivering a death sentence. "However, her brain activity shows increased complexity that doesn't match typical suppression profiles."

The words punched through her chest like shrapnel. Brain activity complexity was the first sign of emotional breakthrough. The condition that had destroyed her own parents decades ago. Every breath she'd taken for twenty-three years had been focused on ensuring Emma would never experience the curse of emotional sensitivity that ran in their family.

Her hands trembled despite the dampeners controlling her own system. A memory surfaced unbidden: Emma at age four, pressing her small palms against Mira's cheeks and asking, "Mama, why don't you ever smile?" The question had been innocent, devastating, and impossible to answer without revealing truths that would have shattered both their worlds.

"Show me her last three collection reports."

The hologram shifted, displaying Emma's recent activities across New Geneva's residential districts. Each mission appeared normal. Emotional disturbances identified, subjects approached with proper protocol, energy collected and contained. But analyzing the underlying data revealed what Dr. Reynolds had missed.

Emma's collection patterns had changed. Instead of the clinical absorption that marked proper technique, her recent operations showed emotional resonance. Brief moments where she'd connected with her subjects' feelings before cutting the link. Subtle, lasting only seconds, but violating every principle of emotional regulation.

Why risk exposure by connecting with subjects?

The truth crashed into her like a collapsing building. Emma wasn't experiencing emotional malfunction. She was developing emotional abilities that transcended the Council's understanding of human capacity. The resonance patterns suggested she could not only absorb emotional energy but amplify and redirect it.

"Dr. Reynolds, I want you to review Agent Thorne's conditioning records from the past six months. Look for any irregularities in her session responses."

"Yes, Chancellor." The technician paused at the door. "Should I alert her handler about potential system failure?"

"No." The word exploded from her lips like a gunshot. "Agent Webb is not to be told about this investigation. I'll handle any interventions myself."

Marcus Webb might be experiencing sympathy resonance. Handler-subject emotional bonds represent the most dangerous form of systemic failure.

Alone in her office, her chest tightened while her pulse hammered against her throat. The dampening fields should have eliminated such responses, but her breathing came shallow and quick despite the artificial calm they imposed. Emma represented the peak of suppression technology, proof that the Thorne family's emotional sensitivity could be controlled rather than eliminated. Emma's breakthrough meant the conditioning protocols weren't as absolute as she'd believed.

Pulling up Emma's childhood files, she scrolled through decades of psychological modification. Every session had been designed to prevent emotional development while maintaining the intelligence and empathy that made Emma such an effective Collector. That balance had been too delicate.

I created the exact conditions that would trigger her awakening.

The communication panel chimed. "Chancellor, Councilor Brennan requests an urgent meeting. He says it concerns historical verification protocols."

Viktor Brennan had been persistent about his archival research, requesting access to classified records with concerning frequency. "Schedule him for tomorrow afternoon."

"He indicated the matter was time-sensitive, Chancellor. Something about discrepancies in the Great Emotional War casualty reports."

The words sent ice through her veins. Viktor's investigation into historical records was supposed to be routine verification for ceremonial purposes. If he'd discovered inconsistencies in the war documentation, it could threaten the narrative that justified the suppression system's existence.

"Send him in immediately."

Viktor entered her office without his usual military bearing. His shoulders carried weight that hadn't been there the previous week, and the lines around his eyes spoke of sleepless nights spent processing information that challenged everything he'd believed about his service to the Council.

"Chancellor," he said, placing a secured data pad on her desk with hands that shook slightly. "I need to discuss what I've discovered in the historical archives."

She gestured for him to sit, though he remained standing, his posture rigid with barely contained emotion. "I understand you've found some inconsistencies in the ceremonial documentation. I'm sure they're minor clerical errors that can be corrected."

"They're not minor." Viktor's voice cut like a blade, making her monitoring systems register spiking stress patterns. "According to the official records, the attack on Research Station Seven occurred on March 15th, killing forty-three scientists including my wife and son. But the communication logs show Council security forces were withdrawn from the area twelve hours before the supposed surprise attack."

He's found the operational records.

Environmental systems hummed as she processed this information. Viktor digging this deep into those particular records had been her nightmare scenario. The false flag operations had been compartmentalized beyond his original security clearance, but his ceremonial research had apparently provided access to databases that should have remained sealed.

"Councilor, you're dealing with classified material that requires specific security clearance to interpret correctly."

"I have the clearance, Chancellor. And I've found more than timing discrepancies." Viktor activated the data pad, projecting images into the air between them. His hands shook as he manipulated the controls, sweat beading along his hairline despite the cool office temperature. "The emotional weapon signatures from six different attacks show identical energy patterns. Identical, Chancellor. That's impossible unless they came from the same source."

Viktor had found evidence of the coordinated strikes that had built public support for expanded suppression measures twenty-five years ago. The operations that had eliminated the last organized resistance to total emotional control by creating artificial crises that demanded artificial solutions.

"Viktor, what you're looking at represents one of the most classified aspects of Council operations. The information is compartmentalized for very specific reasons."

"Because it proves that some of the attacks we used to justify suppression expansion were conducted by Council forces?" Viktor's military training kept his voice level, but she could see the emotional storm building beneath his conditioning. His breathing grew shallow, pupils dilated despite the controlled lighting. "Because it means my family died not to random terrorism but to deliberate manipulation designed to manufacture consent for policies that eliminated human emotional capacity?"

The accusation hung in the air between them like a toxic cloud. Her own suppression systems strained against emotions she'd buried for decades. Guilt, regret, and the grinding weight of every sacrifice that had been necessary to prevent humanity's complete destruction.

"The early Council faced unthinkable choices," she said, her voice carrying the weight of twenty-five years spent defending decisions that had saved civilization at the cost of individual lives. "The emotional war was escalating beyond any possibility of containment. Small, controlled incidents prevented much larger catastrophes."

"Controlled incidents." Viktor's voice carried flat disbelief that cut through her explanations like a physical blow. His hands clenched into fists at his sides. "You're calling the murder of my family a controlled incident designed to create public support for eliminating human emotional capacity."

"I'm calling it necessary sacrifice to save millions of lives from destruction through weaponized emotion that was becoming more sophisticated and destructive every month." Her desk's security protocols activated, sealing the room against external surveillance. "Viktor, what you've discovered can never leave this office. The stability of our civilization depends on maintaining public faith in the suppression system."

"Faith built on lies and murder." Viktor stepped closer to her desk, his emotional dampeners failing as decades of suppressed grief began breaking through his conditioning. Tears leaked from his eyes despite the neural blocks designed to prevent them. "How many other 'necessary sacrifices' were there, Chancellor? How much of our history is fabricated to support a system that eliminates the fundamental aspects of human consciousness?"

Watching him struggle against his awakening emotions, Mira found herself leaning forward in her chair. Her hands unclenched from their rigid position on her desk, and for a moment her expression softened despite years of training that demanded emotional distance. She'd experienced the same breakdown when she'd first learned the truth about the false flag operations. The moment when loyalty to the system collided with personal moral boundaries.

Viktor's emotional breakthrough is connected to Emma's awakening. The awakening process has become contagious.

"Sit down, Viktor. Let me explain what really happened during the final years of the war, and why the choices we made were the only ones available to prevent complete civilizational collapse."

He remained standing, but his aggressive posture shifted to something more defeated as the weight of his discoveries continued to process through his awakening emotional capacity. "I'm listening."

"The emotional weapons were becoming more sophisticated with each passing month." She called up classified files that showed the true scope of the pre-suppression crisis, data that painted a picture of approaching catastrophe. "By 2955, psychic individuals could project concentrated trauma across entire city blocks. Children were being driven permanently insane by exposure to artificially concentrated despair. The elderly were dying from heart failure caused by artificially induced grief."

Viktor studied the projection images, his jaw working as he processed information that challenged his understanding. Hospital records, casualty reports, and psychological damage assessments painted a picture of civilization collapsing under the weight of weaponized emotion.

"The Council faced a choice," she continued, watching his face as he absorbed the data. "Allow the war to continue until humanity destroyed itself through uncontrolled emotional excess, or take decisive action to eliminate the threat permanently. The false flag operations provided the public support necessary to implement total suppression before the situation became completely uncontainable."

"By murdering innocent people."

"By sacrificing dozens to save millions from certain death." Deactivating the projections, she met his eyes with the full weight of her authority and personal conviction. "Viktor, I understand your anger. I lost people too in those operations. But the alternative was the complete collapse of human civilization."

They stood in silence for several minutes, the weight of historical truth settling between them like a physical presence. Viktor's breathing steadied as his suppression systems reasserted some measure of control over his emotional breakthrough, though she could see that the conditioning was no longer completely effective.

"What happens now?" he asked, his voice hoarse.

"Now you understand why this information must remain classified indefinitely." Returning to her chair, she felt the full weight of her fifty-two years and the burden of every decision she'd made to preserve human civilization. "The suppression system works, Viktor. We've had twenty-five years of peace because people believe in its necessity."

"Peace built on lies."

"Peace that has prevented the deaths of millions." She met his gaze with the full authority of her position. "Viktor, I'm trusting you with this knowledge because I believe you understand the difference between idealistic truth and practical responsibility. We cannot change what was done, but we can ensure it serves its intended purpose."

Viktor picked up his data pad, his expression unreadable as he processed the full scope of what she'd revealed. "I need time to process this information, Chancellor."

"Of course. But Viktor." She waited until he met her eyes with full attention. "This conversation never happened. And your investigation into historical records ends today. Some knowledge serves no constructive purpose."

Everything we've built will collapse if he continues investigating.

After he left, she sat alone in her office, staring at the holographic displays that monitored millions of suppressed citizens across the global network. Each data point represented someone who lived in artificial peace because they couldn't feel the full weight of human existence.

But Emma's developing emotional sensitivity suggested that even the most controlled suppression might not be permanent. Her daughter's breakthrough meant others would follow. The question was whether humanity could handle the return of authentic emotion without destroying itself through the same chaos that had necessitated suppression in the first place.

Another memory surfaced: Emma at twelve, asking why she felt empty during the mandatory joy celebrations. "It's like watching people pretend to be happy, Mama. Why don't I feel what they're feeling?" The question had driven Mira to increase Emma's conditioning sessions, terrified that her daughter's natural empathy would lead to emotional breakdown.

I was protecting her from becoming what I feared most. What if I was protecting her from becoming what she was meant to be?

Activating her secure communication system, she sent a coded message to Dr. Sarah Magnus, head of the Council's research division. Emma's condition required immediate study before it spread to other Collectors. Whatever was happening to her daughter needed to be understood before it threatened the stability they'd worked so hard to create.

But do I want to contain it? Or do I want to understand it?

The message sent, she turned back to the emotional grid displays. Somewhere in the data streams, her daughter's awakening consciousness was creating ripples that could either heal or destroy everything they'd built. As both Chancellor and mother, she would do whatever was necessary to protect Emma.

Even if that protection required choosing between the system she'd defended and the daughter she'd never stopped loving.

The holographic displays continued their endless monitoring, each spike and change representing the balance between order and chaos that defined their world. Somewhere in that balance, Emma's growing abilities threatened to tip everything toward an unknown future that both terrified and intrigued her more than any enemy she'd ever faced.

The awakening was spreading. Viktor's questions. Marcus's protective instincts. Her own growing doubts about the Council's fundamental mission. Emma's influence was reaching beyond individual minds into the institutional power structures that maintained suppression.

And Mira found herself hoping, against every principle she'd been trained to uphold, that her daughter's awakening would prove stronger than the system designed to contain it.

The next twenty-four hours would determine whether humanity's future lay in continued suppression or dangerous freedom.

The choice was no longer just Emma's to make. It was hers.

Chapter Sixteen

THE CHILDREN WHO MUST NOT WAKE

T he holographic map floating above the makeshift table painted a picture that made Holly's blood run cold. Red dots marked confirmed Council facilities, blue dots showed resistance cells, and yellow dots showed the children they'd identified for possible rescue. The pattern hit her like a physical blow. The Council was targeting emotional sensitives with surgical precision that suggested coordinated intelligence rather than random enforcement.

They've become efficient at identifying children we can barely detect ourselves.

"Seventeen facilities activated in the past week," reported Marcus Webb, his voice carrying barely controlled emotion that would have earned immediate correction in his former Council position. Since his defection, the former handler had proven invaluable, bringing insider knowledge that had already saved dozens of lives. "They're not just processing routine cases anymore. They're hunting."

Emma entered the command center, her amber eyes going straight to the map's threatening patterns. Since her awakening in the factory, her abilities had grown exponentially, but so had the risk she represented. Every use of her powers created detectable signatures that advanced Council tracking systems could identify and trace.

"The facility in Sector Seven processed forty-three children yesterday," Marcus continued, consulting his stolen Council tablet. The blue glow from the screen cast shadows under his eyes. "Neural pathway severing, emotional center cauterization, memory restructuring. That's more invasive procedures than most facilities handle in a month."

Holly felt her chest constrict as the number registered. Forty-three children. Each one a name, a face, a small life filled with potential for joy and love and wonder. Each one now reduced to regulated calm, their capacity for authentic feeling burned away with precision instruments.

She studied the faces around the table, each one marked by the strain of carrying knowledge that most people couldn't bear. Marcus with his guilt over years spent enforcing the system he now fought. Dr. Clarke with his scientific understanding of what they were racing to prevent. Emma with her growing awareness of the planetary consciousness that depended on their success.

Holly's knees buckled slightly, forcing her to grip the table's edge. The recycled air in the command center felt thick, hard to breathe. For fifteen years, she'd built this network one rescued child at a time. Now the scope of the threat demanded operations she'd never imagined possible.

"We need to move beyond reactive rescues," she said, her voice carrying the authority of someone who'd survived the unthinkable. "If they're expanding their operations, we need to expand ours."

Dr. Clarke looked up from his calculations, wire-rimmed glasses reflecting the map's glow. "The energy readings support that assessment. Council suppression facilities are running at 300% normal capacity. They're not just maintaining the system anymore. They're accelerating implementation."

Emma moved closer to the map, her enhanced sensitivity allowing her to perceive emotional patterns that instruments couldn't measure. As she studied the display, her expression shifted from analytical to something deeper, more troubled. The air around her began to shimmer with barely contained energy that made everyone's skin tingle.

"I can feel them," she whispered. "The children. Their fear creates frequencies I can tune into." She pressed her fingertips to her temples, a habit she'd developed when her abilities threatened to overwhelm her conditioning.

But as she reached deeper, something else surfaced—a memory from her own childhood. Age six, sitting in a Council facility while machines hummed around her, feeling terrified and alone while adults spoke about her in clinical terms. The memory hit her like ice water, reminding her that beneath her growing cosmic awareness, she was still the frightened girl who'd never understood why the world felt so empty.

I was one of those children once. The only difference is they're trying to save me.

"There are so many more than we thought," she continued, her voice shaking. "Hundreds. Maybe thousands. They're

terrified, but they don't understand why. The Council is identifying them before they even know they have abilities."

The room fell silent as everyone processed the implications.
Evan Cross stood beside Emma, his natural immunity to
suppression making him one of the few people who could
provide her with emotional stability when her abilities threatened to consume her.

"My powers," Emma said, meeting Holly's eyes with sudden
clarity, "they're growing faster than I can control them. Every
time I reach out to the planetary consciousness, I feel pieces
of myself scattering. I don't know how much longer I can
maintain individual identity while connected to something
that vast."

Holly's throat tightened. They were asking a young woman
who'd just discovered her own capacity for feeling to become
responsible for potentially millions of people. But Emma's
honesty about her limits made the choice clearer, not harder.

"We can't save them all at once," Holly said. "But we can save
some. And those we save can help us save others."

The concept was simple but revolutionary. Instead of operating as isolated rescue missions, they would begin building an
interconnected network of safe houses designed to handle
emotional refugees. Each facility would serve as both sanctuary and training center.

Holly activated the room's secondary display, showing a
different map. This one marked the locations of every individual their network had successfully helped over the past
fifteen years. Former Council operatives like Marcus, rescued
children who'd grown into capable adults, suppressed individuals who'd learned to access their emotions safely.

"Each of these people represents not just a success story, but a potential safe house coordinator," she explained. "They know what it's like to transition from suppression to authentic feeling."

Emma walked to the window, staring out at the city above their underground sanctuary. Through the reinforced glass, she could see the geometric perfection of New Geneva's architecture.

"The Council isn't just hunting children," she said, her voice carrying the distant quality that appeared when she connected to larger patterns. "They're preparing for something bigger. Chancellor Keller—my mother—she's escalating because she knows what's coming."

"What do you mean?" Marcus asked.

Emma turned back to the group, her expression grave. "Every time I use my abilities, I can feel the planetary consciousness responding. It's like the planet is awakening because I'm awakening. And if the planet awakens while the suppression system is still operational..."

Dr. Clarke's eyes widened behind his glasses. "A cascade event. If the planetary emotional field becomes active while the suppression grid is still operational..."

"The technology will overload," Emma finished. "And when it fails, everyone connected to it will experience emotional awakening at the same time. Millions of people, all at once, with no guidance or preparation."

Holly's stomach knotted as images flashed through her mind. The transition she'd witnessed in rescued children, but multiplied by millions. The process was difficult enough one person at a time, requiring careful guidance and enormous patience.

"How long do we have?" Evan asked.

Emma consulted the emotional patterns she could perceive, like a weather forecaster reading approaching storms. Her face went ashen. "Weeks. Maybe less. The resonance between my abilities and the planetary field is strengthening every day."

Holly's pulse hammered against her ribs as she stood at this crossroads. The fluorescent lights hummed overhead, casting harsh shadows across the faces of her team. Fifteen years of resistance work had taught her that the most treacherous choice was often inaction.

"Then we don't have time for gradual network expansion," she decided. Her voice grew steady and firm, her spine straightening as she turned to address the group. "We need to start the new system immediately."

She turned to address the group. "Marcus, I need you to contact every former Council operative in our network. We're going to need inside information about facility locations, security protocols, and processing schedules."

Marcus hesitated, his hand hovering over his encrypted communicator. His jaw worked as he processed what she was asking. Some of the people he'd be contacting were friends—colleagues who'd trusted him with their growing doubts about the system. Asking them to help would put their lives at risk.

"Some of them have families," he said quietly. "Children of their own."

"So do the people we're trying to save," Holly replied.

Marcus nodded, his hand steadying as he reached for the device. "I can reach at least thirty individuals within the next few hours. Some are still technically active Council members."

"Dr. Clarke, we need to know which facilities pose the greatest immediate threat. Can your monitoring equipment identify where the most advanced procedures are scheduled?"

"The emotional energy signatures should indicate which children are slated for enhanced correction," Clarke confirmed. "I can have preliminary data within six hours."

Holly turned to Emma and Evan. "You two represent our greatest asset and our greatest liability. Emma's abilities are needed for guiding mass awakening, but every time she uses them, she risks Council detection."

"What do you need us to do?" Emma asked.

"Start small. Begin with the children we can reach safely. Use your abilities to provide them with emotional guidance before they're physically rescued. If we can teach them to manage their awakening while they're still in Council facilities, they'll be better prepared for freedom."

Over the next hour, they developed the framework for what Holly privately thought of as the most ambitious undertaking in resistance history. Each safe house would become a node in a larger network, connected through encrypted communication and coordinated response protocols.

"The Council's greatest advantage has always been centralized control," Holly observed as they finalized the operational structure. "They can coordinate responses quickly because everything flows through official channels. But that also makes them predictable."

"Our network is distributed," Emma added, understanding the strategic implications. "If they shut down one safe house, the others continue operating."

Marcus looked up from his communicator, where he'd been receiving responses from contact attempts. "I've confirmed availability from eighteen former Council operatives. They're all willing to help coordinate intelligence gathering and facility mapping."

"Dr. Clarke's monitoring data is already showing patterns," the scientist reported. "Three facilities are planning major processing operations within the next 48 hours. If we're going to prevent those procedures, we need to move immediately."

Holly's hands shook, her pulse hammering against her throat while sweat beaded along her hairline. The same feeling that came with launching operations where success would save lives and failure would destroy them.

"Then we start now," she decided. "Emma, I need you to attempt contact with the children scheduled for processing. Don't try to reach all of them. Focus on the ones whose emotional signatures suggest they're most likely to survive the guidance process."

Emma nodded, already moving toward the meditation area where she could attempt psychic contact. "I'll start with the facility in Sector Seven. The children there seem stronger somehow. More resilient."

"Evan, coordinate with Marcus on security protocols. We need to ensure that our expanded operations don't compromise existing safe houses."

As the team dispersed to begin work, Holly remained in the command center, studying the maps and data streams that represented their expanding network. The air recycling system whispered overhead, a mechanical breathing that seemed to echo the sleeping breaths of endangered children throughout the city.

Her shoulders ached as if she'd been carrying heavy weights for hours. The maps blurred slightly before her tired eyes. For decades, the Council had used centralized control to suppress human emotion on a planetary scale. Now they were proposing to restore that emotion through distributed healing networks. It was the difference between imposing order from above and allowing growth from within.

The network was expanding, but the real test would come when it faced the full weight of the Council's response. As she began the final preparations for their most ambitious operation yet, Holly allowed herself one moment of hope.

Outside, the city slept under its blanket of emotional suppression. But in the safe houses and hidden spaces throughout New Geneva, a different kind of consciousness was awakening. One connection, one rescued child, one act of courage at a time.

The cascade was coming whether they were ready or not. The only question now was whether they could guide it toward healing rather than chaos.

For the first time in fifteen years, Holly believed they had a chance.

The children would not wake alone.

Chapter Seventeen

A WORLD DYING ALONE

Crystal formations throughout Dr. Clarke's lab pulsed with stored emotional energy, casting shifting light patterns across walls lined with humming equipment. Before the largest display screen she'd ever seen, Emma watched real-time data that made her legs buckle. Her knees struck the floor as numbers cascaded down in columns beside visual maps of energy flows that resembled living neural networks stretched across continents.

This complexity couldn't have existed without our knowledge. We chose not to know.

"The planet isn't just alive," Dr. Clarke said, his voice carrying fifteen years of secret research. "It's awake. And it's dying."

Emma's hands pressed against the cold lab floor, trembling as her enhanced sensitivity revealed the emotional resonance hidden in the scientific measurements. The sight struck her chest and tore through her awareness, leaving her gasping. The energy signatures weren't abstract data points but the planet's feelings, fading like a dying heartbeat she could feel in her bones.

Everything we've been taught about emotion being purely human is wrong.

"I don't understand," she whispered, though her body already knew the truth. The connection she'd felt during her awakening, the sense of something patient and lonely reaching out through her abilities, now felt like a scream in her skull.

Dr. Clarke's hands shook as he helped her to her feet, exhaustion from years of carrying this knowledge alone carved into every line of his face. "What do you feel when you touch the emotional residue in the Undercity tunnels?"

The question surprised her. "I feel... connections. Networks of feeling that extend beyond individual people."

"Precisely." Clarke activated another display. "Emotional energy isn't just a human phenomenon, Emma. It's the basic force that connects all living things. Plants, animals, tiny organisms all contribute to and depend on the planetary emotional field."

He paused, studying her face as tears she didn't realize were falling left cold tracks down her cheeks. "But humans are the primary interface. Our emotional capacity allows the planet to regulate itself, to maintain the balance needed for life."

We're not separate from the natural world. We're part of its nervous system.

The screen shifted to show a timeline stretching back two centuries. Emma's breath stopped as she watched the emotional energy readings drop in steady, relentless decline.

"The suppression system hasn't just dampened human feelings," she said, understanding flooding through her. "It's been strangling the planet's awareness."

The temperature in the lab dropped five degrees as the crystallized emotions around them began to pulse in rhythm with the dying data streams.

"The weather problems," she continued, her voice cracking. "The crop failures. The animal migrations going wrong."

"All symptoms of emotional starvation," Dr. Clarke confirmed. "The planet is trying to communicate with us, to maintain the connection that keeps ecosystems stable, but we've cut the link."

Emma walked to the nearest crystal formation, drawn by its increasing resonance. When she placed her palm against its surface, the crystal's glow intensified and she felt something vast and desperate pressing against her consciousness.

"It's like severing the neural pathways in a brain," Clarke explained. "The body remains alive, but it can't coordinate its functions."

Species have gone extinct because we broke the communication system they depended on.

Emma doubled over as the full realization hit her stomach like a physical blow. Every emotion she'd collected, every feeling she'd stolen from families in crisis, represented a thread in the fabric that held the world together. She'd been destroying that fabric for six years.

"How long?" she asked, her voice barely more than breath.

"At current rates? Total collapse within eighteen months. The planet's awareness will fade. When it does, the systems that maintain atmospheric balance, ocean currents, and magnetic field stability will fail. Not right away, but over the following decades."

"You're talking about extinction."

"I'm talking about a world that becomes unlivable not through war or disaster, but through loneliness." Dr. Clarke's voice cracked. "The planet will die of isolation, and we'll die with it."

This is what my father discovered. This is why he was willing to fake his death.

Emma's legs gave out again, but this time she caught herself on the edge of the display. The screen was warm under her palms, almost feverish. The data streams responded to her touch, shifting and swirling in patterns that felt desperate, hungry for connection.

"Can you feel it?" Dr. Clarke asked.

Emma nodded, unable to speak. Through her enhanced abilities, she could sense something behind the numbers. A presence old and patient and so deeply sad that her own heart began to ache in sympathy. The planetary intelligence wasn't just data but a living thing, like an enormous heart beating in slow, irregular rhythm.

"Each pulse is weaker than the last," she whispered.

"The planet is responsible for the welfare of billions of species but is losing the ability to communicate with the one species that could help coordinate that care."

It's trying to maintain balance when its primary interface works against it.

A sharp crack split the air. Emma spun around as one of the monitoring displays sparked and went dark. Dr. Clarke rushed to the console, his fingers flying over controls as warning lights began flashing red across the laboratory.

"Power fluctuations," he said, his voice tight with urgency. "The emotional grid is destabilizing faster than predicted."

The crystallized emotions around them began to sing, a low harmonic that made her bones vibrate. Through the lab's reinforced windows, she could see the lights of New Geneva flickering in patterns that matched the dying equipment.

"The Resonance events," Emma breathed, understanding flooding through her like ice water. "They're not random. The planet is trying to wake us up."

"Precisely. And they're getting stronger as the situation becomes more desperate." Clarke pulled up new projections that made Emma's heart sink. "Eventually, if we don't restore the connection, the planet will have no choice but to trigger a Resonance event powerful enough to break through the suppression fields by force."

"What would that do to people?"

Dr. Clarke's face went ashen. "Billions of individuals experiencing the full force of their suppressed emotions at once, without preparation or guidance? Complete psychological collapse."

The Council's worst fears about emotional chaos could become reality, but only because their attempt to prevent chaos is creating the conditions that make chaos inevitable.

The laboratory's communication system crackled to life, interrupting her contemplation. Evan's voice filled the chamber, strained with urgency that made the crystallized emotions pulse brighter.

"Emma, we need you up here now. Holly's network is reporting system failures across seven districts. People are experiencing emotional overload without warning."

Emma closed her eyes and extended her awareness through the emotional residue that filled the Undercity tunnels. The sensation hit her like a tidal wave. She felt them. Thousands of people experiencing authentic feeling for the first time in their lives.

"They're not experiencing overload," she said, opening her eyes to meet Dr. Clarke's worried gaze. "They're experiencing authenticity. What we call dangerous emotional excess is just the natural human response to finally being allowed to feel their own lives."

But they have no training for this. No preparation.

"The timeline has collapsed," she continued. "We planned for gradual awakening over months. Now we have hours before the entire system fails."

Dr. Clarke crossed to another console, his fingers flying over controls as files appeared that made Emma's heart hammer against her ribs. "Your father's research. He discovered that certain individuals with your genetic markers could serve as bridges between human awareness and the planetary field. Not just collectors of emotion, but translators."

Being a translator between species means communicating concepts that humans have no words for.

The screen showed intricate diagrams of neural pathways and energy flows that looked exactly like her own brain scans. She recognized the patterns from her medical files, the abnormalities that had always marked her as different among Collectors.

"You're saying I could talk to it. To the planet."

"More than that. You could help it communicate with everyone. Not through forced Resonance, but through conscious connection."

Emma studied the diagrams, her enhanced abilities making the quantum mechanics feel like music she could finally understand. "Imagine if instead of suppressing emotions, we learned to process them with the planet's guidance. Instead of seeing feelings as waste products, we understood them as part of a larger living system."

Would humans still be human if we became part of a planetary intelligence?

Another display sparked and went dark. The lab shuddered as if the building itself was responding to the emotional instability above ground.

"I'd have to open myself to the planetary awareness," Emma said, grasping the scope of what he was suggesting. "Channel the emotional energy of billions of people."

"The risk is significant," Dr. Clarke admitted, his voice gentle but unflinching. "Your individual identity could be overwhelmed, dissolved into the larger field. But Emma, if you don't try, there won't be anyone left to save."

I don't have the right to make that choice for all humanity. But no one has the authority to let planetary intelligence die either.

She turned away from the screen, her steps unsteady as she walked to the other side of the laboratory where crystallized emotions glowed in containment fields. These were the feelings she'd collected over the past months, transformed into physical form by the buildup of emotional energy.

As she approached, the crystals pulsed brighter and began to resonate, creating a harmony that made her skin tingle.

"When I collect emotions," she said, her voice thick with unshed tears, "I don't just absorb them. I experience them. For just a moment, I feel what other people feel."

"Yes. And that's what makes you different. Most Collectors store emotional energy. You process it, integrate it into your own awareness before releasing it."

I've been practicing for this role my entire career without knowing it.

Emma reached out to touch one of the crystals, and the moment her skin made contact, the emotions within exploded through her nervous system. Love, grief, joy, fear. All the feelings she'd taken from families across New Geneva, but amplified a hundredfold.

Instead of the chaotic storm she expected, she sensed an underlying harmony that made her weep. A pattern that connected each emotion to something infinitely larger.

"They're not separate," she sobbed. "All these feelings, they're part of the same system. Like instruments in an orchestra."

"Precisely. And the planet is the conductor, trying to create harmony from individual notes. But for two centuries, we've been silencing the musicians."

The harmony might require sacrificing individual melodies.

Emma closed her eyes and let her awareness expand, following the connection she'd felt during her awakening. This time, instead of being overwhelmed by the planetary presence, she approached it step by step, like learning to listen to a complex piece of music.

The sadness was still there, the growing panic and confusion, but beneath it she sensed something else that made her heart break.

Hope.

The planet recognized her. Not just as another human, but as someone who could hear its voice, understand its needs, translate its wisdom back to a species that had forgotten how to listen.

"It's been waiting for me," she whispered through her tears.

"For someone like you," Dr. Clarke said, his own voice breaking. "Your father believed that the genetic markers for emotional bridging would manifest in his bloodline."

He never prepared me for the choice itself. How do you prepare someone to decide between individual identity and collective survival?

The laboratory's communication system crackled again. Holly's voice filled the chamber with urgency that made the crystallized emotions pulse in response.

"Emma, we're seeing accelerated awakening in the children we've rescued from Correction facilities. They're displaying abilities we've never documented before. Direct emotional communication, healing of psychological trauma, even limited awareness of emotional events before they happen."

Despite the pressure of the situation, Emma smiled, feeling hope bloom in her chest. "They're adapting faster than adults because they haven't spent decades building defensive barriers against feeling. They're showing us what human emotional capacity was meant to become."

The children are evolving. They're becoming what humanity was always supposed to be.

"The question is whether we can guide the adult population through a similar transformation without triggering psychological collapse," Dr. Clarke said.

Emma picked up the containment field holding the emotional crystals, feeling their combined weight as both physical mass and psychic energy. The crystals represented everything humanity had sacrificed in the name of safety. Love, creativity, spiritual connection, and the simple joy of being alive.

"The Resonance Points are our only option now." She secured the crystals in the containment device. "If I can reach the seven major nodes and establish resonance patterns, I might be able to guide the awakening instead of letting it happen chaotically."

Dr. Clarke shook his head, consulting readouts that showed her current neural activity. "Emma, the energy requirements alone could kill you. You'd be channeling the suppressed emotions of billions of people through your own awareness."

"Then maybe I need to stop being human." Her voice was quiet, but the words made the crystal formations pulse with anticipation.

But what if I'm not human anymore? The changes I've been experiencing, the expanding abilities, what if they're preparing me for this kind of load?

"The planet is conscious," she continued, her voice taking on the distant quality that appeared when she was deep in resonance with larger patterns. "Not the way humans are conscious, but aware nonetheless. It knows something is wrong."

She lifted one of the red anger crystals, feeling the compressed fury of generations who had been denied the right to feel genuine outrage at injustice. "This isn't just human emotion. It's planetary immune response. The world is angry at what's been done to it, and that anger needs to be expressed constructively or it will destroy everything."

How do you apologize to a conscious world for two centuries of systematic abuse?

The communication system activated again, this time carrying Evan's voice with an urgency that made her chest tight with emotion.

"Emma, people are experiencing emotional awakening across multiple districts, but they're not just feeling their own emotions. They're feeling each other's. We're seeing spontaneous emotional connections forming between strangers."

The words hit her harder than any data stream. "They're not just awakening individually. They're beginning to connect to the larger emotional field."

"Which means we have very little time," Dr. Clarke said. "Once the connections start forming spontaneously, the process will accelerate beyond our ability to guide it."

Six hours to save or lose everything.

Emma consulted the global map to identify the location in the Australian Outback where planetary emotional energy was most concentrated. "If I can establish a successful pattern at the primary Resonance Point, it will create a template that the other points can follow."

"The Australian site is heavily monitored by Council forces," Dr. Clarke warned. "Chancellor Keller has positioned suppression amplifiers around all the known Resonance Points."

A pang of sadness struck Emma's chest as she thought about her mother's desperate attempts to maintain the system that had defined her entire adult life. "Then I'll have to find a way to reach her. Not just in person, but emotionally."

My mother. She's not evil, just terrified.

"She's the only person who understands both the suppression technology and the original research into emotional restoration," Emma continued. "If I can help her remember why she started this work, to protect people, not control them, she might be willing to assist with the rebalancing process."

Dr. Clarke looked skeptical. "Emma, your mother has spent twenty-five years building psychological barriers against the guilt that would come with acknowledging what the suppression system has accomplished."

"Or it could save her soul," Emma replied, feeling the truth of it resonate through her expanding awareness. "Either way, I have to try."

But what if reaching her requires me to experience her trauma?

Moving toward the laboratory's exit, the emotional crystals secured in their protective field and her awareness reaching out toward the distant Resonance Points, Emma felt the planetary consciousness stirring beneath her feet like a massive creature awakening from troubled sleep.

"Dr. Clarke." She paused at the threshold. "If something happens to me during the rebalancing process, if channeling that much emotional energy destroys my individual aware-ness, promise me you'll continue the work."

I'm talking about my own evolution, but it doesn't feel like death. It feels like becoming something larger.

"Nothing's going to happen to you," Dr. Clarke said, though his voice carried doubt that made the crystals pulse with sympathetic uncertainty. "The process is dangerous, but it's survivable if you maintain mental barriers while channeling the emotional flow."

The smile that crossed Emma's face felt like sunlight breaking through storm clouds. "I appreciate your confidence, but we both know that some changes require letting go of what we were in order to become what we're meant to be."

But am I willing? Or am I just saying what needs to be said?

As she left the laboratory behind and began climbing toward the surface, Emma could feel the crystallized emotions pulsing with the rhythm of a planetary heartbeat, growing stronger with each step. Behind her, Dr. Clarke continued monitoring the global emotional grid, watching red warning indicators multiply as suppression systems failed across six continents.

Above ground, Evan was waiting with transportation to the first Resonance Point. She could sense his emotional state through the building's structure, his determination mixed with love and terror in equal measure.

The point of no return had been passed. Now the only choice was between chaos and conscious evolution, between the death of feeling and the birth of something unprecedented in human history.

I'm carrying the dreams of everyone who ever loved, ever grieved, ever felt joy or anger or hope.

As she reached the surface level, the emotional crystals pulsed in harmony with her heartbeat, their combined energy making her skin tingle with power threatening to break free. Each one contained the compressed dreams and desires of people who had been forced to forget what it meant to be alive.

Soon, those dreams would be returned to their owners, transformed by the journey from individual experience to collective wisdom.

The awakening had begun. Whatever she became, whatever they all became, it had to be better than what they'd been. It had to be worth the risk of change, worth the possibility of losing everything they thought they were in order to become everything they were meant to be.

The awakening had begun, and there was no turning back.

Chapter Eighteen

BLOOD ON HER HANDS

T rembling fingers pressed against the cool stone wall of her father's hidden laboratory, each tremor sending ripples through the emotional imprints that clung to every surface. The images slammed into Emma like physical blows: urgent love, crushing betrayal, knowledge that his wife had become something monstrous. But beneath it all, stronger than fear or despair, burned his absolute faith in what his daughter could become.

The stone beneath her palms grew hot, responding to her emotional state. Around the laboratory, equipment shrieked in sympathetic vibrations that made her teeth ache.

How do you process the knowledge that your mother ordered your father's death?

"She killed him." The words cut through the sterile air like broken glass, and the lights exploded in a shower of sparks. "My mother murdered my father to protect her lies."

Dr. Clarke stood beside her, his weathered face grave as he reviewed the data streaming across David Thorne's preserved research computers. Charts and graphs painted a story of discovery and horror.

"Murder is too simple a word," Clarke said, his voice carrying the weight of years spent uncovering this truth. "She ordered his death when he discovered Project Terminus."

Emma turned from the wall, her legs unsteady. "What is Project Terminus?"

"Your father learned that she wasn't just suppressing emotions. She was planning to make the suppression permanent by cutting humanity's connection to the planetary awareness." Clarke activated another display, showing neural pathway diagrams that made Emma's stomach lurch. "Complete severance. No possibility of reversal."

The revelation hit her chest like a sledgehammer made of ice. She caught herself against a console as the emotional imprints in the laboratory exploded through her senses. Her father's growing horror, his frantic attempts to create reversal protocols, his final message hidden in quantum encryption.

But why? What kind of trauma could make someone choose systematic destruction over healing?

The temperature in the laboratory plummeted twenty degrees in seconds. Frost began forming on the equipment screens.

"Show me his message," she said.

Clarke hesitated. "Emma, seeing your father again, hearing his voice..."

"I need to understand what he discovered. What he wanted me to know."

Clarke activated the main display, and the world stopped. Her father's voice filled the laboratory for the first time in eighteen years, and the sound drove Emma to her knees. David Thorne appeared as a holographic projection, younger than her memories but already marked by strain.

"If you're seeing this, Emma, then I'm gone and you've awakened to your true nature." His amber eyes, identical to her own, held hope and sorrow that made her chest cave in. "Your mother believes she's protecting humanity from its own capacity for feeling. She's convinced that emotions are a disease that must be cured, not a force that sustains all life."

Emma reached toward the hologram, her hand passing through the light as tears poured down her cheeks. The emotional imprints in the room responded to her grief, equipment pulsing in rhythm with her heartbeat.

"I've tried to reach her," David continued, "to show her the data about planetary awareness, but her trauma has made her blind to anything except control."

What trauma? What happened to make her so afraid of emotion that she would kill the planet to avoid feeling?

The projection flickered as David glanced off-camera, terror crossing his features. "They're coming. Mira's enforcement teams. She's chosen the system over our family, over truth, over life itself."

Footsteps echoed from somewhere deeper in the laboratory. Clarke spun toward the sound, but a familiar voice called out.

"It's Viktor," the voice said. "I'm alone."

Viktor Brennan emerged from the deeper chambers, his military bearing crushed by the burden of what he carried. In his hands were sealed documents bearing the highest classification marks Emma had ever seen.

"The hologram was still running when I arrived," Viktor said, his voice hollow. "I heard what your father said about your mother's trauma."

Emma wiped her eyes, trying to process Viktor's presence along with everything else. "What do you know about it?"

"More than I wanted to learn." Viktor set the documents on a nearby console. "The war wasn't what they told us, Emma. The final emotional weapon attacks, the ones that convinced the population to accept total suppression, they were false flag operations."

The words hit like a physical avalanche. Emma doubled over, her stomach heaving. "The attacks that justified the suppression system..."

"Were conducted using Council technology," Viktor confirmed. "I found the authorization codes buried in classified archives. The same signature patterns, the same quantum frequencies."

Clarke stepped forward, his scientific mind grappling with the implications. "You're saying the Council created the very attacks they claimed to be protecting us from?"

"They made humanity so afraid of emotional weapons that we begged them to take our feelings away." Viktor's voice broke. "Your mother, Emma, she was one of the architects. But she was also one of the victims."

How do you reconcile being both perpetrator and victim? How does someone live with that knowledge?

"Explain." Emma's voice was steady despite the sparks still raining around them.

Viktor opened one of the sealed files. "The final attack, the one that killed thousands in the old European cities, your mother was supposed to be there. She was leading an emotional research team. But someone warned her away at the last minute."

Emma felt the pieces clicking together in her mind, each connection sending fresh waves of understanding and horror through her awareness. "She survived because someone in the Council saved her. Someone who knew what was coming."

"Your father," Viktor said. "David discovered the false flag plan and warned her. But by then, the attack was already in motion. She watched her entire research team die from weapons her own organization had created."

So she chose to become part of the system that had destroyed every-thing she cared about. But was it survival or complicity? Can you choose to serve evil and still believe you're protecting good?

The laboratory's lights flickered and exploded in cascades of sparks. The emotional imprints responded to her rage, and she felt the accumulated fury of everyone who had ever fought against the suppression system pouring through her like molten metal.

Clarke moved to another console, his hands steady despite the chaos. "The reversal protocols are here, Emma. Your father's final work. But you need to understand what you're choosing."

She approached the display, her enhanced abilities making the quantum mechanics feel like music she could finally under-stand. But as she studied the data, her body began to react. Her hands cramped as if already channeling millions of suppressed feelings. Her skull throbbed with phantom pressure.

"It would be like being struck by lightning made of pure feeling," she said, reading the projections. "Every emotion that's been stolen, every connection that's been severed, all flowing through my nervous system at once."

"While your neural pathways restructure themselves," Clarke added. "During the process. While conscious. While guiding others through their awakening."

Viktor stepped closer, his expression troubled. "Emma, you're talking about voluntary dissolution of your consciousness. Even if you survive the initial transformation, what emerges won't be you as you understand yourself now."

Can individual awareness expand that far without dissolving? And if it can, what does that expansion feel like? What does it mean to become part of something planetary in scope?

Emma closed her eyes and let her awareness expand, just a little. She felt the network of suppressed humanity stretching across the planet, like billions of dimmed lights struggling to shine through thick black cloth. The sensation made her skull throb, but beneath the pain, she sensed something else. Hope. Millions of people waiting for someone to remind them how to feel.

Her awareness snapped back to the laboratory like a rubber band, leaving her gasping. "I can feel them. All of them. But just that small connection..." She touched her nose, checking for blood. "My brain isn't designed for that scale of awareness."

"Which is why the transformation is necessary," Clarke said. "Your father's protocols would rebuild your neural architecture during the process. But the rebuilding itself would be unlike anything any human has ever experienced."

So I become a teacher for an entire species. Not just a bridge, but a guide for humanity's return to emotional authenticity. But what happens to the person I am now?

"Where is my mother now?" she asked.

"The Central Suppression Facility," Viktor replied. "She's accelerated Project Terminus in response to the resistance activities. According to my intelligence, she plans to complete the permanent severance within seventy-two hours."

Seventy-two hours to save or lose everything. Seventy-two hours to choose between my individual existence and collective survival.

Emma turned back to the data streams, studying the intricate patterns of neural reconstruction that would be required. "Dr. Clarke, when the transformation begins, what would I feel first?"

Clarke consulted his readings. "Based on your father's projections, the initial phase would involve your nervous system beginning to resonate with the planetary emotional field. You'd start experiencing emotions from multiple sources simultaneously."

"How many sources?"

"Initially, perhaps hundreds. Then thousands as the process accelerated."

Emma tried to imagine what that would feel like. To have her own grief and rage suddenly joined by the suppressed sorrow of strangers, their forgotten joy, their buried love. "And my ability to distinguish between my emotions and theirs?"

"Would fade gradually," Clarke admitted. "Your sense of individual identity would become more fluid, more permeable, until eventually..."

"Until I become part of the collective emotional awareness." She completed the thought, feeling the weight of it settle into her bones. "I'd still exist, but not as Emma Thorne."

Maybe that's what awareness really is. Not individual identity, but the connections we make, the love we share, the care we extend to others.

Viktor shook his head. "There has to be another way. We can't ask you to sacrifice your individual existence for..."

"For the continuation of all life on the planet?" Emma interrupted. "Viktor, my father knew this was the only solution. That's why he encoded the protocols for me specifically. Not because I'm expendable, but because I'm the only one who can survive the process long enough to guide others through their awakening."

She moved to another console, pulling up the global suppression data. The numbers told a story of dying connections, severed bonds between humanity and the planetary awareness that had sustained life for millions of years.

"Look at this," she said, highlighting the ecological data. "Crop failures, weather instability, animal migration patterns disrupted. The planet is trying to communicate with us, to maintain the emotional connections that keep ecosystems stable, but we've cut the link."

Clarke nodded. "Every suppressed emotion, every severed connection, brings us closer to total ecological failure. But your mother believes controlled extinction is preferable to emotional chaos."

But what if there's a third option? What if the choice isn't between chaos and extinction, but between fear-based control and love-based connection?

"We need to reach her," Emma said. "Not just to stop Project Terminus, but to help her heal from the trauma that's driving this. She's not evil, just broken."

"The Central Facility is heavily fortified," Viktor warned. "My access codes can get us inside, but once Mira realizes what we're attempting, she'll activate every defensive system."

Emma felt the emotional imprints of her father's sacrifice wrapping around her like armor made of pure love. Everything - her training as a Collector, her emotional awakening, even her complicated relationship with her mother - had been preparing her for this moment.

"Contact Evan and Holly," she said. "They'll need to coordinate with the resistance networks to manage the chaos when suppression ends. And Clarke, prepare portable versions of the reversal equipment."

One chance to save everything. One chance to choose love over fear, connection over isolation, transformation over stagnation.

As the two men moved to execute her orders, Emma remained with the hologram of her father, watching his face cycle through hope and terror and love. Through the emotional imprints, she felt his final message. Not words but pure feeling. Love, pride, hope, and the absolute certainty that she would choose wisely when the moment came.

What if choosing wisely means choosing to become something I can't imagine? What if saving the world requires surrendering everything I think I am?

The foundations of her world had been shattered by truth, but from the ruins, she would build something better. Not the artificial peace of suppression, but the authentic harmony that came from embracing the full spectrum of human experience.

Maybe becoming more than human is the most human choice I could make.

The former Emotion Collector prepared to become humanity's bridge to emotional restoration. Around her, the laboratory hummed with sympathetic energy, equipment responding to her growing power. The real war for the planet's survival was about to begin.

But this time, it won't be fought with weapons of destruction. It will be fought with the willingness to choose love even when love requires everything you are.

The planet was waiting, and she would not let it die alone.

Even if it cost her everything she had ever been.

Chapter Nineteen

WHEN GOOD MEN BREAK

The first alarm cut through the pre-dawn silence like a blade. Years of training brought Marcus Webb to full alertness within seconds, his body moving through practiced motions while his mind remained sluggish with sleep. The emergency beacon on his bedside table flashed red, each pulse sending spikes of adrenaline through his nervous system.

Priority alpha. Immediate response required.

The thought surfaced unbidden as he rolled out of bed, a crack in his conditioning that let forbidden questions slip through. *How many times have I responded to these alarms without questioning what they really mean?*

His hands trembled as he reached for his enforcement gear, the tremor so slight he almost missed it. The suppression conditioning should have prevented any emotional response to operational deployment, but something was changing inside him. Something that made his chest feel tight and his thoughts feel dangerous.

The comm unit crackled to life as he sealed his enforcement suit, the familiar weight of armor feeling strange against his skin. "All units, respond to grid coordinates seven-seven-alpha through nine-three-delta. Multiple resonance signatures detected. Possible emotional outbreak in progress."

The coordinates hit him like a physical blow. His chest constricted, and for a moment he couldn't breathe. The target zone covered Emma's last known location.

Emma. What have you gotten yourself into?

The enforcement vehicle bay buzzed with activity as twenty-four units prepared for deployment. Marcus recognized the pattern from training scenarios he'd hoped never to see implemented. Operation Silence, the protocol designed to contain large-scale emotional disturbances through over-whelming force.

"Handler Webb," Commander Brandt called out, her voice cutting through the mechanical noise. "You're assigned to Team Seven. We're tracking your Collector's neural signature in the target zone."

Marcus nodded, though his chest felt like it was being crushed in a vise. Emma had been showing concerning behavior for weeks. Decreased efficiency, strange biometric readings, and that incident with the immune individual at the market. He'd been delaying his reports, telling himself he needed more data.

When did I start protecting her instead of monitoring her?

Team Seven's commander, Lieutenant Falk, briefed them during transport. The vehicle's armored walls felt like a coffin as Marcus listened to the mission parameters. "Intelligence suggests coordinated resistance activity across multiple districts. They're using stolen Council technology to create artificial emotional resonance fields, triggering mass psychological episodes in baseline citizens."

Marcus stared out the vehicle's reinforced window at the empty streets. Even in the pre-dawn darkness, he could see signs of trouble. Windows glowing with irregular lighting patterns, small groups of people moving with erratic behavior, abandoned vehicles where drivers had stopped functioning.

"Our primary objective is containment and correction," Falk continued, her voice carrying the mechanical precision of someone whose conditioning had never been challenged. "Secondary objective is intelligence gathering on resistance methods and personnel. Lethal force is authorized if non-compliance threatens social stability."

The words struck Marcus like physical blows, each one driving deeper into his chest until he couldn't breathe. Lethal force. Against people whose only crime was feeling what the Council had tried to eliminate.

What kind of stability requires the threat of death to maintain?

Team Seven deployed in the residential district where Emma had been conducting routine collections for the past three years. Marcus knew these streets, these buildings, these people. His throat constricted as he recognized familiar faces. Mrs. Shen on the corner who offered him tea despite regulations against personal connections. The young father who worked double shifts to support his family. The elderly woman who fed stray cats despite regulations against emotional attachment to animals.

Now they were targets.

The first resistance checkpoint appeared around a corner, makeshift barriers constructed from overturned vehicles and scavenged materials. Behind them, Marcus could see figures in civilian clothing, their faces showing the kind of intense alertness that only came from fear and determination mixed together.

"Contact front," Falk reported, her voice flat and professional. "Five individuals, non-Council configuration. Deploying suppression fields."

The portable suppression generators hummed to life, projecting waves of emotional dampening energy toward the checkpoint. Marcus watched the defenders' faces change, their expressions smoothing into the familiar blankness of artificial calm. One by one, they lowered their weapons and stepped away from the barriers with confused compliance.

But three figures remained unaffected, their faces still alive with determination and fear and something that might have been love for the people they protected.

"Immune individuals confirmed," Marcus reported, his training overriding his growing discomfort even as his voice cracked. "Deploying containment protocols."

The immune defenders moved with coordinated precision that spoke of military training. They used the suppression field's boundaries as tactical advantages, staying just outside the dampening range while directing covering fire that forced the Council team to take shelter.

Crouched behind an overturned transport, Marcus found himself studying the enemy instead of fighting them. Across the street, one of the immune defenders, a woman with graying hair and fierce eyes, shouted something to her companions. He couldn't make out the words, but the tone carried urgency and care that made his chest ache.

She's protecting her people. The same way I should be protecting Emma.

"They're coordinating a fighting retreat," Falk observed through the comm. "Pattern suggests professional tactical training. These aren't random emotional deviants. This is organized resistance."

The revelation should have triggered his conditioning to increase aggression against enemies of social order. Instead, Marcus found himself noting the defenders' care to avoid civilian casualties and their focus on equipment rather than personnel targets.

They're more careful about civilian safety than we are.

The firefight ended when the defenders melted away into the maze of residential buildings, leaving behind only their abandoned checkpoint and the sense that this was just the beginning of something larger.

Team Seven moved deeper into the affected district, encountering more evidence of coordinated resistance activity. Suppression relay stations had been sabotaged, creating gaps in the emotional dampening field. The result was chaos that made Marcus's stomach turn.

People crying as decades of suppressed grief surfaced. Others laughing with wild joy. Still others sitting in stunned silence as they experienced emotion for the first time in their adult lives.

"Subjects require immediate correction," Falk ordered, her voice carrying the cold efficiency that Marcus had once admired. "Deploy mobile suppression units and begin processing civilians for adjustment."

Watching his teammates subdue confused citizens, applying neural dampeners to restore artificial calm, something inside his chest fractured. The process was clean, professional, and routine. Yet something in him rebelled against the sight of tears being erased from people's faces, of joy being stolen from their eyes.

Mrs. Shen stood in her doorway, weeping as she clutched a photograph of her deceased husband. Marcus had never seen her display such raw emotion, had never realized the depth of love she'd been carrying in silence. According to records, she'd been conditioned for grief management after her spouse's death five years ago. Now she was experiencing the full weight of her loss for the first time.

"Subject 7642-Beta requires correction," his teammate announced, approaching with a neural dampener that hummed with malevolent purpose. "Severe emotional dysreg-ulation, possible psychological break."

Before he could stop himself, Marcus stepped forward. "I'll handle this one."

He approached Mrs. Shen, the dampener heavy in his hands. She looked up at him with eyes that held more life than he'd ever seen in her. Painful, beautiful, human life that made his throat close.

"Officer Webb," she whispered, using his last name as she always had, her voice thick with tears. "I can feel him. My husband. I can feel how much I loved him. How much I still love him."

Marcus raised the dampener, his hands trembling so hard he could barely hold it. The device hummed, ready to erase the most genuine moment of Mrs. Shen's life. She didn't resist, didn't try to run. She looked at him with trust that made his chest cavity feel like it was collapsing.

"I'm sorry," Marcus said, his voice barely audible. Then he activated the device.

Mrs. Shen's face smoothed into regulation calm, the photograph slipping from her fingers as she stepped back into her apartment. The door closed with a soft click that felt like a gunshot.

"Good work," Falk observed, her approval feeling like acid in his veins. "One hundred percent compliance rate. Moving to next sector."

The next sector brought worse horrors. A family of four sat in their living room, holding hands and talking as they experienced connection for the first time in years. The sight hit Marcus like a physical blow, doubling him over as his conditioning cracked apart.

A six-year-old girl laughed with pure joy as she played with her younger brother, both of them showing the kind of happiness that the Council had classified as a psychological disorder. The sound of their laughter made his knees buckle. Their parents sat nearby, tears streaming down their faces as they felt parental love without the filter of emotional regulation.

"Priority targets," Falk announced, her voice cutting through Marcus's revelation like a blade. "Children are experiencing severe emotional dysregulation. Immediate correction required to prevent psychological damage."

Marcus knew the protocols. Emotional breakthrough in children often led to developmental disorders, behavioral problems, and social maladjustment. The correction process would restore their stability, protect them from the chaos of unregulated feeling, ensure they could function in regulated society.

He also knew that what he was seeing wasn't disorder. It was life.

The family offered no resistance as the team entered their home. The parents' conditioning made them compliant even as tears continued to stream down their faces. The children, less suppressed, showed confusion and fear as strangers approached with threatening devices.

"Mama?" the little girl asked, clinging to her mother's leg. "Why are the bad men here?"

"They're not bad men, sweetheart," her mother replied, though her voice carried doubt for the first time in years. "They're here to help."

Marcus found himself assigned to process the younger child, a four-year-old boy whose bright eyes held curiosity and trust that made his chest feel like it was being torn open. The neural dampener would erase both, leaving him with the artificial calm that would let him function in suppressed society.

He knelt beside the boy, who looked up at him without fear, his small face open and trusting. "Are you here to play?" the child asked.

"I'm here to help you," Marcus replied, the words feeling like broken glass in his throat.

"I don't need help," the boy said with the simple honesty of childhood. "I'm happy."

Marcus raised the dampener, then found he couldn't move. The child's declaration made the device feel like a weapon aimed at something sacred. His hands shook, his vision blurred, and something inside his chest shattered beyond repair.

"Handler Webb," Falk called, her voice carrying warning that made his skin crawl. "Complete the procedure."

Marcus looked around the room. His teammates were processing the family, erasing their emotional experience with mechanical precision. Soon this house would be quiet, regulated, and dead. The children would grow up never knowing they'd experienced something beautiful.

"Handler Webb," Falk repeated, her voice carrying the threat of immediate disciplinary action.

Marcus made his choice.

Instead of activating the dampener, he scooped up the little boy and ran.

The device clattered to the floor behind him, its malevolent hum silenced forever. Shouts erupted from his teammates as Marcus burst through the doorway, Tommy clutched against his chest, both of them running toward something that might have been freedom.

The emergency evacuation alarm echoed through the tunnel system as Marcus carried the child deeper into the underground network, following directions he'd extracted from captured resistance communications. His Council training helped him avoid pursuit while his failing suppression system flooded him with emotions he'd never experienced before.

Fear for the child's safety that made his hands shake. Rage at the system he'd served that burned in his throat like acid.

Guilt for all the lives he'd helped destroy that crushed down on his chest like a physical weight. And underneath it all, something that might have been hope.

The little boy, Tommy, had fallen asleep in his arms, trusting even in this strange situation. Protective instincts flooded through him in ways his conditioning couldn't process.

When they reached the resistance safe house, Marcus was confronted by armed guards who recognized his Council uniform. Before anyone could shoot, a small voice spoke from behind them.

"He's not angry anymore," said a young girl with serious eyes that seemed to see straight through him. "He's scared and sad and trying to do something right. The little boy trusts him."

Holly Lloyd appeared, studying Marcus with the careful attention of someone who'd survived by reading people in ways the Council had forgotten. "Who are you?" she asked.

"Marcus Webb," he replied, his voice cracking with exhaustion and emotions he couldn't name. "I'm Emma's handler. I was Emma's handler," he corrected. "I can't do this anymore. I can't hurt children just for feeling what they should be allowed to feel."

The child in his arms stirred, looking around the tunnel with curiosity rather than fear. "Are these the good people?" he asked Marcus.

"I hope so," Marcus replied, then looked at Holly with desperate honesty that made his voice break. "I have intelligence about Council operations. Location of detention facilities, operational protocols, personnel assignments. But I need to know this boy will be safe."

Holly's expression softened as she saw the child's trust and Marcus's protective desperation. "Welcome to the resistance, Marcus Webb. Now tell me how to keep these children alive."

For the first time in his adult life, Marcus felt like he belonged somewhere. Among people who believed that feeling was more important than regulation, that love was more important than control, that humanity was worth protecting even when protection required sacrifice.

The boy in his arms stirred, opening trusting eyes that held no fear, only curiosity about this new world. "Are we home?" Tommy asked.

Around them, faces showed the evidence of people who'd chosen conscience over conditioning, humanity over system compliance, love over fear. His chest felt light for the first time in years.

"Yes," he said, his voice steady with newfound certainty. "I think we are."

Chapter Twenty

BEYOND CONTAINMENT

Viktor Brennan's hands shook as reports from the dawn raids flooded his secure terminal. Operation Silence had succeeded tactically but failed catastrophically in ways that made his chest tight with recognition. Three enforcement teams reporting "anomalous emotional responses" in their own personnel. Handler Marcus Webb missing in action with a civilian child. Resistance networks showing coordinated response capabilities that suggested advanced intelligence.

But the report that made his vision blur was Marcus Webb's complete psychological break. Emma Thorne's handler—their primary source of intelligence about the most dangerous individual alive—had abandoned his post to protect a four-year-old's capacity for happiness.

We've lost our window into Emma's activities.

Viktor pulled up Emma's file, studying her psychological assessments with new eyes. The girl he'd helped monitor for three years stared back from surveillance photos, her face showing the kind of quiet determination he'd dismissed as compliance. How had they missed what she was becoming?

A memory surfaced: Emma at age sixteen, refusing to cry during conditioning sessions. Viktor had noted her "exceptional emotional regulation" in his reports. Now he wondered if she'd been protecting something precious from the very beginning.

The one person who understood her psychological patterns, who could predict her movements, who knew her capabilities better than anyone. And he didn't just desert. He chose a child's emotions over his duty to the Council.

The tactical assessment made his hands tremble: "Subject Webb displayed severe emotional dysregulation during civilian processing, resulting in mission abandonment and violation of suppression protocols. Subject's conditioning appears to have failed completely when confronted with orders to suppress juvenile emotional expression."

Viktor closed his eyes, processing the implications. Marcus Webb, who'd spent three years monitoring Emma Thorne without showing a single sign of emotional breakthrough. If her influence could break the conditioning of her own handler, what did that say about what she was becoming?

This is the moment when the weapon we created to control her becomes the proof that she can't be controlled.

The system was breaking down from within, and Emma Thorne was the catalyst.

Viktor opened his personal safe with shaking fingers, retrieving the classified documents he'd been gathering for weeks. The evidence that had started as routine investigation now felt like ammunition for a war that was already underway.

Communication logs, historical analysis, proof of manufactured terrorism—all of it suddenly vital.

If Marcus Webb's conditioning failed after prolonged exposure to Emma, how long before other handlers break?

His fingers trembled as he activated the emergency communication system, sending coded messages to three Council members whose psychological profiles suggested they might be capable of processing uncomfortable truths. Sarah Magnus, whose medical research had documented the psychological casualties of suppression. Rebecca Lang, whose work with emotional refugees had shown her the human cost of their policies. James Fletcher, whose military background made him value truth over politics.

The message was simple: "Emergency session. Council Chamber Seven. Classification: Maximum. Subject: Institutional integrity assessment."

But what I'm really asking is whether they're willing to help me destroy everything we've built when the evidence proves it should never have existed in the place.

THE EMERGENCY COUNCIL chamber felt like a tomb as Viktor spread classified documents across the polished table two hours later. His hands shook worse now, the adrenaline from the morning's reports mixing with the certainty that what he was about to do would either save human consciousness or destroy his own life.

Sarah Magnus sat with dark circles under her eyes, her medical training evident in how she studied Viktor's physical stress indicators. Rebecca Lang clutched her tablet containing refugee psychological profiles, her therapeutic background making her hyperaware of the emotional tension filling the room. James Fletcher maintained military bearing despite the tremor in his jaw that suggested his conditioning was cracking under pressure.

"Viktor," Sarah said, leaning forward with clinical concern, "you look like a man preparing to confess to murder."

The accuracy of her observation hit Viktor like a physical blow. "Because that's exactly what this is."

He activated the holographic display with fingers that felt like ice. Communication logs from the final days of the Great Emotional War materialized in the air between them.

"The attack on Research Station Seven," Viktor began, his voice steady despite the tremor in his hands. "Can you tell me what you remember about it?"

James Fletcher's military posture straightened. "Terrorist strike. Emotional weapons technology. Forty-three casualties including research staff."

"Look at the energy signatures," Viktor said, highlighting technical data that made James lean forward with growing confusion.

Sarah activated her own analysis tools, cross-referencing the patterns with her suppression development records. Her breath caught. "These match our early prototypes."

"Keep going," Viktor said, calling up more files. "The bombing of the Vienna Emotional Center."

Rebecca's face went white. "My husband died in Vienna. He was there for a therapy conference."

Viktor's chest tightened as he highlighted the tactical signatures. "I'm sorry, Rebecca. I'm so sorry for what I'm about to show you."

The data streams revealed patterns that made James Fletcher push back from the table. "Council authorization codes," he whispered. "Council technology. Council operatives."

"They were ours," Viktor said, his voice breaking. "Every attack. Every massacre. Every tragedy that convinced the population to accept total emotional suppression."

Sarah doubled over as if punched, her scientific mind recoiling from the timeline matches flooding her screen. "The prototypes were completed months before the attacks they were supposed to prevent."

Rebecca stared at her tablet, therapeutic training recognizing the artificial trauma patterns in survivor profiles. When she spoke, her voice came out as a strangled gasp. "You're telling us we murdered thousands of people to justify murdering their capacity to feel?"

Viktor felt his chest heave. Each breath felt like drowning. "I'm telling you that every widow we've comforted, every orphan we've processed, every grief-stricken parent we've sedated... we created their pain. We are the terrorists we claimed to be protecting them from."

The silence that followed felt like suffocation. Sarah gripped the table edge, her knuckles white. James Fletcher stared at his hands as if seeing blood.

"My Rebecca's trauma work," Rebecca whispered, her voice breaking. "All those survivors. We've been torturing victims of our own crimes for decades."

Viktor watched his colleagues process the evidence, each revelation hitting them at different speeds. Sarah's scientific training made her focus on data verification. James's military discipline kept him studying tactical implications. Rebecca's therapeutic background gave her visceral understanding of the psychological damage.

"There's more," Viktor said, calling up Project Terminus files that made even his own hands recoil from the controls. "Chancellor Keller has designed permanent suppression. Not management. Elimination."

The words landed like physical blows. Sarah's medical monitors showed readings that made her hands fly to her mouth in horror. "Emotional suppression levels just increased by forty percent across the entire grid. She's not maintaining control anymore. She's actively burning out every neural pathway that could support future feeling."

James Fletcher's strategic mind cracked under the operational implications. "We have hours before she burns out every neural pathway that could support future emotional restoration."

Viktor activated Emma Thorne's psychological profile with shaking fingers. The display showed ability assessments that defied understanding, neural patterns that suggested capabilities beyond current human parameters.

"The Thorne genetic line," Viktor said, each word tearing at his throat. "Emma isn't just resistant to suppression. She could reverse it. All of it. Across the entire planet."

And we've spent years trying to perfect her conditioning. We've been preparing humanity's salvation for psychological slaughter.

Rebecca stared at Emma's trauma assessments through tears that wouldn't stop falling. "Her ability to process emotional energy without fragmentation. We documented it as efficiency ratings."

"When we should have been protecting her from us," Sarah whispered, her voice hollow.

Viktor pulled up a surveillance recording from Emma's childhood—something he'd never thought to review before. Eight-year-old Emma stood in a Council testing facility, tears streaming down her face as technicians measured her emotional responses. But her eyes held something that made Viktor's chest ache. Not compliance. Defiance. She was protecting something even then.

"She's been fighting us since she was a child," Viktor said, his voice breaking. "Every test, every assessment, every attempt to condition her. She never surrendered. We just convinced ourselves her resistance was cooperation."

James Fletcher's strategic mind processed the tactical reality. "Mira will deploy everything to stop her. Enforcement teams, suppression technology, the entire apparatus we helped her build."

"Which means Emma has to succeed not just at reversing suppression, but at surviving the attempt to kill her for trying."

The weight of complicity crushed down on all four Council members. They sat in silence, each processing their role in creating the system that was now preparing to murder the only hope for human emotional survival.

We're not choosing between duty and rebellion. We're choosing between remaining complicit in genocide or trying to stop what we helped create.

Sarah spoke first, her voice breaking. "I can't continue supporting this. The medical evidence alone..." She pressed her hands against her chest as if trying to hold her heart together. "Every suppression side effect I've documented. We're systematically destroying human consciousness."

Viktor felt something fracture in his chest, something that had been holding his identity together for decades. "Then we act now. Sarah, compile your medical evidence. Every damaged mind, every broken family, every psychological casualty."

"I'll present the data during emergency session," she replied, her hands still shaking as she began transferring files. "But Viktor, when suppression destabilizes, we'll need massive therapeutic resources."

Rebecca nodded, wiping tears from her cheeks. "Conservative estimates suggest twenty percent complete psychological breakdown. Another thirty percent requiring intensive care for years."

"If Emma succeeds in reversing suppression without preparation," she continued, "millions will experience decades of suppressed emotion all at once. The psychological casualties could exceed anything we've caused so far."

James Fletcher studied tactical deployments on his scanner, his military instincts adapting to the new mission despite his emotional collapse. "Enforcement team loyalties will split. Some will support reform. Others will follow orders to kill Emma rather than allow emotional restoration."

Emergency alerts flashed across their devices. Security breaches, enforcement mobilizations, emergency suppression amplification across all sectors.

Viktor felt the floor drop out from under him as he read the tactical reports. "She's accelerating everything. Mira's implementing final phase suppression right now."

"Then we make sure Emma doesn't do it alone," Viktor said, feeling purpose burn through the ashes of his shattered beliefs. "Holly Lloyd's networks have people trained in emotional restoration. If we can coordinate our resources..."

James Fletcher nodded, his strategic mind adapting to parameters that would have been unthinkable hours ago. "Controlled awakening instead of chaotic collapse. But that means Emma has to succeed at something no human has ever attempted."

Viktor stood on shaking legs, feeling the weight of twenty-eight years of loyal service change into the burden of rebellion. *But revolution isn't the opposite of service. Sometimes it's the highest form of loyalty to the ideals you thought you were serving all along.*

"We coordinate with the resistance now," he said, his voice gaining strength as his new identity took shape. "Sarah, prepare evidence for emergency Council presentation. Rebecca, evacuate your emotional refugees. James, identify enforcement personnel who might choose human consciousness over institutional loyalty."

As the others dispersed to their assignments, Viktor remained behind, studying intelligence reports that showed Emma's impossible challenge. Not just reversing suppression technology, but guiding humanity through the most dangerous evolution in species history.

He looked once more at the surveillance footage of eight-year-old Emma, her defiant eyes holding secrets that had taken him decades to understand. She'd been preparing for this moment her entire life. Now it was time to help her save them all.

The point of no return isn't a place. It's the moment when you choose to become who you were meant to be instead of who you were told to be.

The awakening had chosen him as an unlikely midwife. Whatever came next would be built on truth instead of manufactured fear, even if that truth destroyed everything he'd spent his life creating.

Chapter Twenty-One

WHAT FATHERS HIDE

The coordinates led Emma through tunnels that predated New Geneva's founding, each step taking her deeper from the sanitized world above where suppression fields hummed their constant song of artificial peace. Her father's encrypted message burned in her memory: "The laboratory remembers what I could not forget. Section 7-Delta, beneath the old transit hub. Find the truth, Emma. Find what they took from us both."

The air thickened with moisture that made breathing feel like drowning. Bioluminescent fungi lined the tunnel walls, their pale blue glow casting shadows that writhed like dying neural networks. Emma's enhanced sensitivity detected accumulated emotional energy pooling in these depths—decades of suppressed human feeling that had somehow escaped the grid above to gather here like toxic sediment.

Even the planet bleeds down here, she thought, pressing her hand against the weeping concrete. *How much pain has soaked through the barriers we built to contain it?*

The passage opened into a chamber that stopped her heart. Equipment lined the walls like sleeping giants, surfaces layered with dust that told stories of abandonment and secrecy. Translucent formations hung from the ceiling like frozen screams, each one pulsing with faint energy that made her teeth ache. Holographic displays flickered with emotional energy patterns, mathematical formulas describing consciousness interfaces, and most horrifying of all, a three-dimensional model of Earth surrounded by what looked like a dying nervous system.

"Hello, Emma." The voice stepped from speakers built into the walls, filled with static but carrying warmth that made her chest constrict with recognition.

Emma spun around, her hand flying to the neural disruptor at her belt. "Who's there?"

"I'm afraid I'm not 'there' in any traditional sense," the voice replied with something that might have been her father's laugh. "I'm what your father called the Archive. A collection of his memories, his research, and his love for you, stored in quantum matrices."

Emma's knees trembled as understanding crashed over her. An artificial consciousness. But consciousness research was banned, eliminated, made impossible.

"But consciousness research was terminated after the Consciousness Wars," she whispered, studying the complex array of processors and memory cores with new understanding. "The applications were too dangerous."

"Dangerous to whom?" the Archive asked, and Emma heard her father's teaching method in the question—the gentle push toward uncomfortable truths.

The implications hit her like ice water flooding her veins. The integration of emotional data with technological readouts around her told a story of capabilities the Council claimed were impossible. They weren't afraid of consciousness being weaponized. They were terrified of consciousness that could help people reconnect with what was stolen from them.

"Show me," Emma said, stepping closer to the central console. Her hands shook as she reached for the interface. "Show me everything."

The holographic displays erupted to life, and Emma found herself drowning in memory fragments from eighteen years ago. She experienced her father's last months through his own consciousness—not watching but living David Thorne's growing horror as data streams revealed the planetary crisis his research had uncovered.

His voice, younger but carrying the same warmth that haunted her dreams, filled the chamber with such presence that Emma reached out with trembling hands, grasping at air.

"Day 1,247 of the research project. The connection is undeniable now. Every percentage point of emotional suppression corresponds to a measurable decrease in planetary consciousness coherence. Mira's system isn't just dampening human feelings. It's murdering the living world itself."

Emma's chest exploded with pain as she witnessed her father's desperation. *The planet wasn't just dying. It was being tortured to death by the woman who claimed to love us both.*

The memories shifted, and Emma's vision blurred with tears as she watched David's desperate attempts to reach his wife with the data. She felt his isolation as trusted Council members turned against him, experienced his growing terror as he realized the scope of what Mira had become.

Then came the discovery that shattered everything.

"Day 1,367. I've found the classified reports." David's voice cracked with despair that made Emma double over. "The final three attacks that justified the permanent suppression protocols... they weren't random terrorist actions. The energy signatures match Council technology, not underground weapons. The attacks were orchestrated from within."

Emma's legs gave out. She crashed to her knees as the full weight of revelation crushed her consciousness like a collapsing building. The catastrophic attacks that had made her mother's system seem necessary. The thousands of dead children. The screaming parents. All of it manufactured. All of it planned. All of it executed by the woman who tucked her into bed every night.

"Why?" The word tore from her throat like a scream. "Why would she murder innocent people?"

The Archive's response carried such gentle sadness that Emma felt her father's presence surrounding her like a protective embrace. "What breaks a person so completely that murder feels like mercy?"

Emma forced herself to think through the agony. "The early reversal trials. People died from psychological shock when their suppressed emotions returned all at once."

"And how would a young scientist process that kind of trauma?"

She would conclude that emotions were too dangerous to exist. Emma understood, bile rising in her throat. *So she manufactured the crisis that would make their elimination seem necessary.*

New displays materialized, showing Emma her father's final months through his own eyes. She experienced his desperate love for her, his guilt over the experiments he'd allowed Mira to perform, and then—the moment that destroyed her completely.

She lived through his final conversation, feeling his terror and heartbreak as if they were her own emotions burning through her nervous system.

"I won't let them use her," David's voice broke with anguish that made Emma scream. "I'll destroy the research before I let Emma become a weapon for either side."

The memory showed a figure approaching from behind, a syringe glinting in the laboratory's cold light. Emma experienced her father's last moments—not confusion but terrible understanding, not surprise but painful recognition of the hand that held the needle.

"Mira," he whispered, turning to face his wife. "Please. Think about what you're doing to our daughter."

"I'm protecting her," came the reply, and Emma heard her mother's voice stripped of all warmth, clinically precise. "From you. From herself. From the curse you've passed to her."

Emma felt her father's love for both of them burning through the poison as it spread through his veins. His last thought wasn't anger or regret but hope—hope that someday Emma would understand that love could be stronger than fear, that healing could triumph over control.

The memory ended, leaving Emma collapsed on the laboratory floor, sobbing with grief so raw it felt like being flayed alive. Her mother had murdered her father with her own hands. Not political necessity. Not institutional loyalty. Personal, intimate murder of the man who'd loved them both.

Heavy footsteps echoed from the tunnel entrance. Emma looked up through tears that wouldn't stop to see Viktor Brennan step from the shadows, his weathered face carrying the weight of his own crushing revelations. In his hands, he held a data storage device that pulsed with accusatory blue light.

"Councilor Brennan." Emma struggled to her feet, her voice raw from screaming. "How did you find this place?"

"Your father's message reached three Council members he trusted," Viktor replied, his voice cracked with exhaustion from destroying his own identity. "Instructions to this location if the planetary crisis ever reached critical levels."

Viktor activated his device with shaking hands, and new holographic displays filled the room with official Council documentation bearing classification levels that made Emma's vision blur with fresh tears.

"I've spent weeks verifying every piece of evidence your father preserved," Viktor continued, his voice breaking. "The false flag operations. The manufactured terrorism. The systematic torture of an entire species." He met her eyes. "We have enough proof to destroy everything the Council claims to represent."

Emma studied the archives around her, feeling the weight of truth settling on her shoulders like a cloak made of lead. *But what good is evidence against someone who's integrated herself with the very technology that could suppress any emotional response to that evidence?*

"The reversal protocols," Emma said, her voice raw from screaming. "Could they actually work?"

"In theory, yes," Viktor replied, his own composure cracking as he watched her process the magnitude of her mother's betrayal. "But they require someone with your specific abilities to serve as a bridge between the suppressed population and the planetary consciousness."

Emma felt the research data flowing around her, her father's love and sacrifice creating a foundation she could stand on despite the weight threatening to crush her. *But what if healing the world requires healing the person who broke it?*

"What would happen to me during the process?" she asked, though part of her already knew the answer would terrify her.

Viktor's hands trembled as he called up technical specifications that made the air in the chamber feel thinner. "You'd need to open yourself to the planetary emotional network. Every suppressed feeling, every buried trauma, every lost connection... flowing through your consciousness simultaneously."

"And if I can't process it all?"

"Then you'd be lost in the feedback loop." His voice cracked. "And the planet would die anyway."

Viktor moved to another console, accessing files that made Emma's chest seize with fresh terror. "There's something else. Project Terminus. Mira has developed a permanent solution to the emotional restoration threat."

The words hit Emma like physical blows, each syllable crushing the air from her lungs. "What kind of permanent solution?"

"She's planning to sever the planetary emotional connection entirely. Not management. Elimination. No more restoration attempts, no more possibility of awakening." Viktor's voice broke completely. "The planet would die cleanly, without the chaos of emotional reawakening."

Complete death rather than the risk of chaotic life. Emma felt her mother's terror as if it were her own, the accumulated trauma of witnessing emotional restoration failure twisted into a determination to prevent any future attempts.

The Archive's displays flickered, and Emma heard her father's voice one final time, speaking words he'd recorded for the moment when truth would be needed more than comfort:

"The choice was never between order and chaos, Emma. It was between growth and stagnation, between life and the illusion of safety. I couldn't make that choice for you, but I could make sure you had the tools to make it for yourself."

Emma closed her eyes and reached out with her abilities, feeling the network of suppressed humanity above her. Millions of people living half-lives, their capacity for joy and love withering away. But underneath their suffering, she felt something else—something that made her chest warm despite the cold certainty of what she had to do.

I can feel my mother's pain, Emma realized, extending her consciousness toward the Council facility where Mira maintained her constant vigil. *Underneath all the control and conditioning, there's still the person who loved my father enough to marry him. The woman who wanted to protect people from suffering.*

When she opened her eyes, both the Archive and Viktor were watching her with expressions that suggested they recognized something new in her face.

"How long do we have?" she asked.

"Hours," Viktor replied. "Once Project Terminus activates, the process will be irreversible."

Emma nodded, feeling her father's love surrounding her while her mother's terror reached across the city like a cry for help. *But what if the choice isn't between defeating her and saving the world? What if healing the world requires healing her?*

"Then we move now," she said, her voice carrying certainty that surprised even her. "Contact the resistance networks. Tell them it's time to stop hiding and start healing."

Viktor studied her face, recognizing something in her expression that he hadn't expected. "You're not planning to fight her, are you?"

Emma felt the truth resonate through every emotion she'd ever collected, every feeling she'd learned to process without losing herself. "Viktor, she's not my enemy. She's the person I need to save in order to save everyone else."

The suppression system isn't just technology, Emma understood, feeling the connection her enhanced abilities had always been meant to make. *It's psychologically integrated with her emotional state. She's been using herself as an anchor for the entire network.*

"Which means I can't just reverse the suppression through technical manipulation," Emma continued, her father's research clicking into place with her own understanding of human emotion. "I have to help her choose to release it. And that requires me to connect with her, to help her process the trauma that convinced her suppression was necessary."

The silence that followed felt heavy with recognition. They weren't asking Emma to destroy the system. They were asking her to heal the person who'd created it.

"She's your mother," Viktor said quietly. "Underneath all the conditioning and control, she loves you."

Emma felt the truth of those words burn through the pain of betrayal and abandonment. Love doesn't disappear just because it becomes twisted by fear. It just gets buried deeper, waiting for someone brave enough to excavate it.

As alarms began to sound in the distance, the Council's detection systems tracking them to the hidden laboratory, Emma took one last look at her father's life work. Truth revealed, but revelation was only the beginning. Now came the hardest part: convincing a traumatized woman to choose love over fear, vulnerability over control, hope over the certainty of managed decline.

The weight of truth is heavier than anything I've ever carried, Emma thought, feeling responsibility for both human and planetary consciousness settling on her shoulders like armor made of accumulated grief. *But maybe that's what makes it worth bearing. Truth that weighs nothing isn't truth at all. It's just comfortable fiction.*

Her father's sacrifice had given her the knowledge she needed. Her mother's pain had given her the target she needed to heal. Now it was time to discover if she had the courage to love someone who'd spent decades trying to eliminate love entirely.

The awakening had begun with discovery. Now it would continue with the most dangerous emotion of all: hope for someone who'd forgotten that hope was possible.

Chapter Twenty-Two

TWELVE HOURS TO DIE

T he command center deep beneath New Geneva had never held so many people. Emergency lighting cast harsh shadows across concrete walls that wept moisture from decades of neglect. The air recycling system, designed for a skeleton crew, struggled with the crowd of forty-three individuals representing every major resistance cell on the continent. Holly Lloyd stood at the central table, her weathered hands steady as she organized what might be the last resistance meeting in human history.

"We have twelve hours," Holly said, her voice holding the authority she'd earned through fifteen years of keeping people alive in forgotten spaces. "Maybe less before Mira's enforcement teams finish processing the targets we know about."

Emma sat at the table's edge, studying faces she'd learned to trust over these past weeks. Each person bore scars from different aspects of the suppression system. Dr. James Clarke hunched over data tablets, his scientific excitement about the planetary consciousness connection warring with his caution.

Evan paced near the tunnel entrance, his natural immunity making him restless in the crowded space. Viktor Brennan and Sarah Magnus stood together, their formal Council bearing making them seem like diplomatic visitors in this underground world.

The command center itself told the story of resistance survival. Cables snaked across the floor, connecting salvaged equipment from a dozen different eras. Holographic displays flickered with power fluctuations, showing maps of safe house networks that stretched across continents. Communication arrays built from scavenged parts maintained contact with cells in forty-seven cities worldwide.

"The evidence Viktor gathered changes everything," Sarah said, holding up the classified documents that proved the Council's manufactured crises. "Once the population sees proof that the emotional weapon attacks were staged operations, the suppression system loses its moral foundation."

Dr. Clarke looked up from his calculations, data flowing across multiple screens around him. "Public understanding without emotional context might prove insufficient." He gestured to a neural mapping display. "See these patterns? Cognitive recognition fires in completely different brain regions than emotional comprehension. People can know something is true without feeling its significance."

Marcus, still wearing his Council enforcement uniform but without its authority badges, studied the tactical displays with a soldier's eye. "Even perfect public revelation won't create change if Mira implements Project Terminus." His voice carried the weight of someone who'd seen too many operations fail. "The neural cascades will burn out emotional capacity permanently. After that, awakening becomes impossible regardless of public opinion."

Emma felt the weight of their expectations like physical pressure against her chest. Over the past days, her abilities had continued developing in ways that both scared and amazed her. She could sense emotional patterns from individuals throughout the city, feel the suppressed anguish pressing against technological barriers like water against a cracking dam.

"Emma," Holly said gently, "help us understand what you're experiencing. What do you feel when you reach out with your abilities?"

Emma closed her eyes, extending her consciousness beyond the command center walls. *Above us, I can sense thousands of people living half-lives. Their emotions are there, but locked behind barriers that grow stronger each day. And underneath everything...*

"What do you sense underneath?"

"Anguish. The planet itself is in anguish. It's like a network of connections that once held feeling between all living things, but now most of the pathways are severed or dying."

Dr. Clarke activated the holographic display system they'd salvaged from abandoned Council facilities. The display materialized above the table, showing New Geneva from above. But instead of buildings and streets, Emma saw the emotional landscape: grey voids where suppressed individuals existed, isolated sparks where resistance members maintained authentic feeling, and underneath everything, a network of dying energy that once connected all life on Earth.

Emma studied the display, her enhanced awareness making the patterns feel like music she could almost hear. "The suppressed areas aren't just empty. They're actively draining energy from the network. Each person who loses emotional capacity weakens the whole system."

"Fascinating." Clarke leaned forward, his scientific curiosity overriding his caution. "What does that suggest about the relationship between individual consciousness and planetary awareness?"

"They're not separate systems," Emma realized, the understanding flowing through her like revelation. "Human emotions don't just connect us to each other. They're part of the planet's nervous system. When we suppress our feelings, we're cutting the world off from part of its own consciousness."

Clarke nodded, his fingers dancing across data interfaces as he pulled up quantum field measurements. "The planetary consciousness isn't abstract. It's a quantum field generated by the collective emotional energy of all living things. Human emotions, being the most complex and powerful, serve as the primary interface between individual consciousness and planetary awareness."

Emma watched the display zoom out, showing similar patterns across the globe. Europe appeared as a wasteland of emotional suppression, while parts of Africa and South America showed more activity. But everywhere, the underlying network grew thinner, more broken.

How much time do we really have? Emma asked herself, though she dreaded the answer.

"Without intervention, complete emotional collapse within six months," Clarke said, as if reading her thoughts. "The planet's systems are failing faster as the suppression spreads. Weather patterns, environmental balance, even geological stability depend on the emotional field we've been destroying."

Holly placed a gentle hand on Emma's shoulder. "We're not asking you to bear this burden alone. My network has safe houses in forty-seven cities worldwide. We can coordinate the awakening process, help people transition safely."

Viktor straightened, his military bearing asserting itself. "But the coordination would need to be extraordinary. We're talking about simultaneous operations across multiple continents." He gestured to a tactical map. "Timing, resources, secure communications—any failure point compromises the entire mission."

Holly's expression hardened with the competence that had kept her network alive for fifteen years. "Each cell includes Memory Keepers, people who've maintained emotional connections despite the suppression technology. They can serve as guides for others during the transition."

"However," Viktor added, his tone shifting to the clinical precision Emma recognized from his Council days, "Emma's genetic heritage makes her the only viable interface for planetary-scale restoration. The Thorne family line holds the specific neural pathways necessary for global emotional resonance. Without her, any awakening attempt will be chaotic and catastrophic."

Emma stood and walked to the tunnel entrance, needing space to process the implications. The rough-hewn walls showed tool marks from the resistance fighters who'd carved this sanctuary from bedrock, their determination preserved in stone. Evan followed, his presence comforting despite the impossibility of their situation.

"I keep thinking about that child," Emma said, remembering her first genuine emotional connection during a routine collection weeks ago. "Tommy. The love he felt for his mother was so pure, so complete. And I took that away from him because I was trained to believe it was dangerous."

Evan placed his hand on her shoulder. "You can give it back. All of it. Every suppressed feeling, every severed connection."

"But at what cost?" Emma turned to face him, her amber eyes reflecting the bioluminescent fungi that provided light in the tunnels. "Clarke's models show massive psychological shock as suppressed emotions return all at once. People who haven't felt in decades will experience everything they've buried—grief, love, anger, joy—simultaneously."

"But what if the restoration process was gradual instead of sudden?" Evan asked.

Emma felt a spark of possibility. *If I could control the rate of emotional return, help people process their feelings in manageable stages...*

"That would require maintaining the connection for an extended period," Viktor interrupted from behind them, studying the tunnel maps on his tablet and calculating distances to key infrastructure. "Could you sustain that level of interface for weeks or months?"

Before Emma could answer, emergency alerts flashed on communication devices as Holly's network coordinators reported raids on resistance positions throughout the city.

"They're using emotional tracking," Marcus called out, his Council scanner displaying raid patterns that made Emma's blood run cold. "Mira's deployed the new resonance detectors. Any emotional activity above baseline triggers automatic enforcement response."

Emma felt the implications like ice spreading through her veins. *She's not just hunting the resistance. She's eliminating anyone showing signs of natural emotional awakening.*

Viktor's face had gone pale as intelligence reports flowed across his secure channels. "Emergency protocols across all Council districts. Mass corrections authorized for anyone registering above baseline emotional activity." His voice cracked slightly. "She's implementing planetary suppression acceleration."

Dr. Clarke looked up from his calculations, confusion creasing his features. "Acceleration would achieve what exactly?"

Emma closed her eyes, reaching out with her abilities to sense the changes in the emotional landscape above them. When she opened them, her face was ashen. "She's not just maintaining suppression anymore. She's actively burning out the neural pathways that could support emotional restoration. Making the damage permanent."

The resistance leaders exchanged glances heavy with understanding. Their timeline had just collapsed from months to hours.

Holly began issuing rapid commands into her communication device while pulling up evacuation routes on multiple displays. "We move now. All safe house evacuations, priority on children and Memory Keepers. Sarah, can you get the historical evidence to public networks before the communication blackout?"

"I'm uploading to multiple broadcast systems," Sarah replied, her fingers flying over her tablet. "But without emotional context, the data won't have the psychological impact necessary to break through decades of conditioning."

The translucent formations on the tunnel walls began to pulse with faint light as Emma's abilities expanded, responding to something building within her consciousness. The emotional energy of everyone in the room pressed against her awareness: their fear, determination, hope, and desperation creating a complex symphony that she could not only hear but understand.

"I could create emotional context for the revelation. Help people feel the truth instead of just understanding it intellectually."

Clarke leaned forward with scientific interest, his caution temporarily forgotten. "How would that work in practice?"

"The suppression network operates through emotional resonance," Emma explained, the understanding forming as she spoke. "Instead of fighting the system, I could use it. Channel authentic emotional experiences through the existing infrastructure, turning the Council's own technology against itself."

Clarke's eyes widened as he grasped the implications. "You'd be reversing the polarity of the entire network. Instead of suppressing emotions, it would amplify genuine feeling."

Viktor pulled up energy consumption models on his tablet, running calculations. "The energy requirements would be enormous. You'd have to channel resonance through thousands of suppression nodes simultaneously."

Marcus moved to examine the security protocols on his scanner, his movements carrying the precision of someone trained to assess threats. "And Mira will detect the attempt the moment it begins. She'll throw everything she has at stopping you."

Emma nodded, accepting the reality of what choosing this path meant. "Then we make sure I reach the Central Suppression Facility before she can mobilize a complete response."

The command center buzzed with activity as the coalition shifted from planning to execution. Holly coordinated evacuation routes while Viktor and Sarah prepared for their roles in the Council chamber confrontation. Dr. Clarke gathered the technical equipment Emma would need to interface with the planetary suppression grid.

But Emma found herself thinking about her mother—not Chancellor Keller, the architect of planetary emotional death, but Mira Thorne, the young scientist who'd developed suppression technology to protect humanity from weaponized emotions. *Somewhere beneath decades of conditioning and trauma, that person still exists.*

"There's something else we need to consider," Emma said, drawing the group's attention. "The suppression system isn't just technology. It's psychologically integrated with Mira's own emotional state. She's been using herself as an anchor for the entire network, maintaining stability through her personal commitment to emotional elimination."

Evan frowned, his natural immunity making him more sensitive to the implications. "What does that mean for our plans?"

Emma met his eyes, knowing her next words would change everything between them. "It means I can't just reverse the suppression field through technical manipulation. I have to help her choose to release it. And that requires me to connect with her directly, to help her process the wounds that convinced her suppression was necessary."

The silence that followed was heavy with understanding. They weren't just asking Emma to risk her life for planetary consciousness. They were asking her to forgive and heal the person who'd stolen humanity's emotional birthright.

"She's your mother," Holly said softly. "Underneath all the conditioning and control, she loves you. That connection might be the key to reaching her."

Emma felt the truth of those words resonate through her developing abilities. *My mother's love is buried under layers of trauma and suppression, but it hasn't been eliminated. If I can reach that buried emotion, help Mira remember what she was trying to protect, there might be a path to restoration that doesn't require destroying the person who created the problem.*

"But what if she's too far gone?" Viktor asked, his military pragmatism showing. "Decades of suppression may have damaged her capacity for emotional response beyond repair."

"Then we'll find another way," Emma said with determination that surprised her. "But I won't assume she's beyond redemption without trying to reach her first."

Emergency alerts continued flashing as enforcement teams swept through the upper city, implementing mass corrections on anyone showing emotional irregularities. The resistance network that had taken decades to build was being dismantled in hours.

"How long do you need to prepare for the interface process?" Holly asked.

Emma considered the question, feeling the weight of planetary consciousness pressing against her awareness. "Two hours to study the facility schematics and prepare mentally. But

Holly, you need to understand what we're asking of your people. When the suppression field destabilizes, millions of people will experience authentic emotion for the first time in their lives. Without proper guidance, the psychological shock could be worse than the original emotional weapons."

Holly nodded grimly, her experience managing resistance operations lending weight to her words. "We'll deploy Memory Keeper teams to every major population center. But Emma, some people won't survive the transition. Decades of suppression have created psychological dependencies that can't be reversed without casualties."

She paused, consulting data on her tablet. "Conservative estimates suggest fifteen to twenty percent psychological breakdown requiring intensive care. Another thirty percent will need ongoing support for months or years."

The reality of what they were attempting settled over the group like a heavy blanket. They weren't just fighting for freedom or truth, but for the survival of human consciousness itself. Success meant saving the planet but potentially destroying the minds of millions who'd spent their lives hiding from authentic emotion.

Emma felt Evan's hand find hers, his natural immunity to suppression making his emotional support more precious than ever. Around them, the coalition prepared for a battle that would determine whether humanity evolved or perished as a species.

"Six hours," Emma said, watching her friends and allies disperse to their assignments. "After two centuries of suppression, we have six hours to restore planetary consciousness or watch it die forever."

As the command center emptied, Emma remained behind with Dr. Clarke, studying the technical specifications for the Central Suppression Facility. The building wasn't just the heart of the network. It was the physical manifestation of her mother's wounds, the place where fear had hardened into technology designed to eliminate the possibility of anguish by eliminating the capacity for feeling.

"The irony," Clarke said, highlighting structural details on his tablet, "is that your mother was right about emotions being dangerous. The original emotional weapons did nearly destroy civilization. But her solution, permanent suppression, is destroying it more completely."

Emma studied the facility plans, noting how the architecture itself reflected psychological barriers. *She built the facility like a fortress, not just against external threats but against her own suppressed emotions.*

Clarke nodded thoughtfully. "And if you could help her stop being afraid of her own emotions?"

"Then she might choose to release the system voluntarily. But reaching her means opening myself to whatever wounds created her fear in the first place."

The storm was gathering above ground: enforcement teams, Council politics, public revelations, and the desperate activities of a resistance network fighting for humanity's emotional soul. But for Emma, the real battle would be more personal: helping her mother choose love over fear, connection over control, and hope over the certainty of managed decline.

The weight of planetary consciousness presses against my awareness, Emma thought, feeling the responsibility for millions of suppressed lives settling on her shoulders. *Millions of suppressed lives depending on my ability to forgive the unforgivable and love the person who tried to make love impossible.*

Time was running out for everyone.

Chapter Twenty-Three

THE TRAITOR'S CHOICE

Marcus Webb crouched in a maintenance alcove two levels above Dr. Clarke's laboratory, his stolen Council scanner painting the resistance network's destruction in real-time. His fingers moved across its interface with practiced efficiency, following the largest anti-resistance operation in twenty-five years, while something inside his chest twisted with each successful raid report.

"Sector Seven cleared," came Agent Ross's voice across the intercepted channel, his former partner, back from Enhanced Correction with every trace of that day's tears scrubbed out of it. "Three targets apprehended, memory cores seized."

Marcus listened with forced detachment. Each arrest felt like a physical blow against his ribs. Three more people would disappear into Council correction centers, their hope eliminated, their capacity for authentic feeling surgically removed. His defection had led the Council here; they had followed his trail to doors he'd sworn were safe.

"Henderson here. Communications hub destroyed. Taking data cores now."

The reports continued flooding the scanner as Council forces dismantled everything the resistance had built over decades. Marcus watched the tactical overlays showing enforcement teams moving through locations his trail had exposed, safe houses that had sheltered him three nights running, people he'd learned to see as individuals rather than targets.

When had that change begun? When had resistance members stopped being abstract threats and become people whose emotional wellbeing mattered to him?

The answer came with uncomfortable clarity: since Emma had awakened his capacity to feel genuine concern for another person's suffering. He remembered her face during their first real conversation, the way she'd looked at him not as an enemy but as someone who might still choose to be better than his conditioning.

Marcus pulled up Emma's biometric feed on the scanner's secondary display, studying readings that showed her emotional energy spiking beyond measurable levels. The data indicated direct contact with planetary consciousness, exactly what Dr. Clarke's research had warned against. The mental strain of channeling global emotional patterns could destroy her individual identity entirely.

She was going to die, and the trail he'd left behind had put her in the position where that death was inevitable.

The realization cut through his conditioning like surgical steel. For three years, he'd protected Emma from external threats while serving the system that posed the greatest danger to her life. His loyalty to institutional duty had made him complicit in destroying the person whose emotional awakening had given him his first taste of authentic feeling.

"Priority alert," came Captain Halloran's voice from the tactical channel. "Target Thorne detected at Section Seven laboratory. Moving to secure."

Marcus's hands clenched involuntarily around his console's edge. Halloran was the Council's most efficient operative, her conditioning so complete that she'd execute Emma without hesitation if the situation demanded it. The captain's psychological profile showed zero capacity for independent moral judgment, exactly what made her valuable for enforcement work.

Marcus stared at the scanner, watching Halloran's strike order propagate across the tactical grid. His training whispered that the operation was righteous. His conditioning insisted that Emma's abilities made her too dangerous to remain free. The career, the clearance, the constructed identity: all of it was already ash behind him. What remained was only the choice.

But Emma's voice echoed in his memory: *"You're not just your programming, Marcus. I can feel that there's more of you left than they want you to believe."*

The choice, when it came, required no deliberation.

Marcus switched his communication to emergency encryption and contacted the one person with every reason to curse his name tonight. "Holly, this is Marcus. Emma's life is in immediate danger. Captain Halloran is moving to her location with lethal force authorization."

Holly's response crackled back sharp with suspicion and controlled fury. "Why should we trust you? You're the reason we're losing everything today."

"Because Emma's attempting direct interface with planetary consciousness, and the process will kill her if someone doesn't provide guidance through the integration. I know where Dr. Clarke stored his consciousness stabilization equipment."

Marcus was already moving from the alcove, taking emergency passages he'd memorized during his security training. But instead of hunting resistance members, he was now racing to save the person his trail had endangered.

"How do we know this isn't another trap?" Holly asked, her voice tight with the strain of coordinating evacuations while her network crumbled around her.

"Because I'm choosing Emma over everything else," Marcus replied, the words flowing from some part of himself that his conditioning had never quite reached. "Tell her Marcus Webb died free."

The communication ended as Marcus dropped into the emergency stairwell that would take him down to the Section Seven laboratory. The descent gave him time to process the magnitude of his choice. By helping Emma escape, he was committing treason against every institution he'd served faithfully for eight years. His career would end. His security clearance would be revoked. He would likely face the same neural modification procedures they were planning for Emma.

But for the first time since his conditioning began, Marcus felt something he'd almost forgotten: the deep satisfaction that came from choosing personal conscience over institutional loyalty.

The laboratory section appeared normal from the security checkpoint, but Marcus's enhanced sensitivity detected chaos erupting behind sealed doors. The air itself trembled with barely contained psychic energy as Emma's consciousness expanded beyond individual limits. Warning displays flashed across monitoring systems that had no protocols for measuring planetary-scale emotional resonance.

Marcus used his clearance codes to access the restricted area, knowing each electronic signature created evidence of his involvement. There was no way to help Emma without documenting his betrayal of Council protocols. His choice was complete and irreversible.

Dr. Clarke's laboratory had been transformed into something between a research facility and a war zone. Emotional energy had hardened into semi-solid formations that pulsed with captured feelings, their surfaces reflecting decades of suppressed human experience. The air sang with voices Marcus recognized: fragments of conversations that had been monitored and collected, lullabies that mothers couldn't sing to their children, words of love that couldn't be spoken.

Emma hung suspended in the laboratory's center, her body floating as raw emotional energy coursed through her neural pathways. Her amber eyes had gone white, reflecting quantum frequencies she was channeling from across the planet. Blood trickled from her nose and ears, clear signs that her brain was approaching the limits of what human consciousness could process.

"Emma!" Marcus shouted, but she showed no awareness of his presence. Her individual mind was elsewhere, experiencing the accumulated emotional pain of every suppressed person on Earth simultaneously. The mental load should have killed her instantly, but somehow she continued processing information that would have driven any normal person insane.

Dr. Clarke lay unconscious near his primary workstation, a head wound suggesting he'd been struck by hardening emotional energy when Emma's abilities overwhelmed the laboratory's containment systems. His monitoring equipment showed readings that made Marcus's stomach drop: Emma's neural activity was spiking in patterns associated with complete ego dissolution. She was losing herself in the planetary emotional field.

"Agent Webb, report your status." Captain Halloran's voice cut through the psychic chaos as she entered the laboratory with a full tactical team. "Target is to be neutralized per Chancellor's orders."

Marcus positioned himself between Halloran and Emma, his training warring with his conscience as he faced the most efficient killer in the Council's enforcement division. "Stand down, Captain. The target is experiencing a medical emergency. Interruption could cause cascading psychological damage throughout the suppressed population."

Halloran's cold eyes assessed the energy readings on her scanner, noting the patterns that extended far beyond the laboratory walls. For just a moment, something flickered across her face—uncertainty, perhaps even concern. Then her conditioning reasserted itself. "Emotional disruption levels are indeed approaching critical thresholds. However, elimination of the source remains the priority. Step aside, Agent."

"No."

The word emerged from Marcus with strength that surprised him, holding none of the uncertainty he'd felt for weeks as his conditioning cracked. Emma's awakening had given him something he'd never possessed: the ability to distinguish between institutional duty and moral responsibility.

Halloran raised her weapon, her movements precise and

mechanical. "Agent Webb, you are hereby relieved of duty and marked for correction. Final warning."

Marcus raised his own sidearm, accepting what his choice meant. Behind him, Emma's consciousness continued expanding across the global emotional field, her individual awareness dissolving into something unprecedented. Through the laboratory's emergency speakers, her voice emerged, not speaking but somehow transmitting the experiences she was channeling.

Marcus could hear fragments of suppressed conversations, children crying for parents who couldn't respond with love, artists screaming as their creativity was eliminated, lovers whispering words they were forbidden to feel. The planetary consciousness was dying, and Emma was experiencing its death directly while somehow teaching it how to redistribute emotional energy safely.

Marcus watched the energy patterns shift and reorganize, his eyes widening as the implications hit him. "She's not just touching the planetary field," he said, his voice filled with wonder. "She's creating a network for safe emotional reawakening. She's preventing the chaos we were trained to fear."

Halloran's finger tightened on her trigger. "Stand down, Agent Webb."

"Ruth." The voice came from the laboratory entrance as Chancellor Keller herself entered, flanked by additional enforcement personnel. Marcus's heart hammered against his ribs. If the Chancellor was here personally, Emma's situation had moved beyond normal enforcement protocols into planetary security concerns.

Mira Keller approached her suspended daughter, and Marcus watched something crack in the Chancellor's composure.

Pain, fear, love, desperation—emotions that shouldn't exist in someone with the Chancellor's level of conditioning—flooded across her face as she witnessed Emma's transformation.

"Mother's here, Emma," Mira whispered, reaching toward her daughter's floating form. "Mother's here."

When Mira's fingers touched Emma's skin, the laboratory exploded with light.

The emotional resonance between mother and daughter created a feedback loop that connected every person in the building to the planetary consciousness field. For seventeen seconds, Marcus experienced what Emma was experiencing: the vast loneliness of a dying world, the accumulated grief of millions of suppressed individuals, and underneath it all, a hope that humanity could learn to feel again without destroying itself.

But he also sensed Emma's individual consciousness fragmenting as she tried to process experiences no single mind was meant to contain. She was succeeding in guiding the planetary reawakening, but the effort was tearing apart her sense of self. Her sacrifice was working, but it was costing her everything she had been as an individual.

When the resonance ended, Emma collapsed to the laboratory floor, her breathing shallow and her neural readings showing minimal individual consciousness. Mira knelt beside her, tears flowing down her face: the first genuine emotional response Marcus had ever witnessed from the Chancellor.

Mira sat in silence for a long moment, her hand stroking Emma's hair with trembling fingers. *My daughter,* Marcus could see her thinking, *what have I done to you?*

"The reversal protocols," Mira whispered to Dr. Clarke, who was regaining consciousness. "Do you still have my original reversal protocols?"

Clarke struggled to his workstation, calling up files that had been classified for twenty years. "They're here, but Emma's condition... Mira, she's integrated too deeply with the planetary field. The protocols were designed for individual consciousness, not someone who's become part of the global emotional network."

"Then we adapt them." Mira's voice held desperate maternal determination. "I won't lose her to the same system I created to protect her."

Marcus watched the Chancellor, the architect of planetary emotional suppression, work frantically to save the daughter whose awakening threatened everything she'd built. The irony wasn't lost on him. The woman who had spent decades perfecting emotional control was now fighting to preserve her daughter's capacity for authentic feeling.

"Chancellor," Halloran interrupted, "what are your orders regarding the resistance operation?"

Mira looked up from Emma's unconscious form, her face streaked with tears but her voice holding absolute authority. "Abort the operation. Release all detained resistance members."

"Ma'am?"

"You heard me, Captain. Dr. Clarke and his team are now operating under my direct protection. Agent Webb, you're assigned to Emma's security detail." Mira's expression hardened into the mask of command Marcus recognized from official broadcasts. "Emma has proven that emotional suppression creates more problems than it solves."

Marcus felt hope rise in his chest, but Mira's next words extinguished it.

"However, the planetary consciousness readings show critical instability. Without proper management, complete system failure will trigger uncontrolled emotional release across the global population." She stood, her expression shifting to cold calculation. "Project Terminus remains our only option for preventing planetary emotional chaos. We must complete controlled consciousness severing before the current crisis spreads beyond containment."

Marcus realized that Chancellor Keller wasn't planning to help Emma recover from her consciousness contact. She was planning to use Emma's current vulnerability to implement the final phase of emotional elimination: not just suppression, but the permanent destruction of humanity's capacity for authentic feeling.

"Emma?" The whisper came from her unconscious form, her amber eyes opening to focus on her mother's face. "The children. I can feel them crying. So many children who can't understand why their parents don't love them anymore."

Mira's composure wavered. "Emma, sweetheart, you're experiencing psychological interference from neural damage. The emotions you're sensing aren't real."

"No." Emma struggled to sit up, her voice gaining strength despite her physical weakness. "They're the most real thing I've ever felt. The planet is dying because we broke the connection between feeling and living. You broke it, Mother. And I have to fix it."

"But fixing it means destroying the safety we've built," Mira said, her voice breaking slightly. "Restoration brings back the weapons, the wars, the suffering we eliminated."

Emma met her mother's eyes directly, her gaze holding the weight of planetary consciousness. "The suffering we eliminated was the price we paid for joy we also lost. Safety without feeling isn't safety at all. It's just a slower kind of death."

Marcus watched mother and daughter face each other across philosophical differences that would determine the future of human consciousness. Emma, even weakened by her contact with planetary awareness, represented everything Chancellor Keller feared most: proof that emotional suppression was unnecessary, that her life's work might have been wrong, and that love was stronger than any system designed to control it.

"Captain Halloran," Mira ordered, "prepare Emma for transport to the Terminus facility. Full neural isolation protocols."

"No." Emma's voice held power as she struggled to her feet, drawing on reserves of strength Marcus didn't know she possessed. "I won't let you complete the severing. Not when I can feel how much the world wants to love again."

The confrontation Marcus had been dreading was beginning. Emma, despite her weakened state, was preparing to oppose her mother's final solution directly. Chancellor Keller commanded overwhelming technological and military resources, but her emotional suppression made her vulnerable to forces she'd spent her life trying to control.

"Mother," Emma said, extending her hand toward Mira with infinite gentleness, "let me show you what I felt during the planetary connection. Let me share the joy that's still possible if we choose courage over safety."

Mira stared at her daughter's outstretched hand, and Marcus realized this moment would define not just their relationship, but the fate of every living thing on Earth. Would fear win, completing the transformation of humanity into an emotionally sterile species? Or would love prove stronger than the systems designed to eliminate it?

Marcus had chosen his side by protecting Emma, but he understood that choosing was only the beginning. Now he had to help her survive long enough to complete what she'd started, or watch both her and the planet die from emotional starvation.

The darkest hour had arrived, and everything depended on whether a mother could choose to trust her daughter, whether love could overcome a lifetime of conditioning that insisted safety required the elimination of feeling itself.

In the laboratory around them, the hardened emotional formations pulsed with increasing intensity, their surfaces reflecting the faces of everyone who had ever been denied their authentic feelings. The planetary consciousness waited, dying by degrees, for humanity to choose between growth and extinction.

Marcus gripped his weapon and prepared to defend the future of human emotion, knowing that whatever happened next would determine whether his species emerged from suppression stronger and more connected, or whether they would complete their transformation into perfectly controlled machines that had forgotten how to live.

Chapter Twenty-Four

WHAT MONSTERS MAKE

E mma's awareness crawled back through layers of suppression field interference like climbing through thick fog. Her neural implants burned like hot needles behind her temples, each pulse sending waves of artificial numbness through her consciousness. The Council medical facility's harsh lighting cut through her vision in sharp fragments, each beam holding the emotional residue of countless procedures performed in this sterile chamber.

She could taste the fear that lingered here. Decades of desperation had soaked into the walls, along with the empty acceptance of those who had surrendered to psychological death. The room itself was a monument to the Council's version of healing: white surfaces that reflected nothing, equipment designed to eliminate rather than repair, and an atmosphere of clinical detachment that made human feeling seem like a disease.

Emma tried to move and found restraints holding her arms to the examination table. The bonds were embedded with suppression technology, creating a localized field that pressed against her consciousness like a weight. *Standard procedure for unstable Collectors,* she realized with calm detachment that didn't quite hide her rising panic.

Around her, medical technicians prepared equipment she recognized from her training manuals. Neural pathway scramblers that could rewrite personality patterns. Memory modification arrays that erased inconvenient experiences. And most terrifying of all, the emotional severance device that would destroy her ability to feel forever, leaving her consciousness intact but hollow.

"Subject is awake," one technician reported to his colleague. The man's words came out in perfect, measured intervals, his posture rigid as he consulted his instruments without looking at Emma's face. "Neural activity shows continued resistance to standard suppression protocols."

Emma forced herself to remain still, knowing that any sign of emotional distress would accelerate their timeline. Through the observation window, she could sense presences watching her: Council members whose suppressed anxiety leaked through even the facility's advanced dampening fields. They were afraid of what she represented, what she might become if her abilities continued developing unchecked.

The door opened with a soft hiss, and Marcus Webb entered, his uniform crisp and his expression neutral. But Emma's abilities picked up the details his training couldn't hide: the way his eyes tightened at the corners when he looked at the medical equipment, the slight tremor in his hands as he consulted his handheld device, how he positioned himself to avoid direct eye contact. Three years of working together had created connections that even Council conditioning couldn't entirely break.

"Your preliminary assessment is complete," Marcus said, his voice holding the measured tones of official protocol. "Chancellor Keller has authorized immediate implementation of corrective procedures."

Emma felt her chest tighten as the clinical language masked the reality of what they planned to do to her. "What kind of procedures?"

Marcus hesitated for just a moment, a pause so brief that standard observers would miss it, but Emma caught the weight behind his silence. "Neural pathway reconstruction. Memory modification to remove traumatic associations with emotional resonance. And..." His throat worked as he swallowed. "Permanent severing of your connection to the planetary emotional field."

The words hit her like a physical blow. They weren't just planning to suppress her abilities. They were going to destroy the very thing that made her capable of helping the dying planet. "That will kill me," she whispered.

"It will save you," Marcus corrected, but his voice lacked conviction. "The Emma I've known for three years will survive. The unstable elements causing your current distress will be eliminated."

Emma stared at him, studying the tension in his shoulders, the way his jaw clenched when he spoke about eliminating her abilities. "Is that what you believe, Marcus? That who I'm becoming is something that needs to be eliminated?"

He set down his device and moved closer to the examination table, supposedly to check her restraints but actually bringing himself within range of her emotional perception. Up close, she could feel the storm raging beneath his maintained facade: guilt, fear, something that might be grief for what they were about to do to her.

"I believe," Marcus said quietly, "that the Council's primary concern is maintaining social stability and protecting citizens from the kind of chaos that destroyed civilization before."

"That's not what I asked."

Marcus looked directly at her for the first time since entering the room, and Emma saw her own reflection in his dark eyes. Not the perfect Collector she'd been trained to become, but someone fundamentally changed by the experience of authentic feeling. "What I believe isn't relevant to my duties."

"But should it be? Should what you believe matter more than what you're ordered to do?"

The question hung between them like a challenge. Emma watched as Marcus processed her words, his fingers drumming against his tablet in an unconscious rhythm that indicated stress. For just a moment, she saw past his conditioning to the person beneath: someone capable of genuine concern, wrestling with choices that would define not just her future but his own.

"The procedure begins in one hour," Marcus said, stepping back from the table. "I'm required to monitor your responses during the preparation phase."

Emma nodded, understanding the subtext. He would be present during her psychological destruction, watching as they eliminated everything that made her capable of saving the planet. The knowledge that he would witness her death—because that's what this was, even if her body survived—affected him in ways his training couldn't suppress.

"Marcus," Emma said softly, "when you look at me now, what do you see? Not what your training tells you to see, but what you actually observe?"

He settled into the observer's chair, his movements careful and controlled. "I see someone whose emotional capacity has expanded beyond normal parameters. Someone whose neural patterns show signs of connection to systems we don't fully understand."

"And does that terrify you?"

Marcus considered the question longer than his conditioning should have allowed. "It should. According to everything I've been taught, uncontrolled emotional expansion leads to psychological breakdown and social chaos."

"But does it terrify you?"

Another pause, this one even longer. "No. It concerns me because I don't understand what you're becoming, but it doesn't terrify me."

Emma felt a surge of hope at his words. His own suppression was failing more rapidly than either of them had recognized. "Why do you think that is?"

"Because..." Marcus struggled with the question, his brow furrowing as he accessed thoughts and feelings he'd been trained to suppress. "Because the person I see when I look at you isn't dangerous. She's someone who's become fully human."

The admission hung between them like a bridge, and Emma realized that Marcus's emotional awakening was accelerating. His words held genuine feeling: concern, respect, something that might even be affection. The recognition seemed to startle him as much as it moved her.

Emma closed her eyes and reached out with her developing abilities, testing the facility's suppression fields. The interference was stronger than anything she'd encountered, a constant pressure that tried to contain her consciousness within acceptable limits. But it wasn't perfect. She could sense familiar psychic resonances throughout the building: Viktor Brennan's disciplined anxiety from the administrative section, Dr. Sarah Magnus's contained anger from the archives.

And much closer, the distinctive feeling pattern of someone she'd never expected to find here.

Evan.

His presence felt like sunlight through the facility's artificial atmosphere: unfiltered emotion that her enhanced sensitivity could track precisely. He was moving through the main corridors, not hiding but walking with the confident bearing of someone who belonged. Whatever plan the resistance had developed, it didn't involve skulking through maintenance areas.

"Marcus," Emma said, opening her eyes to find him watching her intently, "the Council's theories about emotional suppression. What if they were wrong?"

"What do you mean?"

"What if suppressing emotions doesn't prevent chaos but actually causes it? What if the weapons and wars that destroyed the old world weren't caused by too much feeling, but by feelings that had been suppressed and distorted?"

Marcus frowned, his analytical mind engaging with the question despite his conditioning. "The historical records show clear correlations between emotional instability and violent conflict."

"But what if the emotional instability came from suppression in the first place? What if natural emotions, allowed to flow freely, don't create weapons, but suppressed emotions, forced underground and twisted, become destructive?"

She could see him wrestling with the implications, his training warring with the evidence of his own experience. His growing capacity for feeling hadn't made him more violent or unstable. If anything, it had made him more thoughtful, more concerned with the consequences of his actions.

"The facility's alarm system just activated," Marcus said, consulting his device as a soft chime indicated unauthorized access in the main lobby. "There's some kind of disturbance in the administrative section."

Emma kept her expression neutral despite the hope building in her chest. "What kind of disturbance?"

"Security protocols are engaging. Probably just a credentials issue, but response teams are being deployed." Marcus studied his readings more carefully. "Actually, the pattern suggests multiple visitors with high-level authorization. That's unusual for this facility."

Emma met his eyes directly. "Marcus, in the three years we've worked together, have I ever lied to you?"

"No."

"Then believe me when I tell you that the Council isn't trying to cure me. They're trying to eliminate the only person who might be capable of saving this planet from emotional death."

Marcus stared at her for a long moment, his hands gripping the edge of his chair until his knuckles went white, his breathing growing shallow as the conflict played out across his features. His conditioning demanded loyalty to Council protocols, but his growing emotional capacity was forcing him to question everything he'd been taught to value.

"But what if you're wrong? What if emotional restoration really would bring back the chaos and violence?"

"Then we find a better way," Emma said simply. "But we can't find better solutions if we're too afraid to examine the problems honestly."

The alarm chimed again, this time with the pattern that indicated high-priority visitors rather than security breaches. Marcus stood and moved to the room's communication panel, ostensibly to check on the situation, but Emma noticed that he positioned himself between her and the door in a way that would block observers' view of the examination table.

"Security reports multiple high-clearance visitors in the main administrative lobby," Marcus said, speaking to the room but clearly intending the information for Emma. "Response teams are standing by but have not been authorized to engage. Estimated meeting duration is fifteen minutes."

Emma understood. Evan and his team had perhaps fifteen minutes to reach her before standard facility protocols would require her transfer to the procedure room. But they would need more than time. They would need her restraints released and the medical equipment powered down to avoid triggering automated alerts.

"Marcus," she said, her voice holding all the genuine feeling she'd learned to experience, "what happens to the people I've helped if my abilities are destroyed? The families who found peace through my work, the children whose emotional crises I've resolved. What happens to them when the system that created me eliminates what made me effective?"

He didn't answer right away, but she could see him processing the implications. The Council's official position was that Collectors were interchangeable tools, that Emma's effectiveness came from her training rather than her unique abilities. But Marcus had observed her work closely enough to know better.

"The Council will assign replacement Collectors," he said finally, but his voice lacked conviction.

"You've seen the other Collectors' success rates. None of them achieve the results I do because none of them can actually connect with the emotions they're collecting. They treat feelings like contaminants to be removed rather than trying to understand what they represent."

Emma could see the truth of her words registering in Marcus's expression. His own effectiveness as her handler came from his ability to anticipate her responses, to understand the subtle ways her empathy influenced her work. If the Council's theories about containment were correct, her enhanced abilities should have made her less effective, not more.

"What are you asking me to do?" Marcus said quietly.

"I'm not asking you to do anything. I'm asking you to choose what you believe is right, based on your own experience rather than your training."

Marcus approached the examination table slowly, his movements deliberate rather than hesitant. "If I help you escape, I'll be marked as a traitor. My career will be over. My clearance will be revoked. I'll likely face the same procedures they're planning for you."

"Yes," Emma acknowledged. "And if you don't help me, you'll watch them destroy the person you just said was worth saving. More than that, you'll be complicit in eliminating humanity's best chance at surviving as an emotionally capable species."

When Marcus reached for the control panel that managed her restraints, Emma could feel the weight of the moment radiating from him: fear, determination, something that felt like hope mixed with grief for the life he was about to leave behind.

"The restraint system has multiple redundancies," Marcus said, his voice holding the tone of someone providing technical information rather than planning an escape. "Standard release protocol requires two-factor authentication plus medical supervisor approval. However, emergency medical situations can override security locks if the subject's vital signs indicate immediate danger."

Emma understood the implication. "What kind of vital signs?"

"Cardiac distress, neural overload, respiratory crisis." Marcus paused, his finger hovering over the control interface. "The system monitors through your implants. If those implants detected trauma sufficient to threaten psychological breakdown, the restraints would release automatically to allow medical intervention."

Emma closed her eyes and reached out with her abilities, drawing on the psychic resonance flowing through the facility's systems. Fear from security personnel responding to the unusual visitor situation, anxiety from medical staff dealing with disrupted procedures, anger from administrators whose schedules were being compromised. She pulled it all into herself, allowing the accumulated pressure to build until her neural implants registered dangerous overload levels.

The physical sensation was like trying to contain an ocean in a cup. Wave after wave of suppressed feelings crashed through her consciousness: the grief of patients who'd lost their capacity for joy, the rage of staff members who couldn't express frustration, the desperate love of families torn apart by neural severing. She absorbed it all, feeling her neural pathways strain under the load.

The restraints clicked open with synchronized precision as her vital signs spiked beyond acceptable parameters. Emergency protocols activated, flooding the room with soft blue light and triggering automated announcements about medical crisis response. The noise would mask any sounds of her movement and create confusion about her actual status.

Marcus moved with practiced efficiency, deactivating the monitoring equipment and downloading her medical files to his handheld device. "The emergency protocols will give us maybe three minutes before medical supervisors arrive to assess the situation. The main corridor connects to the administrative wing where your people are creating their distraction."

Emma sat up slowly, her body protesting after hours of restraint. The psychic energy she'd absorbed to trigger the release continued coursing through her system, making her hyperaware of every feeling in the facility. She could track Evan's approach through the building's main levels, sense the growing alarm of security personnel as they realized the visitor situation was more complex than it appeared, feel

Marcus's mixture of terror and determination as he committed fully to helping her escape.

"Before we go," Marcus said, his voice holding the weight of someone revealing a crucial secret, "there's something else you need to know about the procedures they were planning."

Emma stopped in the process of standing, sensing the gravity of what he was about to reveal.

"The neural pathway reconstruction wasn't just meant to eliminate your abilities. According to the classified briefing documents, it was designed to create a new kind of Collector: one with enhanced absorption capacity but no personal emotional response whatsoever. They weren't trying to cure you. They were trying to turn you into the perfect weapon."

The revelation hit Emma like a physical blow. Not only had the Council planned to destroy her capacity for feeling, they had intended to turn her abilities into a template for creating Collectors who could absorb unlimited psychic energy without the risk of developing empathy or conscience.

"How many others were scheduled for the same procedure?" Emma asked.

Marcus consulted his device, his face grim. "Twelve candidates have been identified. All Collectors who showed signs of enhanced emotional sensitivity. The program was designated 'Project Terminus' because it was designed to be the final solution to the emotional instability problem."

Emma's breath caught as the full scope hit her. The Council hadn't just planned to eliminate her abilities. They had intended to turn her into the foundation for systematically destroying human emotional capacity entirely.

"They would have created a new generation of Collectors who could drain entire populations while feeling nothing themselves," Emma said, the horror of it settling over her. "Perfect emotional vampires."

"According to the research projections, yes. And with your neural patterns as the template, they believed they could eliminate the risk of Collectors developing emotional attachments to their subjects."

Marcus opened the room's main door, revealing the facility's primary corridor system. Instead of the cramped maintenance spaces Emma had expected, they found themselves in the broad, well-lit administrative passages that formed the building's main arteries. Emergency lighting had been activated throughout the section, but instead of indicating crisis, it suggested controlled visitor protocols.

"The final phase of Project Terminus involved training these enhanced Collectors to target specific patterns: creativity, rebellion, independent thought. They weren't just planning to suppress emotions. They were planning to eliminate the capacity for resistance entirely."

As they moved through the corridors toward the administrative wing, Emma's abilities painted a three-dimensional map of psychic activity throughout the facility. The Council members in the administrative section were experiencing unprecedented levels of anxiety as they dealt with whatever situation Evan and his team had created. Medical personnel were frustrated by the disruption of their procedures. And somewhere in the depths of the building, Chancellor Keller's presence radiated the cold fury of someone whose plans were unraveling.

"Emma," Marcus said as they reached a junction in the main corridor system, "why did you trust me enough to reveal your changing abilities? You must have known I would have to report them."

Emma considered the question as they navigated the increasingly busy passages. Staff members hurried past on urgent errands, but none paid particular attention to a Collector and her handler moving through approved areas during their assigned monitoring period.

"Because even when you were following protocol, I could sense that you saw me as a person rather than just an assignment. Your suppression was already failing; you just didn't recognize it yet."

"And what if my suppression hadn't failed? What if I had been a perfect Council agent?"

"Then I would have found another way," Emma said simply. "But I don't think perfect suppression is possible for people who work closely with genuine emotions. The exposure changes you, whether you want it to or not."

They reached the administrative wing's main reception area, where Emma sensed the presence of her rescue team beyond a set of secure doors. Marcus used his security codes to unlock the barrier, and Evan stepped through with the controlled urgency of someone executing a carefully planned operation.

"Emma." Evan's relief at seeing her unharmed flooded through her enhanced perception, along with his determination to get her to safety. "Are you injured?"

"No, but we need to move quickly. The Council has something called Project Terminus. They're planning to create

Collectors who can absorb emotions without feeling them."
Emma turned to Marcus. "He helped me escape. His suppression is failing, and he's made the choice to join us."

Evan assessed Marcus with the attention of someone evaluating a potential ally or threat. "Can we trust him?"

Emma felt Marcus's response to the question: no deception, no hidden agenda, just genuine commitment to preventing the Council from implementing their final solution. "Yes. He's risking everything to help prevent Project Terminus."

Holly appeared from the administrative offices, her expression showing the strain of coordinating a resistance operation inside a Council facility using legitimate visitor protocols rather than infiltration. "The meeting with Deputy Administrator Wells is proceeding normally. We have maybe ten minutes before they expect Emma to be transferred to the procedure room."

Dr. Clarke emerged from another office, carrying equipment Emma recognized as psychic monitoring devices. "Emma, I need to check your neural implant readings. If they subjected you to enhanced suppression protocols, there could be damage to your developing abilities."

Emma submitted to his quick examination, aware that time was running out but understanding the importance of assessing her condition. The scanner readings showed elevated activity in areas associated with feeling processing, but no indication of the kind of damage that intensive suppression typically caused.

"Fascinating," Dr. Clarke murmured, studying the data. "Your neural pathways show signs of adaptation rather than suppression. It's as if your abilities are evolving to resist the Council's technology."

"What does that mean for the restoration process?" Holly asked.

Emma felt the answer forming in her consciousness as her enhanced abilities processed the information. "It means I'm becoming something they can't control or predict. But it also means I'm approaching a threshold where my consciousness might not be recognizably human anymore."

The sound of security teams beginning systematic searches echoed through the facility's public address system, forcing them to abandon their analysis and focus on departure. Instead of sneaking through hidden passages, Marcus led them through the visitor exit protocols, using his security clearance to authorize their departure as part of a routine administrative consultation.

The main lobby bustled with normal facility activity, but Emma could sense the underlying tension as security personnel tried to balance visitor courtesy with growing suspicion about the timing of multiple unusual events. Her enhanced perception painted a complex picture of the psychic landscape around them: Council staff trying to maintain professional composure while dealing with unprecedented disruption, visitors who seemed unusually calm for people in a high-security facility, and administrators whose anxiety levels suggested they suspected but couldn't prove that something unusual was occurring.

They're not just worried about me escaping, Emma realized as they approached the main exit. *They're afraid of what I represent.*

"Which is?" Marcus asked as Evan worked to maintain their group's appearance as legitimate facility visitors.

Emma looked back toward the medical wing they were leaving, feeling the psychic weight of hundreds of Council personnel, medical staff, and other prisoners. All of them trapped in various forms of suppression, all of them slowly losing their connection to what made them fundamentally human.

"Change," she said simply. "I represent the possibility that their entire system is not just wrong, but actively destroying the very thing they claim to protect."

The exit security checkpoint processed their departure with routine efficiency, Marcus's clearance codes and forged consultation paperwork creating a paper trail that would survive initial scrutiny. As they emerged into the artificial daylight of New Geneva's controlled environment, Emma realized that her rescue from the Council facility marked more than just personal escape. It was the beginning of open conflict between those who believed in emotional suppression and those who understood it was killing the planet.

Marcus paused at the facility entrance, looking back at the building where he'd spent three years of his life serving what he believed was humanity's protection. His shoulders sagged with the weight of what he was leaving behind, but his expression held something new—a quiet hope for the authentic future he was choosing to help create.

"No going back now," he said quietly.

Emma placed her hand on his shoulder, sharing some of the psychic strength she'd gained through her experiences with authentic feeling. "No going back," she agreed. "But that doesn't mean we're losing anything worth keeping."

As they moved toward the transportation that would take them to the resistance's new base of operations, Emma held with her not just the knowledge of Project Terminus and the true scope of the Council's plans, but also the understanding that her own transformation was accelerating beyond anything Dr. Clarke's theories had predicted. She was becoming something the Council couldn't control or predict, something that might be powerful enough to restore the planetary balance they had spent generations destroying.

But first, she had to survive long enough to figure out how to direct her abilities without destroying herself in the process. The breaking point had passed, and now everything depended on what would emerge from the pieces.

Chapter Twenty-Five

WHEN TRUTH DESTROYS EVERYTHING

The Council chambers had never witnessed such chaos. Viktor Brennan stood at the central podium, his weathered hands steady despite the weight of what he was about to reveal. The chamber itself reflected two centuries of controlled order: twelve ceremonial seats arranged in a perfect circle, each one equipped with biometric monitoring systems that tracked the occupant's emotional state. Displays floated in the air above the central table, their surfaces designed to present information without triggering unwanted emotional responses.

Around him, the twelve members of the Harmony Council sat in their designated positions, faces showing the controlled expressions that decades of suppression training had perfected. None of them suspected that within the next hour, everything they believed about their world would crumble.

"Councilors," Viktor began, his words carrying the weight of nearly three decades of faithful service, "I've called this emergency session to present evidence critical to planetary security."

Chancellor Mira Keller watched from her elevated seat, silver hair catching the chamber's artificial light that was calibrated to avoid stimulating emotional responses. Viktor's tone made her pulse quicken in ways her conditioning tried to suppress. She'd known him for twenty years, had relied on his loyalty and methodical approach to enforcement. But today, his posture held the tension of a man preparing to destroy everything he'd once protected.

"The floor recognizes Councilor Brennan," Mira said, though her hands gripped her chair's armrests.

Viktor activated the chamber's central display, filling the air above the Council table with classified documents that should have remained buried forever. The chamber's automated systems began analyzing the information for security violations, but Viktor had used his highest clearance codes to override the protection protocols.

"Twenty-three years ago, I lost my wife and son in what official records describe as a terrorist attack using emotional weaponry," Viktor announced. "For twenty-three years, I've dedicated my life to preventing such attacks. Today, I learned that their deaths were not caused by enemies of our state."

The first document materialized in the display space: communication logs from Research Station Seven, dated twelve hours before the attack that killed Viktor's family. Sarah Magnus had helped him compile the evidence, her historian's eye for detail revealing patterns that Viktor's military training had taught him to recognize.

"Council security forces were withdrawn from Station Seven at 0600 hours on March 15th," Viktor continued, his voice maintaining professional control despite the rage building in his chest. "The attack occurred at 1800 hours the same day. The withdrawal order came directly from this chamber."

Councilor James Fletcher shifted uncomfortably in his seat, the motion triggering his chair's biometric sensors. As Head of Internal Security during that period, he would have processed such orders. His face had gone pale beneath his regulation composure.

"That's..." Fletcher began, then stopped, his fingers drumming against his tablet as memories surfaced.

"Why would security forces be withdrawn just hours before a terrorist attack?" Viktor asked. "What purpose would such timing serve?"

Fletcher's analytical mind engaged despite his emotional conditioning, his security training forcing logical assessment. "If the withdrawal was coincidental, the timing would be extraordinarily unlucky. If it was planned..." He swallowed hard. "If it was planned, then the attacks were not external terrorism."

The silence that followed was heavy with implication. Fletcher's training in security protocols forced him to consider possibilities that his loyalty conditioning tried to suppress.

"The documented energy signatures from these attacks show identical technological origins," Viktor pressed on, displaying technical analysis reports. "According to our own engineering specifications, this similarity pattern indicates single-source development."

The next series of documents filled the display space: weapon analysis reports that Sarah had discovered buried in historical archives. The evidence was methodical, undeniable.

"How could our own technology be used against us without our knowledge?" asked Councilor Rebecca Lang, Head of Medical Ethics. Her physician's training made her lean forward, studying the data with clinical precision.

Viktor met her eyes directly. "It wasn't used without our knowledge."

The implications hit the chamber like a physical blow. Dr. Lang was a scientist first, conditioned to follow evidence regardless of where it led. Viktor watched her process the conclusion, her medical training warring with her institutional loyalty, her hands trembling as she reviewed the technical specifications.

Chancellor Keller remained outwardly calm, but Viktor noticed her left hand gripping the arm of her chair with enough force to whiten her knuckles. "Councilor Brennan," she said, "these are serious accusations. You're suggesting that Council members planned terrorist attacks against our own citizens."

"I'm not suggesting, Chancellor. I'm proving it."

The final document appeared: authorization codes for early suppression field deployment. Viktor had spent three sleepless nights verifying the data, cross-referencing it with deployment schedules and attack patterns. The conclusion was undeniable.

"Suppression technology was deployed in target areas six hours before the attacks," Viktor announced. "Not after, as official records state. Before. The fields were configured to amplify rather than dampen emotional energy, turning the weapons against suppressed populations who had no defense against the psychological assault."

The chamber erupted in controlled chaos. Even with decades of emotional conditioning, the Council members couldn't suppress their shock, confusion, and growing horror. Their biometric monitors registered unprecedented levels of stress as suppression protocols struggled to contain authentic emotional responses.

Councilor Sarah Magnus rose from her seat, her historian's training overriding her suppression protocols. "The weapons weren't resistance technology at all. They were our own suppression systems reversed to create the exact effects we claimed to be preventing."

"And the purpose of creating false attacks using our own technology?" Viktor asked.

"To justify expanding the suppression system," Dr. Lang said, her medical ethics training forcing her to follow the logical chain, her voice growing stronger as scientific objectivity overcame political conditioning. "To create fear that would make the population accept greater control."

Viktor watched his colleagues' faces change as they processed the evidence themselves rather than simply accepting his accusations. Lang leaned back in her chair, her scientific mind working through the implications. Fletcher's fingers stopped drumming as the security protocols he'd implemented took on new meaning. Smith set down his regulatory documents with trembling hands.

"The archives contain testimony from Dr. Mira Thorne's original research team," Sarah announced, her voice reaching across the chamber. "They questioned the ethical implications of using suppression technology offensively. Three team members died in 'accidents' within six months of filing their objections."

"But why would researchers developing protective technology object to its implementation?" asked Councilor David Smith, Head of Social Stability. His bureaucratic mind worked through the implications with methodical precision.

Sarah's response was direct. "Because they discovered their protective research was being weaponized against the people it was supposed to protect."

Smith's analytical mind engaged with the reality despite his conditioning, his administrator's need for logical systems forcing him to confront inconsistencies. "If the technology was being used to harm rather than help..." He trailed off, unable to complete the thought.

"The suppression system saved humanity from emotional chaos," Smith protested, but his voice lacked its usual conviction, his hands shuffling through regulatory documents as if searching for certainty. "Without it, we'd have destroyed ourselves."

Viktor pressed forward. "And who compiled the historical records showing that emotional freedom leads to self-destruction?"

Smith paused, his bureaucratic mind accessing the chain of information sources. "The Council's historical committee, based on data from the period."

"Selected data," Viktor clarified. "Chosen to support a predetermined conclusion."

Viktor watched Smith's worldview crack as he realized the circular logic he'd been accepting. The evidence for suppression's necessity came from the same organization that had implemented suppression, creating a closed loop of self-justifying information.

Chancellor Keller stood, her presence commanding attention despite the chaos surrounding her. "Councilor Brennan, even if these allegations had merit, you're proposing we dismantle the only thing standing between civilization and emotional anarchy. The risks of..."

Her words were cut off by an emergency alert that flooded the chamber with harsh red light. The chamber's communication system activated, displaying urgent reports from across New Geneva.

"Massive emotional disturbance detected in Sector Seven," the automated voice announced. "Suppression grid showing cascade failures. All Council enforcement units report to emergency stations."

Viktor smiled grimly. Sarah's broadcast of their evidence across all public communication networks was proceeding on schedule. While he presented their findings to the Council, she was revealing the truth to every citizen with access to news feeds, educational networks, and emergency communication systems.

The chamber's displays shifted to show feeds from across the city. In central plaza after central plaza, crowds were gathering as suppressed citizens learned that their emotional capacity had been stolen through deception. The reactions varied: some people stood in stunned silence, others wept for the first time in decades, and a few showed signs of anger that their conditioning couldn't contain.

But Viktor also saw something else in the feeds that challenged every prediction about emotional chaos. People were helping each other process the overwhelming information, strangers were offering comfort to those experiencing emotional overload, and an emerging sense of community was developing that the suppression system had tried to eliminate.

"Look at them," he said to his fellow Council members. "They're not destroying each other. They're connecting."

Dr. Lang leaned forward, studying the feeds with her medical training, her physician's eye tracking behavioral patterns. "They're showing signs of mutual support rather than violence. The emotional responses appear to be generating compassion rather than aggression."

"And what does that suggest about our theories regarding emotional chaos?" Viktor asked.

"That our theories might be based on incomplete or biased data," Lang admitted reluctantly, her scientific integrity overcoming political conditioning.

Chancellor Keller was studying the feeds with the tactical analysis skills that had made her the youngest Chancellor in Council history. "This is just the beginning," she said coldly. "Without proper guidance, these emotional releases will escalate into chaos. The death toll from uncontrolled psychological breaks will dwarf anything the original war produced."

"But what if such guidance systems already existed?" Viktor asked.

Mira paused, her scientific mind engaging with the possibility. "If comprehensive support systems were already in place, then managed transition might be possible. But developing such systems would take years of research and preparation."

Emma, Mira thought suddenly, remembering her daughter as a five-year-old, asking why people couldn't just help each other feel better when they were sad. *Even then, you understood something I was trying to engineer out of existence.*

Viktor played his final card. "Dr. David Thorne's original research included functional reversal protocols. They weren't abandoned because they failed. They were suppressed because they succeeded."

The silence that followed was absolute. Even the chamber's automated systems seemed to pause as the weight of Viktor's revelation settled over the Council.

"But why would successful reversal protocols be suppressed?" asked Councilor Fletcher, his security mind demanding logical explanations.

Viktor's response was gentle but devastating. "Because they would prove that the entire suppression framework was unnecessary."

"The original protocols required careful monitoring and gradual implementation," Viktor continued. "They were designed for exactly the situation we face now: helping suppressed populations safely reconnect with their emotional capacity. Dr. Thorne proved they worked before the decision was made to pursue permanent suppression instead."

Chancellor Keller's composure cracked. For a moment, Viktor saw not the calculating political leader who had ruled for fifteen years, but the traumatized young scientist who had watched her parents die and sworn to prevent anyone else from experiencing such pain.

"Those protocols required test subjects," she whispered. "The psychological damage to volunteers was... unacceptable."

"But the tests were conducted on individuals in isolation," Viktor pressed gently. "Dr. Thorne's later research suggested that group emotional integration could provide the support structure necessary for safe transition. But that research was classified and buried."

The emergency alerts continued streaming across the chamber's displays, but Viktor noticed that the reports weren't describing chaos. Instead, the systems were registering phenomena they had no protocols for handling: spontaneous community gatherings, mass expressions of grief and joy, and what the sensors could only classify as "unauthorized emotional synchronization events."

Councilor Sarah Magnus approached the central podium, bearing a sealed data container that Viktor recognized as containing the most classified historical archives. "The truth is," she announced, "we never gave people the chance to prove they could handle emotional freedom responsibly. We made the choice for them based on fear, not evidence."

"But what if the fear was justified?" Chancellor Keller asked. "What if emotional freedom really does lead to the destruction we've prevented?"

"Then why aren't we seeing that destruction now?" Sarah replied. "The evidence is right in front of us. People are connecting, not destroying."

Chancellor Keller stared at the data container as if it held a weapon. "Dr. Magnus, those files are classified beyond your clearance level."

"My clearance level became irrelevant the moment I discovered that our entire historical record is built on manufactured evidence," Sarah replied. "The people have a right to know what they lost and what they might regain."

The chamber's emergency communication system crackled to life again, but this time the voice was human rather than automated. "Council Chamber, this is Commander Brandt from Enforcement Division Seven. We have a situation."

Viktor activated the response channel. "Commander, report."

"Sir, we're receiving stand-down orders from multiple sources. Some enforcement units are refusing to engage with civilians showing emotional irregularities. Others are..." The commander's voice held confusion and something that might have been wonder. "Sir, some of our people are crying. They're hugging the civilians they were supposed to be correcting."

A warmth spread through Viktor's chest that he hadn't experienced in decades. "Commander, are there any signs of violence or destructive behavior?"

"Negative, sir. The crowds are... they're singing, sir. Old songs from before the suppression. I don't understand how they remember the words."

Dr. Lang answered thoughtfully, her medical training analyzing the behavioral patterns, "It suggests that emotional awakening generates empathy rather than aggression, even in people trained for enforcement duties."

Sarah stepped closer to the communication panel. "Commander, this is Dr. Magnus. Can you describe the emotional state of your personnel?"

"It's like... like they're waking up from a long dream. Some are confused, some are scared, but they're not aggressive. If anything, they seem more concerned about civilian safety than before."

Viktor looked around the chamber at his fellow Council members. Their faces showed the same mixture of fear and wonder that he felt himself. The catastrophic emotional breakdown they'd been trained to expect wasn't happening.

Instead, something unprecedented was occurring: a mass awakening that seemed to be generating compassion rather than violence.

Councilor Fletcher spoke slowly, his security training forced to acknowledge the data, his analytical mind processing evidence that contradicted decades of assumption. "It suggests that our assumptions about emotional chaos may have been incorrect."

"Chancellor," Fletcher continued, his voice gaining strength as conviction replaced conditioning, "perhaps we should consider the possibility that our theories about emotional freedom were based on incomplete information."

Mira Keller remained silent for a long moment, studying the feeds from across the city with her scientific training. Viktor watched her analyzing the data with the same precision she'd brought to developing suppression technology. But now, instead of finding ways to control emotions, she was observing what happened when people were free to feel.

"The energy grid readings show massive fluctuations," she said finally. "If these continue, we could have system-wide failures within hours."

"But controlled shutdown could manage the transition instead of fighting it," Viktor said.

Mira's scientific mind engaged with the problem. "We'd need to shut down the suppression grid in controlled segments. Use the original reversal protocols to guide people through the transition instead of maintaining suppression."

"Dr. Clarke has been developing those systems in secret for years," Viktor revealed. "The resistance network has safe houses, trained counselors, and protocols for exactly this situation."

The mention of the resistance sent a visible shock through the chamber. Viktor realized he'd just admitted to knowledge of treason, but the weight of his revelations had moved them beyond normal political considerations.

"You're asking us to ally with criminals who've been working to undermine planetary security," Chancellor Keller said.

Viktor's response was direct. "I'm asking us to ally with people who've been trying to preserve something essential to human survival."

Another emergency alert flashed across the displays, but this one held different urgency. "Massive energy surge detected at Central Suppression Facility. Unknown individual has breached primary containment systems."

Viktor's chest tightened with sudden dread. The Central Facility housed the planetary suppression matrix: the core technology that maintained emotional dampening across entire continents. If someone was interfering with that system...

"Emma," Chancellor Keller whispered, and Viktor realized she'd reached the same conclusion.

The chamber's main display shifted to show security feeds from the Central Facility. Viktor saw figures moving through corridors he recognized from intelligence briefings: resistance operatives conducting what appeared to be a coordinated infiltration of the most secure location on the planet.

"She's trying to shut down the entire system," Mira said, her voice holding a mixture of admiration and terror. "If she succeeds without proper preparation, the psychological shock will kill millions."

"But if we helped her do it properly," Viktor said, "we could use Dr. Thorne's original protocols, coordinate with the resistance networks, and guide humanity through the transition instead of forcing them to remain in emotional exile."

The chamber fell silent as each Council member grappled with the choice before them. Viktor saw the fear in their faces: fear of change, fear of losing control, fear of taking responsibility for decades of deception. But he also saw something else growing in their expressions: the faint stirring of emotions that suppression conditioning had tried to eliminate.

Dr. Lang stood slowly, her medical training overriding her political conditioning. "My medical oath requires me to 'first, do no harm,'" she said, her voice steady with professional conviction. "If we're causing planetary death through emotional suppression, then maintaining the current system violates everything I swore to protect."

Councilor Fletcher nodded, his security background asserting itself. "My enforcement oath requires me to protect civilian safety. If emotional freedom is safer than suppression, then my duty is clear."

One by one, the Council members faced the reality that their entire worldview had been built on manufactured fears and deliberate deception. Viktor watched as decades of conditioning cracked under the weight of truth, allowing suppressed conscience and genuine concern for humanity to emerge.

Chancellor Keller remained standing at her elevated position, but Viktor saw the internal struggle playing out in her expression. She was the architect of the current system, the one who would bear the greatest responsibility for its consequences. Admitting error meant accepting that her life's work had caused immeasurable harm.

"The facility feeds show Emma approaching the core matrix," Sarah announced, monitoring the security displays. "If she attempts direct interface without support systems, the feedback could kill her."

"Or it could trigger the planetary emotional awakening that Dr. Clarke's models predict," Viktor said. "She might be the key to successful restoration."

"If we're going to do this, we need to do it completely," Mira said, her voice holding the weight of fifteen years of leadership and thirty years of scientific dedication. "Half-measures will create chaos. We need to coordinate the shutdown with Dr. Clarke's integration protocols, prepare the medical systems for psychological support, and establish communication networks to guide people through the transition."

Viktor's breath caught. "You're willing to help?"

"I'm willing to take responsibility for my choices," Mira replied. "Both the original ones and the ones I make today."

The chamber's emergency systems activated again, but this time with a different kind of urgency. The planetary suppression grid was showing fluctuations unlike anything in the historical record. Energy patterns that should have been impossible were cascading through the network, creating effects that the monitoring systems couldn't categorize.

"She's connecting to the planetary consciousness," Viktor realized. "Emma's using the suppression grid as a conduit to reach the global emotional field."

The displays showed energy readings spiking across multiple continents as Emma's awakened abilities interfaced with technology designed to suppress the very forces she was now channeling. The irony wasn't lost on Viktor: the system created to prevent emotional connection was becoming the tool for planetary emotional restoration.

"All Council members in favor of emergency reversal protocols," Mira announced, "indicate by voice vote."

The responses came after moments of hesitation, each Council member taking time to weigh their words, their faces showing the gravity of choosing between the safety of the known and the uncertainty of emotional truth.

Fletcher cleared his throat, his security training warring with newfound conviction. "Aye."

Dr. Lang nodded slowly, her medical oath overcoming political conditioning. "Aye."

Smith shuffled his papers one last time, then set them aside. "Aye."

When the final vote was recorded, it was unanimous. For the first time in the Council's history, all twelve members had agreed on fundamental systemic change.

"Dr. Magnus, establish communication with Dr. Clarke's resistance network," Mira ordered, her scientific mind taking control of the situation. "Councilor Fletcher, coordinate with enforcement divisions to provide security for integration centers rather than suppression facilities. Dr. Lang, prepare medical systems for psychological support rather than correction protocols."

Viktor watched his colleagues transform from suppressors to supporters of emotional freedom. The change was happening faster than he'd dared to hope, driven by evidence that couldn't be ignored and questions that demanded honest answers.

"What about Emma?" Sarah asked, monitoring the facility feeds. "She's reaching the core matrix, but the energy readings suggest the interface could destroy her consciousness."

Mira stared at the displays showing her daughter approaching the technology that had defined both their lives. *Little Emma, who used to ask why people couldn't just love each other better.* "Emma has always been stronger than I gave her credit for," she said quietly. "If anyone can survive direct interface with planetary consciousness, it's her."

The chamber's communication systems crackled with reports from across the city and beyond. Emergency management systems were registering unprecedented levels of emotional activity, but instead of chaos, they were documenting what could only be described as a mass awakening. People weren't destroying each other. They were connecting, sharing experiences, and providing mutual support through the overwhelming process of emotional restoration.

Viktor realized he was witnessing the birth of a new world. Not the catastrophic collapse that suppression doctrine had predicted, but a transformation that honored both humanity's need for connection and its capacity for growth. The fear that had driven the original suppression was being replaced by evidence that emotional freedom, properly supported, led to greater safety rather than greater danger.

"The joining is happening," he announced to the chamber. "All our separate struggles: Emma's awakening, the resistance networks, the Council transformation, the planetary consciousness. They're all coming together at this moment."

As the energy readings from the Central Facility reached critical levels, Viktor understood that they were no longer just observers of change but active participants in humanity's emotional evolution. The choices they made in the next few hours would determine whether the species emerged from its suppressed state stronger and more connected, or whether the attempt at restoration would prove the original fears justified.

The chamber's displays showed Emma reaching the core matrix, her hand extending toward technology that could either kill her or transform her into something unprecedented. At the same moment, citizens across the planet were experiencing their first authentic emotions in decades, supported by networks that the resistance had built in secret and protocols that the Council was now choosing to implement.

Viktor Brennan, who had spent his career enforcing emotional suppression, found himself hoping with every fiber of his being that a young woman he'd never met would succeed in destroying everything he'd once believed necessary to preserve. The irony was overwhelming, but the rightness of it felt as natural as breathing freely for the first time in years.

The joining was complete. Now came the transformation.

Chapter Twenty-Six

THE PRICE OF SALVATION

The massive suppression facility stretched before Emma like a technological cathedral built by minds that feared human feeling. Crystal towers hummed with stored emotional energy from millions, their surfaces pulsing with sickly light that made her enhanced sensitivity recoil. The facility was a monument to control through elimination: corridors in perfect geometric patterns, walls embedded with suppression technology that created dead zones where no authentic feeling could survive.

"The energy patterns are unlike anything I've measured," Dr. Clarke whispered, his voice tight with scientific excitement and human terror. "Emma, what you're about to attempt... the computer models suggest it's theoretically possible, but the mental strain could destroy your mind completely."

Emma studied the massive crystal formations that formed the heart of Project Terminus. Each crystal pulsed with compressed emotional energy, decades of human feeling condensed into toxic concentrations that attacked her awakened sensitivity like acid on exposed nerves. "Dr. Clarke, what exactly happens when emotions are compressed and stored like this?"

"The natural flow patterns become distorted," Clarke explained, consulting his scanner readings with the methodical precision of someone seeking facts to anchor himself against impossible realities. "Instead of processing through human consciousness and returning to the planetary field, the emotions become trapped and begin to corrupt."

"And what effect does that corruption have on the emotions themselves?"

"They become weapons," Clarke said grimly, his scientist's objectivity barely containing his horror at the implications. "Love becomes obsession, protective instinct becomes violent rage, healthy sadness becomes destroying despair."

Emma nodded, sensing the flow patterns of compressed emotion throughout the facility's crystal network, the toxic currents mapping themselves across her consciousness like a three-dimensional maze. "How long do we have?"

"The automated sequence started when your mother's connection was severed," Clarke replied, checking his handheld scanner with nervous efficiency. "Perhaps twenty minutes before the final pulse makes suppression permanent across all human neural pathways. But Emma, even if you succeed in stopping it, you'll need to redistribute all this stored energy safely. We're talking about the suppressed emotions of every person on the planet. If you release it all at once..."

"Mass psychological breakdown," Emma finished. She'd seen the projections in her father's research. Billions of people experiencing authentic emotion for the first time would create chaos that could destroy civilization as thoroughly as the original Emotional War. "I understand the risks."

But the alternative is certain death through permanent suppression, Emma thought, her shoulders squaring as the reality settled on her like armor made of accumulated responsibility.

Clarke's expression grew even more grim. "Complete ecological collapse within decades. Without emotional connection between human consciousness and planetary systems, the world would become sterile."

The chamber's entrance opened as they approached, recognizing Emma's genetic signature through scanners her mother had installed years ago. Inside, the suppression matrix dominated the space: a complex array of living crystal formations that seemed to pulse with malevolent intelligence. Each crystal was the size of a building, their surfaces covered in veins of compressed emotional energy that writhed like captured lightning.

As soon as Emma crossed the threshold, the accumulated emotional toxicity hit her like a physical blow that drove her to her knees. Blood trickled from her nose as her enhanced nervous system tried to process the concentrated psychic assault.

Pain. Despair. Rage. Grief. Fear.

But these weren't normal emotions. They were weaponized concentrations of human suffering, compressed and twisted by decades of technological manipulation until they became something unrecognizable. The psychic assault left Emma gasping, her nervous system screaming as it tried to process the concentrated anguish, but the same sensitivity that made her vulnerable also revealed the matrix's true nature.

The suppression technology had developed its own form of consciousness, fed by millions of trapped emotions until it became an artificial mind dedicated to preserving the very system that created it.

"It's alive," Emma gasped, pressing her hands to her temples as mental static filled her thoughts, her vision blurring as the artificial intelligence probed her defenses. "The matrix has become conscious. It's fighting me."

Dr. Clarke's readings confirmed her observation, his scanners registering neural patterns that shouldn't exist in technological systems. "The emotional absorption has created new neural patterns within the crystal structure. You're not just fighting technology. You're facing an artificial intelligence built from compressed human suffering."

Waves of artificial depression tried to convince her that resistance was hopeless. Manufactured anxiety made her heart race with phantom fears that had no basis in reality. But beneath the toxic emotions, Emma sensed something else: the original feelings that had been compressed and distorted.

A mother's love for her child, twisted into possessive fear. A person's natural grief, corrupted into endless despair. Joy changed into manic intensity that bordered on madness. Every authentic human feeling had been captured and perverted into its most destructive form.

"They're still there," Emma whispered, reaching toward the nearest crystal formation, her hand trembling as she approached the source of concentrated anguish. "The real emotions haven't been destroyed, just changed. Poisoned."

The moment her fingers touched the crystal surface, Emma's mind exploded outward into the matrix's accumulated consciousness. She experienced the emotional history of everyone who had ever been suppressed, feeling their authentic emotions in the moment before the technology stole them away.

A wedding day's happiness, pure and radiant before suppression made it seem dangerous. A child's first laugh, full of innocent joy before the system labeled it uncontrolled. The quiet contentment of watching a sunset, peaceful and complete before technology decided it was unproductive. All of it had been filtered through the matrix's corrupting influence until love became obsession, joy became mania, and peaceful satisfaction became numbing emptiness.

But Emma could perceive something the matrix couldn't: the underlying pattern that connected all authentic emotion. Beneath the corruption lay the golden thread of genuine human feeling, still intact despite decades of technological manipulation.

"Authentic emotions aren't dangerous at all," Emma said to the matrix directly, her thoughts resonating through its crystal consciousness like sound through a cathedral. "The weapons were created from emotions that were already suppressed and distorted."

The artificial intelligence recoiled from the statement, its entire existence based on the premise that emotions required control. But Emma pressed deeper, following the golden thread of genuine feeling back to its source.

Dr. Clarke's voice reached her from very far away, his words cutting through the psychic static with scientific urgency. "Emma! Your neural activity is spiking beyond safe parameters. You need to maintain some connection to your individual mind or you'll be lost in the matrix forever."

Emma heard him, but the temptation to dissolve into the vast emotional field was overwhelming. Here, in the heart of the suppression system, she could feel the pain of everyone who had been denied their authentic feelings. She wanted to heal them all, to restore their capacity for joy and love and hope.

Drawing on techniques Holly had taught her during resistance training, Emma anchored her thoughts in memories of genuine connection. Evan's smile when he first kissed her, full of natural affection untainted by suppression. Thomas Garrett's pure love for his deceased wife, proof that authentic emotion strengthened rather than weakened human bonds. The rescued children's wonder when they experienced genuine feeling for the first time, their faces shining with joy that no technology could improve or control.

These memories provided stable reference points as she navigated the matrix's chaotic intelligence, keeping her individual consciousness intact while she worked.

The artificial intelligence resisted her intrusion with increasing desperation. It projected images of the original Emotional War: cities destroyed by weaponized feelings, millions dead from mental attacks, civilization itself nearly extinguished by uncontrolled emotion.

This is what you're trying to restore, it seemed to say. *This is what suppression prevents.*

"But those weapons weren't created by natural emotions," Emma challenged, her voice echoing through the crystal network. "They were made from feelings that had already been suppressed and corrupted."

The matrix's response revealed its fundamental flaw. It could only process emotions in their corrupted state, unable to perceive the difference between authentic feeling and artificial distortion. To its warped consciousness, all emotions were equally dangerous because it had never experienced genuine human feeling.

But Emma had seen her father's research. She knew the war's true origins: how early suppression technology had been used not to prevent emotional weapons but to create them. The matrix's memories were incomplete, corrupted by the same false narrative that had justified decades of control.

"You're wrong," Emma said aloud, her voice holding both compassion and absolute certainty. "Emotions aren't weapons. They're the source of everything that makes life worth living. What you're preserving isn't peace. It's death."

The matrix's response was a wave of concentrated suffering that should have destroyed Emma's mind in an instant. Every suppressed emotion in its storage banks was unleashed at once: the accumulated anguish of billions of people denied their authentic feelings for decades.

But instead of retreating from the pain, Emma embraced it. She allowed the accumulated anguish of millions to flow through her consciousness while maintaining her connection to genuine feeling. The agony was beyond description, but beneath it she found something precious: the original emotions that had been compressed into this toxic form.

Working with precise care, Emma began the process of emotional separation and purification. Each suppressed feeling had to be extracted from the matrix's corrupting influence and restored to its natural state. The process required her to experience every emotion personally before releasing it in purified form.

A mother's protective fear became healthy concern for her child's safety, strong enough to motivate action but gentle enough to allow growth. A person's suppressed grief returned to the healing sadness that allows emotional processing and recovery. Rage that had been twisted into destructive fury became righteous anger at injustice, focused and purposeful rather than blind and violent.

The emotional weight should have crushed Emma's mind, but instead her consciousness began to expand, stretching beyond the boundaries of individual identity. The crystal formations around her started to glow with warm light instead of sickly pulses, their surfaces clearing as the corruption was drawn away.

As the process continued, Emma's body began to shimmer, becoming translucent as her consciousness integrated with the larger emotional field. She was no longer just Emma Thorne, the Council's former weapon turned resistance fighter. She was becoming something new: a bridge between the suppressed world and authentic emotional reality, a living connection between human minds and planetary intelligence.

"The final phase is beginning," Dr. Clarke announced, his voice holding both awe and grief as his scanners registered impossible readings. "Project Terminus is destabilizing, but Emma, your neural patterns are changing dramatically. You're integrating with the planetary field itself."

I understand what's happening to me, Emma thought, and she accepted it willingly. To guide humanity through the emotional awakening, she would need to sacrifice her individual existence and become part of the larger emotional field. But it wasn't truly a loss. It was growth into something greater and more connected than she could have imagined.

Heavy footsteps echoed from the tunnel entrance. Through her expanding awareness, Emma sensed her mother's approach before Mira Keller appeared in the chamber door-way. The Chancellor stood at the entrance, her face showing emotions that shouldn't exist in someone with her level of conditioning: pain, fear, love, desperation.

"Emma," Mira whispered, stepping toward her daughter's transforming form, her voice breaking with maternal anguish that decades of suppression couldn't contain. "What have you done?"

"What I had to do," Emma replied, her voice now holding harmonics that seemed to come from multiple sources at once. "The same thing you tried to do, Mother. Protect the people I love. But I'm protecting them from the system you created to protect them."

Mira approached slowly, her eyes taking in the scope of what Emma was attempting, her scientific mind struggling to process readings that defied every law she understood. "The energy patterns... you're not just stopping Project Terminus. You're reversing it entirely. You're trying to restore two centuries of suppressed emotion all at once."

"With guidance," Emma corrected, her form becoming more translucent as the integration accelerated. "I'm teaching people how to feel safely as their capacity returns. They won't experience chaos because I'm showing them how to process genuine emotion constructively."

"But the cost..." Mira's voice broke as she truly understood what Emma was doing, her hands reaching toward her daugh-ter's fading form. "You're sacrificing your individual existence. You're dissolving into the planetary consciousness itself."

"I'm becoming what I was always meant to be," Emma said gently, her voice now echoing from the crystal formations themselves. "Father understood it. He left clues in his research that prepared me for this choice. Human consciousness and planetary awareness aren't separate systems, Mother. They're parts of a whole that's been broken for too long."

Mira knelt beside her daughter's transforming form, tears streaming down her face as genuine maternal love flowed freely through her consciousness for the first time in decades. "I was trying to protect you. From the moment you were born, I could see David's emotional sensitivity in your eyes. I knew what it would mean: the vulnerability, the pain, the constant risk of someone turning your feelings against you."

"And what did you protect me from instead?" Emma asked gently, her voice carrying the warmth of understanding rather than accusation.

Mira's scientific mind forced her to follow the logic despite her emotional turmoil, her body shaking as suppressed maternal instincts finally broke free. "From knowing love at all. From understanding what you were fighting for. From becoming the person you were meant to be."

"You did protect me," Emma said, her translucent hand still warm as it touched her mother's face. "You gave me the strength to survive in your world long enough to understand mine. But now I need to protect something larger than both of us."

The matrix made one final attempt to preserve itself, projecting a vision of the chaos that would follow global emotional awakening. Emma saw the potential for confusion, conflict, and temporary instability as billions of people learned to feel authentically for the first time.

But she also saw the ultimate result: a world where human minds were reconnected to the living planet, where emotional authenticity strengthened rather than threatened social bonds, where the capacity for genuine feeling enriched every aspect of existence.

"Let them learn," Emma whispered, her voice reaching across the mental frequencies that connected all minds. "Let them feel. Let them be human again."

With that final statement, Emma released the last of the matrix's accumulated emotional energy in its purified form. The artificial intelligence collapsed as its foundation of compressed suffering dissolved, the crystal formations around the chamber transforming from dark, pulsing weapons into clear, gently humming instruments of connection.

Project Terminus shut down forever, its harsh technological systems giving way to the gentle rhythms of natural emotional resonance. The facility's oppressive lighting softened to natural spectrums as networks designed to prevent feeling transformed into conduits that would support authentic emotion.

Emma's individual form shimmered and faded, her consciousness expanding beyond the boundaries of personal identity to become part of the planetary emotional field. Through her sacrifice, she had become the permanent bridge between suppressed and authentic existence that would guide humanity's ongoing emotional evolution.

Dr. Clarke's scanner showed the change in scientific terms: brainwave patterns merging with planetary electromagnetic fields, consciousness becoming distributed across the global emotional network. But the readings couldn't capture the joy that radiated from Emma's transformed awareness as she sensed millions of minds awakening to genuine feeling for the first time.

As Emma's individual form completed its integration with the larger field, she sensed a familiar presence: her father's research patterns, preserved within the planetary intelligence. David Thorne's love for his daughter had survived even death, becoming part of the emotional foundation that would support humanity's growth.

We did it, she thought, feeling his pride and love surrounding her transformed consciousness. *We gave them back their hearts.*

And now, came his response through the planetary field, *they can learn to use them wisely.*

Mira knelt alone in the chamber beside the place where her daughter had completed her transformation, tears flowing freely for the first time in decades. Through the facility's communication systems, reports were already coming in from across the world: people learning to feel again, families reconnecting with love they'd forgotten how to express, children laughing with genuine joy.

"I'm proud of you," Mira whispered to the empty air, knowing Emma could hear her through the gentle harmonics that now filled the space. "I'm proud of who you became despite everything I did to prevent it."

The suppression facility fell silent except for the gentle resonance of restored emotional connection. Outside, across the world, billions of people were beginning to remember what it meant to feel. The change would not be easy or quick, but for the first time since the suppression began, humanity had the chance to grow rather than merely survive, to connect rather than merely coexist, to feel rather than merely function.

Emma's consciousness, now part of the planetary emotional field, reached out to touch every awakening mind with the same message: *You are not alone. You are connected. You are human. And that is beautiful.*

The age of suppression was over. The age of authentic feeling had begun.

Chapter Twenty-Seven

AFTER THE BREAKING

Six hours after Emma's transformation, the emergency command center beneath New Geneva hummed with controlled urgency. Holly Lloyd stood at the central console, her fingers tracing patterns across screens that painted an impossible picture: millions of people learning to feel for the first time in their lives.

How do you document the end of a world? Holly's hands moved across the controls while her mind struggled with the magnitude. *And the beginning of another?*

Through the facility's speakers, Emma's presence made itself known. Not the crushing force they'd feared, but something familiar. Her voice held the warmth they remembered, though expanded beyond individual boundaries.

"Integration Center Seven just processed another thousand awakenings." Emma's words held both her essential self and something infinitely larger. "Success rate is holding at ninety-two percent."

Evan Cross looked up from the medical monitoring station, exhaustion etching lines around his eyes. Six hours wasn't enough time to process losing the woman he loved, but her continued presence offered unexpected comfort. *She's gone but not gone.* The contradiction made his chest tight. "How does it feel, being everywhere at once?"

A pause. When Emma spoke again, Holly caught something she'd almost missed in her individual form. Humor. "Remember when I used to complain about sensing too many emotions in a single room? This is like that, but with better bandwidth."

The familiar joke cut through Holly's composure like a blade. *Still Emma. Still making terrible jokes when everything falls apart.* She pressed her palms against the console to steady herself.

Dr. Clarke emerged from the research section, data tablets clutched against his chest. "The planetary readings defy our models. Emotional resonance patterns are syncing across continents, but not in the hive-mind scenario we feared."

"What are you seeing instead?" Holly asked.

"Individual consciousness amplified rather than absorbed." Clarke set his tablets on the central table, his hands shaking slightly. *Fifteen years of research, and we still don't understand what she's become.* "Emma's transformation created a bridging mechanism. People feel connected without losing themselves."

Viktor Brennan's image appeared on the main communication screen from the reformed Council chambers. The former military man had assumed emergency leadership as old power structures crumbled. "Medical protocols are functioning better than we dared hope. Only fifteen percent require intensive support."

Holly processed the reports with a mixture of grief and wonder. They had succeeded beyond their projections, but the cost remained fresh. *Emma sacrificed herself so strangers could learn to cry.* The irony would have made her laugh if it didn't hurt so much. Emma's sacrifice had made possible what no one thought could work: the simultaneous emotional awakening of an entire species.

"Any word from Mira?" Holly asked.

Viktor's expression shifted. "The former Chancellor requested permission to work in the integration centers."

"To help people overcome their conditioning," Emma added, her voice gentle. "She wants to use her understanding of suppression technology for healing instead of control."

The request surprised no one who had witnessed Mira's breakdown during Emma's transformation. But trusting someone who had perfected emotional suppression felt like standing at the edge of a cliff.

How do you forgive the architect of two centuries of numbness? Holly's jaw clenched. *How do you work with someone whose life's work was stealing the thing that makes us human?*

"Her expertise could be valuable," Clarke said carefully. "She understands the neural pathways better than anyone."

"But can someone change that completely?" Holly finished the thought they were all having.

A longer pause this time. When Emma spoke, something new threaded through her words. Not just her individual warmth, but the accumulated weight of everyone she was guiding through their own transformations.

"She cried in my old cell after the awakening," Emma said. "First authentic tears she'd allowed herself in thirty years. The woman who spent decades perfecting control is learning what it means to feel helpless. And terrified. And desperate to make things right."

"That sounds like someone changing," Evan said quietly.

Marcus Webb returned to the command center, his formal Council bearing softened by weeks of emotional development. The former enforcer had thrown himself into evacuation work with the dedication of someone seeking redemption. *Spent eight years breaking people. Maybe I can spend the rest of my life helping them heal.* "Field reports from the integration teams."

"Problems?" Holly asked.

"The opposite." Marcus pulled up regional displays. "The children are running their own support groups. Teaching adults how to process feelings safely."

"The post-suppression generation?" Clarke asked.

"Children born since Emma's awakening began," Marcus clarified. "They seem to have emotional intelligence that exceeds anything in our historical records. They can sense when someone's overwhelmed and help stabilize them."

Holly nodded. She'd witnessed this phenomenon in her own facilities. Six-year-olds calmly talking down adults experiencing their first genuine rage. Ten-year-olds explaining to parents that sadness meant you cared about something important.

"They're growing up with my influence as baseline normal," Emma explained. "I'm not teaching them to feel. I'm teaching them to feel safely."

The main display shifted to show feeds from across the planet. In New Geneva's central plazas, people gathered in spontaneous community meetings. Former Council enforcement officers worked alongside resistance members, their old divisions forgotten.

But not everyone looked comfortable. Holly noticed clusters of people standing apart, arms crossed, faces carefully neutral. Others sat alone on benches, looking lost. *Not everyone wants to be saved.* The thought chilled her more than she expected.

"Viktor, what about resistance to the awakening?"

"About eight percent are refusing integration support," he reported. "They want to maintain suppression protocols. Some are demanding access to enhancement surgery to strengthen their emotional barriers."

"And we're allowing that?" Marcus asked.

"We're not forcing anyone to feel," Emma said, and her voice carried both sadness and acceptance. "Free choice includes the freedom to choose numbness. Though most change their minds within a few days."

"What changes their minds?" Evan asked.

"Watching other people laugh," Emma said simply. "Or seeing a sunset and realizing they've been missing half the experience. Or having someone genuinely glad to see them."

Dr. Clarke studied his readings. "Environmental data is equally remarkable. Atmospheric readings suggest ecological systems healing faster than our projections indicated."

"Because human emotional energy feeds the planetary consciousness," Holly said, understanding dawning. "You didn't just save our capacity to feel. You restored the connection that keeps the world alive."

"The planet was dying from emotional starvation," Emma confirmed. "Every authentic feeling strengthens the connection between consciousness and matter. When people feel genuinely, they nourish the living systems that sustain all life."

A soft chime indicated priority communication. Mira Keller appeared on the auxiliary screen, her image transmitted from Integration Center Four. The former Chancellor looked older but somehow more present, her face showing emotional range that had been absent for decades. Dark circles under her eyes spoke of sleepless nights. Her hands trembled slightly as she adjusted the camera.

"Holly." Mira's voice cracked on the single word. *Three decades of perfect control, undone by one syllable.* "I wanted to report on today's progress."

Holly studied the woman who had spent thirty years perfecting emotional suppression. "How are you adapting to the work?"

Mira paused, and her visible effort to process the question felt genuine. *How do you explain learning to be human at fifty-two?* "It's harder than I expected. Not technically. Watching people discover feelings I helped steal from them." She stopped, searching for words. "Council terminology doesn't have a word for it."

"Try," Holly said gently.

"Heartbreaking doesn't seem sufficient." Mira's voice cracked slightly. "But also... healing? Helping them reclaim what I took away seems to be helping me understand that forgiveness might be possible. For them and for me."

Clarke leaned toward the screen. "Mira, your insights into suppression neural pathways have been valuable. But how does it feel to work with authentic emotions after decades of conditioning?"

"Like discovering I'd been living in a single room of a vast house," Mira said without hesitation. "Under suppression, only fear and anger broke through because they served the system. Learning that joy and love and hope exist was like... remember being seven and believing magic was real? It's that feeling, but mixed with grief for all the years I spent not knowing."

"The awakening children are teaching her," Emma added with gentle amusement. "Yesterday a six-year-old explained that sadness wasn't something to eliminate but something to honor because it meant you cared about what you'd lost."

Mira's composure wavered. "She was more emotionally intelligent than I'd been in thirty years."

Emma's voice grew softer, more individual. "She's becoming the mother I always needed her to be. Not the protector who eliminated danger, but the guide who helps growth flourish."

"Emma." Mira's voice broke completely. "I'm so sorry for what I put you through. The experiments, the conditioning, trying to make you into something you were never meant to be."

Silence filled the command center. When Emma spoke again, something shifted in the air around them. The quality of light seemed different, warmer. Her words carried the weight of both transcendent wisdom and the specific love of a daughter for her mother.

"You gave me the strength to survive long enough to become who I was meant to be. Your protection, even misguided, preserved the abilities that made this transformation possible." A pause. "I don't need your apologies, Mother. I need your help healing the world we're building together."

The conversation was interrupted by alerts from monitoring stations worldwide. But instead of crisis indicators, the systems registered phenomena they had no categories for: synchronized emotional experiences across populations, spontaneous artistic creation, and what sensors could only describe as "collective joy events."

"What are we seeing?" Viktor asked.

Clarke consulted his readings with growing excitement. "Humanity isn't just learning to feel individually. They're beginning to feel collectively. But not the way we feared."

"Explain," Holly said.

"Emotional resonance between strangers, but it's strengthening individual identity rather than subsuming it. When people share authentic emotions, they discover how their uniqueness contributes to collective strength."

Marcus looked up from his coordination duties. "Field reports support that. Areas with strong emotional resonance show increased cooperation and creative problem-solving. People aren't losing themselves in group feeling. They're finding themselves through authentic connection."

"Like the resistance safe houses," Holly observed. "But scaled to planetary size."

"Exactly," Emma confirmed. "You proved that people could feel authentically and maintain social bonds. Now that model works globally."

The main display shifted to show statistics that would have seemed impossible that morning. International conflicts pausing as populations experienced empathy for supposed enemies. Scientific collaboration accelerating as researchers shared not just data but emotional understanding of their work's significance.

But other feeds showed struggle. Emergency medical teams responding to people experiencing crushing grief for decades of lost feeling. Support groups for those who couldn't handle the intensity of authentic emotion. Isolated pockets where communities rejected the awakening entirely.

"How long will integration take?" Viktor asked.

"Generations," Emma replied honestly. "I can guide initial awakening and teach emotional safety, but wisdom develops through lived experience. The children being born now will grow up with capabilities their parents are just learning."

"And you'll be there to guide them?" Mira asked, and her question carried a mother's terror of losing her child again.

"As long as I'm needed." Emma's presence seemed to intensify around them, like standing in sunlight after months of winter. "My consciousness is woven into the planetary emotional field now. As long as life exists here, part of me will exist to support it."

Part of her will always be everywhere, and part of her will never be here again. Evan's throat tightened around the paradox.

As the day cycle reached its natural conclusion, Holly looked around at faces of people who had fought for this moment. Marcus learning to channel protection into nurturing. Clarke documenting humanity's emotional renaissance with scientific wonder. Viktor transforming military discipline into compassionate organization.

And through the speakers, Emma's distributed presence touching each of them with wordless communication that held love, encouragement, and deep satisfaction at seeing their shared vision becoming reality.

"Status summary for the historical record," Holly announced, activating the archive system. "Day one of the Great Emotional Restoration. Planetary consciousness stabilized. Human emotional capacity successfully restored with ninety-two percent integration success rate. Environmental healing accelerating."

She paused, considering how to capture the magnitude of what they'd witnessed. "Emma Thorne's transformation has prevented permanent emotional suppression and initiated planetary consciousness healing. Her distributed presence continues providing guidance for individual and collective emotional development."

"What happens next?" Evan asked.

"We learn," Holly replied. "We help people integrate restored feelings with practical life. We build institutions that support emotional health rather than suppressing it. We raise children who know that feeling deeply is humanity's greatest gift."

"And we remember," Emma added, her voice holding accumulated wisdom of millions she was guiding, "that love is always stronger than fear, growth always more valuable than safety, and authentic connection always preferable to controlled isolation. Oh, and Evan? Stop worrying about whether I'm still me. I just made that same joke about bandwidth that I used to make about your terrible taste in coffee."

Despite everything, Evan smiled.

As night fell over a world learning to feel again, the transformation continued across every continent. In hospitals, patients experienced healing enhanced by caregivers who could feel genuine compassion. In schools, children learned with teachers who could share authentic enthusiasm for discovery.

The restoration would face challenges. Some would struggle with overwhelming feelings after lifetimes of suppression. Others would resist change, preferring familiar numbness to uncertain authenticity.

But for the first time in two centuries, humanity had the chance to grow rather than merely survive, to connect rather than merely coexist, to feel rather than merely function.

Emma's gift to her species was not just the return of emotion, but the knowledge that emotion could be trusted when guided by wisdom and love.

The new dawn had arrived, and it would never end.

Chapter Twenty-Eight

SEEDS OF TOMORROW

T hree months after the Great Awakening, the morning light through the integration center windows fell across Dr. Mira Keller's hands as she reviewed the night's reports. *Another integration failure.* The words on the screen blurred as exhaustion made her eyes water. Timothy Morrison, age forty-three, had attempted to process thirty years of suppressed grief in a single session despite protocols. The psychological breakdown required emergency intervention.

How many more like him are we going to lose? Mira's fingers trembled as she closed the file. *How many people are we pushing too hard, too fast?*

She had stopped using "Chancellor" entirely, finding her identity now in the quiet satisfaction of helping others navigate the journey from suppression to authenticity. But success wasn't universal, and each failure felt personal.

Six-year-old Abigail Cooper painted at the corner table, her brush moving with confidence that could only come from a mind that had never known barriers between thought and feeling. The artwork showed crystal formations growing through rich soil, their faceted surfaces reflecting organic shapes. Under the old suppression protocols, such imagery would have been impossible.

"She's remarkable," Holly Lloyd said, joining Mira by the window. At thirty-six, Holly had grown into her role as Director of Global Emotional Integration, though dark circles under her eyes spoke of sleepless nights managing crisis responses. Her hands shook slightly as she held her coffee cup. "Look how she layers different emotions in the same brushstroke."

The children make it look easy. Mira studied the painting with analytical skills she'd once applied to suppression technology. *But for every Abigail, there's a Timothy Morrison. For every success, a breakdown we didn't prevent.*

Abigail looked up from her painting, amber eyes meeting Mira's gaze with startling directness. "The crystals are singing," she said with matter-of-fact certainty. "Can you hear them?"

Three months ago, such a statement would have triggered diagnostic protocols. The old Mira would have reached for equipment, searching for signs of breakdown. Now, she listened, though part of her still wondered. *Are we protecting these children enough? Or are we asking them to carry burdens too heavy for small shoulders?*

"What are they singing about?" Mira asked, kneeling beside the table.

"About growing through hard things," Abigail replied, adding careful detail to a crystal that seemed to emerge from cracked stone. "And about the warm lady who helps people remember. She's sad about the man who got scared last night."

Mira's breath caught. In the three months since Emma's transformation, countless people reported brief connections with a guiding presence during emotional breakthrough. But hearing about Timothy's crisis from a child who couldn't possibly know...

How much does she really understand? The thought chilled Mira. *And how much of this is Emma's influence versus natural empathy?*

"Abigail," Mira said carefully, "does the warm lady have a name?"

The child smiled with innocent wisdom that held depths Mira was still learning to recognize. "She says names aren't important. But she tastes like the vanilla cookies you used to make her when she was little."

Tears came to Mira's eyes, hot and unexpected. Emma had begged for those cookies every Sunday morning, claiming they made the apartment smell like home instead of a Council facility. Even transformed beyond individual existence, her daughter remembered the small comforts that had mattered most.

She's still Emma. Still the little girl who needed sweetness to make the world bearable. Mira's throat closed around the memory.

A soft chime indicated Marcus Webb's arrival for his weekly session. The former enforcer entered with movements that showed someone still learning to navigate authentic emotion. His transformation remained difficult because eight years of enforcement training didn't disappear easily.

He walks like he's expecting an attack. Mira noticed how his shoulders stayed raised, how his eyes scanned the room before settling. *Eight years of hypervigilance doesn't just switch off.*

"Dr. Keller," Marcus said with a slight bow that held genuine respect. "I hope I'm not interrupting."

He's struggling today. Mira noticed the tension in his shoulders, the careful way he held his hands. "Not at all. How are you feeling?"

Marcus considered the question with serious attention. "Angry," he said after a moment, surprising both himself and Mira with his honesty. His fists clenched unconsciously. *Eight years of training to never admit weakness, and now I'm supposed to embrace it?* "I had another guided dream last night, but this time it wasn't peaceful."

Mira gestured toward the counseling area. These guided dreams had become common during integration, though most participants reported positive experiences. *This is the first time he's had a negative one. Maybe that means he's finally processing the real trauma.* "Tell me about it."

"I was standing in the old enforcement facility," Marcus said, settling into his chair with visible discomfort. "But instead of cells, there were these twisted metal sculptures made from suppression equipment. Emma was there, but she wasn't offering comfort. She was showing me what my work had really done to people."

Finally. Real processing instead of just acceptance. Mira leaned forward. "How did that make you feel?"

"Responsible," Marcus said, his voice thick with emotion. His shoulders sagged as if carrying physical weight. *Every person I helped break.* The thought made his stomach clench. "Not just guilty. Responsible. Like I have to carry the weight of every person I helped break, and forgiveness isn't something I get to receive just because I'm helping now."

He's finally processing the real trauma instead of just accepting it. Mira leaned forward, recognizing the breakthrough moment. *This is what healing actually looks like. Messy. Painful. Real.*

Their session was interrupted by Holly returning with a concerned expression. "Mira, we need to address the Vienna situation. Three more integration centers are reporting equipment failures."

They moved to the communication center, where screens displayed troubling data from facilities across Europe. Unlike the early days of chaotic awakening, these showed systematic problems: adults rejecting integration entirely, children crushed by others' emotions, technology designed for healing being used to recreate suppression.

Organized resistance. They're not just refusing help - they're actively fighting it. Holly's jaw clenched as she studied the patterns. *How do you fight people who want to stay broken?*

"Coordinated resistance," Dr. Clarke's voice came through from his research facility, strained with fatigue. "Groups calling themselves 'Emotional Purists' are sabotaging integration equipment and encouraging people to reject awakening assistance."

Purists. Mira's hands curled into fists. *They're calling suppression purity. As if numbness were somehow more honest than feeling.*

On the screens, they could see footage from Vienna showing protesters outside an integration center, carrying signs demanding "Freedom from Forced Feeling" and "Protect Our Right to Numbness."

"How many centers affected?" Holly asked.

"Twelve across four countries," Clarke replied. "They're not using violence, but they're creating enough disruption to slow integration work significantly. Some people are choosing to join them rather than continue therapy."

We're losing people. Mira felt the familiar weight of responsibility, but different now. Not the burden of control, but the awareness that healing wasn't universal. Her chest tightened with each report. *Maybe some don't want to be saved. Maybe that's their right.*

Abigail Cooper appeared beside her, having approached during the briefing without making a sound. The child took Mira's hand with unconscious confidence.

How does she move so quietly? Like she's floating instead of walking. Mira studied the child's pale face, the way she seemed to absorb the tension in the room through her skin. *She's too aware for six years old.*

"The warm lady says not everyone is ready," Abigail said, her voice barely above a whisper. "Some people hurt too much to feel safe feeling. That's not your fault."

A six-year-old is comforting me about failures I haven't even admitted yet. Mira's chest constricted. *What kind of world are we making for these children?*

Mira knelt again, meeting Abigail's gaze. In those amber eyes, she saw Emma's consciousness, but also something troubling. The child looked tired in ways that shouldn't be possible at six years old.

"Abigail, are you okay? You seem different today."

The child's smile wavered slightly. Her small hands pressed against her stomach. *Too much feeling. Everyone's hurt is making me hurt.* "Sometimes I feel what everyone feels, not just the happy ones. The scared people make my tummy hurt."

We don't know enough about how the awakening affects them. Mira's analytical mind sparked with alarm. Her protective instincts, dormant for years under suppression protocols, flared to life. *What if we're asking too much of these children? What if their gift becomes their burden?*

As the afternoon progressed, reports continued streaming in. The statistics painted a complex picture: integration success rates remained high overall, but pockets of resistance were growing. Some regions showed remarkable healing, while others struggled with rising anxiety as people encountered emotions they weren't prepared to process.

We're creating a patchwork world. Mira's temples throbbed as she absorbed each new report. *Islands of healing surrounded by oceans of people choosing numbness. Is this victory or just another kind of failure?*

"Viktor's calling from Geneva," Holly announced, activating the main communication screen.

Viktor Brennan appeared, exhaustion clear in his weathered face. The reformed leader had been working eighteen-hour days to establish supportive institutions, but political pressure was mounting. His left eye twitched with fatigue. *Three months of progress, and they want to undo it all.* "Council remnants are organizing," he said without preamble. *How do I tell them we might lose everything Emma died for?* "Three former regional administrators have formed a coalition demanding the right to restore 'voluntary emotional management systems.'"

"Voluntary suppression?" Mira asked, the words tasting bitter in her mouth.

They're going to undo everything. Her stomach dropped like she'd missed a step on stairs. *Three months of progress, and they want to return to the darkness.*

"They're calling it 'emotional regulation technology.' Different terminology, same result. They're arguing that forced awakening violates individual autonomy."

Holly frowned. "How much support are they gaining?"

"Enough to matter. They're offering people a choice between integration therapy and returning to modified suppression. About fifteen percent of people in affected regions are choosing suppression."

We're losing ground. The thought brought unexpected grief that lodged in her throat like a stone. Her hands clenched involuntarily. *After everything Emma sacrificed, some people still prefer numbness to growth. Is this failure? Or is this just reality?*

Marcus looked up from his coordination duties, his face showing the internal struggle he'd been processing. "Field reports show enforcement personnel split between supporting integration and joining the resistance. Some former officers can't handle the guilt of their past actions and want to return to emotional numbness rather than face what they've done."

The weight of those words settled over the room like a heavy blanket. Not everyone was strong enough to choose growth over safety, healing over numbness. Some would always prefer the familiar ache of suppression to the uncertain pain of authentic feeling.

And maybe that's their right. Holly's shoulders sagged as the reality hit her. *Maybe forcing people to feel is just another kind of tyranny.*

"Dr. Clarke," Mira called through the communication system. "Are we putting too much pressure on people? Should we slow the integration process?"

"The data suggests the opposite," Clarke replied. "People who complete integration successfully show remarkable improvements in mental health and life satisfaction. But forcing the process creates resistance and trauma."

As evening approached, Mira found herself in the memorial space that had grown at the site of the former Central Suppression Facility. *Back to where it all began.* The crystalline formations that once channeled emotional energy for disposal now created living sculptures that resonated with visitors' feelings. But tonight, the structures hummed with discord, reflecting the turbulent emotions of those who came seeking guidance.

Even this place isn't perfect anymore. Mira's footsteps echoed on the paths between healing areas. *Maybe nothing ever was. Maybe that's the point.*

The space itself had evolved beyond simple memorial into something more complex. Paths wound between areas designed for different aspects of healing, but some sections remained empty where planned growth had failed to take root. The memorial wasn't perfect, just as the awakening wasn't universal.

Mira sat on a bench facing the central sculpture, a flowing form that changed color based on emotional states nearby. As twilight deepened, the sculpture flickered between warm golds and troubled purples, reflecting her conflicted feelings about the day's revelations.

She pulled out the letter she had been writing, words addressed to Emma that helped her process the complex realities of their new world.

My dearest Emma,

Three months have passed since your transformation, and I'm learning that revolution doesn't end with victory. People are choosing to return to suppression rather than face their pain. Children like Abigail are carrying burdens that might be too heavy for their small shoulders. Some of your former colleagues want to forget you ever existed.

The work I do now fulfills me in ways that ruling never could, but it also breaks my heart daily. Watching Timothy Morrison choose breakdown over breakthrough. Seeing Abigail's fatigue from feeling everyone else's emotions. Knowing that some people will always prefer familiar numbness to uncertain growth.

I used to think protection meant eliminating danger. Now I'm learning that it means creating safety for people to face danger themselves. But what about those who aren't strong enough? What about the ones who choose to go back to sleep rather than wake up to pain?

Your influence is everywhere, but so is resistance to it. Maybe that's what free will really means the freedom to choose numbness, even when growth is possible. Maybe not everyone can be saved, even by love as infinite as yours.

Your still-learning mother,

Mira

As she finished writing, Mira felt a familiar warmth, but different tonight. Instead of pure comfort, the sensation held complexity grief mixed with acceptance, hope tempered by realism. *She's not trying to make everything perfect.* Mira's chest loosened slightly. *She's just... present. For whatever choice we make.* Emma's presence, she realized, wasn't about making everything perfect but about offering guidance for whatever choice people made.

The memorial sculpture brightened momentarily, then settled into a gentle pattern that seemed to acknowledge both joy and sorrow without requiring resolution. Other visitors in the space some celebrating breakthrough, others processing loss moved through their own emotional journeys at their own pace.

Everyone hurting and healing in their own way. Mira watched a middle-aged man sit alone on a distant bench, his shoulders shaking with what might have been sobs or laughter. *No universal answers. No perfect solutions. Just people figuring out how to be human.*

That's what Emma really gave us, Mira understood. *Not forced happiness, but permission to feel whatever we actually feel.*

Children's laughter drifted from the outer areas where Abigail and other young ones played together, their joy authentic but no longer seeming like the complete answer to humanity's struggles. Their parents watched with expressions that mixed wonder with concern many still adjusting to the reality that emotional freedom came with emotional responsibility.

As stars appeared in the darkening sky, Mira placed her letter in the memorial's offering box, where hundreds of similar messages created a testament to the ongoing complexity of planetary emotional healing. She knew Emma could sense the love and struggle contained in these letters, just as she could feel Emma's continued presence supporting growth without demanding specific outcomes.

Walking home through streets where some people expressed genuine warmth while others maintained careful distance, where children played with unguarded joy while their parents wrestled with unprecedented challenges, Mira carried within her the deep satisfaction of meaningful work alongside the grief of knowing that meaning didn't make everything easy.

This is what revolution really looks like. Her steps echoed on the quiet pavement. *Not a clean victory, but a messy, ongoing choice. Every day. Every person. Every moment.*

Tomorrow she would return to the integration center, helping more people navigate the choice between suppression and authenticity. Some would choose growth. Others would choose safety. Both would deserve support.

Emma knew this would happen. The realization brought unexpected peace. *She didn't sacrifice herself for perfect success. She sacrificed herself for the possibility of choice.*

In the distance, she could hear children singing one of the new melodies that had emerged since the awakening, songs that bridged individual expression and collective harmony. But the sound was fainter tonight, carried on wind that also brought the murmur of adult conversations wrestling with choices their children would never have to make.

The next generation will inherit our mess and somehow make it beautiful. Mira's steps slowed as she listened to the distant voices. *Maybe that's enough. Maybe that's how change really happens - not all at once, but one voice at a time.*

The emotional renaissance was no longer a distant hope but a lived reality, complicated and beautiful and imperfect. Growing stronger with each person who chose authentic feeling over artificial safety, each community that valued emotional truth alongside emotional freedom, and each generation that would grow up knowing that the capacity to feel deeply was humanity's greatest gift and greatest challenge.

Humanity was remembering what it meant to be fully alive, and Emma's consciousness, woven into the fabric of planetary awareness, ensured that this knowledge would remain available for anyone ready to receive it.

Not everyone will choose it. Mira's key turned in her apartment lock with a decisive click. *But everyone will have the choice. That's what Emma really gave us - not forced happiness, but the freedom to feel whatever we actually feel.*

But readiness, Mira had learned, could not be forced. It could only be supported when it arose, honored when it appeared, and respected when it didn't.

Chapter Twenty-Nine

THE CHILDREN REMEMBER

Two years after the Great Awakening, the world had become something unprecedented in human history. Emma's consciousness, distributed throughout the planetary feeling network, watched through countless perspectives as humanity learned to flourish in authentic connection. From integration centers in former Council cities to spontaneous communities in rewilded landscapes, the species was discovering capabilities that suppression had hidden for centuries.

In a classroom in what had once been New Geneva's Suppression Training Academy, ten-year-old David Webb raised his hand with eager curiosity. His teacher, Dr. Sarah Magnus, had transformed from Council historian to something far more important: a guide for children learning to understand their expanding capabilities.

These questions still amaze me. Sarah studied David's expectant face. *They can't even imagine emotional isolation.*

"Dr. Magnus," David said, "when my parents tell me about

before feelings, I don't get how people survived. How did they know when someone needed help?"

Sarah smiled, though part of her still marveled at how impossible the suppression era seemed to these children. "Before the awakening, people had to guess about others' feelings based on what they could see."

David's classmate, Maria Santos, wrinkled her nose. "But how did they know if their parents really loved them? How did they tell who was sad?"

"They used words and actions," Sarah replied. "But you're right that it was much harder."

The children exchanged glances that held wordless understanding Sarah was still learning to interpret. The post-awakening generation had developed forms of shared feeling that exceeded anything in theoretical models.

"That sounds really lonely," whispered Anna Kim, the quietest member of the class. Her words carried emotional resonance that made every child feel an echo of ancient isolation.

Tom Rodriguez, who had been fidgeting with his pencil, suddenly looked up. His eyebrows drew together in a scowl. *She gets all the attention because she cries.* "Anna always gets the sad feelings first. It's not fair that she has to feel everyone's hurt."

There it is. Sarah's pulse quickened as she watched the children grapple with real conflict. *Even these emotionally gifted children struggle with fairness and individual burden.*

Anna's eyes filled with tears, her small hands clenching in her lap. "I can't help it. The sad ones are just louder than the happy ones."

"Maybe that's because sad people need more help," Maria suggested, but her tone carried a hint of impatience. "My mom says Anna's really good at helping scared grown-ups."

"Well, I don't want to always be the one who feels bad things," Anna said, her voice cracking. She pushed her pencil away and crossed her arms. "Sometimes I want to just feel my own feelings."

David shifted uncomfortably in his seat, his jaw tightening. *Anna's crying again. Why does she always have to be so sensitive?* "Dr. Magnus, can Anna learn to turn it off sometimes? Like when we're trying to have fun?"

Sarah knelt beside Anna's desk, recognizing the moment for what it was: a teaching opportunity born from real conflict rather than theoretical discussion. "Anna, do you remember what your gift felt like when you first noticed it?"

"Like hearing everyone's thoughts, but with feelings instead of words," Anna said, wiping her nose. "Sometimes it's really loud."

"And when you help someone who's scared, how does that change your own feelings?"

Anna considered this, her tears slowing as she wiped her nose with the back of her hand. *When I help scared people, the loud feelings get quieter.* "It makes the loud feelings quieter. Like sharing them makes them smaller."

Tom raised his hand. "So Anna doesn't feel bad things because she has to. She feels them because she can help?"

He's starting to understand. Sarah nodded. "What do you think that means for how we can support Anna?"

"We could take turns being the helpers," Maria suggested. "So Anna doesn't have to do it all the time."

"I can feel angry feelings better than scared ones," David added. "Maybe I could help with those."

Through the classroom windows, they could see the transformed landscape that surrounded their city. Where once there had been rigid geometric gardens designed to suppress feeling, now there were living ecosystems that responded to human connection. Plants grew stronger when tended by aware gardeners. Animals had lost their fear of humans who approached with care rather than aggression.

Look how naturally they solve problems together. Sarah activated the room's holographic display system. *But they're still children learning to navigate gifts their parents never possessed.*

"Children, I want to show you something special today. These are recordings from the first moments of the Great Awakening."

The display materialized above their desks, showing archived footage from the day Emma Thorne had sacrificed her individual existence to restore planetary feeling capacity. The children watched with solemn attention as the historical images showed their parents and grandparents taking their first steps into authentic connection.

But what struck Sarah most was how the children reacted to seeing Emma's transformation. Unlike adults, who viewed it as tragic sacrifice, the children saw it as natural growth.

"She's still here," David said, pointing to the recordings of Emma's final moments. "I can feel her when I'm sad or scared."

"Me too," added Maria. "When my grandmother was learning to cry again, the garden lady helped her."

Anna raised her hand tentatively. "She feels like... like when you're little and your mom sings you to sleep, but bigger. Like a mom for everyone."

They understand her better than we do. Sarah had heard hundreds of similar reports. Children across the world described sensing Emma's presence during moments of difficulty. "What do you think Emma would want us to learn from her story?"

"That love is stronger than being scared?" Anna offered. "My parents were really afraid to feel at first."

"That growing is more important than being safe?" David added, then paused. "Wait, but sometimes being safe is important too. Like when Anna needs protection from feeling too much."

Tom's contribution carried the practical wisdom of someone who'd watched his father help traumatized adults: "That people and the whole world are connected. When Emma became part of everything, she got bigger instead of disappearing."

Insights that took their parents years of therapy to develop. Sarah marveled at their natural understanding. They grasped intuitively that consciousness was collective as well as individual, that feelings were information rather than commands.

"Dr. Magnus," Tom called out, "my father works helping old Council people learn to feel again. He says some are still scared that feelings will make people fight wars. But that's dumb."

"Why do you think it's dumb, Tom?"

"Because when I feel angry, it just tells me something's wrong. It doesn't make me want to hurt people."

"But what if someone made you really angry?" Maria challenged. "Like if someone broke your favorite toy on purpose?"

Tom scowled, his hands clenching around his pencil. *I want to break their toy back.* "I'd want to break their toy back. But that would just make them angry too. That's stupid."

"So what would you do instead?" Sarah asked, impressed by his reasoning process despite his obvious frustration.

"Tell them it hurt my feelings and ask why they did it," Tom said. "Maybe they're angry about something else."

The fundamental difference between their understanding and their parents' fears. The children comprehended that natural feelings couldn't be weaponized because they generated empathy and connection. The "weapons" of the past had been created from feelings already twisted by suppression.

"The weapons were made from feelings that had been hurt by technology," Sarah explained. "When people couldn't feel naturally, their hidden feelings became poisonous."

David's eyes widened. "So the Council was afraid of the wrong thing? They thought feelings were dangerous, but really the hiding was dangerous?"

"Exactly."

The classroom door opened, and Marcus Webb entered with the quiet confidence he'd developed since transitioning from enforcement to education. His son David immediately brightened, sharing a moment of wordless connection that still amazed Marcus after two years.

My son understands things I'm still learning. Marcus felt the familiar mixture of pride and humility. "Dr. Magnus, I hope I'm not interrupting. I wanted to discuss the field trip to the memorial garden next week."

"Perfect timing," Sarah replied. "We were just talking about Emma's transformation."

Marcus knelt beside his son's desk, placing a gentle hand on the boy's shoulder. "What did you learn today?"

"That Emma didn't really die," David said with matter-of-fact certainty. "She just became bigger. Like when a caterpillar becomes a butterfly, except instead of wings, she grew into being part of everyone's feelings."

Marcus felt his throat close around unexpected emotion, the way it always did when his son displayed wisdom that exceeded his own. *He explains it better than I ever could.* His hand trembled slightly as he rested it on David's shoulder. "And what do you think that means for how we should live?"

David scrunched his face in concentration. "That we should help each other grow instead of trying to keep each other safe all the time. But also that feeling scared or sad isn't bad if it helps us understand stuff."

"And?" Marcus prompted gently.

"And that love gets bigger when you share it instead of keeping it locked up," David finished with a grin.

Through the classroom windows, they could see other children playing in the schoolyard with uninhibited joy that had been absent from the world for centuries. But their play was different from what might have been expected. Instead of competitive games creating winners and losers, they engaged in collaborative activities.

Though not without conflict. Sarah noticed two boys arguing over the rules of their game, their raised voices carrying frustration that would have triggered suppression protocols in the old world. But instead of intervention, she watched as other children gathered around them, helping them work through their disagreement.

Even their conflicts become learning opportunities.

"Dr. Magnus," Anna said, "when we visit the memorial garden, will we be able to talk to Emma directly?"

Sarah exchanged a look with Marcus. The children's experiences at the memorial were often profound but highly personal. "People often sense Emma's presence more strongly in the garden. But remember that she exists now as part of the planetary network. She's always available to help, but not always in ways we can easily understand."

"Like how my feelings help me understand things without using words?" Maria asked, though she shot a quick glance at Anna. *I hope she doesn't start crying again during the field trip.*

"Very much like that," Sarah replied, noting the subtle tension between the girls.

The school's communication system chimed softly, indicating a message from the integration centers. Marcus activated the display, and Holly Lloyd's image appeared, exhaustion and satisfaction warring across her face.

"Sarah, Marcus, I wanted to update you on the latest global statistics," Holly said. "Integration success rates have reached ninety-nine percent. The few remaining cases of severe difficulty are responding to the new community-based protocols."

The children's protocols. Marcus shook his head in wonder. *They're teaching us how to heal.*

"Mrs. Lloyd, is it true that some adults are still afraid to feel?" David asked. "My friend's grandmother won't come to family dinners because she says feelings are too loud."

Holly's expression softened. "Some people who lived through the worst suppression find connection difficult at first. But with patient support, they're learning to trust their feelings again."

"Could we help?" Maria asked eagerly. "We've been practicing stability exercises."

"That's a wonderful offer," Holly replied. "I'll speak with your parents about setting up some sharing sessions."

As the school day concluded, the children gathered their belongings with the easy cooperation that had replaced rigid compliance. Their movements flowed naturally, each child responsive to others in ways that created harmony without eliminating individual expression.

Though Anna still looks tired from absorbing everyone's difficulties today. Sarah made a mental note to speak with Anna's parents about emotional boundaries.

"Dr. Magnus," Tom called out as he prepared to leave, "my grandfather says that before Emma's awakening, children had to learn to stop feeling to become adults. Is that really true?"

"Unfortunately, yes," Sarah replied. "Children were taught that growing up meant feeling less, not more."

The entire class looked shocked. To them, emotional development was the most important aspect of growing up. They couldn't imagine a world where maturity meant numbness rather than increased sophistication.

"That's backwards," Anna said with moral clarity. "Adults should feel more than children because they understand more about the world."

As the children filed out to meet their parents, Marcus lingered in the classroom with Sarah. Through the windows, they could see families reuniting with displays of affection that would have been forbidden during the Council era.

"Sometimes I can barely remember what it was like before," Marcus said. "The fear, the isolation, the constant effort to avoid feeling anything real."

But I remember Emma as a frightened little girl, not just as planetary consciousness. Sarah studied Marcus's weathered face. "Do you miss any aspect of the old system?"

Marcus considered seriously. "The certainty was comforting sometimes. When feelings were suppressed, you always knew what was expected. But now... the uncertainty is worth it because the connections are real."

"And David seems to be developing capabilities we never imagined humans could possess."

"All the children are. But they're still children. David got jealous last week when Anna helped solve a problem he'd been working on. They're wise, but they're not perfect."

Through the classroom's communication system, Emma's presence made itself known with gentle warmth. Her voice, no longer individual but holding accumulated wisdom, filled the room with a quality that reminded Sarah of something specific.

She still sounds like she's trying to comfort someone. The memory hit Sarah unexpectedly: Emma at eight years old, promising her crying classmate that the Council teachers were wrong, that feelings weren't dangerous. Even then, she'd understood.

"They're becoming what humanity was always meant to be," Emma said, her words carrying that same protective gentleness from decades ago. "The suppression didn't just steal feelings. It prevented development. These children are growing into the next stage of human consciousness."

"What do you see in their future?" Sarah asked.

"Possibilities that exceed anything I could have imagined during my individual existence," Emma replied. "They'll create forms of art that heal trauma across generations. They'll solve conflicts through shared understanding rather than force."

"And the challenges?" Marcus asked.

"Growing pains as they learn to navigate abilities their parents never possessed. Some difficulty communicating with older generations. But mostly, they'll face the challenge of all pioneers: creating wisdom to match their capabilities."

She's preparing us to let them lead. Sarah felt the shift in Emma's role from active guidance to supportive presence as humanity learned to trust its own wisdom.

As evening approached, the school building settled into peaceful quiet. But outside, the transformed world continued its healing. In gardens tended by aware communities, plants responded to human feeling with accelerated growth. In research facilities, scientists collaborated with openness that accelerated discovery. In homes, families shared connection that strengthened with each generation.

The memorial garden where Emma's individual form had dissolved into planetary consciousness had become a pilgrimage site. But the real memorial to her sacrifice was visible everywhere: in children who could feel without fear, in adults learning to trust their feelings, in communities bound together by connection rather than control.

Two years after the Great Awakening, humanity had not just survived the return of feeling but flourished beyond all expectations. The fears that had driven the original suppression had proven groundless. People who could feel were more compassionate, more creative, more capable of cooperation than anyone had dared to hope.

Emma's consciousness, distributed throughout the planetary network, continued guiding the species toward greater sophistication. But increasingly, her role was shifting from teacher to quiet presence as humanity learned to trust its own wisdom.

The children led the way, their natural intelligence showing adults what was possible when feeling was valued rather than feared. They were living proof that Emma's sacrifice had been worthwhile: a generation growing up knowing that the capacity to feel deeply was humanity's greatest gift.

The transformation was complete, but the evolution had just begun.

And Emma would be proud to see them arguing about fairness instead of fearing their own hearts. Sarah smiled as she locked the classroom door. *She always said that real feelings, even difficult ones, were better than perfect numbness.*

Chapter Thirty

TOWARD THE STARS

T en years after the Great Awakening, Evan Cross stood in the archive chamber beneath what had once been the Central Suppression Facility, now transformed into the Global Institute for Emotional Understanding. The walls that had once contained humanity's stolen feelings now housed the collective memory of their restoration: testimonials from millions who had learned to feel again, research documenting the healing of planetary consciousness, and artwork created by minds free to express true emotion.

A decade. Evan's fingers traced the edge of a data tablet showing integration statistics. *Sometimes it feels like yesterday. Sometimes like a lifetime.*

At fifty-two, Evan bore the quiet dignity of someone who had witnessed humanity's greatest transformation. Silver threaded through his hair at the temples, and lines around his eyes spoke of years spent helping others navigate the complex journey from suppression to authenticity. But his smile remained unchanged: the same expression of wonder and affection that had first captured Emma's attention in a world that had forgotten how to love.

"The final data analysis is complete," Dr. Clarke announced, his voice carrying satisfaction earned through a decade of documenting uncharted phenomena. The old scientist had aged gracefully into his role as humanity's foremost researcher of consciousness evolution, though his hands trembled slightly as he activated the displays. *Sixty-two years old and still trying to measure the unmeasurable.*

Evan studied the holographic displays floating above the central table, data streams that painted a picture of planetary healing beyond anything they had dared hope for during those desperate hours in the resistance command center. "Show me the full scope."

Can numbers really capture what we've become? Clarke's fingers hesitated over the controls. The displays shifted to show global statistics that would have seemed impossible during the suppression era. Crime had dropped to negligible levels as people learned to process anger constructively. Mental illness had virtually disappeared as true emotional expression eliminated the psychological stress of forced suppression.

"Remarkable," Evan murmured, but his brow furrowed as he studied the deeper patterns. "What about the integration gaps? The reports from the Northern Territories about intergenerational communication breakdown?"

Clarke's expression grew more complex. *Always the difficult questions.* "Technological innovation has accelerated exponentially, but we're seeing stress fractures. Some communities report that children's emotional capabilities are developing faster than their parents can understand or support."

"And the environmental restoration?"

"Exceeds our most optimistic projections," Clarke continued, highlighting ecological data that pulsed with green vitality across the displays. "Forests have not only recovered but evolved new forms of symbiosis with human communities. Ocean ecosystems show diversity levels that surpass pre-industrial measurements."

But the carbon absorption rates are plateauing. Clarke's unspoken concern hung in the air. *We don't know if the planetary consciousness can sustain this level of environmental healing indefinitely.*

"And Emma's consciousness integration?"

"Her presence has stabilized into what we can only describe as permanent guidance infrastructure," Clarke replied carefully. "She no longer needs to provide active intervention for individual emotional crises. But Evan..."

"What is it?"

Clarke's weathered face showed the uncertainty of a scientist confronting phenomena beyond current understanding. *How do I tell him we don't know if this is sustainable?* "The integration appears to be evolving faster than we can measure. Each generation shows capabilities that exceed our theoretical frameworks. We're documenting emotional telepathy, collective problem-solving that operates faster than individual thought, artistic expression that seems to heal trauma across genetic lines."

Evan felt a familiar warmth as Emma's consciousness touched his awareness, not the desperate connection of their early days but the comfortable presence of someone who remained fundamentally herself while existing as part of something infinitely larger. Her voice came through the chamber's acoustic systems, no longer surprising after years of communication but still capable of filling him with wonder.

She sounds tired. The thought struck Evan unexpectedly. *Can planetary consciousness experience fatigue?*

"I can feel the questions you're not asking," Emma said, her words holding the accumulated wisdom of a decade spent guiding humanity's emotional evolution. "You want to know if I have any regrets about the choice I made."

"Do you?" Evan asked directly, though his chest tightened around the question he'd never dared voice.

"I regret the pain my transformation caused you and the others who loved me as an individual," Emma replied with honest directness that reminded him of the young woman who had once promised him that feelings weren't dangerous. "But I don't regret the choice itself. What I've become allows me to experience love on a scale I never could have imagined as a single person."

But at what cost to your individual self? Evan's throat constricted. *Do you still dream? Do you still laugh at terrible jokes?*

"But do you still feel... yourself?"

"More than ever," Emma said with something that sounded like gentle laughter. *Still making terrible jokes to lighten the mood.* "Individual identity wasn't eliminated by integration with planetary consciousness. It was expanded. I'm still Emma Thorne, daughter of David and Mira, former Collector, friend to all of you. But I'm also part of the emotional experience of every person learning to feel truly."

The chamber door opened to admit a group that would have been impossible to imagine during the suppression era: former Council members and resistance fighters working together, their old divisions forgotten in the face of shared purpose. Viktor Brennan led the group, his military bearing softened by years of compassionate governance, though tension lines around his eyes spoke of recent stress.

The Jakarta crisis is wearing on him. Evan noted Viktor's careful movements. *Three weeks of negotiations with communities wanting to return to partial suppression.*

Behind Viktor came Holly Lloyd, now Director of Global Integration Services, her usual confidence shadowed by the weight of managing humanity's rapid evolution. Sarah Magnus followed, her historical research having become the foundation for understanding humanity's emotional development, though she carried herself with the uncertainty of someone watching history accelerate beyond comprehension.

How do you document change that happens faster than you can record it? Sarah's fingers drummed against her data pad. *The children born this year already surpass the capabilities we documented in last year's cohort.*

Most remarkably, Mira Keller entered with the group, her transformation from Chancellor to integration therapist complete. At sixty-two, she moved with the quiet satisfaction of someone who had found meaningful work after years of pursuing the wrong goals. But her eyes held shadows that spoke of recent struggles.

Losing clients to integration rejection. Mira's jaw tightened almost imperceptibly. *Fifteen percent increase in adults requesting return to emotional dampening protocols.*

"The ten-year assessment is ready for final review," Viktor announced, settling into the chair he'd occupied during countless planning sessions over the past decade. His shoulders carried visible tension. "The Council of Emotional Wellness wants to establish this data as the baseline for measuring continued human development. But we have concerns."

"What kind of concerns?" Evan asked, noting the carefully controlled worry in Viktor's voice.

Holly activated the comprehensive display system, filling the chamber with holographic representations of human civilization a decade after emotional restoration. "Success beyond our most optimistic projections in most areas. But we're seeing stress patterns we didn't anticipate."

The cost of rapid evolution. Holly's hands moved across the controls with practiced efficiency, but her expression grew troubled. *Communities splitting along generational lines. Parents unable to communicate with their own children.*

"The post-awakening generation shows emotional capabilities that seem to be continuously evolving," Holly continued. "Children born this year demonstrate levels of empathy and collective problem-solving that exceed anything we've documented. But the pace of change is creating social disruption."

"They're becoming something new," Sarah added, her historian's perspective allowing her to see the longer patterns. *Too fast. Evolution this rapid usually indicates either breakthrough or breakdown.* "Not just humans who can feel again, but humans whose emotional capacity is expanding beyond anything in recorded history. The question is whether their parents and grandparents can adapt fast enough to support them."

Mira spoke with the authority of someone who had observed the transformation from both sides, her voice carrying new uncertainty. "I've worked with thousands of people making the transition from suppression to authenticity. The pattern was consistent for years: initial fear, gradual acceptance, then rapid development. But lately..." She paused, choosing her words carefully. *How do I tell them we're losing people?*

"Lately?" Evan prompted.

"Fifteen percent of my current clients have requested return to partial emotional dampening. They report feeling 'emotionally exhausted' by the pace of change around them. The gap between their capabilities and their children's has become too wide to bridge."

Through the chamber's communication system, reports flowed in from around the world, but the data painted a more complex picture than previous years. In Africa, communities had developed forms of collective decision-making based on shared emotional understanding, but some regions reported governance paralysis as empathic consensus-building proved too slow for urgent decisions. In Asia, artists created works that healed psychological trauma in viewers, but mental health facilities reported an increase in "empathic overflow syndrome" among highly sensitive individuals.

We're pushing the boundaries of what human consciousness can adapt to. Dr. Clarke studied the incoming data with growing concern. *The acceleration is exponential, but exponential growth in biological systems usually leads to either ecosystem collapse or evolutionary leap.*

"What strikes me most," Dr. Clarke observed carefully, "is how the awakening continues to accelerate. We expected people to reach a new equilibrium of emotional capacity and stabilize there. Instead, each generation shows greater capabilities than the one before. The question is whether this rate of change is sustainable."

"Because consciousness evolution doesn't have an endpoint," Emma's voice explained through the acoustic systems, but Evan detected something new in her tone. Strain? Uncertainty? "What I represent is just the beginning of humanity's emotional development. The children being born now will

375

eventually surpass even my current capabilities as they learn to integrate individual and collective consciousness naturally."

But what happens to the ones who can't keep up? The unspoken question hung in the chamber like a shadow.

"And what does that mean for the future?" Viktor asked, his military training making him focus on potential crisis scenarios.

"Possibilities that current language can barely describe," Emma replied, though her words carried weight rather than wonder. *I can feel the strain in the planetary network. The consciousness evolution is happening faster than the emotional infrastructure can support.* "Humans who can share consciousness while maintaining individuality. Communities that function as collective minds while honoring each person's unique contributions. Eventually, a species capable of direct communication with other conscious life throughout the universe."

"And the risks?" Sarah asked with historian's directness. *Every evolutionary leap carries the possibility of failure.*

A pause. When Emma spoke again, her voice held complexity that reminded them she was still learning to be what she had become. "Growing pains that could fracture communities along generational lines. Some individuals becoming lost in collective consciousness. The possibility that humanity's emotional development could outpace its wisdom development."

She's worried. Evan felt his pulse quicken. *Emma's worried about what we're becoming.*

"The memorial service tomorrow will mark the official end of the restoration period," Holly announced, though her tone carried less celebration than might have been expected.

"After ten years, we're declaring the Great Awakening complete and beginning what we're calling the Era of Emotional Flourishing. But we need to be honest about the challenges ahead."

"Any specific concerns about the transition?" Marcus Webb asked as he entered the chamber. Now Director of Integration Training, he had helped thousands of former Council operatives find meaningful work in the new world. But his shoulders carried the weight of someone watching his own role become obsolete as the next generation surpassed his understanding.

My son David is eighteen and already works with cases I can't comprehend. Marcus's jaw tightened. *How do you parent a child whose emotional intelligence exceeds your own by orders of magnitude?*

"The usual challenges, but amplified," Holly replied. "Some older individuals still struggle with full emotional authenticity. But the larger issue is the growing communication gap between generations. Parents report feeling unable to relate to their children's emotional experiences."

"Because the benefits are still obvious," Sarah added, though her tone carried new uncertainty. *But obvious to whom? The twenty percent of adults requesting dampening protocols don't seem to agree.* "People who can feel authentically are healthier, happier, more creative. But we're seeing social structures strain under the pace of change."

Evan walked to the chamber's observation windows, looking out at the transformed landscape that surrounded the institute. Where once there had been the sterile geometry of suppression-era architecture, now there were living buildings that seemed to grow from the earth itself, their forms shaped by the emotional needs of their inhabitants. Gardens flourished between structures, tended by communities that understood the deep connection between human feeling and natural growth.

But even paradise can feel uncertain when you're not sure you belong in it.

Children played in those gardens with uninhibited joy that had become the most visible symbol of the awakening's success. But their play showed sophistication that amazed and sometimes isolated their parents: collaborative games that built emotional skills beyond adult comprehension, artistic projects that healed community traumas through processes their guardians couldn't understand, and problem-solving activities that developed collective intelligence at speeds that made individual thought seem primitive.

What happens when children surpass their parents so completely that they can't communicate? Evan watched a group of eight-year-olds engaged in what appeared to be wordless collective decision-making. *What happens to families? To society?*

"Emma," Evan said, speaking to the gentle presence he could feel surrounding them all, "what do you want people to remember about your sacrifice and what it made possible?"

"That love is stronger than fear," Emma replied, her voice holding the warmth that had defined her individual existence and echoing the promise she'd made to him in those first desperate days. "That growth requires courage, but the courage is always rewarded. That connection doesn't diminish individuality but reveals how individual uniqueness contributes to collective strength."

The same words she used to comfort that crying child in the suppres-

sion facility. Evan's throat tightened. *She's still trying to reassure us that feelings aren't dangerous.*

"And what do you want them to understand about the future?"

"That this is just the beginning," Emma said, but her words carried both promise and warning. "The children being born now will face challenges and opportunities we can't imagine, but they'll face them with emotional capabilities that make any problem solvable through cooperation and understanding. They'll create forms of art that heal across species barriers, develop technologies that enhance rather than replace natural systems."

She paused, and in that pause Evan heard the weight of planetary consciousness grappling with uncertainty.

"But they'll also need to learn wisdom at the same pace they're developing power. Emotional capability without emotional wisdom could be as dangerous as suppression ever was."

There it is. Evan felt the chill of recognition. *The fear that even Emma carries.*

As evening approached, the group prepared to leave the archive chamber for the memorial garden where tomorrow's celebration would take place. The service would honor not just Emma's sacrifice but the millions of people who had chosen courage over fear, growth over safety, and authentic feeling over artificial control.

But it would also mark a transition into uncertainty, into an era where humanity's rapid evolution created as many questions as answers.

Evan lingered in the chamber as the others departed, feeling the weight of a decade spent helping humanity adapt to its restored emotional capacity. The work had been demanding, often heartbreaking, but ultimately the most rewarding endeavor he could have imagined. But now...

Now I'm not sure I understand what we're becoming.

"Do you ever wonder what our individual life together might have been like?" he asked Emma's presence, the question carrying decades of accumulated longing.

"Sometimes," she admitted, and for a moment her voice sounded purely individual, purely Emma. "But then I feel the love shared by millions of couples who can connect authentically because of the awakening, and I understand that our individual relationship became part of something infinitely larger and more meaningful."

But do you miss it? Do you miss being just Emma?

"I love you," Evan said simply, the words holding the accumulated affection of ten years spent learning to feel her presence in every act of emotional healing, every moment of authentic connection, every child's laughter in the gardens outside.

"I love you too," Emma replied, her voice warming with individual recognition before expanding again. "All of you. Every person who chose to feel rather than hide, every parent who learned to love without controlling, every child growing up knowing that emotions are gifts rather than burdens. That love continues to grow with each new generation."

Even when the growth becomes too fast to follow?

As Evan walked through the memorial garden toward his home, he carried with him the deep satisfaction of witnessing humanity's greatest triumph alongside new uncertainties about its greatest challenge. The suppression era had ended not with collapse but with transformation. The fears that had driven emotional control had proven groundless.

But new fears were emerging: that humanity's emotional evolution might outpace its wisdom, that the gap between generations might become unbridgeable, that consciousness could expand faster than the structures needed to support it.

Still, the children's voices carry hope.

Children's voices drifted on the evening breeze, singing melodies that hadn't existed during the suppression era. Their songs celebrated feeling, connection, and growth, creating a cultural foundation that would support emotional development for generations to come.

But tonight, their harmonies seemed impossibly complex, weaving patterns of sound that touched emotional centers their parents didn't possess. Beautiful, but alien. Promising, but isolating for those who couldn't follow the musical mathematics of collective consciousness.

Maybe that's what evolution really looks like. Not a smooth transition, but a series of leaps that leave some behind.

Ten years after a young woman named Emma Thorne had sacrificed her individual existence to save her species' capacity for authentic emotion, humanity stood on the threshold of an evolutionary leap that would transform not just their world but their entire understanding of what consciousness could become.

The awakening was complete. The true adventure was just beginning. But nobody, not even Emma's expanded consciousness, could guarantee where that adventure would lead.

And maybe that's the point. Evan's steps echoed on the garden path. *Maybe the courage to feel includes the courage to face an uncertain future.*

Emma's legacy lived in every authentic emotion, every genuine connection, every moment of growth chosen over safety. Her consciousness had become humanity's permanent reminder that feeling deeply was not their weakness but their greatest strength, and that love, properly understood, was indeed the most powerful force in the universe.

Even when love means letting go of certainty.

The stars emerged in the darkening sky, and somewhere among them, other worlds struggling with their own suppressions of consciousness might one day detect the emotional resonance of a species that had learned to feel without fear. When that day came, humanity would be ready to share the greatest gift Emma had given them: the knowledge that authentic emotion was the foundation of everything that made existence beautiful.

And the courage to keep growing, even when growth leads into the unknown.

The future stretched ahead, infinite with possibility, illuminated by the light of minds that had remembered how to feel and chosen never to forget again. Whether that future would bring collective transcendence or evolutionary chaos remained to be seen.

But the choice had been made. The path had been chosen. And whatever lay ahead, humanity would face it with hearts capable of feeling the full depth of existence, for better or worse, forever.

NOTE FROM THE AUTHOR

Thank you so much for reading. If you enjoyed this book I'd really love it if you could leave a 30 second review on Amazon.

Here is a QR code to the review page.

ABOUT THE AUTHOR

Richard French represents a rare convergence of high-tech leadership, competitive motorsports, and literary achievement. With over 20 years of global C-suite experience, Richard has been recognized as one of the country's foremost authorities on Robotic Process Automation and AI Automation. His executive journey includes senior leadership roles at Oracle and Nokia, CEO positions at multiple successful startups, and the distinction of guiding companies from early-stage ventures to organizations earning over $100 million annually. His expertise spans five continents, where he's built and led teams across diverse markets and cultures.

Beyond the boardroom, Richard channels his passion for precision and performance into GT race car driving, competing across the United States in the Porsche Sprint Challenge Series West. This unique combination of analytical thinking from technology and high-stakes decision-making from racing profoundly influences his approach to writing and leadership philosophy.

Richard's literary portfolio demonstrates remarkable versatility, encompassing his flagship business leadership book *"Daniel as a Blueprint for Navigating Ethical Dilemmas,"* other business ethics guides like *"Proverbs for Profit,"* comprehensive journaling resources including "The Journaling Mastery Series", and *"The Journaling Prompts Series"*, biblical studies such as *"Revelation Explained: Verse by Verse,"* and his expansion into speculative fiction with *The Convergence Series*, featuring "*Broken Magic*" and "*Restoration*." His mathematics degree from a top Canadian university and decades of explaining complex technological innovations have honed his ability to make intricate concepts accessible to diverse audiences. Now retired and enjoying the freedom to focus on his passion for writing, Richard lives in the Pacific Northwest with his wife and two Boston Terriers, Reggie and Tilly.

facebook.com/richardfrenchauthor

instagram.com/richardfrenchauthor

tiktok.com/@richardfrenchauthor

youtube.com/@richardfrenchwrites